I0787268

POPPY

SOSEKI NATSUME

Translated by
SHELLEY MARSHALL

SHELLEY MARSHALL

ISBN 978-1-959002-09-3

www.jpopbooks.com

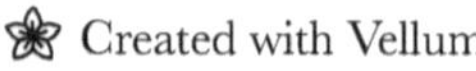 Created with Vellum

CONTENTS

しぬほど上げる頭の上には微笑なる春の宝の

毎に過ぎ、襟はして、吹けば梅を……と怪しまず……する……

探しつつ中へ……して、どうすると

云はぬ許りに叡山が聳えてゐる。

「恋し」い……園写山だ……と四……な胸を

出して一寸櫛の状に身を伺たせて欲しはふと

「あんに見えるんだから。欲はふはい……と

は叡山を軽蔑した様なうを云ふ。見える……つて、見え……は今朝て

直つ吟ふて見えて、尾ら。第師へ……叡山が……朝病を

PRESS RELEASE FOR POPPY, MAY 28, 1907

Last evening, I strolled to Morikawa-chō with Toyotakako (Komiya Toyotaka) and bought two flowering plants. I asked the gardener, "What is this flower called?"

He said, "That's a poppy."

I was struggling with the title for a serial novel and felt awful about missing the deadline for the press release. It seemed right, so I borrowed the flower's name. One will adorn the first page.

In the evening shadows of the waning spring, while clusters of pure white, dark red, and intense purple piled into several layers of crumpled flower petals, its elegance that places many crowns, glorious but too heavy, on heads devoid of leaves so coarse saws are deceived, is said to gleam and evoke the sensation of enchanting beauty. Whether my novel will share the essence of this flower is hard for me to judge unless I write it.

The company said the press release must have a title. The word *poppy* does not have to be in the title, but it was a bit too convenient. I've briefly explained the origin of *Poppy*. The creation of *Poppy* begins now.

CHAPTER 1

"It's pretty far. Where do we start the climb?" asked one man, stopping to wipe his brow with a handkerchief.

"I'm not sure where. I was wondering that, too, because I can see the mountain over there," casually answered the man with a square face and body.

While thick eyebrows moved under the brown brim of his tilted fedora, above his head as he looked up, Eizan [Mount Hiei] soared into the deep indigo from the bottom of the light blue summer sky and towered into a place so supple he wondered whether it would move if blown on.

"That mountain is unyielding," he said, sticking out his square chest and leaning on his cherrywood walking staff.

"There's no reason because we can see so much."

This time he spoke with slight contempt for Eizan.

"You say we can see it, but I could see it when we left the inn this morning. It would be awful if Eizan disappeared while on the way to Kyōto."

"It's good that we can see it, right? If you walk without making irrelevant comments, naturally, you'll reach the top of the mountain."

The tall, slender man didn't answer. He took off his hat and fanned his chest. Only his broad forehead was noticeably pale. The brim of his hat blocked the intense rays of the summer sun that dye the canola flowers.

"Well, it'll be a problem if we rest now. Let's go faster," said the square man.

His companion seemed to resent his black hair sticking to his sweaty forehead and not flying back as he wished when exposed to the summer breeze. Gripping his handkerchief in one hand, he roughly wiped his forehead, face, and around to the nape of his neck. He gave no sign of being upset by the suggestion.

"You said that mountain is unyielding, right?" he asked.

"Yes, wouldn't it look like this if it moved?" asked the square man, further squaring his square shoulders. As his free hand created a relative of a *turbo sazae* sea snail, he demonstrated the position if it moved slightly.

"Saying if it moved is like saying it doesn't move but it could," he said, looking down at his companion from the corners of his narrowed eyes.

"That's right."

"Can that mountain move?"

"Ah, ha, ha, ha. You're doing it again. You were born a man who makes irrelevant comments. Okay, let's go."

He walked out as soon as he raised his thick walking staff to his shoulder, nearly making it whistle. The slender man stored his handkerchief in his sleeve and followed.

"It would have been nice to have enjoyed the day at Heihachi Teahouse in Yamabana. We just started the climb but are only halfway there. About how far are we from the natural summit?"

"It's about two and a half miles to the summit."

"From where?"

"Who knows from where? It's a Kyōto mountain with a known height."

The slender man said nothing and only grinned. The square man continued speaking with authority.

"When taking a trip with a man like you who only plans and

does not execute, I miss seeing things everywhere. A companion is a pleasant nuisance."

"A companion who recklessly rushes out like you will be a nuisance. First of all, if you went out with a companion and left him, would he know where to start climbing, where to look, or where to descend?"

"What did the plan say about trivial matters? Is that mountain tall?"

"That mountain's fine, but do you know how many thousand feet high that mountain rises?"

"Do I know? That's trivia. Do you know?

"I have no idea."

"It's a marvelous sight."

"You shouldn't act so superior because you don't know. Neither of us knows the mountain's height. If you don't know how long it takes to reach the summit or what to look at once we're there, the schedule will not progress as planned."

"If we don't progress, we will only adjust. While considering extraneous matters as you do, we can adapt any number of times," said the square man and quickened his pace. The slender man trailed behind in silence.

In the springtime, every object easily became a poem in Kyōto from Shichijō Avenue to Ichijō Avenue. Between the smoky willows, white cloths splashed with warm water were wrung out countless times at the dry riverbed of the Takanogawa River. Most people naturally approach the mountain from the right and left on long, winding roads stretching north for more than five miles. Gentle echoes flowed to the feet from all around, from over here, from over there, bending to the point of breaking.

If you enter the mountain in late spring and reach the summit, spring will still be chilly with lingering snow. On a strip of road stitching a skirt to the towering peak and running into dark shadows, an Oharame, a peddler maiden from Ohara, rose into view in the distance. Cows appeared, too. A Kyōto spring lingers and is serene like the endless urine stream from a cow.

"Heeey!"

The man falling behind stopped and called to his friend in the lead. As his shouting voice, carried by the spring wind, traveled down the road glowing white and slowly faded away, he collided with the mountain at a dead end of only silvergrass. The square shadow walking one block ahead stopped.

The lean man stretched his long hand above his shoulder and gestured twice for his companion to come back. Before the cherry-wood walking staff was warmed by the sun, he walked back with it twinkling in front of his shoulder.

"What is it?"

"Not what is it. The climb will start here."

"Starting the climb at a place like this is a little strange. Crossing this log bridge is odd."

"When thoughtlessly walking like you, we'll walk right into Wakasa Province."

"It doesn't matter if we enter Wakasa. Do you know any geography?"

"I just asked the Oharame. It seems if we cross this bridge, head down that narrow path, we'll go up two-and-a-half miles and come out."

"Come out where?"

"At the top of Eizan."

"We should come out somewhere on Eizan's peak."

"I don't know where. I won't know unless I climb up."

"Ha, ha, ha, ha. It looks like even you, who loves planning, didn't ask that much. Too wise to make a mistake? I'll cross by following your instructions. You'll finally climb. How about it? Can you walk?"

"Can I walk? I have no choice."

"Of course, you're a philosopher. With a little more clarity, you may develop to your full potential."

"Either way is fine. You go ahead."

"Will you follow me?"

"It's all right, please go."

"If you're inclined to follow, I'm off."

The two shadows crossed the bridge dangerously spanning a

mountain stream. Their figures were hidden in a path that came out with little effort at the summit overgrown with grass on the grassy mountain. The grasses were dry stalks still holding last year's frost. Sunshine beaming directly above passed through clouds melted into wisps and returned to steam. Only their cheeks flushed from their warmth.

The man in the lead turned and called, "Hey, Kingo."

Kingo's slender frame, well-suited to the narrow mountain path, stood erect and looked down.

"Huh?" he answered.

"You're about to give up and are a weak man. Don't look down," he said, swinging his walking staff from left to right as usual.

The Takanogawa River shining as a silver thread in his eyes glimmered far away and ended at the tip of the swinging walking staff. On both sides, dense growths of blooming canola flowers rubbed together until they burned and crumbled. Before this back-drop, a far-off, light purple mountain was drawn in the distant haze.

"Of course, the scenery is magnificent," said Kingo. He twisted around his tall frame, slipped down, and stood still on a perilous sixty-degree incline.

"We climbed this high in no time. That was fast," said Hajime, the square man.

"That may be the same as descending into corruption or becoming enlightened without realizing it."

"Day becomes night. Spring becomes summer. The young become the old. They're all the same. In that case, I'll swiftly under-stand, too."

"Ha, ha, ha, ha. So how old are you?"

"You're older than me."

"I know."

"I know that."

"Ha, ha, ha, ha. Of course, it seems to be a secret."

"A secret? No, I know."

"So how old are you?"

"You say it first," said Hajime, not moving at all.

"I'm twenty-seven," said Kingo with ease and undaunted.

"Really? Well, I'm twenty-eight."

"You're the old guy."

"Stop joking. It's only a year difference."

"So it's both of us. They'll say we're both old."

"If it's both of us, I'll overlook it, but only I'm——"

"You'll overlook it? You're still young if that's worrying you."

"What do you mean? Do people become idiots during a climb?"

"During a climb, they get in the way. Move aside a little."

A carefree-looking woman ambled down the road of a hundred or a thousand turns without a straight stretch for thirty feet and excused herself as she passed by—a large bundle of twigs taller than her pressed on her dark hair with raven-black highlights. While carrying the overgrown dry grass thatching on her head, untouched by her hands, she slipped past Hajime.

The eyes watching her figure from behind as she carried the rustling, thickly overgrown, withered silvergrass were captured by a red *tasuki* cord holding back her kimono sleeves slipping off diagonally in the blackness of dark streaks. Even when more than two miles away, the straw-thatching that appeared to stick to the tip of a pointing finger was probably the woman's home. Much the same as long ago at the fall of Emperor Tenmu, lingering haze sealed off the mountain hamlet of Yase forever, and serenity prevailed.

Hajime said, "All the women around here are pretty. I'm impressed. It's like a picture."

"They're probably Oharame."

"What? These women are Yaseme, peddlers from Yase."

"I've never heard of Yaseme."

"Nonetheless, I'm sure they're from Yase. If you think I'm lying, I'll ask the next one we meet."

"Nobody said you're lying. But aren't those women usually called Oharame?"

"Are you sure? Will you vouch for it?"

"Doing it that way is poetic. Somehow, that would be elegant."

"For now, I'll use an alias."

"An alias is a good idea because many aliases exist in the world:

constitutional government, pantheism, loyalty, honesty, filial piety, respect for one's elders. There are all kinds."

"Of course, a lot of soba shops are named Yabu. All butcher shops have Iroha in their names."

"Yes, it's the same when scholars introduce themselves to each other."

"That's dull. If it comes to that situation, it would be better to drop the alias."

"From here on, you will assume the alias of a diplomat."

"Ha, ha, ha, ha. I can't take that alias. The fault is there are no examiners possessing elegance and grace."

"How many times have you failed? Three?"

"You know that's ridiculous."

"Two times?"

"What? You know exactly how many times. I only failed once out of fear."

"Because you took it once, but in the future ..."

"When I don't know how many times I'll do something, I get a little discouraged, too. Ha, ha, ha, ha. Sometimes, my alias is good, but what are you going to do?"

"Me? I will climb Eizan. Hey, stop rolling down those stones with your back leg. It's dangerous to whoever's behind you. Aaah, I'm exhausted and will rest here," said Kingo. Rustling sounds rose as he collapsed onto his side in the pampas grass.

"Hey, have we already failed? Various aliases are chanted only in words. Mountain climbing is no good from here," said Hajime. He gently tapped the top of sleeping Kingo's head with his walking staff. With each tap, the tip of the walking staff mowed down pampas grass with a rustle.

"All right. Get up. The summit is just ahead. If you rest, do it after you succeed. Come on. Get up."

"Aah."

"Aah, what? Let's go."

"I think I'm going to throw up?"

"Throw up and fail? Come on. You have one option. I'll take a break, too."

Kingo pushed his black hair into the yellow grass. Although his hat and umbrella had rolled down the hilly road, he lay on his back, gazing at the sky. Nothing blocked the view between his face shaven to a pale shadow and the vast heaven of feathery clouds floating out to infinity and serenely vanishing. Vomit spewed over the ground. The world separated, the ground separated, and the ancient and modern worlds separated in his eyes facing the immense sky. There was only the vast sky.

Hajime took off his formal *haori* coat with its Yonezawa splash pattern, folded it into a rectangle using the *sode-tatami* technique, and placed it over his shoulder. He recalled a memory and thrust out both hands with full force from his chest. He swiftly stripped to the waist and exposed a padded haori vest beneath. Shaggy fox fur stuck out of the back of the vest. This treasured vest was a gift from a friend who went to China. The friend said, "The skins of one thousand sheep are not worth the armpit of one fox. You wear this vest all the time. When I see the splotches and random bald spots on the fox skin worn on your back, you're no different than a wild fox with a mean temper."

"Are you climbing the mountain? Do you need directions? Ha, ha, ha. This is an odd place to sleep."

The woman with black-streaked hair was on her way down the mountain.

"Hey, Kingo. You're sleeping in an odd place. Even the women are making fun of you. Why don't you behave and get up?"

"Women make fun of everyone," said Kingo, still gazing at the sky.

"Calmly sitting on your butt there is a problem. Are you going to throw up again?"

"If I move, I'll puke."

"Well, that's a problem."

"All the throwing up happens when I move. Gallons of vomit are spewed into the world with one word, *move*."

"What? You don't actually intend to vomit? How dull. If there's more, will I have to descend to the foot of the mountain with you on my back? Deep down, I'm a little tired of this."

"It's not your concern. And nobody is asking you to—"

"You're a man devoid of charm."

"Do you know the definition of charm?"

"What are you saying? The thing to do is to try not to move any more than needed for a minute. You are a ludicrous man."

"Charm is ... a soft weapon that knocks down a stronger opponent."

"Then brusqueness is a sharp weapon that pushes around an opponent weaker than oneself."

"Is that logical? If you try to move, charm becomes necessary. Is there charm in a man who knows he'll vomit if he moves?"

"It's awful to use fallacious arguments. In that case, excuse me while I go ahead. All right?"

"Do as you wish," said Kingo, of course, gazing at the sky.

Hajime wrapped both empty sleeves around his waist, yanked and tucked in the hem of the striped fabric coiled around his hairy shins, and similarly folded around and tucked in the white crepe.

He quickly hung the haori folded a short time ago over the end of the walking staff. In a carefree voice, he said, "With one sword, I'll face the world alone." Then he disappeared on the steep mountain road that ran out in ten steps at an abrupt left turn.

After that came silence. Within the quiet, when we recognize the lives entrusted to us in our veins after all trivial matters are peacefully resolved, our spirited young blood transcends the vastness of Heaven and Earth.

Our blood moves in deep contemplation having lost the pulsing sounds of flowing blood. The body in silence is unadorned, is ignored in the state of mind of spiritual enlightenment without forgetfulness, and assumes a boundless, lively spirit.

When aware it is alive, the spirit discards the shadowy troubles of the transitory world and leaves a mountain cave in the clouds, similar to the change from morning to evening in the empty skies. The spirit transcends all concerns.

The past and present are empty. One foot steps into a world apart from the world that expands to the east and west. If this were not so, I would want to become a fossil. All reds and blues and yellows and purples are absorbed. I want to become a pitch-black fossil that knows nothing about returning to the original five colors. If not, I'd like to die.

Death is the end of everything and the beginning of everything. Hours accumulate to become a day. Days accumulate to become a month. Months accumulate to become a year. In other words, everything piles up and ends in a grave.

All the rowdiness around the grave pours the unneeded oil of humanity on a withered skeleton. Fate is separated by a single layer of meat and is a comedy of dancing all night long by an unwanted corpse. The one with a faraway spirit admires the far-off country.

Kingo unthinkingly conjured these thoughts and finally got up. He had to walk again and looked at Eizan, the thing he didn't want to see. Among countless useless beans, the useless traces of mountain climbing must remain for a few days as a painful memorial. If this memorial is required, the counting never ends until the hair turns gray. A fissure reaches the marrow and never disappears.

Ten or twenty beans swelled up on the soles of his feet for no reason. The moment he looked down at the heel of his boot laced halfway on the sharp edge of the cutting stone, the stone's surface changed to a hard surface, and the leg he was about to raise slid down nearly two feet.

Kingo quietly chanted, "I don't see a road thousands of miles long." He put force on the umbrella and scrambled up the abrupt turn in the steep mountain road. The sharp turn in the incline had a charm that invited the people coming from below to the sky. He neared the summit and stood.

Kingo waved the visor and looked up at the peak where the hill ran in a straight line from the bottom. From the top where the hill ended, he looked up at the endless sky swollen with the unlimited colors of spring in faint light.

He chanted, "I see simply thousands of miles of sky."

He sang the second line in the same soft voice.

When he reached the top of the grassy mountain and climbed up four or five steps into a cluster of assorted trees, he thought darkness instantly cloaked his shoulders and dampened the soles of his climbing boots. The road crossed from west to east behind the mountain. In a flash, he left the grass and found himself in the forest.

Forest richly colored the skies over Ōmi. Unless it moved, the tree trunks and the branches above stacked layer upon layer, extending for many miles. The greenery from long ago seemed to fold into blackness each year and buried two hundred valleys, three hundred portable shrines, and three thousand depraved warrior monks. Buddhists who had achieved supreme and perfect enlightenment were completely buried beneath the many leaves.

The lush forest soaring halfway into the sky was cedar, there since the days of the great Buddhist missionary Denkyō Daishi. Kingo passed alone under the cedars. Like two hands thrust out from the right and left, the roots of cedar trees thwarted the passage of people, pierced the ground, split apart rocks, dug deep into the ground, and bit into the soil, or with extra power, leaped back and crossed the dark road, gradually rising to an inch.

Natural railroad ties rested on a ladder of rocks. While short of breath, Kingo climbed the comfortable steps, a gift from the mountain spirit.

Hikage vines crawled toward the cedar trees lining the road as if leaking out of the darkness. If the growth wrapped around one's legs, the full length of the pulled vine would be revealed. Out-of-reach decaying fern swayed erratically on the windless day.

"Over here. Over here," said Hajime, his voice, sounding like a *tengu* goblin, quickly rose above his head. When Kingo stepped on the ground of layers of decayed grass, the ground did not spring back to hide his deep boot prints. He finally thought of pushing on his Western-style umbrella to climb to the tengu's seat.

"Well done! Fantastic! I've been waiting quite some time for you. What took you so long?"

"Yeah" was all Kingo said. Suddenly, he let go of his umbrella and dropped his butt onto it with a thud.

"Are you going to throw up again? Before you do, please take in this view for a moment. It would be terrible to throw up while you're looking," he said, pointing his walking staff between the cedars. The sparkling lake at Ōmi glimmered through the gaps neatly standing between the old trunks framing the sky.

"Of course," said Kingo, straining to see.

There was no satisfaction in simply opening a mirror. The tengu goblins on Eizan avoided the brightness of the famous Biwa mirror and drank themselves into a stupor on sacred sake stolen in the early evening. Like cloudy breaths blown over a surface, hazy hot air spread throughout the fields and valleys. The spring scenery brimming with colors collected on the paint palette of a giant and effortlessly smeared with a brush faded over a radius greater than twenty miles.

"Of course," said Kingo again.

"All you can say is of course? No matter what you're shown, you are never pleased."

"Show me? You didn't make this."

"That sort of ingratitude marks a philosopher. You study the lack of filial piety and are out of touch with day-to-day people."

"I'm truly sorry.

"So I'm a scholar of the lack of filial piety? Ha, ha, ha, ha. You can see white sails. Over there, nothing is moving before the background of the blue mountain on that island. No matter how long I watch nothing moves."

"Sails are boring. The nondescript parts resemble you. But it's beautiful. Hey, I'm here, too."

"And there are more far off by the purple shore."

"Oh, yes. There they are. All of it is boring and featureless."

"It's all like a dream."

"What is?"

"What is? The scene before your eyes."

"Really? I thought you were remembering something. You are better at handling objects. If it's a dream, it's no good to stand there with your hands in your pockets."

"What are you talking about?"

"Of course, what I'm saying is only a dream. Ah, ha, ha, ha, ha. Where did Taira no Masakado exhale fire in the old days?"

"That's on the other side because we're looking down on Kyōto. It's not this way. He was a fool, too."

"Masakado? Well, rather than merely breathing out fire, a philosopher will vomit."

"What sort of things does a philosopher vomit?"

"To become a true philosopher, you become cerebral. You simply think. A full *daruma*."

"What is that smoky-looking island?"

"That island? It's shrouded by a murky haze. That's probably the huge Chikubu Island."

"Are you sure?"

"What? Behave. I adhere to the doctrine that an alias doesn't matter if it's the truth."

"Does that truth exist in this world? Thus, an alias is necessary."

"Is everything human like a dream? Goodness."

"Only the thing called death is the truth."

"That's awful."

"If you bump into death, the fickleness of human beings never ends."

"Because it's fine that it never ends, there's no chance of that encounter."

"Never is coming now. When it comes, then they'll think, Oh, I see."

"Who?"

"People who like intricate carving with small knives."

If you descend the mountain and step onto the Ōmi plains, you will be in Hajime's world. Gazing at a distance from a high, dark, sunless place and never approaching the bright world of spring is Kingo's world.

CHAPTER 2

A WOMAN RESEMBLES A RICH PURPLE DOT EXTRACTED FROM springtime at the height of a day in March wrapped around crimson, and the dot vividly trickles down in sleeping Heaven and Earth.

Fine gold legs hammered with crystalline slivers of iridescent shells are set to tame folded-back side locks of black hair, a dream world more fascinating to gaze at than a dream. On the quiet day, the observer's heart carried off to some distant world is jolted back to reality by the twitching of her dark eyes.

During the spread of half of a drop, her intense eyes steal the moment, create the power of a swift wind, and exist in, yet dominate the spring. When her eyes swim against the current and reach the border of magical powers, bones whiten in paradise and never return to this mortal world. This is not a simple dream. While the fuzzy dream grows, a brilliant point of a star portending disaster draws closer to the purple eyebrows, it says, "Look at me until I die." The woman is wearing a purple kimono.

On this serene day, the woman gently pulled out a bookmark and read the heavy volume adorned with gold leaf on her lap.

> ... she said [kneeling before his grave]: "Dear Antony, I buried thee
> but lately with hands still free; now, however, I pour libations for

thee as a captive, and so carefully guarded that I cannot either with blows or tears disfigure this body of mine, which is a slave's body, and closely watched that it may grace the triumph over thee. Do not expect other honors or libations; these are the last from Cleopatra the captive. For though in life nothing could part us from each other, in death we are likely to change places; thou, the Roman, lying buried here, while I, the hapless woman, lie in Italy, and get only so much of thy country as my portion. But if indeed there is any might or power in the gods of that country (for the gods of this country have betrayed us), do not abandon thine own wife while she lives, nor permit a triumph to be celebrated over myself in my person, but hide and bury me here with thyself, since out of all my innumerable ills not one is so great and dreadful as this short time that I have lived apart from thee."

The woman raised her head. Her sheer make-up floated slightly when she stiffened her pale cheeks as if excess matter were stored in the bottom layer. The man keen to discern what was stored in that layer became her prisoner. Spellbound, his mouth shifted slightly. When the shape of his mouth crumbled, this man's will had already fallen prey to his rival. Her lower lip was deliberately colored. The instant she started to speak but did not, the one under attack always failed to deflect.

The woman only moved her eyes to glance, like a falcon strike from the sky. The man grinned. The contest was already over. A crab flicking its tongue to the front of its jaw and foaming at the mouth is a clumsy strategy in a fight against crows and herons. Pounding drums push an army to victory in battle.

A reluctant pledge to surrender is the most ordinary strategy. A strategy that blows needles containing honey and forces sake drinking to deliver poison still has not reached its full potential.

The exchange of even one word is not allowed in the supreme battle. A flower picked as a greeting over a long distance away is silent and unspoken. In a moment of hesitation, as expected, evil spirits that strike the emptiness write *indecisive*, write *delusional*, and write *a lost child*, and abruptly withdraw.

In the will-o'-wisp of life's successes in this world, characters written indiscriminately with blue phosphorous blown onto the tip of a writing brush are not easily erased by sweeping them away with a brush of gray hairs. He smiled, but in the end, had no reason to retract his smile.

"Seizō," called the woman.

"Huh?" the man promptly answered with no time to fix his collapsed mouth.

A smile appeared half unconsciously over his lips until the wave of his heart was written in cursive characters when he had nothing to do.

When on the verge of running out of characters, he worried the second wave that should be written would not come. The exclamation "Oh?" of a timely offer easily slipped from his throat.

From the beginning, the woman was a schemer. Having elicited the "Oh?" she said nothing for a moment.

"What is it?"

The man managed to speak. If he couldn't continue, they would get along very well. If they can't get along, they'll feel uncomfortable. Taking notice of the other person always evokes this emotion, even among royalty. Not to mention, in addition to the purple woman, from the beginning, speechlessness was foolish in the man's eyes that reflected nothing.

The woman remained quiet. A sword-bearer wearing a boy's *chigomage* topknot mingling with the young pine in a Yōsai painting hanging in the alcove possessed the tranquility of long ago. The fawn-colored horse's owner, dressed in a *kariginu* kimono, could not see the moving scenery in the routine of a courtier accustomed to peaceful days.

Only the man was anxious. A first arrow missed the mark. Where the second arrow struck was uncertain. If it missed, she must keep trying. The man held his breath and stared at the woman's face. The emotion of expectation filled his slender face, lacking in flesh. While wondering about the odds, he wished for a hopeful sign from the ample lips.

"Are you still here?" the woman calmly asked. This was a surprising response.

The bow pulled and aimed at the sky seemed to return the gourd-shaped feather perilously above his head. She forgot about the man's ego and returned to watching her companion.

From the beginning, the woman seemed to forget about the man seated before her and was lost in the book opened on her lap. As was her habit, when the woman discovered the beauty of the gold leaf on the book, she yanked it from the hands of the man carrying it and began reading.

The man only said, "Oh."

"Does she intend to go to Rome?"

The woman looked at the man's face with an unconvinced expression that made no sense. Seizō had to take responsibility for Cleopatra's behavior.

"She's not going. She's not going," he said as if pleading with an unrelated queen.

"She didn't go? I wouldn't go," she finally said in agreement.

Seizō barely slipped out of the dark tunnel.

"If you look at works written by Shakespeare, women with that personality appear often."

Seizō exited the tunnel, jumped on a bicycle, and flew off. *A fish dances in deep waters / A kite spreads its wings and soars in the sky.* Seizō was a man who lived in a land of poems.

A place where the pyramid's sky burns, a place that embraces the sands of the Sphinx, a place where the long river harbors crocodiles, and a place where the enchanting Cleopatra embraced Antony two thousand years ago while her beautiful skin was gently cooled by an ostrich-feather fan are excellent subjects for paintings or themes for fine poetry, which was Seizō's specialty.

"When I look at the Cleopatra depicted by Shakespeare, I get a peculiar sensation."

"What sort of sensation?"

"While pulled into an ancient hole, unable to get out, and in a daze, the purple Cleopatra is vividly projected before my eyes. From among peeling colorful woodblock prints, only one person suddenly blazed in purple came floating out."

"Purple? You often mentioned purple. Why purple?"

"Why? That is how it feels."

"Well, is this the color?" she asked while deftly waving her long sleeve half spread out on the blue tatami mat before the tip of Seizō's nose. Cleopatra's scent struck the depth between his eyebrows.

"What?" He abruptly returned to his senses. Like a little cuckoo that skims the sky and pierces through the bottom of falling rain faster than a carriage pulled by a team of four horses, strange colors briefly flickered and quickly faded away. She placed her beautiful hands, resting so quietly they seemed to lack a pulse, on her knees.

The scent of Cleopatra gradually escaped his nose. He longingly pursued the receding figure of the shadow that unexpectedly called out from two thousand years ago. Seizō's heart was lured to a far-off boundary and pulled back to a moment two thousand years ago.

He said, "This is not the love of a gentle breeze, the love of tears, or the love of grief. This love of a torrential rainstorm and the love of deluges, not recorded on calendars, are the loves of a dagger."

"Is that love of a dagger purple?"

"The love of a dagger is not purple. The love of purple is the dagger."

"When the love is cut, does purple blood spill out?"

"When love angers, the dagger is said to flash purple."

"Did Shakespeare write that?"

"I evaluated the writings of Shakespeare. When Antony married Octavia in Rome, and when a messenger brings news of the marriage to Cleopatra, then Cleopatra's ..."

"Purple is dyed darker with jealousy."

"When purple is scorched by the Egyptian sun, a cold short dagger shines."

"Is this darkness all right?"

Soon after she asked, a long sleeve flashed again.

Seizō was interrupted. Even if he sought something from his

companion, she was a woman who wouldn't consent unless shown deference. Looking pleased, the woman who removed the malice confidently gazed at his face.

"Then what did Cleopatra do?"

She held him down but loosened the reins again. Seizō had to dash away.

"She thoroughly questioned the messenger about Octavia. The questioner is interesting because the interrogation brings out Cleopatra's personality. Is Octavia tall like me? What color is her hair? Is her face oval? Is her voice soft? How old is she? She questioned the messenger about every little thing."

"How old was the person asking all the questions?"

"Cleopatra was just thirty."

"So she's a little old like me?"

The woman cocked her head and giggled. The man was captured by her mysterious dimples and a bit confused. If he agrees, it becomes a lie. A simple denial is customary. The man was unable to answer until the point where a sparkling line of gold mingled with her shiny white teeth and disappeared again. The woman was twenty-four. For a long time, Seizō knew there was a three-year difference in their ages.

A beautiful woman older than twenty and without a husband counts one, two, three in vain. It's a mystery why to this day at the age of twenty-four she had not yet become a bride. Amid the futile aging of a spring residence, watching the shadows of flowers in full bloom on long days soon to be gone, and playing a koto with a bitter expression are the habits of women in the world of the late to marry. Echoes resembling the sounds from a biwa are heard on the koto's bridge in the occasional non-existent sounds swept away by a priest's *hossu* brush. More mysterious was their interest and enjoyment in its unnatural tones. The details are not understood any more than at the beginning. Sometimes, the shadows of the words exchanged between this man and this woman are peered into, and unneeded speculation secretly predicts the signs of divination of a nebulous love.

"As I age, will the jealousy worsen?" she asked Seizō again.

Once more, Seizō was unnerved. A poet must understand people. He was duty-bound to answer her question. However, he had no reason to answer about things he knew nothing of. The man who has never seen the jealousy of the middle-aged woman could not help despite being a poet and a literary man. Seizō was a literary man proficient in letters.

"Well, let me see. It depends on the person."

Instead of being direct, his response was muddy. She was not a woman who would let the matter rest.

"When I become that woman of a certain age, no, now I am that woman. Ha, ha, ha. What should I do, if I reach that age?"

"You will ... Now, you ... are jealous."

"I am."

The woman's voice coldly slashed the quiet spring breeze. The man who happily lived in a poetic land quickly lost his footing and fell into the mundane world. If he falls, he is an ordinary person. The other person looks down on him from a high, inaccessible cliff. He had no time to think about who kicked him down to this place.

"How old was Kiyohime when she transformed into a serpent after her love was rejected?"

"Of course, if she weren't in her teens, there never would have been a play. She was perhaps eighteen or nineteen."

"And her obsession Anchin?"

"Wasn't he around twenty-five?"

"Seizō."

"Yes."

"How old are you?"

"Me? ... Well, I'm ..."

"Don't you know without thinking?"

"No, what? I'm the same age as Kingo."

"Oh, yes, you're the same age as my brother. However, he looks much older."

"What? That's not true."

"Yes, it is."

"Shall I indulge you?"

"Yes, please do. Although your face is not youthful, you are young at heart."

"Can you see that?"

"You look like a pampered rich boy."

"How sad."

"It's actually cute."

Twenty-four years old for a woman is thirty years old for a man. The reason is not known. The fallacy is not known, too. Why the Earth rotates and why it settles down, of course, are unknown. While the great stage of all ages develops with no bounds, you don't know from the beginning what position you'll occupy and what role you'll play. The clever person is only glib.

A woman cannot make the world her rival, turn around to face the people of a nation, and handle matters before the eyes of the masses. A woman understands the trick of having only one rival. In a one-on-one fight, the woman always wins. The man always loses. The woman is raised inside a metaphorical cage, pecking at feed grains and happily fluttering her wings. In her small heaven in the cage, any competitor to the woman in singing bird calls will always be defeated. Seizō is a poet. Because of that, only half of his head is poking inside this cage. Seizō entirely failed to chirp.

"That's adorable. Exactly like Anchin."

"Anchin is horrible."

His apology was unspoken, but he understood this time.

"You're dissatisfied," said the woman, smiling with her eyes.

"But ..."

"But what is horrible?"

"I'm not running away like Anchin."

This is called being put on the defense by failing to escape. The rich boy did not know about seeing a chance and cleanly withdrawing.

"Ha, ha, ha. I'll chase after you like Kiyohime."

The man was quiet.

"Am I a few years too old to become a snake?"

An untimely springtime flash of lightning emerged from the woman and pierced the man's chest. The color was purple.

"Fujio."

"What is it?"

The man who called and the woman who was called sat facing each other. The six-tatami-mat sitting room was isolated by dense green shrubbery, even the echoes of vehicles passing back and forth were faint. In the lonely transient world, they were the only two people alive. In the tatami area with a brown border, when their faces were just two feet apart staring at each other, society receded far from them.

The Salvation Army is striking large drums and parading through the city. Hospitalized patients afflicted with peritonitis are taking faint breaths. Nihilists in Russia are throwing bombs. At the railway station, pickpockets are being arrested. Fires are burning. Babies are born. At the parade grounds, new soldiers are being upbraided. People are jumping to their deaths. Others are being killed. Fujio's older brother and Hajime are climbing Eizan.

The figures of a man and a woman calling each other's name deep in the pleasure quarters weighed down by the fragrance of flowers brightly dance on the shadow of spring sinking into the depths of death. The universe is the universe of this couple.

The door of the heart crisscrossed by the blood vessels of three thousand veins and arteries and surging with young circulating blood opens with love and closes with love, and vividly draws the motionless man and woman in the depths of the vast sky.

Their fates are determined in this dangerous moment. If a body is moved slightly to the east or west, it ends.

Calling is not a simple matter, nor is being called. Obstacles greater than life and death await them.

Will explosives covering everything be detonated or detonate? The bodies of the two motionless people are two fiery masses.

"Welcome home."

A voice echoed in the entryway. Wheels grinding down the gravel came to a stop. The opening of the sliding screen door was heard. The sounds of lightly trotting footsteps traveled down the hallway. The tense postures of the two people collapsed.

"My mother has returned," casually said the woman, remaining seated.

"Oh," the man answered, sounding relaxed.

As long as your heart is not exposed to the outside, it is not a crime. A solvable puzzle is weak as evidence in a court of law. Inadvertently, the pair entertaining each other were at ease while tacitly approving of what happened between them. The whole world is at peace. No one can point fingers behind their backs. If they can, they're at fault. The world will be peaceful to the very end.

"Was your mother out?"

"Yes, she did a little shopping."

"I should be going," he said and adjusted his seating position before standing. He was a man who worried about ruining the pleats of his pants and always sat as relaxed as possible.

He lifted his backside, grabbing onto a support when needed. He placed both hands on his knees. Cuffs like snow covered the backs of his hands. From beneath his dull gray sleeves, sparkling his-and-hers cloisonné buttons appeared.

"Please, there's no need for you to go. My mother has returned, but we have no urgent tasks," said the woman, showing no sign of welcoming her mother home. The man did not attempt to stand.

"But," he said as he searched his pocket and retrieved a thick cigarette. The smoke from the cigarette mostly distracted him. The cigarette was an Egyptian brand and sported a golden mouthpiece tip. In the dark color blown into a ring, a mountain, or a cloud, with his hip raised, he adjusted his sitting position, which made it possible for him to shrink the space between Cleopatra and himself.

As thin smoke slowly drifted out and passed over his black mustache, as expected, Cleopatra gave a clear order, "Please, sit down."

The silent man sat more comfortably. The spring day was endless for both of them.

"I can't stand the loneliness these past days of only having women around."

"When will Kingo return?"

"When will he come home? I haven't the slightest idea."

"Has he sent any messages?"

"No."

"Kyōto is probably quite interesting this time of year."

"It would have been nice if you had gone, too."

"Well, I ..." said Seizō but stopped.

"Why didn't you go?

"I have no particular reason."

"But aren't all of you old friends?"

"Are we?"

Seizō rudely let his cigarette ashes drop onto the tatami. When he said, "Are we?" his hand jerked involuntarily.

"Didn't you live in Kyōto for a long time?"

"So you know each other?"

"Yes."

"Because the friendship is fairly old, I didn't feel like going."

"You're too heartless."

"What? That's not so," said Seizō somewhat seriously and breathed the Egyptian cigarette into his lungs.

"Fujio. Fujio."

A voice called out across from the sitting room.

"Oh, is that your mother?" asked Seizō.

"Yes."

"I should probably be going."

"Why?"

"You may have things to do?"

"Does it matter if I do? Aren't you a scholar? A professor comes to teach, does it matter who comes home?"

"But I've hardly taught you anything."

"Well, I'm beginning to be taught. If I've learned only that, it has been a lot."

"Is that so?"

"Haven't you taught me about Cleopatra and many other things?"

"If you like Cleopatra, there's much to learn."

"Fujio. Fujio," her mother sharply called.

"Please, excuse me for a moment. Please wait. There's something I wish to ask you."

Fujio left. The man stayed in the six-tatami sitting room. Traces of residual smoke, spilled ashes, and undisturbed ashes lay on an antique Satsuma incense burner placed on the floor. Fujio's room was quiet yesterday and today. The warmth of the room waiting for the owner at the abandoned sitting cushion of twilled fabric was quietly swept away by a light spring breeze.

Seizō said nothing and looked at the incense burner and the futon. In a corner floating above the tatami of a broken lattice, a shiny object was wedged deep inside.

Seizō turned his head slightly to the side and thought about searching for the shiny object. It looked like a watch. He hadn't noticed it until that moment.

When Fujio got up, the futon might have flexed, brushed against the silk partition, and exposed the hidden object. There was no need to hide a watch under a futon. Seizō peeked under the futon again.

He folded over the chain of connected links formed from pine needles and revealed the front. An edge with a raised *nanako* pattern slightly rose in the depths reflecting fine light rays. It was a watch. Seizō tilted his head.

The gold was rich in color purity. Those who love wealth and rank always love this color. Those who beg for honors always choose this color. Those who achieve fame always adorn themselves in this color.

Just as a magnet attracts iron, this color turns every head. Anyone who does not kneel in reverence before this color is rubber with no elasticity. He can't pass through the world alone. Seizō thought, This is a good color.

From the direction of the opposite sitting room, the rustling sounds of silk approached, transmitted along the curved veranda. Seizō quickly averted his peeking eyes, feigned innocence, and found himself staring at a Yōsai hanging scroll when two figures appeared at the threshold.

One wore a black silk crepe kimono with three family crests stylishly draped over her shoulders and a dull half-collar. Only her traditional hairstyle shined.

"Ah, welcome," said the mother, slightly bowing and sitting near the open-air veranda.

Instead of the songs of bush warblers, in the garden thoroughly swept clean until not a speck of dust was seen, a lone, overly tall, pine tree stood as if it owned everything. This pine and this mother could be thought to be one and the same.

"Fujio has been only trouble for you. She speaks so selfishly because she is nothing more than a child. Must she always greet people with 'Please, make yourself at home.' As she has gotten older, it has become rude.

"In truth, she's a baby, only fusses, and quibbles endlessly. However, I am grateful to you for instilling a fondness for English in her. Lately, she seems to have been reading challenging works and has become fairly skilled.

"Since her brother is here, it would be nice if he taught her. Perhaps siblings are incapable of doing that."

The mother's eloquence was impressive. Seizō found no pause to interject one word, was seduced, and ran off, but his destination was never clear. Fujio silently opened the book borrowed from Seizō a short time ago and continued reading.

After making this lamentation and crowning and embracing the coffin, she ordered a bath to be prepared for her. After bathing, she lay down and enjoyed a splendid banquet. And there came one from the country bringing a basket; and on the guards asking what he brought, the man opened it, and taking off the leaves showed the vessel full of figs.... After feasting, Cleopatra took a tablet, which was already written, and sent it sealed to Caesar, and, causing all the rest of her attendants to withdraw except those two women, she closed the door. As soon as Caesar opened the tablet and found in it the prayers and lamentations of Cleopatra, who begged him to bury her with Antonius, he saw what had taken place. At first he was for setting out himself to give help, but the next thing that he did was to send persons with all speed to inquire.

But the tragedy had been speedy; for, though they ran thither and found the guards quite ignorant of everything, as soon as they opened the door they saw Cleopatra lying dead on a golden couch in royal attire. Of her two women, Eiras was dying at her feet, and Charmion, already staggering and drooping her head, was arranging the diadem on the forehead of Cleopatra. One of them saying in passion, "A good deed this, Charmion."

"Yes, most goodly," she replied, "and befitting the descendant of so many kings."

She spake not another word, but fell there by the side of the couch.

Now it is said that the asp was brought with those figs and leaves, and was covered with them; for that Cleopatra had so ordered, that the reptile might fasten on her body without her being aware of it. But when she had taken up some of the figs and saw it, she said, "Here then it is," and baring her arm, she offered it to the serpent to bite.

After the sentence, *Yes, most goodly … and befitting the descendant of so many kings*, the entire page seemed subtly blurred, as though the delicate last wisp of burning incense was drawn into emptiness.

"Fujio," called her unobservant mother.

The man, at last relaxed, was generous and looked toward the one being called. She was looking down.

"Fujio," her mother called again.

Her eyes finally left the page. Beneath her white forehead touching her billowy traditional *hasashigami* hairstyle was her thin but not bony nose. Her lips tinted red ... her lips smoothly slipped. The edges of her cheeks blended firmly with her chin. Her throat gracefully abandoned her chin and gradually emerged in the real world.

"What?" answered Fujio. A response between day and night from the woman standing between day and night.

"Oh, you're too indifferent. Is that book that interesting? Please read it later. Aren't you being rude?

"Your naive selfishness is troublesome. Did you borrow that

book from Seizō? It's quite pretty. Please, don't sully it. You don't value books ..."

"I'm being careful."

"Well, that's good, not like that last time ..."

"That was Kingo's fault."

"What did Kingo do?" asked Seizō, opening his mouth to speak, as usual for the first time."

"No, you are a gathering of selfishness. From the beginning to the end, all you do is argue like a small child. Lately, your brother's books ..."

Her mother looked at Fujio and wondered whether to keep speaking. Blackmail with compassion is a game preferred by older people and used against younger ones.

"What happened to Kingo's books?" Seizō timidly asked.

"Shall I tell him?"

Half smiling, the older woman held back. Her spirit was as if she thrust out a toy dagger.

Ignoring her mother, Fujio said, "I threw my brother's books into the garden."

Her pointed answer was hurled to strike between Seizō's eyebrows. Her mother forced a smile. Seizō's mouth hung open.

"As you know, her brother is quite the eccentric," said Fujio's mother, indirectly humoring her daughter, who was given to despair.

"Has Kingo returned home, yet?" asked Seizō, finding the perfect moment to change the subject.

"He's exactly like you, a bullet. He leaves and doesn't return. He complains constantly about his terrible health.

"If that's so, I suggested he take a short trip. But he kept on fussing. Finally, Hajime asked the immovable man to accompany him.

"However, he is truly a bullet. Young people are ..."

"Kingo's young and exceptional. He's special because he excels in philosophy."

"I guess so. Although I don't know anything ... Hajime is a care-free fellow and is truly a bullet. That is a problem."

"Ah, ha, ha. He's full of life and an interesting fellow."

"Speaking of Hajime, where is that object you had earlier?" asked Fujio's mother, raising her keen eyes and scanning the room.

"It's here," said Fujio, leaned over, stood, and smoothly slid the twill sitting cushion on the new tatami. The signs of wealth and nobility swelled on the nanako lid coiled three times by a chain.

She reached out her right hand. While she considered making the shiny object ring out, the chain slipped from her palm and dropped to the tatami. When stopped by its length at one foot, excess force pulled it to the side. The decorative garnets affixed to the edge and the long object swung back and forth several times.

This first swing hit Fujio's white forearm with a deep red jewel. The second swing moved toward Kanze, the goddess of mercy, gently touching her cuff. When the third swing quieted down, she sprang to her feet.

She sat in front of Seizō who was gazing blankly at the scene of beautiful colors moving quickly and jumbled together in duos or trios.

"Mother," she said, looking back, "Do this and it will stand out." She turned back around.

The gold chain shaped like pine needles passed through the button holes on the front of Seizō's padded vest and glittered radiantly against the dark, felt-like melton fabric.

"Well?" asked Fujio.

"Of course, it's quite fetching," said her mother.

"What's going on?" asked Seizō while being wrapped in smoke. Fujio's mother giggled.

"Shall I give it to you?" asked Fujio, glancing to the side. Seizō said nothing.

"Well, we should stop," she said, stood again, and took the gold watch from him.

CHAPTER 3

On this rainy day, long, thin strands of smoke hanging like a willow tree were blown in columns. In the darkness of a navy blue business suit hanging on a clothes rack, black tabi socks were turned down by a third and curled into balls. An elegant carry-all cloth bag sat on top of narrow staggered shelves. Loose strings listlessly dangled down. Beside it, toothpaste and white toothpicks said, "Good morning." Threads of white rain passed through the glass of the tightly closed *shōji* sliding door and shined in long, narrow lights.

"Kyōto is a terribly cold place," said Hajime, as he put a padded meisen-silk workman's apron over his rented *yukata* summer kimono. He sat boldly with his legs flung out and his back supported by the alcove's pine post. While glancing outside, he began talking to Kingo, who was sitting with a camel hair blanket covering his lap and an air cushion puffing up his black hair.

"More than cold, this is a sleepy place," he said, slightly shifting his head. His combed, damp hair joined the discarded tabi socks by the bounce in the air.

"All you do is sleep. You came all the way to Kyōto to sleep."

"Uh-huh. This is a relaxing place."

"Then relax. That's fine. Your mother was worried."

"Hmph."

"'Hmph' is your response. Even so, I'm going to a lot of trouble that is unknown to others to get you to relax."

"Can you read those characters [僝雨僽風] in that picture?"

"Let me see. It's unusual. Is it read *sen u shū hū*? I've never seen it before. I see the radical for person [亻], so does it have something to do with people? People write unnecessary characters. What was it originally?"

"I don't know."

"Not knowing is all right. More than that, this fusuma sliding screen is interesting. The gold paper pasted on one side is magnificent. The wrinkles here and there surprised me. It looks like a prop in a shabby kabuki theater. Take those three bamboo shoots over there. They were drawn economically. What do you think? Hey, Kingo, this is a mystery."

"What's a mystery?"

"I don't know, but it's a mystery because something with an unknown meaning is drawn."

"Is it a puzzle because you don't understand the meaning? It's a mystery because it has meaning."

"But I think anything devoid of meaning is a mystery to a philosopher. I'm thinking as hard as possible. It's like bursting a blood vessel to study a crazy move discovered in a shōgi checkmate problem."

"Well, a crazed painter probably drew these bamboo shoots."

"Ha, ha, ha, ha. If you reason like that, the problem vanishes."

"Do the world and bamboo shoots go together?"

"Isn't there a legend called the Gordian Knot? Do you know about it?"

"You think everyone else is a middle-school student."

"Even if I don't think so, please listen. If you know it, tell me."

"What a pain you are. I know about it."

"So, tell me. A philosopher often deceives others because he's a person who is too obstinate and unable to confess not knowing no matter what he's asked ..."

"I don't know which of us is too obstinate."

"Either one is fine. Now, tell me."

"The Gordian Knot is a legend from the age of Alexander the Great."

"Yes, I know. And ..."

"A farmer called Gordias dedicated a cart to the god Jupiter ..."

"Hey, hey, wait a minute. Did that happen? And then ..."

"You ask if that happened. Don't you know?"

"I didn't know that much."

"What? You have the habit of not knowing yourself."

"Ha, ha, ha, ha. The teachers didn't teach that when I was in school. I'm sure those teachers didn't know that much."

"Anyway, no one could untie the knot tied by the farmer at the cart shafts and the crosspiece."

"Of course, that is the Gordian Knot. So? That knot was a problem to Alexander, so he cut it with his sword. Am I right?"

"Alexander didn't say it was a problem."

"All right. Go on."

"When he heard the oracle say the knot would be untied by whoever would rule all of The East, Alexander said, 'In that case, I'll do this ...'"

"I know that. I was taught that by my schoolteacher."

"Then, you understand now?"

"It's good. I think it's unacceptable if people don't understand his saying 'It doesn't matter how it's undone.'"

"That's fine, too."

"That is fine, too. This isn't a rivalry. No matter how much he thought about the Gordian Knot, he could not unravel it."

"Was cutting it the solution?"

"No, it wasn't, but it worked well given the situation."

"The situation? He was not a coward given the situation in the world."

"So the reason is Alexander became a big coward."

"Do you think Alexander is that great?"

The conversation briefly broke off. Kingo turned over. Hajime, still sitting with his legs flung out, opened up a travel guide. The rain came down at an angle.

When the lonely drizzle falling on the old capital city intensified enough to bounce off the back of a swallow showing its red belly to the sky as it darted off, the gentle rain dampened Shimokyō, the district bustling with merchants, and Kamikyō, the home of nobility and aristocrats. At the green base of the thirty-six peaks, the only sounds were the flowing waters dissolving the reds of Yuzen silk dye and water pouring over the flowers of vegetables.

"You're upstream, and I'm downstream ..."

If he removed the weight of the hand towel hiding his eyebrows at the gate where parsley was being washed, he could see the giant Daimonji character on the mountainside.

Generations of springtimes have grown moss over the emperor's consorts, Matsumushi and Suzumushi. Only their graves remain in a thicket where bush warblers should be singing.

At Rashōmon Gate where demons appeared, the gate was torn down after demons no longer came out. No one knows the fate of the demon's arm lopped off by the warrior Watanabe no Tsuna. The spring rain of the old days fell. Rain falls on the temples in Teramachi, on bridges along Sanjō Avenue, on cherry blossoms in Gion, on pine trees at Kinkaku-ji Temple, and on Kingo and Hajime on the second floor of the inn.

Kingo wrote in his diary while lying down. He opened a bit of the brown cloth binding to bend a corner stained with sweat. After turning a couple of pages, he found a page about a third empty and began writing. He picked up the pen with spirit.

> Rain falling on a beautiful house
> People ancient and modern sit in tranquility

He wrote this Chinese verse and then thought for a moment. He seemed at a loss for what words to add.

Hajime flung aside the travel guide, startling the tatami with a thud, and went out to the veranda.

A one-legged rattan stool, perfect for the veranda, sat in the dampness as though waiting for someone. The sitting room in the house next door could be seen through scattered weeping golden bell flowers. The shōji screen was shut tight. Sounds of a koto escaped from inside.

> Sounds of a koto suddenly heard
> A weeping willow droops in resentment

Kingo wrote this ten-character verse on another line but looked displeased and immediately drew a line through it. The rest of his entry was plain prose.

The universe is a mystery. Each man solves the mystery as he wishes. Solving it his way and calming himself are happiness. If you doubt this, even a parent is a mystery. Even brothers are a mystery. A wife, children, and even seeing oneself are mysteries.

A person is born into this world to push against mysteries, become old and gray, and agonize in the dead of night.

To solve the mystery of parents, you must become one body with your parents. To solve the mystery of your wife, you must have the same heart as your wife. To solve the puzzle of the universe, you must have the same mind and body as the universe. If you can do this, your parents, wife, and the universe become suspect. It is an insolvable mystery. It is painful. At the moment the unsolvable mysteries are the parents and siblings, the preferred new mystery of a wife usually becomes distress over one's financial position and being entrusted with other people's money.

The problems of only having the new mystery of a wife or forcing the painful birth of a new mystery within a new mystery accumulated interest for the entrusted money and another person's earnings managed as one's own. All suspicions throw out the body and can find the solution for the first time. The problem is how does one throw the body away. Death? Death is too ineffective.

Before Hajime settled down on the rattan stool, he was listening to the koto next door. Within the chill of early spring at the Omuro Imperial Palace, he should not know the elegance of an expert biwa performance. There is no elegant pursuit that nobly thinks about the thirteen strings stretched into a shape resembling a southern iris and the lacquered tongue decorated with gold set in ivory. Hajime listened casually.

The small garden was not even one hundred square feet. Opposite the yellow weeping golden bell flowers trickling over the fence, shadows of many varieties of moss crept out of a thicket of Narihira bamboo. Eizan moss crawled over the entire surface. The sounds of the koto were coming from this garden.

Rain is first. In winter, raincoats freeze. In fall, lamp wicks dwindle. In summer, loincloths are washed. In spring, with flat silver ornamental hairpins dropped onto the tatami, the sounds of strumming and plucking were beside the gleaming red, gold, and indigo undersides of the shells used in the *kai-awase* shell-matching game. Hajime is surely listening to the plucked sounds.

"Shapes are seen in the eyes," said Kingo and wrote another line.

"The ears hear voices. Shapes and voices are not the true substance of an object. Although nothing proves an object's true substance, both shapes and voices are meaningless.

When some object is caught deep inside this, both the shape and voice become an entirely new shape and voice. This is an abstraction. An abstraction is a way for a mystery that is fundamentally empty to be seen by the eyes and heard by the ears."

The hands coming to play the koto gradually became frequent. Pauses were threaded through the rain. White claws seemed to fly several times over the bridge. A warm melody seemed to alternate plucking to intertwine the notes of the thick strings and the delicate notes.

> Listening to a stringless koto, for the first time, I sense the meanings of the artistic modulations of the opening, middle, and climax.

When Kingo finished writing, Hajime leaned back on the stool and looked down on the neighboring house. His voice carried from the veranda into the room.

"Hey, Kingo, I can't say why, but it would be good to listen a little longer to that koto. She's quite good."

"Yes, I've been listening attentively for some time," said Kingo, setting down his diary.

"You can't listen carefully while asleep. Please come out here. I'm ordering you to take a business trip to the veranda."

"What are you talking about? I'm fine here. Stop bothering me," said Kingo, showing no signs of rising from his tilted air cushion.

"Hey, I have a clear view of Higashiyama."

"Really?"

"Hey, some guy is walking along the Kamogawa River. It's actually poetic. Some guy's walking by the river."

"Walking is good."

"How does that saying go? *Like many sleeping figures wrapped in futons on* wherever. Maybe people will sleep anywhere on a futon. Will you please come here and tell me?"

"No."

"While you're doing that, the waters of the Kamo are rising. It's bad. Oh no, the bridge looks like it's gonna collapse. Yikes, the bridge is collapsing."

"Even if it does, it won't affect me."

"The bridge falling won't affect you? It won't trouble you even if you can no longer see The Miyako Odori in the evening."

"No. Not at all," said Kingo, who looked bothered. He turned over in bed and gazed sideways at the bamboo shoots on the unremarkable golden sliding screen door.

"If you're so calm, there's no use. The only option for me is to surrender," said Hajime. At last, he yielded and entered the room.

"Hey, hey."

"What now? You are a pain."

"You probably heard that koto."

"Didn't I say I heard it?"

"You know, it's a woman."

"Of course."

"How old do you think she is?"

"Hmm, how old?"

"There's no competition with your indifference. If you're going to tell me, then clearly say, 'Please, tell me.'"

"Who says that?"

"You won't say? If you don't, then only I'll speak. Oh, that's Shimada."

"Is the tatami room open?"

"What? The tatami room is shut tight."

"As usual, that's a lame alias."

"The alias is the real name. I saw that woman."

"Why?"

"I want to listen."

"Not listening to anything is fine. It's more interesting to study these bamboo shoots than to listen to that. As I lie here and look to the side at these shoots, I wonder why they appear shorter."

"It's mostly because your eyes are looking from the side."

"What is the fate of the three lines drawn on the two sheets of thick paper?"

"Because it's pretty bad, it probably should lose one point."

"Why are the bamboo shoots deep blue?"

"It may become the mystery of food poisoning when eaten."

"Yes, it's a mystery. Can you solve mysteries?"

"Ha, ha, ha, ha. Sometimes I try to solve them. Although earlier I said I would solve the mystery of Shimada, I believe the inability to find a full solution is an absence of enthusiasm, which is unbecoming for a philosopher."

"If you want a solution, then solve it. You're that pretentious and not a philosopher who defers to others."

"Well, for now, my solution is trivial. Later, I'll lower my head. That koto's owner ..."

"Yes."

"I saw her."

"I just heard her."

"Oh? There's nothing else to talk about."

"If there isn't, that's fine."

"No, that's no good. Then I'll talk. Yesterday, when I finished my bath, I dried off and cooled off on the veranda. You'll probably want to hear this.

"I calmly looked around at the view of Ōtō. I felt good. The moment I lowered my eyes to look at the house next door the young lady slid open the shōji door halfway, leaned against the door, and looked at the garden."

"She's a beauty."

"Yes, she's lovely, not as pretty as Fujio but better looking than Itoko."

"Really?"

"That's all you have to say. You possess too little altruism. Out of courtesy, you should say, 'That's unfortunate. It would have been nice if I saw her, too.'"

"That's unfortunate. It would have been nice if I saw her, too."

"Ha, ha, ha, ha. So I tried to show her to you, I told you to come out to the veranda."

"Wasn't the shōji shut?"

"At some point, it might have been open."

"Ha, ha, ha, ha. If it were Seizō, he'd probably wait until the door opened."

"That's true. It would have been good to bring along Seizō and show him."

"Kyōto is a good place for a man like him to live."

"Yes, it's very Seizō-like. I told the general to come or whatever, but in the end, he doesn't show."

"He says he has to study during the spring vacation."

"Can you study during the spring vacation?"

"I can't study when it's like that. A literary man is carefree and must not."

"That's a bit too close to home because I, too, am not very serious."

"No, a simple literary man is only a little hazy from drunkenness. He has no character because he can't sweep away the haze and discover his true self."

"A hazy drunkenness? A philosopher contemplates extraneous

matters and makes pained expressions. He's probably drunk on saltwater."

"Despite climbing Eizan, as you saw, a man who can go deep into Wakasa is drunk on rain showers."

"Ha, ha, ha, ha. It's strange because each one of us is drunk."

Kingo's black hair finally rose from the pillow. When air heavy with moisture pressed down by the glossy hair bulged out by elastic forces, the pillow's position turned slightly on the tatami. At the same time, as the camel-hair lap blanket slipped down, he turned it over and folded it in half. His flat, narrow obi sash sloppily tied around his waist was exposed.

"Of course, I'm drunk," quickly commented Hajime, sitting properly on the pillow. With his arms extended in two steps and holding up his thin frame and his torso supported on the palms of his hands, Kingo scowled as he scanned his hips.

"You do look drunk. Aren't you sitting up unusually straight?" he said, staring at Hajime for a long time from under his upper, single eyelids.

"That's because I'm sober."

"You only sit like you're sober."

"My mind is also sober."

"Wearing a padded kimono and sitting properly while drunk, you smugly believe nothing will go wrong. That's funny. It's fine to look drunk when drunk."

"Really? Then, please excuse me," said Hajime and immediately switched to sitting cross-legged.

"You are admirable because you don't insist on being foolish. You're not so absurd as to be a fool and think you are wise."

"What you said about me seems to flow smoothly when you heed advice."

"Despite being drunk, if that's so, it's all right."

"Why are you so cocky? While knowing you are drunk, you probably can't sit cross-legged or kneel properly."

"You're a loafer just waiting around," said Kingo and smiled sadly.

Hajime went over determined to speak but suddenly looked serious. When he saw Kingo's smiling face, Hajime had to look serious.

Of the many expressions of many faces, some never fail to touch the human heart. They do not make the muscles on the face scramble to dance. They do not spark lightning in each strand of hair on the head. They do not cut the connections to the tear ducts to see a torrent of tears.

Pointless fury is like a swaggering young man brandishing a sword and cutting the floor. The motions are shallow. It's a play at a Hongō theater. Kingo's laughter wasn't laughter for the stage.

A wave of elusive compassion from the bottom of his heart barely flowed through a pipe as fine as a strand of hair. Momentary shadows were cast during the day in this transient world.

An expression that comes and goes is different. If you stick out your head and notice the transient world, you instantly return to the inner sanctuary. The one captured before turning back wins. If the capture fails, Kingo cannot be understood over a lifetime.

His laughter was thin and mildly cold. Within its docility, quickness, and fading away, his life will be vividly sketched. His acquaintances will understand the meaning of this moment.

Kingo was placed at the border of savagery. Parents and children have difficulty understanding this sort of person. Even brothers are strangers. Placing him at the border of savagery and, for the first time, sketching out his character becomes a crude novel. Savagery will not recklessly emerge in the twentieth century.

A spring trip is peaceful. Kyōto's inns are quiet. The two men are safe. They joke. Between them, Hajime understands Kingo, and Kingo understands Hajime. This is the world.

"Are you a loafer just waiting around?" asked Hajime, starting to twist the leather straps of the camel-hair lap blanket.

"Will you be a loafer forever?" he asked but didn't look at his companion's face. He repeated "forever" like a question, a soliloquy, or as though speaking to the camel-hair lap blanket.

"Even if I loaf right here, I am determined," said Kingo. Now, for the first time, he half rose to his feet and turned to face his companion.

"It would be nice if your father were alive."

"What? My father being alive may have been a problem."

"Maybe so," said Hajime, drawing out the last word.

"In short, if I give the house to Fujio, it'll all be settled."

"Then what will you do?"

"I'll be a loafer."

"At last, you will be a true loafer."

"Yes. It doesn't matter if I inherit the house, I'll loaf around, or don't inherit, I'll loaf around."

"But you can't. First of all, your mother will be troubled."

"Oh, Mother?"

Kingo made a strange face and looked at Hajime.

If I have doubts, even I can be deceived. At the intersection of interests of people other than me, the thickness of the skin that filters away the dust of losses is not easily measured. A close friend gave that assessment of my mother. Was the assessment of her interior only understood outside of her?

Inescapable feelings hide somewhere in me or a demon deceives me. They say he, a relative on my father's side, is my best friend. Heavenly secrets are hard to divulge in a roundabout way.

Were Hajime's words intended to trick me into examining the depths of my heart about my feelings toward my stepmother? Even after seeing this, if Hajime is the same as always, then that's it. If he's a man who plays tricks, after pulling out my thoughts, there's no guarantee things won't be turned upside down.

Do Hajime's words echo his honest intent, without duplicity, to sincerely understand my mother's inner feelings? Making assumptions from aspects of his life, that may be so.

Perhaps, having been asked by my mother, I will stop my cowardly behavior of throwing a weighted probe into the bottom of the frightening, even to me, abyss of my sorrowful heart.

However, the honest person is more easily used. Though aware of my cowardice and being reduced to a pawn, I accept the wishes of my mother who misjudged me out of kindness to me. The mutually uninteresting results might come to light in the family before an inevitable time. In any case, a mouth that doesn't interrupt does not speak.

The two were silent for a short time. Next door, the koto was still being played.

"Is that koto being played in the style of the Ikuta school?" asked Kingo, changing the subject.

"It has gotten cold. I'm putting on my fox vest," said Hajime, changing the subject. The two conversed about two different subjects.

He opened the chest of his padded kimono robe and took down his usual strange padded undershirt from the top of the staggered shelf. When he leaned his body and passed his arms through, Kingo asked, "Is that vest handmade?"

"Yeah. A friend who went to China gave me the fur. Itoko sewed the front for me."

"It's genuine. It's well done. Itoko is different from Fujio and is practical, which is a good thing."

"It's good? Marrying her off is a little troublesome."

"Are there no good proposals?"

"Good proposals?" asked Hajime, glancing at Kingo. He said with no interest, "It's not that there are none ..."

As his words trailed off, Kingo changed the subject.

"When Itoko marries, it'll be your father's problem, too."

"It's a problem, and nothing can be done, but the trouble will come. But more than that, will you marry?"

"I ... uh ... I can't earn a living."

"So as your mother says, you should inherit the house ..."

"That's no good. Whatever she said, I'm not doing that."

"It's strange. Sorry. Because you are unsure, Fujio probably can't marry."

"It's not that she can't. She won't."

Hajime said nothing and twitched his nose.

"Don't force me to eat eel again. We eat eel all day every day. My stomach is stuffed with small bones. The truth is Kyōto is a foolish place. Why don't we go home?"

"You can go home. If it's the eels, you don't have to go home.

However, your sense of smell is extremely keen. Can you smell the eel?"

"You can't? They're constantly being baked in the kitchen."

"With your level of intuition, my father possibly did not have to die in a foreign country. He seemed to have a dulled sense of smell."

"Ha, ha, ha, ha. Have your father's belongings been delivered?"

"They might have arrived by now. A fellow named Saeki from the diplomatic mission should bring them to us. There's probably nothing. A few books, maybe."

"There may be his customary watch."

"Yes. That watch he bought in London and was so proud of? That will probably come. That watch has been Fujio's toy since childhood. Once she had it in her hands, she rarely let it go. She was fascinated by the garnets in its chain."

"Thinking about it. That watch was an antique."

"Perhaps. He bought it on his first trip to The West."

"Please, give it to me as a memento of your father."

"I was thinking that, too."

"When your father went overseas this last time, he promised to give it to me as a graduation present when he returned."

"I also remember that. This time, Fujio may seize it again and make it her toy."

"Can't Fujio let go of that watch? Ha, ha, ha, ha. It doesn't matter. I'll get it anyway."

Kingo was silent and stared for a long time at the space between Hajime's eyebrows. On the lunch trays were the eels predicted by Hajime.

CHAPTER 4

Kingo's diary has these lines.

People who see colors don't see shapes. People who see shapes don't see substance.

Seizō is a man who sees color and lives in the world.
Here is another line from Kingo's diary.

The connection between life and death never ceases. Madness appears in a world of colors.

Seizō is a man who lives in a world of colors.
He was born in a dark place. Someone said he was born out of wedlock. Friends bullied him when he wore a workman's *tsutsusode* kimono to school. Dogs barked at him wherever he went. His father died. He had bitter experiences in the outside world and no home to return to. Out of necessity, others took care of him.

Seaweed at the bottom of the sea drifts in dark places and knows nothing about the sunny places on the shore where white sails float by. Waves tease by trembling to the right and fluttering to the left. Sometimes, it is defiance. The waves are used to it and don't care.

Waves have no time to think about any object. Naturally, the question of Why am I buffeted by the waves? is not a problem. It is impossible to make it better.

They say fate sprouts in dark places and can grow there. Fate is said to move in the morning and the evening. Therefore, it is moving.

Seizō was seaweed at the bottom of the sea.

In Kyōto, Kodō-sensei took care of him. The sensei had a kimono with a splash pattern made for him. Every year, the sensei gave him a monthly allowance of twenty yen. From time to time, he also taught him about books. He learned about the tour of cherry blossom trees around Gion. The sensei showed him the scrolls of Chion-in Temple, and he recognized their great value. He began eating full servings of meals. The seaweed on the bottom of the sea separated from the ground and eventually floated up.

Tōkyo dazzles the eyes. Someone who lived a hundred years ago in the Genroku era had a shorter life than someone who lived for three days in the Meiji era.

In other places, people walk on the soles of their feet. In Tōkyo, they walk on their toes. They do handstands. Move to the side. Impatient people rush in.

Seizō moved tirelessly around Tōkyo. After his dogged circling, he opened his eyes and saw the world was changing. It changed even after he rubbed his eyes. When he thought, This is strange, the change was bad.

Seizō moved forward without thinking. His friends said, "He's a genius." His teachers said, "He's full of promise." In the boarding house, they said, "Seizō. Seizō."

Seizō moved forward without thinking. When he advanced, the emperor awarded him the gift of a silver pocket watch. The seaweed floating out held white flowers on the water's surface. Things without roots go unnoticed.

The world is a world of colors. If these colors are savored, the world is savored. The world's colors are vividly reflected in the eyes along with one's success. A life surpassing a brocade in brilliance is precious. Seizō's handkerchief sometimes carries the scent of the flowers of a heliotrope.

The world is a world of colors. Shapes are the remains of colors. The man who criticizes the remains and does not understand the essence inside does not know how to clear off the foam rising on sake and clings to its square vessel. The plate cannot be eaten no matter how closely it is examined. Sake that does not touch the lips is flat. A conventional man hugs a bottomless sake cup of morality and huddles on the side of the road.

The world is a world of colors. Mischievously, it is called a world of carnal desires or a world you can see but not touch like a flower reflected in a mirror or the moon reflected on the water. The absolute reality of the ultimate nature of all things is a delusion in which people with deformities who are rejected in the world sweep away intolerable hatred in dreams during daytime naps.

A blind man strokes a three-legged kettle. If he cannot see color, he wants to study the shape. A blind man without hands doesn't dare stroke anything. The handless blind man searches for the substance of an object beyond using his eyes and ears.

A flower arrangement sat on Seizō's desk. The first winds of summer blew through the weeping willows outside the window. His eyeglasses with gold rims hung on the tip of his nose.

The natural order is to cross over a gorgeous region and enter with humility. Long ago, we were called babies and dressed in red outfits. Most things grow up inside of paintings. Then from the light colorings of the Shijō school of painting, we grow old in India-ink drawings of the Unkoku school and become familiar with the ephemeral nature of a coffin.

Reminiscing about the past, one sees memories of a mother, an older sister, sweets, and carp streamers. The further back he looked, the more magnificent it became.

Seizō's inclinations were different. By retracing the natural path, the roots are shaken and cut from the dark earth and drift to the bright shore of waves transmitting the sun. Born at the bottom of a hole, he took twenty-seven years to draw nearer step-by-step to a more beautiful transient world. When he peeked through a knothole into the twenty-seven-year history, the further he looked back, the darker it became. A solitary red point flickered faintly along the way.

When he came to Tōkyo, he adored and longed for the redness and was not bothered by recurring cold memories. Again and again, he peered through the knothole into the past. He lived elegantly through long nights, eternal days, and occasional rain showers. Now, the red has mostly receded. The colors also faded considerably. Seizō came to neglect looking through the knothole.

The knothole into the past was plugged by satisfaction with the present. The current times are in an economic slump but will create the future. Seizō's present moment is a rose, the bud of a rose, a promising young man. He lacks the need to shape the future. If the budded rose fully opens, naturally, this is his future. When gazing through a knothole into the future through a special tube, the rose is already open. It seems if he extended his hands, he could grab it. Somebody whispers near his ear, "Grab it quickly." Seizō was resolved to write a doctoral dissertation.

Will I become a doctor after I write a dissertation or will I write the dissertation to become a doctor? I don't know unless I ask a doctor, but I must write the dissertation. It will not be a simple thesis but will certainly be a doctoral dissertation.

The doctor is magnificent, the most colorful of scholars. Each time he peers through the tube of the future, the word *doctor* burns a golden color. Beside the word *doctor,* a gold watch dangles down from heaven. The red garnet stones under the watch sway like flames of the heart.

Fujio, with her dark eyes, also reaches out a slender arm to beckon him. This creates a beautiful picture. The poet's ideal vision becomes the people in this picture.

Long ago, there lived a man named Tantalus. It is written that he met a bitter fate as punishment for committing a terrible crime. His body was plunged into water up to his shoulders. Above his head, branches were heavy with delicious fruits.

Tantalus is thirsty, but when he tries to drink water, the water recedes. Tantalus is hungry, but when he tries to eat fruit, the fruit evades him. Even if he moves his mouth a foot, the fruit moves a foot. If his mouth moves forward two feet, the fruit moves forward two feet. Whether he foolishly moves three or four feet or travels one thousand miles, Tantalus remains hungry and parched. Even now, he probably walks in pursuit of water and fruit.

Each time Seizō peers through the tube into the future, he feels like a follower of Tantalus, but that is not all.

Sometimes, Fujio is haughty. Her long eyebrows shorten, as though they're being pressed together, and she glares. The garnet blazes. The figure of a woman is enveloped by flames and vanishes.

The word *doctor* gradually thins and darkens as it peels off. The watch plummets down like a meteorite from far off heaven and breaks up. At that moment, he hears a snap. Being a poet, Seizō sketched a variety of futures.

He stuck his chin propped on his hand at the front of the desk. As always, he peeked at his future in the camellia flower covering a colored glass vase for a single flower. In a future with several paths, today's results were worse than usual.

The woman said, "I'd like to give you this watch."

"Thank you," Seizō said and reached out. She tapped his open hand and said, "I'm sorry, but the engagement has already been settled."

He asked, "The watch is not included, but are you?"

She said, "Me? Of course, I'm attached to the watch," and then turned around and briskly walked out.

Seizō tried to create the future up to this moment but was surprised despite the excessive time remaining. When he tried to start from the beginning again and held up his chin in slight pain, the shōji screen door slid open.

"A letter, Sir," said a maid, who moved forward and set down the letter.

When he saw the letter addressed to *Ono Seizō-sama*, written in the calligraphic style of the Sugō school, Seizō swiftly tensed both elbows and pulled back his body supported by the desk as if he were about to leap. Simultaneously, the camellia tube for peeking at the future trembled. A crimson petal fell without a sound onto a collection of Rossetti's poems. In a flash, the entire future crumbled.

Seizō leaned on the desk, leaving his left hand extended. He tilted his head and gazed from a distance at the letter resting on the palm of his hand but did not rush to turn it over. Despite not turning it over, he thought he knew what was written. If he was correct, turning it over became more difficult. If he turned it over and his guess was right, he could not go back.

One time, a tortoise was asked a question. He stuck out his head and was hit. While thinking he would be hit, if possible, he stayed hidden in his shell. Even if he sees he's on the verge of the fate of being hit, a bit of his neck wants to shrink in an instant. Presumably, Seizō may be a turtle of a university student who narrowly escapes the judgment of facts. Sooner or later, the turtle pokes out his head. Seizō turns over the envelope now.

After staring for a short time, the palm of his hand itches. After he craves a moment of calm, he wants to turn it over and know once and for all to put his mind at ease.

Seizō makes up his mind, turns over the envelope, and places it on the desk. The name written on the back is *Inoue Kodō*. The cursive characters written using a generous amount of ink in bold characters on a white envelope jump off the paper, as though the tips of needles had been lined up and fixed in Seizō's eyes.

Seizō takes both hands off the desk as if letting a sleeping dog lie. Only his face faces the letter on the desk. However, the desk and his lap break the connection with a foot-long gap. His hands pulled from the desk seem to effortlessly come out of his shoulders.

Should I break the seal? If someone comes and says to break the seal, I will give a reason not to break it and feel relief. However, if I can't make others surrender, I can't surrender either.

A little-known jujitsu practitioner has not proven himself a jujitsu professional until he throws a man one time in the streets. A weak argument is similar to weak jujitsu. Seizō thought a visit from this friend since his Kyōto days would be nice.

The student lodger on the second floor started playing a violin. Seizō recently began violin lessons, too. Today, however, he was not interested at all. He was jealous of the student he considered to be happy-go-lucky. Another petal fell from the camellia.

Holding the vase with a single flower, he slid open the shōji door and stepped onto the veranda. He threw flowers into the yard followed by the water. He held the flower arrangement in his hand. He was about to toss out the flower arrangement but stood on the veranda holding it. There were hinoki cypress trees and a fence. On the other side was the second floor. A rain umbrella was hung out to dry in the dried-up yard. Fallen flowers stuck two petals to the black border of a snake eyes pattern. There were many other things but all were meaningless. Everything was mechanical.

Seizō shuffled back inside the room dragging his heavy feet. He didn't sit but stood in front of the desk. The knothole to the past opened, and the history of long ago appeared long and narrow in the distance. It was dark. A point in the darkness caught fire and moved closer. Suddenly, Seizō bent over, reached out his hands, and broke the seal.

Greetings,

As the bright season of spring opens, I hope to find you in good health. As always, I persevere. Sayoko is in good health, too. I hesitate to ask you to rest.

At the end of last year, I announced I would move to Tōkyo. Subsequently, various situations unfolded. This culminated in favorable circumstances. Soon, I intend to take decisive steps, as you know. Twenty years ago, I moved out of Tōkyo. Other than the two times I visited on short stays of five or six days, I've heard little news of my hometown. I will arrive in total ignorance and am asking for your assistance.

Tsutaya, my neighbor, has offered to buy my old home and residence for many years. I entered discussions with him and signed a contract.

I've sold off all of my bulky belongings here and intend to have an easy move. Sayoko only wishes to take her koto to Tōkyo. Old items are hard to discard. Please take pity on a young woman's feelings.

As you know, five years ago, I sent for Sayoko to come to Kyōto. She hopes for a quick change of residence and to be educated at a Tōkyo school. As for her future, we agree for the most part and have nothing in particular to report. I'd like to meet with you after I arrive.

The exhibition will be held in your town and crowded. I will depart on an express night train. An express train is important to passengers in a rush, but it is difficult to plan while en route to Tōkyo for one or two days. The deadlines are set, and I will notify you in a timely manner. First, I will see to that business.

Seizō finished reading but remained standing in front of the desk. The unfinished letter gently dropped from his right hand. The folded paper with Seizō-sama ... Kodō written in a margin settled like a wave pattern on the blue cashmere desk cover.

Seizō ran his hand along half the cloth away from him and looked down until the color faded on the desk cover. When his downcast eyes stopped, inevitably, his eyes turned to gaze at the Rossetti poetry collection. He looked at the two scattered red petals printed on the front cover. Drawn in by the red, he seemed to stare at the colored glass vase that should be set on the right corner. The vase was not going anywhere. The camellia inserted the day before yesterday had lost its silhouette and shape. The tube for peering at a beautiful future disappeared.

Seizō sat in front of the desk. A peculiar smell floated from inside his benefactor's letter weakly folded up. A stale, musty-smelling rose. It was a smell from the past. The present and the past bind the ends of a hairline that resists being forgotten and connects them until they vanish at the fine edge. This smell unites the present with the past near the face.

If the history of half a lifetime is long and questioned in reverse back to the hopelessness of a point, it becomes gloomier the further back traveled. If a bud emerges and becomes a stem, it is fortunate a drill's power sharpens at the end of a withered branch with veins having no pulse. Rather than saying it is unnecessary to pierce the life of memory, it is tragic.

The god Janus has two faces, one looks forward and the other, backward. The fortunate Seizō has only one face. With his back facing the past, his eyes reflected only bright prospects. A north wind blew toward his back. Yesterday and today when the memory of this cold place was excised with difficulty, the cold object was chased from the cold place. Until now, simply forgetting was fine.

While the future unfolds with warmth and vibrancy, if he were surrounded and driven back to the past by just one step, it ends. The living past is quietly embedded in the dead past. While fearing it will move, it will probably be okay. Movements on that day become only a long series of panoramas that look back. His chest is caressed at a point that does not move.

However, when he makes light of the distant past and now looks through the tube into the past, everything is in motion. As he continues to leave the past behind, it gets closer. It draws near.

The quiet before and after and the dryness to the left and right are overcome and come swaying like the flame in a paper lantern lighting the night. Seizō began turning around in the room.

Nature does not exhaust nature. Before that extreme is reached, something will happen. Monotony is the enemy of nature.

When Seizō turned around in the room and not yet standing up, the maid's head poked out from behind the shōji door.

"You have a guest, sir," she said, smiling. Why was she smiling? It made no sense. She smiles when she says "Hello," "Welcome home," or "Dinner is served."

The way she looks at people and smiles for no reason is proof of always seeking something from others. This maid was seeking a reward from Seizō.

Seizō appeared indifferent and only looked at her. She despaired.

"Shall I bring him through?"

"Uh, yeah," Seizō replied listlessly.

The maid despaired again. She smiled impulsively because she was attracted to Seizō. From her perspective, the guest, unattractive to her, did not have the value of half a *mon*. Seizō understood this intellectually. The connection to his popularity with the maid until today was entirely based on this realization. Seizō was a man who did not like to fall into delusions even concerning his popularity with maids.

Long ago, a philosopher said two objects cannot occupy the same space at the same time. The simultaneous presence of charm and anxiety in Seizō's brain was contrary to the inventions of this philosopher. Charm receded and anxiety crept in. The maid collided with his troubles. Charm receded and anxiety crept in. A false philosopher thinks charm is a mere facade and anxiety has substance.

Upon a landlord entering a house, charm settles private matters, and anxiety is transferred to the renters. Nevertheless, the maid saw Seizō's predicament.

"Shall I bring the guest through?"

"Yes. All right."

"Shall I tell him you're out?"

"Who is it?"

"Asai-san."

"Oh, Asai."

"Are you out?"

"Yes, okay."

"You're not here?"

"What should I do?"

"Which one, sir?"

"I'll see him."

"I'll show him in."

"Wait. Wait a minute."

"Yes, sir?"

"No, nothing. It's fine."

There were times when he wanted to see friends, and times when he didn't. If he was clear, there was no trouble. When he didn't, the excuse that he was out was employed. Seizō was a bold man who used that excuse as long as the visitor's feelings wouldn't be hurt. The only problem was his wanting to meet a guest, not wanting to meet a guest, leaving from the front, or returning by the back. Even the maid made fun of him.

From time to time, he encountered people he knew while out and about. If they had a brief exchange, that was it. Then as before, they became total strangers. Sometimes, however, both avoided the other by moving to the right or the left at the same time.

When he didn't want the encounter, he began to move to the opposite side and altered his gait. However, the other person also changed his mind and crossed to the opposite side. When they realized their opposites were the same and corrected again, they corrected in the same way at the same instant. Both tried to do it again but hesitated. After the hesitation, they tried again. Their confusion remained as they rocked back and forth like the pendulum of a wall clock. In the end, both wanted to bad mouth the other as a dope. The popular Seizō was called a dope by the maid a few times.

Asai entered. He was an old friend from his days in Kyōto. In no time, he gripped his slightly broken-in brown hat with his right hand as if trying to crush it and tossed it onto the tatami.

"The weather's great today," he said, sitting down cross-legged. Seizō had forgotten about the weather.

"It's a lovely day."

"Have you been to the exhibition?"

"No, I haven't gone yet."

"You should go. It's fun. I went yesterday and ate ice cream."

"Ice cream? Yes, yesterday was very hot."

"The next time, I'm going to eat Russian food. Why don't we go together?"

"Today?"

"All right, today is good."

"Today is a little ..."

"You can't go? Studying too much will make you sick. You'll soon be a doctor and are probably thinking about marrying a beautiful wife. What a rude guy."

"No, it's not that. I've lost interest in studying."

"Your nerves may be frayed. You don't look so good."

"I don't? I am feeling out of sorts."

"It shows. The young lady Inoue-san will worry. Eat some Russian food soon, and you'll get better."

"Why?"

"Why? Because she's coming to Tōkyo."

"Is she?"

"Is she? Of course, you should have been notified.

"Were you notified?"

"Yes, I was. Will you be?"

"No, I was."

"When was that?"

"A little while ago."

"Finally, you're getting married."

"Why would I do that?"

"You're not then? Why?"

"Why? The situation with them is gradually becoming more serious."

"What situation?"

"We'll have an unhurried talk about that. Inoue-sensei has been a great help to me. I will do anything within my power for Sensei. But marriage is not something I can rush into, as you may believe."

"But you will get engaged."

"At one time, I thought about discussing that with you, too, but I sympathize with Sensei's feelings."

"That's probably so."

"If the sensei comes, we can have an unhurried discussion. The problem is he has taken things for granted."

"What did he take for granted?"

"After reading his letter, he seems to have decided."

"That's because his thinking is old-fashioned."

"Once he's made a decision, he doesn't budge. He's stubborn."

"Lately, his family finances haven't been good."

"I was thinking about that. It'll be a problem."

"Could you look at your watch and tell me what time it is?"

"Two-sixteen."

"Two-sixteen? Is that watch a gift from the emperor."

"Yes."

"You're a smart fellow. It would have been nice if I got one, too. If I had one, my reception in the world would be very different."

"That's not true."

"But it is because the emperor would be my supporter."

"Are you going somewhere after this?"

"Yes. The weather is too nice not to enjoy. Will you come?"

"There's some business I must attend to, but we can go that far."

Seizō said goodbye at the gate and proceeded toward the Kōno estate.

CHAPTER 5

With one step through the temple gate, the greenery of an ancient world assaulted their shoulders from the left and right. The only sounds were the footsteps of Kingo and Hajime falling on a path wider than six feet of variously shaped natural stones neatly laid in a line.

From this direction continuing endlessly down a straight, narrow strip, the men could look up and past the final stones of the path and see the temple. Thick cedar shingles undulated from the left and right in an inner ring and formed two large wings. A small roof extended onto a small wing where both large wings gathered at a steep spine. They wondered whether the vents were for air or light. At the same time, Kingo and Hajime looked up from the side at an angle that presented the most charming view of this temple.

"It's bright," said Kingo and stopped his walking staff.

"That temple looks nearly indestructible despite being a wooden structure."

"In other words, its fine construction created a handsome design. This may be consistent with Aristotle's notion of *form*."

"It's fairly complicated. Aristotle doesn't matter. But it's curious that all the temples around here evoke strange feelings."

"An interest in ship-plank fences or religious light offerings are different. The priest Musō Kokushi built them."

"Look up at the temple. The slightly weird feeling is you turning into Musō Kokushi. Ha, ha, ha, ha. Musō Kokushi can say a few words."

"Because we become Musō Kokushi and the zen master Daitō Kokushi, there is value in strolling around a place like this. What is sightseeing?"

"If Musō Kokushi became a roof and lived until the Meiji era, that's fine. It's far better than a cheap bronze statue."

"Yes, it's obvious."

"What?"

"What? The landscaping of the temple grounds. There are no curves at all. It's bright no matter where you are."

"Just like me. So I'll probably feel good when I enter the temple."

"Ha, ha, ha. Maybe so."

"When I look at it, Musō Kokushi resembles me. Don't I resemble Musō Kokushi?"

"Whatever. It's nice. Shall we rest a little?" Kingo asked and sat on the railing of the stone bridge crossing a lotus pond. At the base of the railing, the four-inch thick branches of a large, three-tier pine looked out over the water. Spots of moss on the stones budded a faint blue. Beneath the moss encroaching deeply into a purple matter mixed with gray, yellow stalks of withered lotus smoothly poked through last year's frost into springtime.

Hajime took out a match and a cigarette. He struck the match and tossed the burning remains into the pond waters.

"Musō Kokushi was not mischievous like you," said Kingo. He used both hands to carefully bring the head of his walking staff to the tip of his chin.

"Only in that is he inferior to me. Copying Munechika Kokushi is a good idea."

"You'd probably be a better bandit on horseback than a revered Kokushi priest."

"Because a bandit diplomat on horseback is a little weird, I'll rightly be stationed in Peking."

"As a diplomat specializing in The East?"

"Asian administration. Ha, ha, ha, ha. Someone like me is not suited for Western countries. What will happen if I undertake training? Will I turn out like your father?"

"It would be terrible if you die in some foreign country like him."

"What? That doesn't matter because I'll leave what's left to you."

"That's a big nuisance."

"I won't simply die but will die for the nation. At least, doing that should be fine."

"I already have too much to do for myself."

"By nature, you're too selfish. Are there any thoughts of Japan in your mind?"

Until now, a cloud of jokes obscured the seriousness. That cloud finally cleared, and seriousness floated up from below.

"Have you thought about Japan's fate?" asked Kingo. He pressed down on the tip of his walking staff and tipped back the vital part he was holding.

"Fate is what gods ponder. People are fine if they move like people. Look at the Russo-Japanese War."

"If I can recover from a cold, I think my life will be long."

"Are you saying Japan has a short life?" Hajime pressed closer.

"It's not the war between Japan and Russia. It's the war between one race of people and another."

"Of course."

"Look at America. Look at India. Look at Africa."

"Because of that, your father died in a foreign country. The logic is I will also die in a foreign country."

"From proof more than theory, doesn't everyone die?"

"Is dying the same as being killed?"

"Usually, you are killed while you don't know what's happening."

Kingo, who withdrew from everything, tapped the tip of his walking staff on the stone bridge and shrunk his shoulders in horror. Hajime jumped to his feet.

"Look over there. Look at that temple. Didn't the monk called Gazan say the temple was rebuilt from only one bowl of alms begged for by a monk? Moreover, death came at or before fifty. If you don't think that will happen, you can't stand up chopsticks lying on their sides."

"Look there from the temple," said Kingo, still sitting on the railing and pointing in the opposite direction.

The temple door that cut the world into vertical slices opened quickly, red things passed through and blue things passed through. Women passed through. Children passed through. With spring coming to Saga, scattered streams of people from Kyōto moved in continuous tumult to Arashiyama.

"There it is," said Kingo. Again, the two went out into a world of color.

If they turned left before the temple gate of Tenryū-ji temple and turned right at Shaka-dō temple, they came to Togetsukyō bridge. Even in Kyōto, it was famous as a beauty spot.

The two men looked at the shops that haphazardly lined both sides of the street and sold famous products or inscribed products. The feet of those wearing traveling clothes for more than seven days moved toward the station with a mind to travel.

Everyone they met was from Kyōto. Every half hour during the flowering season, a train arrived from Nijō and emptied. The new arrivals, all nice-looking young men and women, were blown towards the flowers on Arashimayama.

"It's beautiful," said Hajime, forgetting about the crowds in the world. No other place has women who wear clothes as fine as those in Kyōto. The world's trends cannot rival the elegance of Kyōto's women.

"The women of Kyōto are dancing the Miyako Odori day and night. They're so carefree."

"That's why I say it's so like Seizō."

"However, the Miyako Odori is wonderful."

"It's not bad. Somehow, business is good."

"No. When I see that, I hardly feel any sexual attraction. When women's dress is decorated that much, they lose to adornment and have fewer human molecules."

"Yes, the extreme of that ideal is the Kyōto Doll. A doll is not tawdry when it's mechanical."

"The danger is with the ones who wear light makeup, are active, and have the most human molecules."

"Ha, ha, ha, ha. I guess any type of philosopher would be in danger. However, the Miyako Odori presents no danger to the diplomat. We are in total agreement. It's good we came to enjoy ourselves in a safe place for both of us."

"Human molecules are good when the first principle is active, but usually decay because the tenth most important principle is randomly activated."

"About which principle are we at?"

"We're no higher than the second or third principle because human beings are superior."

"Really?"

"Even if what I say is trivial, you have charm."

"Thank you. What activities constitute the first principle?"

"The first principle? The first principle cannot be fulfilled if blood is not seen."

"That's dangerous."

"When blood washes away the frivolous perspective, the first principle is evoked. People are that superficial."

"Is it my blood or someone else's?"

Instead of answering, Kingo stared at the teacups of powdered green tea displayed at a kiosk. The handmade ones were molded from clay and filled three shelves. They all looked silly.

"Those dopey things are no good no matter how much they're washed in blood," said Hajime, trailing behind him.

"This one is …" said Kingo, picking up a teacup to examine it. Not noticing, Hajime jerked his sleeve. The teacup smashed into pieces on the ground.

"Oh no."

Kingo gazed at the scattered fragments.

"Hey, did it break? That doesn't matter. Come here and look. Hurry."

Kingo stepped over the threshold into the dirt-floor room.

"What is it?"

He looked over his shoulder past a man behind him who belonged to Tenryū-ji to see a typical Kyōto Doll strolling away.

"What is it?" asked Kingo again.

"Oh, she's gone. Too bad."

"Who's gone?"

"That woman."

"What woman?"

"The one next door."

"Next door?"

"The koto's owner. The young lady you wanted to see. I did my best to show her to you, but those worthless teacups got in the way."

"That's unfortunate. Which one is she?"

"Which one? Can I still see her?"

"It's unfortunate about the young lady, but the teacup was a tragedy. It's your fault."

"There are so many. You just can't wash that teacup. It's a problem that can't be fixed if broken. There's nothing I dislike more than the implements owned by tea masters. Everything is twisted. I want to gather all the tea implements in the world and smash every last one to pieces. Because something comes next, why not break a few more teacups?"

"Hmph, how much does one cost?"

They paid for the teacup and headed to the train station.

The Kyōto train that brings the libertines to the flowers returned to Nijō from Saga. The ones not returning passed through the mountain and exited in Tanba. The two men bought tickets for Tanba and descended to Kameoka. The rapids of the Hozugawa River streamed down from this station. The waters flowing downstream gently passed before their eyes and created the charm of blue oil. The shore opened. Horsetail picked by children in the countryside also grew there. The boatmen maneuvered the boat to the shore where sightseers awaited.

"What an odd-looking boat," said Hajime. The bottom was constructed from one flat board. The decking on the gunwale was barely a foot above the water. An ashtray tipped over onto a red blanket. The two men sat a good distance away from each other.

"You can move to the left. The waves don't hit there," said the boatman.

There were four boatmen. At the bow, one man held a twelve-foot bamboo pole, followed by two men on the right side holding oars, and another standing on the left with another bamboo pole.

The oars creaked. The men's neck muscles were roughly hewn, flattened oak wrapped by a wisteria vine. A rounded shape greater than a foot told of tightly gripping hands. The height and blackness of the knuckles of the gripping hands seemed to stand up as blue streaks in a small pine branch and pass a powerful paddling stroke through the veins.

The oar held down by a wisteria vine bent the scruff of the neck with each stroke, scraped the wisteria, and rubbed against the decking while the powerful nape of the neck stood up straight. The oar squeaked with each stroke.

The shore was hit by several swells. The soundless water was continuously sent forward with no time to stop. Ripples of water came one after another. In the springtime, mountains encircled a mountain castle and rose above their heads like a folding screen. The approaching waters were forced to enter between the mountains.

When the sun shining on hats seemed to lose the shadows momentarily, the boat had already entered the gorge. The rapids of the Hozugawa River began there.

"We're finally here," said Hajime, looking about three feet past the boatmen's figures in the narrow space between the shores. The water roared.

"Of course," said Kingo. When he stuck his head over the side of the boat, the boat slid into the rapids.

The two men on the right relaxed their grips to cut through the waves. The oars flowed and reached the side of the boat. The man standing at the bow kept the pole on the side. The tilting boat going down like an arrow reverberated with stomping at the feet and the buttocks seated on the bottom of the boat. When they worried the boat would rupture, it had already broken free of the running rapids.

"Over there," said Hajime. Looking past his pointing finger, he saw white foam fall headlong and bite into an area of one hectare. Faint sunshine and shadows spreading over the valley scrambled to win thousands of jewels.

"Splendid," said Hajime with great pleasure.

"This or Musō Kokushi, which is better?"

"This is more distinguished than Musō Kokushi."

The boatmen could not be any more nonchalant. Apparently unconcerned about a boulder hugging a pine tree that looked about to fall but didn't, they moved the oars to approach and manipulated the poles to move away. The passing rapids rotated in various directions. With each rotation, a new mountain leaped into view. Swift currents robbed the travelers of time to count the stony mountains, mountains of pine trees, and mountains of assorted small trees, and propelled and thrust the boat into the rapids.

The huge boulder was round and avoided the nuisance of being covered by moss. It waited for the boat to reach the center where the greenery collapsed. Water droplets smashed against its naked purple body and scattered, showering from the waist in the spring chill.

Was the boat an arrow, a shield, or some other object? With resolve, the boat aimed and lunged at this large boulder.

Water could not be seen leaving in a vortex from a crack on the other side of the boulder. How far down did the eroded slope drop to the river bottom? The passengers were mystified by the destinations of the waves. Will the boat be catapulted into the boulder and smashed to pieces, or be engulfed by the unseen beyond and plunged into the depths? The boat pressed forward.

"We're gonna hit," said Hajime, raising his hips. A giant purple boulder rose and pressed on the boatman's black hair.

"Uh," grunted the boatman as he put his strength into the bow. The boat easily slipped under the giant belly of the boulder eating the waves with power great enough to shatter it. The boatmen adjusted their grips on the poles at the side. With both hands raised high above their shoulders, they steadily maneuvered the boat. From the tip of the pole pushing away from this beast, the boat slid at an angle across the bottom edge of the boulder with less than a foot to spare and fell on the other side.

"At any rate, this is far superior to Musō Kokushi," said Hajime as they dropped.

When the rapids abated, an empty boat climbed toward them from the other side. Naturally, if the poles weren't being used, the oars were. Fists strained to push off at the corners of the boulder.

A thin rope wrapped around the striped fabric sloping off of shoulders connected the long distance to pull the boat back. He headed toward a shore that was hard to detect except for the flow of the water by leaping to rocks, crawling over boulders, and bending forward at the waist until his sandals disintegrated.

Both hands dangling down immersed only fingertips in the blocked and swirling whirlpools. Boulders were naturally rubbed and eroded by the persistence of superhuman power for generations and gradually and easily received the backs of legs being dragged forward. The long bamboo poles being passed over here, there, and above the boulder is said to be the strategy to slide quickly without the pulled rope opposing our force.

"It has calmed a bit," said Kingo, looking at the shores on both sides. Far above the towering mountains where footholds could not be seen, the cuttings sounds of a hatchet were heard. A black shadow moved high in the sky.

"That has to be a monkey," said Hajime. His pharynx protruded when he looked up at the cliff.

"You can do anything once you get used to it."

His companion also shaded his eyes with his hands to see.

"How much do you think he gets paid for a day's work?"

"My guess is not much."

"Can I ask from down here?"

"The current is too fast. There's not even a little leeway. It runs all the time. If there aren't places like this here and there, you can't go."

"I want to run faster. Earlier, when we went around that boulder's protruding belly, in a way, it was great fun. I wanted to borrow the boatman's pole and steer the boat."

"If you had, we'd be in heaven now."

"What? It's fun. Better than looking at a Kyōto Doll?"

"Everything in nature acts according to the first principle."

"By doing so, nature is a model for humans."

"What? A human is nature's model?"

"Of course, it's a Kyōto Doll."

"A Kyōto Doll is nice. Naturally, you're a fan of the lifelike doll."

"The Kyōto Doll is nice. She is close to nature. The first principle has some meaning. The problem is ..."

"What is the problem?"

"Isn't there a serious problem?" asked Kingo.

"On a day with problems, there is no plan. The reason is the model disappears."

"You say it's fun to ride the rapids because there is a model."

"You're asking me?"

"Yes."

"So I am a man of the first principle."

"While riding the rapids, it's the first principle."

"Does an ordinary person ride the rapids? Oh, my."

"Before nature translates a person, of course, the model is a person because the person is transferred to nature. The emotional uplift of going down the rapids is the uplift in your belly acting on the first principle and transferring to nature. That is the translation of the first principle and its interpretation."

"Inseparable friends probably exist because the first principle acts mutually."

"First of all, that is certain."

"Is there a place in you to be an inseparable friend?"

Kingo said nothing and gazed at the bottom of the boat. Long ago, Lao Tzu explained this as *He who speaks does not know*.

"Ha, ha, ha, ha. That's the reason the Hozugawa River is my bosom buddy. It's a joy. Delightful," said Hajime, clapping his hands a few times.

The currents flowing around the jumble of rocks on the left and right separated as in an embrace. The transparent, partly green waves drawn by Ogata Kōrin drew curves resembling early bracken ferns and leisurely crossed over the corners of the boulders. The river eventually neared Kyōto.

"When we go around that nose, we'll be at Arashiyama," said the boatman, setting the long pole inside the gunwale. Propelled by the screeching oars, they slipped out as though sliding through a deep abyss. The rocks on the left and right naturally opened up. The boat landed below Daihikaku.

The two men crawled up among the pine trees, cherry blossoms, and swarms of Kyōto Dolls. After slipping under the sleeve connected to the curtain, they came out between the pines at Togetsukyō Bridge. Hajime tugged on Kingo's sleeve again.

A thatched-roof teahouse stood at the foot of the bridge shielded by two red pines and boasted of the brightening shadows of flowers on the waves of the Ōi River. A geisha with her hair in the Takashimada style was resting there.

The oval face of the beautiful woman, wearing an old-fashioned bun often allowed these days, peeked at the flowers but could not stand the wind and cast down her eyes to stare at the famous dumplings to avoid people.

If her knees properly met on a lightly dyed satin figured covering, the colors of the clothes folded beneath her could not be seen. A patterned collar, less conspicuous than the top collar, under her kimono immediately caught Kingo's eyes.

"There she is."

"Who?"

"The woman who played the koto. I'm sure her father is the fellow wearing the black haori jacket."

"Really?"

"That isn't a Kyōto Doll. She's from Tōkyo."

"How do you know?"

"The maid at the inn said so."

Amid boisterous laughter, small groups of fools with gourds filled with alcohol flailed their arms and pushed from behind.

Slightly leaning their bodies forward, Kingo and Hajime passed by the swaggering people. The world of colors was at its height.

CHAPTER 6

A PALE GREENISH-BROWN ORCHID FLOWER INSIDE THE LAPEL reflected a hint of sorrow on a round face, blew a faint aroma onto the skin, and spilled onto the chest of the woman wearing the kimono. Itoko was this sort of woman.

A finger is used to point at a person. Four fingers are folded onto the palm and the remaining index finger points to that right there. A pointing hand unmistakably forms a line. If all five fingers are extended to indicate look at that, west and east are correct, but the feeling of being right is dulled.

Itoko is a woman who lined up all five fingers to point. It can't be said that the impression is misunderstood. However, it is strange. The situation is unsatisfactory when the pointing finger is too short. It may be more satisfactory when the pointing finger loses length. Itoko is a woman who lines up her five fingers simultaneously. It cannot be said to be satisfactory and is not evaluated as better than satisfactory.

When flesh is lost in the slender fingertip of a finger pointing at a person, a clear feeling gradually gathers in the fingertip and constructs a point of focus.

Fujio's fingers extended beyond the red of the fingertips and ended with sharpness like sewing needles. Eyes seeing this hurt at once.

Anyone who doesn't understand this detail will not cross the bridge. One who understands this detail too well crosses over the railing. The fear is the one who crosses over the railing will fall into the water.

Fujio and Itoko were in a war of five fingers versus the tips of needles in the six-tatami-mat sitting room. Everything about their conversation was war. Women's conversations are, for the most part, war.

"I haven't seen you for quite some time. It's wonderful you're here," said Fujio to her hostess.

"My father has been quite busy, so I haven't been able to keep in touch."

"Have you been to the exhibition?"

"No, not yet."

"And Mukōjima?"

"I still haven't gone anywhere."

Fujio thought that only staying at home could be fulfilling.

A shadow of a smile shaded the corners of Itoko's eyes each time she answered.

"You're that busy."

"Although nothing was that important—"

Most of Itoko's answer was cut off.

"It's harmful when you don't go outside, even briefly. Spring only comes once a year."

"You're right. I think so too, but—"

"Although it's once a year, if you die, wouldn't this year be your last?"

"Ha, ha, ha, ha. My goodness, dying is so gloomy."

Their conversation pierced the word for *death* and flew apart to the right and left. Ueno is the road to Asakusa. At the same time, it is the road to Nihonbashi. Fujio would accompany her companion to the other side of the grave, but her companion knew nothing about that side.

Itoko said, "Now if my brother is given a bride, I will leave."

A home-loving woman has a home-centered answer. Nothing is as pitiful as a woman who realizes she was born to fulfill a man's needs. Fujio snorted to herself. These eyes, these sleeves, this poem, and this song are not types of pots or charcoal scuttles. They are beautiful shadows that move in a beautiful world. When labeled with the word *practical,* a woman … a beautiful woman loses her true essence and is greatly insulted.

"When does Hajime intend to marry?"

Only these words slipped from Fujio and moved forward. Before responding, Itoko raised her head to look at Fujio. They eased into war.

"If a lady comes along, I think he'll marry."

This time, before Fujio answered, she stared at Itoko. Needles, unexpectedly prepared, did not emerge from inside her eyes.

"Ha, ha, ha, ha. No matter how fine a wife she'll be, she'll quickly become proficient."

"If true, that's wonderful," said Itoko, twisting halfway around to the back. Fujio felt a slight need to flee.

"Who does he have in mind? If Hajime decides to marry, I will search in earnest."

Not knowing whether a lime stick would reach far enough to catch a bird, the bird would surely escape. However, she had to take one more step.

"Yes, please search as if looking for an older sister for me."

Itoko had pushed a little too far into dangerous territory. A twentieth-century conversation is an ingenious art form. If mentioned, the essential point is not understood. If too much is said, she will be slapped.

"You're more like the older sister," said Fujio. She cut the rope for a search entered by her opponent and flung it back. Itoko was still unaware.

"Why?" she asked, tilting her head.

A released arrow missing the mark was clumsiness. Pretending without having a response despite being right is incompetence. A woman is disappointed by incompetence more than clumsiness.

Fujio lightly bit her lower lip. She understood winning and could not come this far and stop.

"You're saying you don't want to become my older sister," Fujio said, feigning innocence.

"Oh."

A color showing she forgot herself appeared on Itoko's cheeks.

The enemy saw that and sneered in her heart.

The following proverb was decided after a consultation between Kingo and Hajime.

People who do not act on the first principle can't mutually illuminate the deepest friendship between each other. The younger sisters of the two men were fighting at the outer fortification of a close friendship. Is it war that pulls one inside a close friendship or war that drives one outside a close friendship? The philosopher has evaluated twentieth-century conversations and said war obscures close friendships.

On top of that, Seizō came. He was chased by the past and walked around and around inside the room in the lodging house. Despite going around many times he didn't try to escape, he tried to see past friends and reconcile the past and the present. Still, he was uneasy because reconciliation may or may not be possible. Of course, he lacked the courage to seize anyone brave who pursued him. Seizō inevitably had hope for the future and came running. One proverb says to hide in the sleeve of the imperial dragon, meaning imperial power. Seizō tried to hide in the sleeve of the future.

Seizō weaved and staggered here. Unfortunately, it's difficult to explain the meaning of weaved and staggered.

"What's wrong?" asked Fujio.

Seizō was worried and still had not ordered the formal kimono with the family crest. The philosopher once explained all people of the twentieth century should have two or three crested kimonos prepared.

"Your complexion looks terrible," said Itoko. Sadly, the anticipated future holds the sword in reverse and digs up the past.

"I haven't been able to sleep for the past few days," he said.

"I see," said Fujio.

"What happened?" asked Itoko.

"Lately, you've been writing a dissertation. That's it, isn't it?"

Fujio both asked and answered the question.

"Yes."

Seizō's answer was a boat at the crossing. If told to board any boat, Seizō had to give in and board. Nearly all lies are like the boat at the ferry launch. He boards because it's there.

"Oh," Itoko gently replied.

A domesticated woman has no connection to whatever dissertation will be written. This woman is only concerned about sickly complexions.

"Even after graduating, you'll be busy."

"He has graduated and received a silver watch. In the future, he will obtain a gold watch for the dissertation."

"That's wonderful."

"Isn't that right? Seizō?"

Seizō smiled.

"Well, you intended to go with my brother and Kingo on the pleasure trip to Kyōto. My brother is blasé about things. I think it's fine to lose a little sleep."

"Ha, ha, ha, ha. Then he's better than my brother."

"I don't know how much better Kingo is," said Itoko without reserve. She quickly realized this and crumpled the fine habutai silk handkerchief on her knees into a ball.

"Ha, ha, ha, ha."

Gold stripes coloring the corners of the front teeth reflected into the outside world from the space between her moving lips. The enemy fell into her trap. Fujio began a second victory song.

This time, Seizō asked, "Is there news from Kyōto?"

"No."

"A postcard may come."

"Didn't someone call him a *bullet*? The bullet that goes forward, sacrifices itself for others, and never returns."

"Who?"

"Oh, my mother probably said that. She said both are bullets. Itoko, Hajime, especially, is a big bullet."

"Who? Did Auntie say that? There are many bullets. I can't

worry about where he'll fly off to if a bride is not quickly found for him."

"Please, hurry and find someone for Hajime. Seizō, together, can't we find a nice lady for him?"

Fujio looked meaningfully at Seizō. Their eyes locked and trembled.

"Yes, we'll be the matchmakers to find a good woman," said Seizō, taking out a handkerchief, and patting his thin mustache. A faint scent struck him. Strong ones are said to be vulgar.

"You probably have several acquaintances in Kyōto. Please have the people in Kyōto take care of Hajime. Many beautiful women live in Kyōto, am I right?"

Seizō's handkerchief lost a bit of its energy.

"What? The truth is they're not beautiful.

"When they return, ask Kingo, and you'll understand."

"Does my brother talk about such things?"

"Then ask Hajime."

"My brother says there are many great beauties."

"Has Hajime been to Kyōto before?"

"No, this is his first time, but he sent me a letter."

"Oh, so he's not a bullet. A letter came."

"What? It was a postcard. A Miyako Odori postcard came. In his shame, he wrote that all the women in Kyōto are pretty."

"Really. They're that beautiful."

"How? I don't understand all those white faces lined up. But if I saw them, I might like them."

"Simply looking at them, they're only white faces lined up. They may be pretty, but they have no expression and aren't very interesting."

"And he writes more."

"A lazy person doesn't do that. What does he say?"

"The koto player next door is better than you."

"Ha, ha, ha. Hajime is incapable of critiquing the koto."

"Is that a slight at my expense because my koto playing is dreadful?"

"Ha, ha, ha, ha. Hajime can do some awful things."

"More than that, he writes, They're prettier than you. It's odious."

"Hajime is brazen. I have no desire to see him."

"But he praises you."

"Oh, in what way?"

"He writes, She's prettier than you but not as pretty as Fujio."

"Well, that's terrible."

Fujio brightened her eyes with a mixture of triumph and contempt, and pulled back her slender neck. In a display of waves comparable to a horse's mane, only the violet of a jeweled abalone radiated like the beautiful light of a star.

Again, Seizō's eyes met Fujio's eyes. The meaning was lost on Itoko.

"Is Seizō staying at an inn called Tsutaya on Sanjō Avenue?"

The man, who forgets himself in the bottomless black eyes and is entirely sucked into the future he clings to, falls back to the past in an instant. When escaping the past in pursuit of you, there is no time to determine the enjoyment of elegance in the shadows of the purple clouds rising from a portable incense burner. It is difficult to deem this covetous. In the instant eyes meet, he wakes from an unfulfilled dream and is thrown into the past. A snake is in the grass. Stepping incautiously onto the green is not allowed.

"What is Tsutaya like?" Fujio asked Itoko.

"What? Tsutaya is the inn where Kingo and my brother are staying. I wondered what kind of place it was and asked Seizō."

"Seizō knows."

"It's on Sanjō Avenue? Tsutaya on Sanjō. I remember having been there but ..."

"Well, it's not a famous inn," said Itoko, looking innocently at Seizō's face.

"Yes," Seizō answered wistfully. This time was Fujio's turn.

"It's not famous. Isn't that good? The koto can be heard in the back sitting room. Naturally, my brother and Hajime are awful. Seizō, however, would be interested. On a quiet day with a gentle spring rain falling, isn't it poetic to hear the beautiful woman next door in an inn playing the koto and easily turning over in your sleep?"

Seizō was uncharacteristically quiet. Even his eyes did not look toward Fujio but gazed idly at the yellow rose in the alcove.

"It's wonderful," answered Itoko in his place.

A person ignorant of poetry has no right to step into a problem of taste. If she began with satisfaction in searching for support for 'It's wonderful' from a domesticated woman, the spring shower, the inner sitting room, and the sounds of a koto are not spoken about. Fujio was dissatisfied.

"I can imagine and create an interesting picture. What sort of place should it be?"

Why did this question come to the domesticated woman? The entire meaning cannot be explained. There was no choice other than to be silent and refrain from taking unnecessary actions. Seizō must speak up.

"What do you think was nice about it?"

"Me? Well, I, well ... The back part of the rooftop is pleasant. A bit of the Kamo River can be seen from the veranda. Seeing the Kamo River from Sanjō is nice."

"Yes, it can be seen depending on your location."

"Are there willow trees on the banks of the Kamo River?"

"Yes, there are."

"Those willows appear to be on fire in the distance. Higashiyama rises above them ... Higashiyama is a pretty, round mountain. That mountain is blanketed by a thick haze like a blue offering. In the haze, the dim five-story pagoda is ... What is the name of that pagoda?"

"Which one?"

"Which one? Can't you see one at the right corner of Higashiyama?"

"I don't recall," said Seizō, cocking his head.

"There is. There absolutely is," said Fujio.

"You know there's a koto next door," Itoko said.

These words broke the vision of a woman poet. It's similar to a domesticated woman born to destroy a beautiful world. Fujio frowned weakly.

"This matter is urgent."

"What interesting thing are you asking? What does that five-story pagoda do?"

The five-story pagoda does nothing. Some people go down to a kitchen only to gaze at sashimi. Those wishing the five-story pagoda would do something are pragmatic people who have learned they can't stand not eating sashimi.

"Well, enough about the five-story pagoda."

"It's interesting. The five-story pagoda is interesting. Right, Seizō?"

In this world, when a pleasant mood is opposed, someone will always apologize. The imperial wrath of a queen cannot be repaired by a votive offering, such as a pot, a kettle, or a miso strainer. A useless five-story pagoda must be enshrined like a tumor in a mist.

"A five-story pagoda is nothing more than that. What should a five-story pagoda do?"

Fujio's eyebrows jerked in surprise. Itoko wanted to cry.

"Oh, I hurt your feelings. I'm sorry. The five-story pagoda is truly interesting. This is not flattery."

If you stroke a hedgehog, the spines stand up the more it's stroked. Seizō had to do something before he exploded.

If he mentioned the five-story pagoda, he might spark her anger. The notes of the koto are taboo to him. Seizō wondered whether it would be better if he somehow mediated. The conversation would benefit if he left Kyōto behind. However, if he recklessly broke off and maintained no connection, he would invite contempt, just like Itoko. He must steer the conversation to another topic to avoid subjecting himself to agony. This seemed a little too difficult for one with enough brilliance to receive a silver watch.

"Seizō, you probably understand," Fujio interrupted.

Itoko was shut out as a clueless outsider. He would mediate between the two women because it would be horrible for him to watch a duel of unpleasant words. He wouldn't need to get involved if the rival of fireworks crossing swords between gentle, elaborate eyebrows could look down at her opponent as unworthy. The kindness of including the excluded person among friends only occurs when the excluded person relentlessly pesters. If done gently, excluding and looking down on someone are not related to his interests for the time being. Seizō no longer needed to consider Itoko to be important. He would not be wrong to get along with Fujio who was first.

He said, "I understand. The life of a poem is more certain than facts. However, many people in the world have no understanding of this."

Seizō had no intention of scorning Itoko but valued Fujio's high spirits. Moreover, his answer was the truth. The truth hits weaklings hard. Seizō sacrificed for poetry and love. Morality did not shine in the heads of weaklings. Itoko felt helpless and alone. At last, Fujio felt good.

"Well, should I speak to you about what's next?"

They say if you curse someone, dig two graves. Seizō had to agree.

"Yes."

"Just three stepping stones below the second floor seemed to be arranged diagonally. The tips abut the well curb. The blossoms of a dwarf cherry blossom bush are barely open. Each time the well bucket is touched, several petals flutter into the well."

Itoko quietly listened. Seizō said nothing and listened, too. A hazy spring sky gradually slipped in. Heavy clouds laid one over the other. A gloomy March pressed down as the day slowly darkened.

Five feet away from the shutter storage box, magnolia flowers sliding off the low gate at the entrance arranged enchanting colors in a line. While looking hard through the thicket of trees, occasionally, two or three rain streaks appeared intermittently. If you thought you saw slanted streaks, they soon disappeared. It was hard to believe something was falling from the sky and harder to believe something was falling to the earth. The life of a streak lasted a little more than a foot.

The place moved the mood. Fujio's imagination darkened with the sky.

She said, "I saw a dwarf cherry blossom bush from the railing on the second floor."

"It's no longer there."

"This will be a rainy day. It looks like a little rain will fall," she said, looking toward the garden. The sky grew darker.

"And behind the dwarf cherry blossom bush is a hedge fence of Kenni-ji Temple. Beyond the hedges, you'll hear the sounds of a koto."

Finally, the koto appeared. Itoko thought, Of course. Seizō thought, This is it.

"When you look down from the railing on the second floor, the neighbor's garden can be seen.

"Shall we talk about the creation of that garden?" asked Fujio, laughing loudly. Cold streaks lightly grazed the magnolia flowers.

"Ha, ha, ha, ha. That's awful. It's getting dark. The cloud of flowers looks like a ghost."

The approaching dark clouds slowly transformed into a thin streak. The clouds promptly crossed over a thicket of trees and took up a fast pursuit. As she watched, several trees passed through together. Finally, the rain came down hard.

"It looks like the deluge has begun."

"I have to excuse myself now that it's raining. Excuse me for leaving the conversation. It's been quite enjoyable," said Itoko and stood. The conversation collapsed with the spring rain.

CHAPTER 7

In the instant a match is struck, fire enters darkness. If several layers of colorful dress are rolled up, a plain border is formed. The enjoyment of spring was used up during the two men's youth. The man wearing a padded vest goes out into the world with his journal in his pocket, beginning the journey home with the man who harbors one hundred years of sorrow.

In the capital covered in ancient temples and shrines, divine forests, and Buddhist mounds, the day finally came to an end with pressing matters left unsolved. The evening was boring. Everything had disappeared, leaving behind only the stars, but even that was not obvious. Twinkling seemed to melt away in the lazy sky. The past started to move from its innermost slumbering part.

One hundred worlds are in the life of a man. Sometimes he enters a world of dirt. Sometimes, he acts in a world of wind. At other times, foul rain bathes the world of blood. Lumps that gather the world of one man in the mind and lumps that mix good and evil are layered one upon the other and vividly reveal one thousand real worlds in one thousand people.

Each world sets its respective center at the intersection of fates. The circumference of one's station in life is drawn to the right and left.

The circle drawn from the center of rage moves swiftly as if flying. The circle that swings from the center of romantic love burns the remains of flames in the sky.

Some pull at the thread of morality. Some suggest being surrounded by wickedness.

Since the worlds flying wildly about in all directions, left, right, front, back, up, and down, are different, it is unlikely people so far apart would find themselves on the same boat.

Having been drained of excitement, Kingo and Hajime were returning east after the pleasure trip, which lasted the last month of spring. Kodō-sensei and Sayoko shook up a slumbering past and were heading east. By chance, two different worlds clashed on the eight-o'clock night train.

Sometimes, there are suicides when my world differs from my world. There is self-destruction. When my world and the world of another are different, sometimes, both collapse. Sometimes, they break apart. Or heat is sharply drawn in, endlessly breaking things apart.

If an amazing difference occurs once in a lifetime, I am the main character who stands on stage when the curtain is pulled, naturally, the leading man in a tragedy. The characteristics conferred from heaven begin at this time and are lively in the first principle.

The different world on the eight-o'clock night train is not violent. However, if the connection is merely sleeves brushing past each other, even under a starry spring evening in the simply charming Shichijō Avenue, there's no need for such a difference. This novel carves and polishes nature. Nature itself does not become a novel.

The two worlds were different inside a car close to five hundred miles long as if they never end, or don't last, like phantoms, or dreams. The nearly 500-mile-long car is indifferent to whether cows are riding, horses are riding, or the eventual fates of the people carried away to the east. The train wheels unafraid of the world go round and round. Later, it plunges into darkness at breakneck speeds.

They become faces waiting impatiently to meet someone again, have no joy in going on and returning from a trip, and are accustomed to traveling on trips with no more interest in wandering. Nonetheless, they are bundled together and all treated like clay figures. The night cannot be seen. Heavy black smoke continues to blow.

Everyone who lives in the sleepy nights moves toward Shichijō Avenue in the fires of lanterns. When the handlebar of a rickshaw is lowered, a dark shadow quickly brightens and enters a waiting room. Dark shadows appear one after another from the darkness.

The interior of the station is buried under living dark shadows. One might think the rest of Kyōto is hushed.

The activities of Kyōto center on one point on Shichijō Avenue. The train continuously belches smoke to push a haphazard bundle of one thousand and two thousand worlds of gathered activities to a bright Tōkyo by dawn.

The dark shadows spark an avalanche. The clumps are split into points. These points move from the right and left.

In a short time, unrivaled noises rise. The locking doors of the train cars make a racket.

Suddenly, a platform widens to sweep away the people gathered there. Only a large clock catches the eye from behind the window. Then, a whistle rings out from far behind, and the car moves with a thump.

While not knowing how the relationships of the mutual worlds interweave, going into the darkness led by their noses, Kingo, Hajime, Kodō-sensei, and the sweet Sayoko boarded the same car. The unknowing car clanked into action. The unknowing four people entered the dark night while in four versions of the world.

"This train is packed," said Kingo, looking around the car.

"Yeah, all the people from Kyōto on this train are probably going to the exhibition. Many have boarded."

"That's true. The waiting room was a crush of people."

"Kyōto is probably a lonesome place about now."

"Ha, ha, ha, ha. Really. It's a quiet place."

"It's a mystery because even people in that place move. Perhaps, they have various tasks to do even there."

"There are probably people who live and die in the quiet," said Kingo, placing his left knee on his right.

"Ha, ha, ha, ha. Are living and dying a task? The parent and child living in the house next door to the establishment Tsutaya are in that group. It's a tranquil way of life. Nothing is said. It's a mystery because they say they're going to Tōkyo."

"They're probably going to attend the exhibition."

"No, they're probably leaving their home and moving to another.

"Really. When?"

"I don't know when. I didn't ask the maid that much."

"That young lady may become someone's bride," said Kingo, as if talking to himself.

"Ha, ha, ha, ha. She may be," said Hajime, laughing as he sat and placing the sack slung around his neck on the shelf. His companion turned his face to the side and looked through the window. Outside was only darkness pierced by the train without hesitation. A roar was the only sound. People have no power.

"It's really fast. Do you know how fast we're going?" asked Hajime, sitting cross-legged on his seat.

"I have no idea. No matter how fast we're going, it's pitch black outside."

"It's dark outside. Isn't that fast?"

"I can't tell because I can't see anything to compare it to."

"You can't see. It's fast."

"Do you know?"

"I absolutely do," said Hajime confidently, adjusting his crossed legs. The conversation broke off again. The train accelerated. It made a hat on the shelf across the aisle tilt and caused the mountain summit to tremble. The attendant left the car from time to time. Most of the riders faced each other and stared at the faces of others.

"This is a fast train. Hey!" said Hajime, reviving the conversation. Kingo's eyes were half-closed in sleep.

"Huh?"

"We're going at a breakneck speed."

"Really?"

"Yeah. So, it seems fast."

The train ran with a roar. Kingo only grinned.

"The express train feels good. If it didn't, I wouldn't feel like riding."

"Is it superior to Musō Kokushi?"

"Ha, ha, ha, ha. It's acting on the first principle."

"The Kyōto train may be vastly different."

"The Kyōto train? That is defeat. It's always the tenth principle or higher. It's a mystery because it's moving."

"Because there are passengers."

"Too many passengers. They're laying tracks over there. They say those are the best in the world."

"That's probably not true. They're too primitive to be the best in the world."

"But if they're laying the best tracks in the world, the progress is also the best in the world."

"Ha, ha, ha, ha. It's in harmony with Kyōto."

"That's true. This is a famous historic train spot. It's the Kinkaku-ji Temple of trains. The words of praise say it has run continuously for ten years."

"Isn't it like the Chinese verse by Libai about crossing hundreds of miles in a day to return home?"

"Between ramparts hundreds of miles apart."

"That refers to Takamori Saigō."

"Oh? I thought it sounded odd."

Kingo held back his response and shut his mouth. The conversation broke off again. The train ran with the usual roar. For a short time, the pair's world disappeared while they were shaken inside darkness. At the same time, the world of the other two appeared under electric lights illuminating a long, narrow path, like a string, through the night.

The evening was born in the shadows of a pale, waning moon. At the home in Kyōto of a father and a child who live frugally without a mother, the hanging lanterns for the Bon Festival of Lanterns had been hung five times. This autumn, after a long hiatus, the spirit of the deceased mother would be welcomed by a fire lit in Tōkyo. As usual, white hands from inside long sleeves were placed one on the other. Empathy for things gathered on the shoulders of this petite woman. The anger about boarding eased into a smooth silkiness that slipped into the edge of compassion.

The one who took pride in purple made the invitation. The one with emotions deep in yellow chased from behind. Spring in the east and west stretched for nearly five hundred miles of railroad tracks. The truth of love was in a thread of desire. While a cloak draped over the hair trembled, it weaved through the long night.

The dream was five years old. With the force of a dripping paintbrush, the old dream was splashed with color through the haze. Through the deepest memories, the dream can be seen boiling up each time those days turned over in her mind.

Sayoko's dream, more vivid than life, rode the black streak of cars traveling east while continuously warming this bright dream in her pocket in the chilly weather of early spring. The car raced east intent on holding onto the dream. The one carrying the dream tightly embraced the blazing object so it wouldn't fall. The car made a singular advance.

Green poked out in the fields. Clouds pierced the mountains. Stars raced by on the starry night.

While rushing past, the one tightly hugging a dream cut loose the vivid dream from far away in the darkness and tossed it before reality. As the car advanced, the gap between the dream and reality narrowed.

Sayoko's journey brought the vivid dream to a brilliant reality and reached the border where they were indistinguishable. The time was still deep in the night.

Kodō-sensei seated beside her was not carrying so important a dream. Every day he gripped the scraggly, graying beard under his chin and thought about the past. It was long ago, deep in his twentieth year. He stayed inside and didn't readily go out.

Something was moving inside the expanse of dust in the world.

People, dogs, trees, or grass were not hazy. A person's past became the true past, after people, dogs, trees, and grass became indistinguishable.

The greater the lingering attachment to those long ago days when I possessed enduring love was coldly abandoned, the more chaotic people, dogs, grasses, and trees became. Kodō-sensei yanked his salt-and-pepper beard.

"How old were you when you came to Kyōto?"

"It was right after I left school. So it was the spring when I was sixteen."

"So this year is what?"

"This is my fifth year."

"So this becomes the fifth year. Time flies. Recently, I was thinking about that." He tugged his beard again.

"When I came, you took me to Arashiyama. We went with Mother."

"Yes, yes. In those days, the flowers bloomed too early. Arashiyama has changed a lot since then. Those famous dumplings were yet to be made."

"No, the dumplings were there. Didn't we eat beside the Sangen Teahouse?"

"Maybe so. I don't quite remember."

"Oh, Seizō said he only ate green food. Wasn't that funny?"

"Of course, at that time, Seizō was there. Mother was healthy, too. I didn't think she would die so soon. Nothing is harder to understand than people. Seizō changed a lot since then, too. We haven't seen him in five years."

"That's all right because he's healthy."

"Yes, after coming to Kyōto, his health improved greatly. When he came, his face was ghostly pale. Somehow, he seemed timid all the time but gradually relaxed as he became more comfortable."

"His nature is kind."

"He is kind. Too kind. Even so, it's wonderful he received a silver watch for his excellent graduating grades.

"He's helped by others. If a man with his good nature were left alone, he wouldn't know where to go and how to get in."

"That's true."

A vivid dream draws a ring and begins to turn inside the chest. There is no dead dream. The deep memories carved from the foundation of five years are separated and fly up a short distance.

The woman fixed her eyes and watched, from all directions, the scene vividly passing before her eyes in the unfolding dream.

The person robbed of spirit while looking at a dream forgets the whiskers of an elderly father. Sayoko kept quiet.

"Seizō may meet us at Shimbashi."

"He may be there."

The dream danced again. While she refrained from jumping up and plunged trembling into the night, she dashed into the dark. The old man let go of his beard. Soon his eyes were sleepy.

In the ancient world in which people, dogs, grasses, and trees are not reflected, the black curtain cascades down. The world that runs while continuing to dance in her small chest, to spin around, and to hold back illuminates darkness like fire. Sayoko embraced this bright world and fell asleep.

The long car pushed aside the enveloping night and crashed into wind blowing the other way.

Beyond the billowing blue smoke of a country at dawn when gods of the other world in pursuit are smacked by a powerful tail and finally emerge. Competitions arise everywhere.

While suspicious of the limitless never-ending fields gradually rising closer to heaven, when the surviving dream is eliminated, and the eyes run halfway to heaven, the world of the sun dawned.

The wings spanning over one thousand miles of a golden chicken resounding the age of gods in the sky flapped for a short time. Eternal snow slid down and cascaded outward into the center of an expanse where swelling clouds opened in the world. As the force pressing on the fields of Hasshu spread to the left and right, the waist down was buried inside a vast blueness. The whiteness pierced through as if looking at the sky. If the stage of whiteness is exhausted, purple pleats and indigo pleats fold at a slant. The white material is torn into several irregular stripes.

People looking up follow the shadows of creeping clouds. From the dark blue foot of a mountain, deep indigo and purple reach the pure white on top while weaving among lightning flashes. Eyes pop open. The whiteness entices all the riders in the bright world.

"Look, you can see Fuji," said Hajime as he slid down the seat and softly closed the window. The morning breeze wafted in from the broad plain at the foot of the mountain.

"Yes, I noticed a while ago." Surprisingly, Kingo, his head covered by a camel blanket, showed little interest.

"Oh, haven't you slept?"

"A little."

"Why's that on your head?"

"It's cold," said Kingo from beneath the lap blanket.

"I'm hungry. Have you eaten?"

"If I don't wash my face before eating ..."

"You're right. You're a man who speaks reasonably. It's nice to look at Fuji."

"Better than looking at Mount Eizan."

"Eizan? What is Eizan? It's just a Kyōto mountain."

"You sound contemptuous."

"Yeah. What do you think about this grand matter? It's bad if people don't go there."

"You must calm down."

"Is the Hozugawa River the best you can expect? Even the Hozugawa is superior to you. You're probably at the level of Kyōto's trains."

"Kyōto's trains are fine because they run."

"Do you ever move? Ha, ha, ha, ha. The camel was brushed aside and moved," said Hajime, pulling down his sack from the shelf. It's getting noisy in here. The train running through the bright world breathed at Numazu. He would wash his face.

Kodō-sensei poked his thin face halfway out the window. The morning breeze blew each black or white hair of the scraggly beard.

"Excuse me. Two bento lunchboxes please."

He grabbed a few silver coins with his right hand, took the boxes with his left, and extended his right hand again for the change. His daughter ordered tea inside the car.

"Let's see what we have." He took off the lid. Grains of boiled white rice were stuck to the underside. Out of desperation, he only pushed his head to the boundary of the meal. Lying beside the light brown of Chinese yams, a bit of rolled omelet was stuffed in and flattened yellow.

"I still don't want to eat," said Sayoko, setting the box down without picking up the chopsticks.

"Oh, well," said the sensei, taking the teacup from his daughter. He gulped down his meal while looking at the chopsticks thrust into the box on his knees.

"We'll be there soon."

"Ah, that makes no sense," he said, yams moving toward his beard.

"The weather is wonderful today."

"I'm happy in this weather. Fuji was a beautiful sight."

Yam fell off his beard and back into the box.

"Do you think Seizō has looked for a place for us to stay?"

"Yes, he has looked," said the sensei between bites. He ate a little while longer.

"I'm going to the dining car," said Hajime. In the next car, he scratched the collar of his kimono with the splash pattern. Kingo's lanky form dressed in a suit stood. When he crossed over and knocked over a leather briefcase in the aisle, Kingo turned around.

He warned, "Hey, that's dangerous."

Kingo pushed open the glass door and stepped into the adjacent car. He was halfway there and intending to go straight through when Hajime jerked back the bottom of his suit jacket from behind.

"Your food is getting cold."

"That's all right, but it's too hard.

"When you're my age, what is frightening is the stiffness in my chest."

"Would you like tea ... shall I pour it?"

Without saying a word, the young man slipped into the dining car.

This small world jumbles together each day and night and flies back and forth across the world. While thinking about going to distant horizons everywhere in this world with no time limit, like arranging the eggs of silkworms willingly planted at the fineness of silk threads, four small universes were lined up in the dead of night traveling on a heartless train as faces pretended not to be in opposition.

The world of stars swept down. In the window that rises and must not hide the bright sunshine that cleanly stripped off the skin of the heavens, the universes of the four people created opportunities and missed each other this time. Two small universes missed each other in passing but now sat with white tablecloths and flattened ham and eggs between them.

"Hey, that was them," said Hajime.

"Yes, it was," said Kingo, answering while staring at the menu.

"Finally, they seem to be going to Tōkyo. I didn't see them last evening at the station in Kyōto."

"I had no idea."

"I didn't know they boarded the next car. We'll see them."

"We see them a little too much. This ham is only fat. Is yours like that?"

"It's the same. It's like the difference between you and me," said Hajime, turning over his fork and thrusting a large slice into his mouth.

"Maybe, we see ourselves as pigs," said Kingo then somewhat pitifully stuffed his cheeks with the flavor of white fat.

"Pork is fine. That's a mystery."

"I've heard the Jewish people don't eat pork," said Kingo, suddenly sounding detached.

"Forget about them, that woman ... is a little mystery."

"Are we meeting too often?"

"Yeah. Waiter, tea please."

"I'll have coffee. This pork is awful," said Kingo, again avoiding the subject of the woman.

"How many times have we seen them? One, two, three times. We've seen them three times."

"If this were a novel, this would develop into a bond. Just that seems safe," said Kingo and gulped his coffee.

"Because just that seems safe, we're both probably pigs. Ha, ha, ha, ha. But I can't say anything. You're in love with that woman—"

"True," said Kingo, cutting off his companion's words.

"Even if that weren't so, because I'll see her about this much, there won't necessarily be a relationship in the future."

"With you?"

"What? Is there some other relationship? It's not a romantic one."

"Yes," said Kingo. While supporting his chin with his left hand, he stared lazily as his right hand held the cup of coffee up to his nose.

"I want a tangerine," said Hajime. Kingo said nothing. After a short time, he said, not looking the least bit worried, "Do you think that woman's going to get married?"

"Ha, ha, ha, ha. Should I ask?" He seemed to have no intention of greeting or asking her.

"A bride? Do I want to marry her that much?"

"Therefore, I don't understand why you won't ask."

"What about your younger sister? I'm sure she wants to marry." A solemn Kingo asked this odd question.

"Itoko? She's a baby but cares about her big brother. She's a virtuoso at sewing and made that fox vest for me. She could make elbow pads for you."

"Maybe."

"Do you need one?"

"It's not that I don't but ..."

The two concluded the elbow pad was impractical and left the table. As they passed through Kodō-sensei's car, the sensei was holding open *The Asahi Shimbun* newspaper in front of his face. Sayoko's small mouth nibbled on an omelet.

Each of the four small worlds was alive with activity. While passing each other by chance again on the train, similar to worrying or suspicious about their mutual fates in one's own family's distant future, the unquantifiable world of tomorrow was embraced as the train entered Shimbashi Station.

"Wasn't that Seizō I saw run off earlier?" asked Hajime as they left the station.

"Was it? I didn't notice," answered Kingo.

The four small worlds collided at the station and momentarily dispersed.

CHAPTER 8

AT DUSK, AN ASAGI CHERRY BLOSSOM TREE CLOUDED OVER THE garden. The spotless veranda was quiet outside the tightly shut shōji sliding door. Inside, a *tetori* iron kettle boiled on a small oblong brazier. In front of the brazier, shibori-dyed, habutai silk futon sitting cushions were laid out.

Kingo's mother sat with dignity on a futon cushion. Threads of nerves passed through the back at the corners of her taut eyes. Dark, crinkly skin shrouded and seemed to pierce her forehead. She looked tenderhearted.

After gripping a needle stored in a sponge, she smoothed an ointment over her tender hands to soothe the scratches. Where possible, she placed her lips on bloody spots and showed no ulterior motive.

Kingo once wrote in his diary.

People born in the twentieth century must know this at least. Those who expose their bones perish.

She heard footsteps on the quiet veranda. New-looking, white tabi socks appeared to be on the verge of ripping on her long, narrow feet. A foot gently dragged back the thick colorful kimono hem border and slowly slid open the shōji door.

The mother in this dwelling slightly tilted her thick eyebrows toward the doorway.

"Oh, please come in."

Fujio said nothing and soundlessly closed the door behind her. She sat near the brazier across from her mother. The iron kettle whistled.

Her mother looked at Fujio's face. Fujio was looking down at the newspaper folded in half beside the brazier. The kettle kept whistling.

Little truth comes from a lot of talk. Letting the iron kettle shriek, the mother and child mischievously faced each other. The veranda was quiet. The pale Asagi cherry blossoms invited the twilight. Spring continued to slip away.

After a time, Fujio raised her head.

"Hello."

The mother's and daughter's eyes suddenly met. Truth filled those glances. When the heat becomes unbearable, bones are exposed.

"Uh-huh."

A long *kiseru* pipe was tapped to clean out the tobacco remnants.

"What does he intend to do?"

"Yes, what will he do? Even as his mother, I know nothing of his intentions."

Smoke from finely shredded Kumoi tobacco blew from the nostrils of her prominent nose.

"After he comes home, the situation will be the same."

"The same. It has been that way his entire life."

The mother's irritated nerves swelled from the back to the front.

"Is being the heir to this family so horrible?"

"What are you saying? All he does is talk. That is why it's bad. By saying that sort of thing, he intends to provoke us.

"If the fortune or anything is not truly received, or if he does something, isn't that good? He complains every day. It's been two years since he graduated. No matter how much he talks about philosophy, he hasn't decided what to do. He must not be indecisive. Each time I see his face, I burn with exasperation."

"Speaking in a roundabout manner seems to get through."

"Even if he understands, he pretends not to."

"Well, that's awful."

"It's true. If he does nothing for me, I can do nothing for you."

Fujio kept herself from answering.

Love brims with all vices. While she held back her response, she was determined to sacrifice everything. Her mother continued.

"Didn't you turn twenty-four this year? After twenty-four, few women are not married.

"If I try to talk to him about getting married, he says please don't. His reason is he wants you to take care of me. He may think he will work independently, but every day he shuts himself off in his room and stays in bed.

"He tells others he intends to be a vagabond and give the family fortune to Fujio. Isn't it a shame if it looks as though we are the nuisance and driving him out?"

"Where did he say that?"

"He said that when he visited Hajime's father at home."

"His personality is not manly. More than that, I think it would be better if Kingo marries Itoko soon."

"Her father is probably interested in getting everything."

"I have no idea what Kingo intends to do. However, Itoko wants to marry him."

Her mother removed the whistling iron kettle and picked up the charcoal scuttle. Several strands of indigo knotweed traced flowing waves, and pure white cherry blossoms were whimsically scattered on a small Satsuma teapot made of ceramic crackle pottery dyed by oozing persimmon with no gaps. Leaves of high-grade *uji* tea of finely twisted green clustered in the teapot cooled in a mound while decaying in the day's hot water.

"Shall I make tea?"

"No, thank you," said Fujio. The overpowering smell wafted from a teacup having the same color as the teapot. As she tapped the bottom of the yellow flow, more than she imagined, the color closer to the edge intensified. The dark water was stagnant and did not push bubbles to the surface.

In the pile of ashes frequently raked by the mother, white residue from thoroughly burned charcoal made from oak had crumbled. She pushed the red part hidden in the center to the side and selected the black ring in the warm hole in the debris with sparks of life.

The springtime light in the room thoroughly warmed the mother and child.

This author dislikes charmless conversations. In a dark world of suspicion and discord, a venomous tongue without a speck of brilliance does not have the elegance of a poet whose beautiful writing brush flows a pleasant spring onto paper. When vulgar words are untouched by half a drop of refinement and do not dwell under the heavens, and the heavens resemble the songs of people who reign over beautiful flowers quietly blooming and an unadorned koto, these words are aligned, but a tiny amount of ink sludge clinging to the tip makes it hard to write with a brush guided by both hands.

The high-quality tea from Uji; the small, fine teapot from Satsuma; and shards of premium charcoal from Sakura steal moments of tranquility. It is a clever strategy to give the reader the comfort found in detachment in a single stroke. However, the Earth has been rotating since ancient times. Light and dark do not discard day and night. This author has the agonizing duty to provide the simplest description of one aspect of the unhappy mother and daughter. The writing brush that appreciates tea and describes coal must return to their conversation. At the very least, the mother and daughter's conversation must hold more charm than before.

"Speaking of the Munechikas, Hajime is a funny fellow. He talks big despite being unable to do scholarship or anything else. Otherwise, he is a splendid young man."

The horse stable and chicken coop are the same place. In the words used to evaluate a mare, nothing would be known about crowing like a rooster or laying eggs. That makes sense.

"He failed the diplomat exam and wasn't the least bit embarrassed. If he were a normal man, wouldn't he have worked a little harder?"

"He's a bullet."

Her mother did not understand what she meant, but Fujio's assessment was blunt. Fujio touched the skin on her velvety cheek and flashed a grin. She was a woman who analyzed poetry. The old-fashioned bullet-shaped *dagashi* candies were balls of black sugar. The bullets of an artillery arsenal were cast in molten lead molds. In either case, bullets were bullets. The mother was serious to the end but remained clueless about the meaning of her daughter's smile.

"What do you think of him?"

Unexpectedly, the daughter's smile sowed doubt in her mother. They say parents know their children best. That is wrong. The situation in a conflict-free world resembles a child whose distant, foreign parents are China and India.

"What do I think? Nothing in particular."

The mother stared at her daughter from beneath sharp eyebrows. Fujio perfectly understood the meaning. She knew her opponent but made no fuss. Fujio calmed herself and waited for her mother's snap decision. Bargaining also occurs between parents and children.

"Are you disposed to marrying him?"

"To Hajime?"

Her caution appeared to be a maneuver to wait for the right moment to strike.

"Oh," the mother said softly.

"He's awful."

"Awful?"

"Is he awful? Yes, he's uninteresting," said Fujio, breaking in and creating a breeze like the one caused by cutting a bamboo shoot into round slices. The breeze stirred at her tense eyebrows. Something trapped by her shut lips flashed and disappeared. Her mother uttered a brief exclamation in agreement.

"I don't like men with so little promise."

Being uninteresting differs from having no promise. A blacksmith's hammer hits with a clang. An exclamation hits with "uh-huh." Even so, the hit is the same sword.

"I'd like to see a clear rejection now."

"A rejection? Are we engaged?"

"Engaged? There's no engagement. However, Father said he would give that gold watch to Hajime."

"Why would he do that?"

"You turned that watch into a toy. You only played with that and a red ball ..."

"And ..."

"In front of everyone, he said half-jokingly to Hajime, 'And this watch has a deep connection to Fujio. I'll give this watch to you but not now. That will happen when you graduate. However, Fujio probably wants the watch and repeatedly comes to wear it.'"

"Do you think that's a mystery now?"

"He seemed to be sounding out Hajime's father's feelings."

"How idiotic."

Fujio's sharp words hit a corner of the oblong brazier and resonated immediately.

"So it's idiotic."

"I'll take that watch."

"Is it still in your room?"

"It's kept in the library."

"Oh, you want it that badly. But should you have it?"

"It's fine with me."

The garnet burning at the end of the chain emits a mysterious light from the bottom of a lacquered stationery box elevated with a design in gold of reeds and geese beckons Fujio.

Fujio stood up suddenly.

Her tall figure slipped out from under the eaves that, for a brief time, protected the life of the day about to vanish as sunset neared. The Asagi cherry blossoms were unchanged and not dimmed by twilight. As she turned, she tilted one side of her slender face, silhouetted on the papered shōji sliding door.

"It's all right if I give that watch to Seizō."

She could not hear the response from behind the shōji door. Spring ended for the mother and child.

At the same time, ample light lit the sitting room of the Munechika home. White light from the lampshade of a Western lamp brought back sunshine on a quiet night and gracefully filled the room. A copper-nickel oil bottle that lit an arabesque pattern high on one side boasted colors not darkened in the evening. As far as the light reached, every face was animated.

"Ah, ha, ha, ha, ha."

First, a laughing voice was heard. All the conversations around the light appeared to start with laughter.

"So you didn't see the Sōrintō pillar, either," someone shouted. The voice came from an elderly man. The jaw held back the flesh of healthy cheeks hanging down too much and forced to fold in two. He patted his balding head from time to time. The Munechika patriarch's patting his head revealed his bald spot.

"What's a Sōrintō pillar?" asked Hajime, sitting cross-legged casually before his father.

"Ah, ha, ha, ha. I don't know why you climbed Eizan."

"Kingo, we didn't come across that along the way."

In front of his teacup, Kingo joined the front of a kimono made from a dark, two-colored striped fabric and properly adjusted the collar of his black haori jacket.

When Kingo was asked the question, Itoko's smiling face quivered.

"I don't believe there was a Sōrintō," said Kingo, placing his hands on his knees.

"There is no path. We had no idea where the climb began. At Yoshida?"

"Kingo, what was that place called? Where we climbed."

"I don't know what it was called."

"Father, we crossed one bridge."

"One bridge?"

"Yes, you crossed one bridge. If you had gone a bit further, you would've ended up in Wakasa Province."

"Would we soon come out in Wakasa?" Kingo immediately took back his previous remark.

"Isn't that what you said?"

"That was a joke."

"Ah, ha, ha, ha. That would have been terrible if you came out in Wakasa."

The old man seemed delighted. Itoko moved the curves of the double eyelids on her round face closer.

"You two only walked forward quickly like a postman. That was no good. The pagodas of Tōtō and Saitō, and the temple complex at Yokawa are on Eizan. Those three places are expansive and every day welcome people in pursuit of knowledge. If you only climbed up and came down, isn't that the same as climbing any mountain anywhere?"

"What? I intended to climb a simple mountain."

"Ah, ha, ha, ha. So you climbed as blisters erupted on your feet."

"Yes, there are blisters, and they are your fault," Hajime said, smiling and looking at Kingo. The philosopher doesn't only look sullen. The light brightly swayed.

As Itoko raised her sleeve to her mouth and lifted her head wearing a smile about to collapse, her eyes moved to the man with the blisters. She tried to shift her eyes, but her face moved first. She was like a thief stealing at the scene of a fire. She planned to become a homemaker. Right away, Kingo feigning innocence presented the next problem.

"Uncle, what are Tōtō and Saitō you mentioned?"

"They're areas of Enryaku-ji Temple. On the vast mountain, these sections are clumped into one. At this place, these parts and the monks are gathered into one. Therefore, this area is divided into three parts. They are properly thought of as Tōtō, the Eastern Pagoda; Saitō, the Western Pagoda; and the rest."

"Oh, you'll study something like law, medicine, or literature at college," said Hajime from the side, sounding like a know-it-all.

"Well, that's true." The older man immediately agreed.

"As the poem goes, *If the east is carnage, / The west is closer to the capital. / Life inside the Yokawa River is good.* Yokawa is the loneliest place and a fine place to study. You must enter about four miles from Sōrintō we talked about."

"Somehow, you passed it without knowing," said Hajime again to Kingo who said nothing but listened intently to the elder's explanation. He spoke with confidence.

"This may be in the Noh play about the boat-haunting samurai ghost Funa Benkei, who in life was the warrior monk Musashibō Benkei and lived beside Saitō. Benkei was chased into Saitō."

"Benkei was a student of Buddhist teachings. You are in the literature course at Yokogawa. Father, who's the administrator of Eizan?"

"The administrator?"

"Eizan's …, that is, the man who built Eizan."

"You mean the founder? That was Dengyō Daishi."

"Building a temple in a place like that is exasperating. Inconvenience is inevitable. Men of old were eccentric. Am I right, Kingo?"

Kingo muttered an unhelpful response.

"Dengyō Daishi, like you, was born at the foot of Eizan."

"Of course, now that you say that. Kingo, you know about that.."

"What?"

"A stake marking the birthplace of Dengyō Daishi was erected in Sakamoto."

"I was born there."

"Oh, really? Kingo, you probably realized that."

"I didn't realize that."

"Because I was distracted by blisters."

"Ah, ha, ha, ha."

The older man was amused.

A spectator sees nothing. Ancient people taught that the imagination is supreme. Typically, in the world, people vainly write the truth that flowing waters never abandon day and night. The truth is written. Unexpectedly, the truth just written rides on the departing waves and silently leaves.

Chants of the Lotus Sutra in the temple, the carving of

Buddha's leg in stone, the sōrin ornament on the pillar, and the pure land in the temple only record the name, year, and history. When I think the end has come, I will embrace a corpse and vividly imagine a person restored to life. One sees not for fame. One watches not to be seen. The most supreme being separates from having a form and enters universal compassion for all. For this reason, Kingo climbs Eizan and does not know Eizan.

The past is dying. A Dharma drum resonates. A Dharma spiral shell blows. A Dharma banner is raised high. The demon gate of the imperial castle is guarded. The past is not known. Buddha sleeps in the main temple building. An old temple where spider silk stretches across the dome is excavated today from the imperial reign of Kanmu. In an unneeded discussion, the dirt of antiquity being washed away is the action of a loafer during day and night in a forty-eight-hour day.

The present carves out the time and waits for me. An ever-changing world drops before our eyes. Both arms cut through the wind and resound throughout the world. Thus, Hajime knew none of this as he climbed Eizan.

Only the older man is tranquil. He explains the world's destiny is Eizan as eternity thinking about going through a complete change in appearance every day and night under the momentary direction of Eizan. From the beginning, he explained out of kindness toward the somewhat troubled young man.

"Speaking of inconvenient. That mountain was selected and opened deliberately for training. Because today's universities are located in places that are too convenient, all of them have become extravagant. The students' habits include Western-style sweets and whiskey."

Hajime made a strange face and looked at Kingo. Unexpectedly, Kingo looked serious.

"Father, Eizan's priest goes out around eleven at night to the distant Sakamoto for soba."

"Ah, ha, ha, ha. Does he?"

"What? It's true. Right, Kingo? No matter how inconvenient, if you want to eat something, you want to eat it."

"He's probably a lazy priest."

"And we're probably lazy scholars."

"You fellows are better than lazy."

"It's nice we're better, but it's nearly five miles of mountain roads to Sakamoto."

"It's probably that far."

"He comes down at eleven in the evening, eats soba, and climbs back up, so ..."

"What do you mean by so?"

"This work can't be done if you're too lazy."

"Ah, ha, ha, ha."

The older man's belly burst with laughter. His voice seemed to startle the lamp shade.

"But long ago, wasn't there a serious priest?"

This time, Kingo asked as though something suddenly came to mind.

"Even now, he is. As though there are few serious men in this world, not many are found among priests and monks. Now, however, it's not that none exist. In any case, that's because the temple is old. It was first called Ichijōshikan-in Temple and much later became Enryaku-ji Temple. Unusual verses remain from that time. He probably lived in seclusion on the mountain for twelve years."

"There's no place to eat soba."

"Why? Because he's never come down the mountain."

"What's the point of growing old on the mountain?" Hajime seemed to be talking to himself.

"Ah, the pursuit of knowledge. You fellows shouldn't be so lazy and would do well to emulate them."

"That's no good."

"Why?"

"Because there's nothing I can't do. On that day, the reason is we would defy your orders."

"What orders?"

"Don't you say each time you look at a person's face, get a wife, get a wife? If I secluded myself on a mountain for the next twelve years, I'd be hunched over when I got a bride."

Everyone burst into laughter. Hajime's father slightly raised his head and stroked forward on his bald head. The drooping flesh of his cheeks seemed to quiver. Itoko dropped her head and stifled her voice Her eyelids flushed pink. Kingo's stiff mouth loosened.

"No, training is just training, but not finding a wife is a problem. Anyway, both of you have this problem.

"Kingo must find one. Shouldn't you?"

"Yes, but it's too soon."

His response was half-hearted. In his heart, he felt seclusion for twelve years on Eizan was preferred to taking a bride. Kingo's heart was nimbly reflected in Itoko's eyes that missed nothing. Her small chest was weighed down in an instant.

"However, your mother is probably worried."

Kingo didn't answer. The older man also understood his mother to be a typical mother. Not one person in this world saw into his mother's heart. If he could not see through his mother, he shouldn't feel sorry for himself. Kingo hung between Heaven and Earth as an inconsequential figure. He felt like the sole survivor on the day of the world's destruction.

"If you are dawdling, Fujio may also be troubled. When a woman is not doing what is expected given her age, unlike a man, fixing it is onerous."

Hajime's father, a man worthy of respect and love, was an ally of Fuji and her mother. Kingo couldn't respond.

"Hajime can't accept. Because I'm older, and there may be issues at some time."

In his heart, the father supports the mother's heart. Despite being a parent, too, the hearts of parents are different. However, it is impossible to explain.

"I failed the diplomat exam. So for now, it's not a good idea," Hajime spoke from the side.

"You failed last year. You don't yet know this year's result."

"You're right, I still don't know. But I'll probably fail again."

"Why?"
"In the end, I may do more than loaf around."
"Ah, ha, ha, ha."
The evening's conversation began and ended with laughter.

CHAPTER 9

Golden lace patrinia bloomed in the field where katsura vines grew. Loneliness drifted by, elegantly avoiding the autumn winds at the remorseful tall figure cutting through the pampas grass. Autumn turned to winter with late seasonal rains. In an endless winter, in the flakes of frost falling on brown and black, a fragile life is bound with little reliance on day or night.

Winter didn't mind the five long years. A lonely flower escaped the chilly night and got lost in the world of spring brilliant with color that knew nothing of poverty.

Everything is set ablaze as spring winds spread over the earth and the sky. Rich colors and hidden yellows are received at a thin branch. It feels like we are breathing out with restraint while feeling small and afraid in an uninhabitable world.

Until now, dreams more vivid than precious stones have been embraced. Our eyes were captured by, our bodies given to, and our hearts entrusted to a diamond set in pitch-black darkness, thus, giving no time to worry about anything. The light of a jewel carried in a pocket radiated into the night. When a far-away road nearly five hundred miles long was picked from a bag of darkness, the precious stone lost the brilliance of many yesterdays in the brightness of reality.

Sayoko is a woman of the past. She embraces dreams of the past. Past dreams embraced by a woman of the past are not rapids that split with reality at the double gate and meet again. If they sneak in occasionally, a dog barks. She thinks, I don't know whether I come from anywhere. The dream held in a pocket feels like a sin that must not be embraced but stored in a wrapping cloth to hide it from view and be met with suspicion on the streets.

Will she return to the past? A drop of oil mixed in water cannot easily return to the oil can. Whether it likes it or not, the oil must flow with the water. Will the dream be discarded? If it can be thrown out, it will be tossed out without flowing out to the bright sea. If thrown out, it will leap back into dreams.

Her world is split in two. When the split world starts to operate in its own way, a painful contradiction occurs. Most novels successfully depict this contradiction. When Sayoko's world collided at Shimbashi Station, it fractured and later broke. The novel begins now. Nothing is more pitiful than the life of the person who begins to write a novel.

Seizō shares these circumstances. The abandoned past pushes a billowing dust of dreams to the side. An aging head emerges from the dustbin of history. He jumps to his feet and walks over. Unfortunately, the roots of life were not kept when abandoned. However, living is inevitable because life is revived without warning.

Withered autumn grasses mistake the season of fickleness. Being brought back to life amid the shimmering warmth of hot air is miserable. Beating to death the one revived contradicts a poet's elegance. If this is reached, it must be appreciated.

Seizō never committed one unfortunate act since birth and has no intention of doing so in the future. To avoid acting in an unfortunate way and resolve matters himself, he watched slightly hidden behind a sleeve of the future.

If the purple scent grew intense and a ghost of the past approached, the moment he gathered his courage Sayoko arrived at Shimbashi. A fissure opened in Seizō's world, too. The author also finds Seizō as pitiful as Sayoko.

"Is your father in?" asked Seizō.

"He stepped out for a moment," said Sayoko, a bit timidly. Because they would move to a new home the following day, the bustling spring household of the father and daughter had no time to run a comb through their sweaty hair. Her threadbare everyday clothes were reflected in the eyes of the poet.

She faced a mirror and focused on applying make-up. The fragrance of a rose in a glass jar wafted in the air. When her beautifully styled hairdo was wetted, an amber comb untangled dark green strands.

Seizō suddenly remembered Fujio. Because of that, his heart told him the past was not worth it.

"He's probably busy."

"We still haven't touched the luggage."

"I came to see how I could help. I had meetings yesterday and the day before."

Seizō's daily invitations to meetings were proof of his reputation in his field. But which field? Sayoko could not imagine. She thought it was far beyond her and a field she couldn't begin to approach. Sayoko looked down at the gold ring shining on the middle finger of her right hand resting on her knee. Of course, it did not compare to Fujio's ring.

Seizō raised his eyes and glanced around the room. He noticed visible knotholes at two spots on the faded wood of the low ceiling. Stains penetrated from a leaking roof. The soot mistaken for spiders hardened and cast scattered dark spots.

A cedar chopstick horizontally pierced the center of the fourth crosspiece from the left. The longer end bent down lower than expected. A rope passed through by a long-gone renter might have dangled an ice bag to cool the chest.

Two layers of thick printed paper covering the sliding door that closed off the adjacent room regularly arranged dozens of patterns resembling English hollyhock set in gold foil on Western-style paper. The black paint on the edges found in mansions was vulgar.

A garden in name only curved freely along the veranda that crossed two rooms but was no wider than a brown obi sash. A cypress tree not quite ten feet tall served no purpose in the spring.

After last year's leaves hardened to a point and wasted away, the conversations next door taking place at the unstable high fence could be heard.

Seizō had brokered the house for Kodō-sensei. However, it was primitive. In his heart, Seizō thought, This residence is awful but at least he has a home. Magnolia kobus trees stood beside the low fence at the gate. A pine moss carpeted the shadow of the evergreen perennial plants. I want to live where a newly tailored handkerchief flaps in the spring breeze.

He heard Fujio would be given that house.

"Thanks to you, we have a fine home," said Sayoko, who knew nothing about boasting. It's a shame if she truly regarded this to be a fine home. If *yakkō* eel were gifted to someone, that person would first say thank you and praise the delicious meal of eel. From then on, the man who gave the treat seemed to show contempt for this person.

Occasionally, an agreement exists to make light of a pitiful person. Seizō belittled Sayoko and her heartfelt thanks. However, he didn't notice the fleeting endearing spots because purple cast a curse. When cursed, eyeballs become triangles.

"I thought you wouldn't like it but prefer a nicer house. I visited others. Unfortunately, nothing was suitable—" he began, but Sayoko interrupted and contradicted his words.

"Oh no, it's wonderful. Father is also delighted."

Seizō thought his words had been mean-spirited. Sayoko suspected nothing.

She pulled her slim face slightly inside and observed him through raised eyes. He has changed over five years. His eyeglasses are now gold. His suit is tailored from sturdy, blue-striped Kurume fabric. His close-cropped hair now glistens. He has grown his mustache to a gentleman's length. Almost overnight, Seizō grew a black mustache. He's no longer the student of the old days. His collar stands up. A decorative pin sparkles with each movement of his shoulder. The gift of a watch is in the pocket of a fine brown vest. The gold watch is never seen in dreams of Sayoko with her small heart. Seizō is changing.

Every day and night for five years, Seizō with a brighter dream than the unforgettable life in his heart is not this man. Five years is long ago.

He understands the opposites of east versus west and long versus short. The barrier of deep mutual love is stopped by the clouds at twilight, bringing an end to the sorrow of separation. It's unthinkable that no change would occur over the years that kept two people, separated by distance, from meeting.

He lived with thoughts such as if the wind blows or rain falls, change will come, and change is found in the moon and flowers. However, he silently prayed there would be no change and stepped down to the platform.

The way Seizō changed logically extends into the past and was not how Lü Meng, a courageous general and brilliant strategist, would have changed. The past of faded colors is defiantly pinned down. The remarkable present hastily changes to finish the evening before the arrival of his companions at Shimbashi. He does not approach Sayoko. Even if a hand is extended, he does not reach out. A man who wants to change, but doesn't, becomes bitter. Naturally, Seizō changed and withdrew.

The father said, "You came to meet us at Shimbashi, hired a car, and took us to our lodgings. Despite your busy life, you put a great deal of effort into making plans. You also rented a retreat for a snail parent and child to sleep. Seizō, you are as kind as in the old days."

The daughter had similar thoughts but didn't move closer.

As soon as she stepped down to the platform, she mentioned her luggage. He took her small handbag, which didn't qualify as luggage, the lap blanket, and walked ahead. When she saw the retreating figure walking with quick steps, she thought, This is it.

The one going first was not guiding the two who traveled a long distance to this place but appeared to have overtaken the parent and child who lagged behind the times.

The proof is to tear a piece of paper in half and later compare the halves for a match. More than a day in heaven, the precious dreams she protected were pulled from a sack of *time* leaking perfume for five long years and brought into the present. A comparison would yield no mistake, but the present quickly moved far away. The gripped paper scrap went unused.

At first, the glare made him think he was emerging from a hole. When he felt slightly more comfortable, he visited a first, second, third, and fourth time with the dying sun as his crutch. Each time, Seizō became more courteous. As his politeness heightened, Sayoko found it harder to approach him.

She pulled in her long jaw that easily slid into her throat, gazed up at Seizō's figure, and looked at his new eyeglasses. She looked at his new mustache. She looked at his clothing, which he changed to match the style of his new mustache. When she saw everything had changed, she released a soft sigh from the bottom of her heart. Aaah.

"How are the flowers in Kyōto? They're probably late."

Seizō promptly changed the subject to Kyōto. Sickly people are consoled by talking about illness. A poet's sympathy jumps into an unpleasant past and, with gratitude, reverses the unraveled braids of memories. Sayoko quickly moved closer to Seizō.

"They're probably late. Before we left, we visited Arashiyama. The flowers were nearly open, about eighty percent."

"That much? They bloom earlier on Arashiyama. That was nice. Who did you go with?"

Throngs of people view flowers as they do on starry nights. However, her only companion in Heaven and on Earth has been her father. If it wasn't her father, she spoke no other name, even in her heart.

"Of course, your father?"

"Yes."

"You had a nice time?" he said at the front of his mouth. Why did Sayoko feel miserable? Seizō started over.

"Originally, Arashiyama was quite different."

"Yes. Fine buildings were built at the hot springs at Daihikaku ..."

"Really?"

"Do you know about the grave of the beautiful koto player, Kogō no Tsubone?"

"Yes, I do."

"Everything over there is a roadside tea house. That place is lively."

"Every year, they become more commonplace. It was much nicer in bygone days."

The Seizō who thought he couldn't get closer collided with the Seizō in dreams. Sayoko had a sudden thought.

"The old days were truly ..."

She started to speak and deliberately looked at the garden. Nothing was there.

"It wasn't as busy the time we went."

Seizō was the Seizō in a dream. Her eyes looking at the garden glanced in the opposite direction. The gold-frame eyeglasses and sparse black mustache reflected in her pupils. Her companion was no longer the man of the past.

Sayoko stifled her throat about to let slip hints of nostalgic stories but closed her mouth without a word. When she gained confidence and was about to turn the corner, a snag developed. The conversation between the refined lady and gentleman clashed from beginning to end in their hearts. Seizō took his turn to speak again.

"You haven't changed, even a little, from that time."

"Oh?" Sayoko answered half-heartedly as if she agreed with him and doubted herself. Even if she changed, she wasn't that worried. Only their ages changed. A striped pattern that grew playfully and a well-used koto were a reproach. The koto stood covered in the alcove.

"I probably have changed a lot."

"You are in such fine form, I barely recognized you."

"Ha, ha, ha, ha. Forgive me. From now on, I intend to change one thing after another. Just like Arashiyama."

Sayoko didn't know what to say. Keeping her hands on her knees, she looked down. Her small earlobes slipped nicely through the ends of her side locks. The seam of her cheeks and neck invisibly traced a curve like a halo. It was a splendid picture. Seizō didn't understand he was seated directly across from disappointment. A poet loves the aesthetics of beauty. He rarely saw flesh fattened this much, flesh pulled back this much, and the extent of color under the lighting. If Seizō grabbed a beautiful picture at this moment, the heels of high-laced boots might have turned around so much that they sunk into the earth and jumped back into the past in the reverse flow of five years. Seizō sat facing disappointment. He thought, This woman is simply uninteresting and lacks poetry.

At the same moment, a wave hit. The aroma of the sleeve fluttering at the tip of his nose scrunched the deep-purple space between his eyebrows. Seizō soon wanted to go home.

"I'll visit again," he said while closing his suit jacket.

"Oh, you must leave now," said her voice quietly, trying to hold back.

"I'll come again. Give your father my regards when he returns."

"But ..." She hesitated.

Her companion rose and waited impatiently for the rest. He seemed to be in a hurry. The one who couldn't approach moved further away. It was discouraging.

"But ... my father ..."

For some reason, Seizō's heart felt heavy. The woman had increasing difficulty broaching a subject.

"I'll come again," he said and stood. He didn't wait to hear what she had to say. The one leaving strayed from the path with no purpose. With no regrets, he left without the slightest bow. Sayoko returned from the entryway to the sitting room and sat close to the veranda in a daze.

Faint spring light from inside the sky that tried to rain but failed shined across the surface while being blocked by pale clouds. Somehow, the gloom above their heads, pressing down on their tranquility, seemed to be lifting.

The sounds of a koto reverberated somewhere. Without wiping away the dust, I should play that lonely covered instrument held up by the wall between two parcels of printed cotton fabric. If I took off the saffron cover .... That piece of music is surely for accomplished hands. A pick lightly pressed and plucked back and forth between frets. The jumble of colors was rich only in the springtime. While listening, the rain was reminiscent of yesterday's.

"It's been raining all morning and I'm bored," her father told the flickering daytime fireflies and weeping forsythia trickling down the bamboo fence.

The satin cuffs easily slid to her wrists. Fine, long silk threads passed through the eyes of needles pricked into the dark crimson of the pin cushion. The long trunk of a bulging, old paulownia tree awakened her eyes. Several of the numerous threads passing through the needles bent like upside-down letter Vs were held down and several others were brushed away.

She was sure Kogō composed the piece. When it seemed wild fingers had kneaded the sorrowful afternoon to splinters, her father poured her tea in gratitude for her efforts.

The capital is the capital of the springtime, the rain, and the koto. Of these, the koto complements the capital. Of course, I, who love the koto, have lived in the quiet capital.

I came from the old capital and saw a crow break through the darkness and fly off. The blackness surprised me. The night trying not to come back seemed to burst into daybreak.

In this case, learning to play the piano instead of the koto would have been fine. English, too, was a thing of the past and mostly forgotten now. Father says a woman has no need for such things. To Seizō, people who live in the past will be so far behind in the coming age that they won't be able to catch up. The world of people who live in the past will not last for long.

If the old-fashioned people are ahead and the modern people are behind when today becomes tomorrow, a life measured in those days is treacherous in words and reason.

The lattice opened. The ancient man returned home.

"I'm back. The dust is awful."

"Even with no wind?"

"There's no wind, but the ground is parched. Tōkyo is a horrible place. Kyōto is much better."

"We'll quickly move to Tōkyo. We're moving there. Haven't you been saying that every day?"

"I said what I said, but after coming here and seeing this place, it's a different matter."

The old man wearing tabi socks adjusted his seat on the veranda.

"I see the tea cups are out. Was there a visitor?"

"Yes. Seizō was here."

"Seizō? This is ..." he said as he carefully untied the cord tying the large package he held.

"Today, I thought about buying sitting cushions. I got on the train but forgot to transfer and had a terrible time."

"Oh my." The daughter smiled with a bit of compassion. "But you went out to buy cushions?"

"I only bought these cushions and came home. That's why I'm late."

He took the imitation Hachijō yellow-stripe-patterned fabric from the package.

"How many did you buy?"

"Three. I think three are enough for now. Lay one down and let's see," he said and passed one to Sayoko.

"Ha, ha, ha. Why don't you set one down?"

"I will and you should, too. They look quite nice."

"The cotton feels slightly coarse."

"That can't be helped. For cotton, the price is the price. But I missed my train to buy this."

"Didn't you switch trains?"

"Well, I asked the conductor for a transfer but got upset and walked home."

"You must be tired."

"What? My legs are still fit. However, I can thank the walking for my beard choked with dust."

Four fingers of his right hand ran down his chin instead of a comb. As expected, faint black specks stuck to his thighs.

"Please, have a hot bath."

"What is this dust?"

"But it wasn't windy."

"It's odd the dust stirred up despite no wind."

"Nonetheless ..."

"No, not nonetheless. As a test, go outside and see for yourself.

I'm most surprised about the dust in Tōkyo. Was it like this the time you were here?"

"Much worse."

"It may be getting worse every year. Today, for instance, there's almost no wind," she said and looked outside from under the eaves.

The sensation of a cloudy sky lessened. Spring seemed to flow by. They could hear the sounds of a koto.

"Someone's playing a koto. She's quite skilled. What is the song?"

"Can you tell me?"

"I'll try. Ha, ha, ha. Your father has no idea. Hearing the koto brings back memories of Kyōto. The quiet of Kyōto is wonderful. Old-fashioned people like me do not journey to a tumultuous place like Tōkyo. This place is for young people like you."

The old-fashioned father deliberately moved to dusty Tōkyo for Seizō and her.

"Well, should we return to Kyōto?"

A smile rose on her forlorn face. The old man understood her filial devotion that pitied a man detached from the world.

"Ah, ha, ha, ha. Will you really go back?"

"I would truly return."

"Why?"

"Why not?"

"But we've just arrived."

"Our recent arrival is not a problem."

"Not a problem? Ha, ha, ha. You're joking."

The daughter looked down.

"So Seizō visited."

"Yes," she said, still looking down.

"Seizō ... What did he want?"

"Well?"

She raised her head. The old man looked at her face.

"Seizō stopped by."

"Yes, he did."

"What happened? Did he mention anything?"

"Nothing in particular."

"He didn't say anything? Though he should have waited."

"He said he was in a hurry and would come again. Then he went home."

"All right. He didn't come for any particular reason. I see."

"Father."

"Yes?"

"Seizō has changed."

"Changed? Oh, he's become a fine man. When I met him in Shimbashi, I barely recognized him. Well, that's wonderful for both of you."

She looked down again. Her words seemed unable to convey what she meant to her unsuspecting father.

"I haven't changed much from the past. He said I haven't changed at all."

The last part echoed in Kodō-sensei's head as if he stepped barefoot onto the end of a vibrating string.

"He said you haven't changed?" he pressed.

"Well, that's all right," she said softly. The old man tilted his head. "What did Seizō say?"

"Nothing in particular ..."

The same question and same answer were repeated. If you step on a water wheel, you'll only go around. No matter how long you step, you don't move forward.

"Ha, ha, ha, ha. You mustn't worry about such trivial matters. Spring is a depressing time. Today is not good weather for your father."

Fall is the depressing season. They know it's mochi but say it's the fault of sake. A person who is comforted is a person who is made a fool. Sayoko was silent.

"Why don't you play a little koto? It will be relaxing."

The daughter charmingly tilted her glum face and looked at the alcove. The hanging scroll dropped lifelessly, vertically cutting the edge of the too-black wall. The saffron cover failed to hide the spring.

"He may break it off."

"Break it off? If he breaks it off, then he should cancel it completely.

"But lately Seizō has been busy. He may soon finish his doctoral dissertation."

Sayoko thought, He doesn't even need a silver watch. One hundred doctors were useless to her.

"That's why he's agitated. Anyone absorbed in learning is like that. Don't worry too much. Even if he wanted to slow down, he has no options, he can't. Huh? What is it?"

"That's so."

"Yeah."

"He's very busy."

"Yes."

"So he went home."

"He went … home? Without doing anything? Nothing can be done because he loves it and is immersed in his studies. Didn't he say he'd set aside a day to go to the exposition with us? Didn't you discuss that?"

"No."

"You said nothing? Maybe, you should have. You said Seizō came, but what did you do? A woman must at least speak up."

After being raised not to speak up, why ask why didn't I speak up? Sayoko had to admit all her mistakes. Her eyes burned.

"Well, it's fine. This is nothing to be sad about. I'll inquire by letter. Don't berate yourself. Now, what's for dinner?"

"There's only rice."

"Rice without side dishes is fine. The maid I requested will come tomorrow. Once we've become more familiar with Tōkyo, it will be just like Kyōto."

Sayoko went to the kitchen. Kodō-sensei started to untie the package in a furoshiki wrapping cloth in the alcove.

CHAPTER 10

A MYSTERY WOMAN ENTERED THE MUNECHIKA HOME. WHEREVER the mystery woman is waves form into mountains, and charcoal briquettes turn into crystals. At Zen temples, they say "willows are green, flowers are red" or "a sparrow chirps, and a crow caws." Everything has its place in nature. The mystery woman must make the crow chirp and the sparrow caw.

After the mystery woman was born, the world instantly became chaotic. The mystery woman places a person approaching her in a pot and with square cedar chopsticks, repeatedly mixes in innermost emotions. If you don't recognize the importance of your existence, you do not approach the mystery woman.

The mystery woman is like a diamond. She radiates a brilliant light. No one knows the source of that light. If looked at from the right, it shines to the left. If looked at from the left, it shines to the right. A mixture of lights is reflected from a variety of surfaces. As many as twenty Kagura masks exist. The inventor of Kagura masks was a mystery woman. The mystery woman entered the Munechika home.

Daioshō, the most virtuous high priest, of the honest and cheerful Munechika home could never imagine a troublesome woman descending from heaven to live and frequently stir the bottom of the pot.

A copybook of the calligraphy masters of the Tang Dynasty rested on the exotic wood desk. The man sitting on a thick sitting cushion chanted a Noh poem about rising smoke in the province of Shinano and a burning tree inside a big-bellied pot. The mystery woman inched closer.

The witches in the tragedy *Macbeth* tossed worldly ingredients into a cauldron.

FIRST WITCH

>Round about the cauldron go;
>In the poisoned entrails throw.
>Toad, that under cold stone
>Days and nights has thirty-one
>Sweltered venom sleeping got,
>Boil thou first i' th' charmed pot.
>[*The Witches circle the cauldron.*]

ALL

>Double, double toil and trouble;
>Fire burn, and cauldron bubble.

SECOND WITCH

>Fillet of a fenny snake
>In the cauldron boil and bake.
>Eye of newt and toe of frog,
>Wool of bat and tongue of dog,
>Adder's fork and blindworm's sting,
>Lizard's leg and howlet's wing,
>For a charm of powerful trouble,
>Like a hell-broth boil and bubble.

The reader is frightened.

That is a play. The mystery woman is not that disturbing. She lives in the capital. The time is the twentieth century. She stepped inside at midday.

Charm boiled up from the bottom of the pot. Waves of laughter drifted by. The mixing implement was called The Chopsticks of Kindness. The quality of the contents from the pot was good. The mystery woman stirred and mixed slowly and quietly. Her hands echoed a Noh performance. Understandably, Daioshō was not afraid.

"Oh, you've gotten too hot. Please, take this."

He handed a large fan to the woman on the cushion. She remained seated by the entryway and posed her hands as usual.

"After that ..."

"Please, take it."

His large hands thrust out.

"I've stepped out for a short time and left the house empty. While thinking about going out, it has been a long time since I've seen you."

Daioshō looked about to interrupt. What was he going to say? The mystery woman immediately added.

"Please, forgive me."

Her black hair dropped to the tatami.

"No, it's fine."

She was not a woman who readily raised her head even after being given leave.

Someone said, "A woman whose etiquette is too polite is distressing."

Another said, "A woman who bows too courteously is a nuisance."

A third person said, "The sincerity of a person is directly proportional to the time the head is lowered."

There are various views. However, Daioshō was annoyed.

The black hair lay on the tatami. Only a voice emerged from her mouth.

"At home, everyone is the same. Every time Kingo or Fujio appear they are a nuisance. I enjoyed your delicious treat the other day and should have thanked you earlier, but I've been so busy."

At last, the head rose. The father sighed with relief.

"It was nothing ... a little gift. Ah, ha, ha, ha. It's finally getting warm."

He seized on an opportune moment to glance at the garden. "How are the cherry blossoms at your home? They should be in full bloom around now."

"This year, it may be the weather's fault, but they bloomed a little earlier than usual. They were at their best four or five days ago. The winds the day before yesterday damaged many of them."

"Is it that bad? Your cherry blossoms are amazing. What are they called? Asagi cherry blossoms. Yes, that's it. Their color is fantastic."

"They're tinted blue and a stunning sight in the evening."

"Is that so? Ah, ha, ha, ha. Along the Arakawa River, the cherry blossoms called hizakura are spectacular."

"Everyone says so. Many have double petals, but the pale ones are not rare."

"They're not. But enthusiasts say there may be a hundred varieties of cherry blossoms."

"Really? Oh my," said the woman, sounding surprised.

"Ah, ha, ha, ha. Even cherry blossoms can't be made light of. Recently, Hajime said he climbed Arashiyama on his way back from Kyōto. I asked him about the flowers, but he only said they had single petals but knew nothing else. These days he's a carefree fellow. Ah, ha, ha, ha.

"Would you like a snack? It's persimmon yōkan from Gifu."

"No, thank you. Please, don't worry about me."

"They're not that good but are a little unusual," said the elder Munechika. He picked up his chopsticks and put a yōkan slice from the dish in his hand. He gobbled it down alone.

"Speaking of Arashiyama." Kingo's mother interrupted. "Kingo may have inconvenienced you again the other day but expressed his delight and gratitude for your advice on various matters. Because he's also selfish, he must be a nuisance to Hajime, too."

"No, he's been a great help to Hajime."

"Excuse me. Kingo is not a man capable of helping others. At his age, he doesn't seem to have a single friend."

"One who studies too much may find it difficult to socialize with just anyone. Ah, ha, ha, ha."

"He doesn't seem to understand women at all and is always somewhat depressed. If Hajime didn't spend time with him, he'd have no companions."

"Ah, ha, ha, ha. Hajime is the exact opposite. He'll associate with anybody. Even when home, all he does is tease his younger sister. That too is a problem."

"No, his cheerfulness and open heart are wonderful. I'm constantly telling Fujio it would be nice for Kingo to be half of what Hajime is and become a little more lighthearted. However, because everything is the fault of his illness, I think my current complaints are unavoidable. I worry not only about my child I did not bear but also about the world."

"That makes sense," answered the elder Munechika somberly and tapped the bamboo spittoon. The metal-tipped pipe with silver leaf fell onto the tatami. Excess smoke flowed from the neck of the pipe.

"After returning from Kyōto, shouldn't he be a little better?"

"Thanks to you."

"The other day, when you visited this house, you seemed to enjoy the idle chatting with everyone."

"Really?" She was thoroughly impressed. "I'm truly at a loss." She drew out her words as if perplexed.

"Well, then ..."

"Given his illness, I don't understand why I worried so much until now."

"If made to marry, a change of heart may be good."

The mystery woman forces others to speak her thoughts. Doing it herself becomes a mistake. She quietly waits for the other person to slip and tumble down. She only prepares a slippery muddy sea without the other person noticing.

"I spend all day and night talking about his marrying. No matter what I say, he never agrees with even a positive utterance. As you see, I'm getting older. Because his father suddenly died overseas and to eliminate worrying on my part, I'd like to see him settle down one day sooner for his sake. Honestly, I don't know how many times I've brought up the subject of marriage. However, each time I bring it up, he flatly rejects it."

"I saw him recently and briefly touched on it. I told him only your mother worries you'll never stop being stubborn. It's a pitiful sight. And it would be nice if you settled down soon to give her peace of mind."

"Thank you so much for your kindness."

"No, your worries are mine. The two of us must take up the burden and do what must be done. Ah, ha, ha, ha. What is it they say? No matter how old they become, the worrying never stops."

"You are fine here, but I … if he keeps saying, 'I'm sick. I'm sick' all the time, he won't marry. If something happens, I could not face my late husband in the afterlife.

"Goodness, why won't he listen? No matter what I say, he says, 'Mother, with this body, I can't handle the problems of this household. Please marry off Fujio and make her care for you. I won't take one *sen* of the fortune.' That's how it is. If I were his birth mother, I could tell him he's selfish. As you know, because I am not, I can't act with such ingratitude to others. I'm truly at a loss."

The mystery woman stared at the high priest. The priest's huge belly protruded. He was deep in thought. The bamboo spittoon rang. A rosewood lid was carefully set in place. The kiseru pipe rolled over.

"Of course."

The priest's voice was restrained, nothing like his usual voice.

"Even so, I, a mother to no one, have no problem being tyrannical. When I rashly speak, I'll cause confusion you don't want to hear about."

"Yes, that is a problem."

The priest took a saffron cotton tea towel from the shallow drawer of the portable tobacco tray and hospitably wiped off the vine of whales.

"Shall I speak frankly? If you say no ..."

"I'm sorry for making you worry so."

"Then we'll see what happens."

"What will you do? If you can make him listen when his nerves act quirky."

"Why? Because he'll agree, I intend to speak so I don't hurt his feelings."

"But if he gathers that I intentionally asked you to speak to him, pandemonium will erupt."

"He is weak. His neurosis will heighten."

"It's like aggravating a swelling."

"Hmm," said the priest, folding his arms. Since the seams of his kimono sleeves were short, his thick elbows seemed impolite.

The mystery woman guides the man through a maze and makes him say, "Of course," "Hmm," makes the spittoon clang, and finally makes him fold his arms.

Twentieth-century taboos are talking impulsively and acting rashly. If a gentleman and a lady were asked why, their answers would be the same. Impulsive words and hasty actions easily have legal repercussions. The mystery woman's politeness was least prone to those repercussions. The priest folded his arms and said, "Hmm."

"If he decides to leave home, I would see that and have no reason to stay silent. However, for some reason, he never listens to me."

"A groom? When he becomes a husband ..."

"No, if that happens, it would be horrible. However, if the most unlikely case is not considered, it'll become a problem at a critical moment."

"Yes, that's true."

"Thinking about that, he may be ill but will get better. While he doesn't become a little more levelheaded, there's no reason to marry off Fujio."

"That's true," said the priest, tilting his head.

"How old is Fujio?"

"At the beginning of the year, she turned twenty-four."

"So soon. Until recently, she was only this tall," he said,

extending his large hand to touch his shoulder and seeming to peer from under his open palm.

"My body is so big, it has become useless."

"If I calculate, she's twenty-four, then my Itoko is twenty-two."

The conversation left this topic and flowed somewhere else. The mystery woman was forced to humor him.

"Even here, I talk too much about my worries rather than Itoko or Hajime. No doubt, you probably think I am a carefree woman who is unaware of others' feelings."

"No, but you're welcome. The truth is I thought I wanted to discuss this situation. Amid this turmoil, Hajime is saying he may or may not become a diplomat. Although this won't be fixed in a day or two, he must take a bride sooner or later."

"Certainly."

"And that would be Fujio?"

"Yes."

"If she's the one, he knows her disposition. And I'll have peace of mind, too. Naturally, Hajime has no reason to refuse. I think it'll be fine."

"Yes."

"Well, as her mother, what are your thoughts?"

"I'd like to thank you for sharing the details on that matter with me."

"That's all right, isn't it?"

"If that happens, Fujio will be happy, too, and I will have peace of mind."

"But if she's dissatisfied and you're not ..."

"There is no dissatisfaction. No situation is better than asking and making it come true. Only she will be trouble. Hajime is an important man who is the heir in the Munechika family. I have no idea whether Fujio will be pleased or not. However, after she accepts and is given away, Kingo, like me, will be forlorn."

"Ah, ha, ha, ha. There are no limits to worrying. If Fujio becomes a bride, naturally, your thoughts will change because Kingo will take on the responsibilities. That's what will happen."

"Will what you are saying happen?"

"As we agreed, it will also be what you said a while ago. If that happens, the dead should be satisfied, too."

"Thank you for your kindness. If my husband were alive, it ... it would be nice not to have these sorts of worries alone."

The mystery woman's words slowly dampened. A writing brush tired of the world hates this moisture. When slowly coming this far into the mystery woman's maze, the brush would have a horrible time moving forward. God who creates everything, the day, night, sea, and shore is said to have rested on the seventh day. The brush skillfully wielded by the mystery woman enters another world touched by the sun and must sweep away the dampness.

An older brother and a younger sister are active in another world touched by the sun. The brightness beamed from the south into the six-tatami-mat mezzanine floor was not enough. Outside the shōji sliding door left open for a pleasant feeling, a two-foot-tall pine swelled up its roots coiling inside a Shigaraki pot. Its shadow bent like a crooked finger hit the eaves. A rubbing of ancient Chinese characters on a white background was pasted on the six-foot, thick sliding door paper. A plover flew over the waves at the handle. In the next three feet taken up by a makeshift alcove, the stem was avoided, and a single lightweight flower was tossed into a flower arrangement basket.

Itoko jumbled up the multicolored sewing in the alcove and placed a sewing box with two drawers pulled open and spilling out threads closer to the window. Her brother's loud voice trampled the soft sounds of the needle creating springtime at each stitch in the path of the sewing thread.

Lying on his belly in the style of the Yayoi people, he ruled the spring in the world while asleep. He frequently tapped the threshold with the tip of a ruler.

"Itoko, your sitting room is bright. It's very classy."

"Shall we switch?"

"There's no point in switching, ... however, it's too high-class for you."

"Too high class? Is it all right because no one uses it anyway?"

"It's nice. Nice is nice, but it's a little too high-class. And isn't this decor best suited to a young lady?"

"What do you mean?"

"This pine. Surely, the garden shop Taiseien sold it to father for twenty-five yen."

"Yes. That bonsai is valuable. It would be awful if it were knocked over."

"Ha, ha, ha, ha. That's like Father being pressured to buy this for twenty-five yen. And it's like you to lug it up to the second floor. Despite the gap in your ages, the father and daughter cannot quarrel."

"Ha, ha, ha, ha. You are one silly man."

"Silly? Just like you, Itoko. We're brother and sister."

"Oh, no, no. Of course, I'm silly. I am silly, but you are silly, too."

"Silly, huh? Isn't it okay because we're both silly?"

"I have proof."

"Proof of silliness?"

"Yes."

"That is Itoko's great invention. What kind of proof is it?"

"That bonsai."

"Oh, this bonsai?"

"That bonsai knows nothing."

"What do you mean it knows nothing?"

"I hate it."

"Oh my. So this is the great invention. Ha, ha, ha, ha. Why did you bring something you hate here? It looks heavy."

"Father brought it here."

"Why?"

"The sun hits the second floor, which is good for the pine."

"Father is kind, too. So your dear brother has been made a fool. Does a father's kindness, a silly child make?"

"What? Now, wait a minute. Was that the beginning of a poem?"

"It sounds like one."

"It seems so, but it's not a true poem."

"I will conduct a careful investigation. More than that, today, you've sewn a superb piece. What is that?"

"This? This is Isezaki silk."

"It's quite shiny, isn't it? Is it for me?"

"It's for father."

"You only sew for Father and rarely anything for me. As far as I can see, nothing since that fox vest."

"You're horrible. You're simply lying. I sewed the clothes you're wearing now."

"This? This already looks bad. Look at this."

"Ew. The collar is grimy. You've only been wearing it for a short time. Hajime, you're too greasy."

"Even if I am, it's still awful."

"Well, if I sew this for you, I'll sew it right now."

"It'll be like new."

"Yes, I'll wash and stretch it."

"A gift bestowed by Father? Ha, ha, ha, ha. Sometimes, you are mysterious, Itoko."

"How so?"

"Because father is old, he only wears new things. On the other hand, a young man, such as myself, is forced to wear old things. That's a little strange. Moving in this vein, he wears a Panama hat, but you can say I wear an ancient soldier's hat found in a storage room."

"Ha, ha, ha, ha. You are too glib."

"Am I only eloquent? What a shame."

"You have other talents."

Hajime didn't answer, rested his chin on his hands, and peered down on the plants in the garden through a gap in the railing.

"You do. A few," said Itoko, her eyes never leaving the needle. She tied up the seam gripped in her left hand. When she released her whitened fingertips, she looked at her brother's face.

"There's more, Hajime."

"What? I'm only a great talker."

"But you have other merits." She held the eye of the needle up to the shōji sliding door and narrowed her charming eyelids.

Still resting his quiet spirit in his hands, Hajime gazed at the garden.

"Will you tell me?"

"Uh-huh."

He couldn't move his lower jaw resting on his hands. His response came from his throat and out his nose.

"Your legs. You know that?"

"Yeah."

Her lips moistened a navy blue thread and formed a point with her fingertips in a woman's plan to pass the thread through the eye of the needle missed before.

"Itoko, is a visitor here?"

"Yes, Kingo's mother."

"Kingo's mother? She's in good health, but her son's dreams will never come true."

"But he's a decent man and doesn't insult people like you."

"Yes, I'm hateful and fail at helping others."

"You tend not to be helpful."

"Ha, ha, ha, ha. In gratitude for fixing my fox vest, would you like to go cherry blossom viewing in the next few days?"

"Haven't the petals already scattered? What's the point now?"

"No, Ueno and Mukōjima are no good, but they're in full bloom in Arakawa. We'll go from Arakawa to Kayano, pick primulas, go around to Ōji, and return home by train."

"When?" Itoko stopped sewing and stabbed the needle at her head.

"Or we can go to the exhibition, have tea at the Taiwan Hall, enjoy the lighted outdoor decorations, and return home by train? Which will it be?"

"I want to see the exhibition. If I finish sewing this, we'll go. All right?"

"Yes. Therefore, you must value your older brother. There aren't many kind older brothers like me in all of Japan."

"Ha, ha, ha, ha. I'll cherish you. Please, hand me the ruler."

"While you are diligently at work, I'll buy a diamond ring for my bride."

"You are skilled ... only at talking. Do you have that much money?"

"Money? Not now."

"Hajime, why do you always fall short?"

"Because I'm exceptional."

"What happened to the scissors?"

"They're next to the cushion. No, a little more to the left. Why is there a monkey attached to those scissors? Is it a joke?"

"This? Isn't he cute? Mr. Silk Monkey."

"Did you make him? Your handiwork is impressive. Is there anything you can't do? This is quite clever."

"Anyway, I can't compete with Fujio. Hey, please stop dropping your cigarette ashes on the veranda. Here, use this."

"What is that? Oh, it's decorative paper pasted on a thick card. I guess you made this. You have too much free time. What is this for? Needles? Scraps of thread? Hmm."

"Hajime, you like women like Fujio, don't you?"

"I like women like you, too."

"I'm a different type. Aren't I?"

"There's nothing wrong with you."

"You're hiding. That's weird."

"Weird? It's all right to be weird. Auntie Kōno often speaks in confidence."

"Depending on the situation, she may talk about Fujio."

"Does she? Should I go ask her?"

"Please, stop doing that. There is a charcoal iron around here you could use as an ashtray, but I hesitate to go and get it."

"It's harmful to be restrained in your home. Shall I fetch it?"

"There's no need to, but please stop doing that. Go downstairs now. Our little talk is over."

"You're very insecure. I'm suppressing yawns. Should I lie down?"

"It's all right to yawn."

"Well then, can I yawn and lie down?"

"Please don't lie down. With poor manners like that, you will fail the diplomat exam."

"It's possible that the examiner agrees with you. That's a problem."

"A problem? Of course, Fujio probably agrees."

Itoko stopped her sewing hand but hesitated to pick up the charcoal iron. She pulled off the thimble used when stitching a traditional *irikobishi* diamond pattern. She accidentally dropped the lid beautifully painted with a *jorinmoku* fish-scale pattern behind the pincushion where silver raindrops pierced a pink fabric.

Her palm supported her earlobe reddened by the long day beside a window. Her right elbow rested on a sewing box. Below her spread-out work, the slant of her hidden elbow collapsed.

The dark color mixed with flowers on the sleeves of her undershirt slid noiselessly over her supple arm. The pillar of flesh brighter than usual was vivid under the ribbon hanging like a butterfly.

"Hajime."

"Yeah? Are you finished? You look a bit muddled."

"Fujio is no good."

"No good? What do you mean?"

"She has no intention of coming here."

"You asked her?"

"Am I so rude I'd ask something like that?"

"How do you know without asking? You're a shrine maiden through and through. Your chin jutting out, resting on your hands, and leaning on the sewing box depicts a superb scene in the world. Although you're my younger sister, you cut a splendid figure. Ha, ha, ha, ha."

"Please, calm down. Although people speak kindly to you ..."

As she spoke, Itoko's white arm supporting her head flopped down. Her fingers dangled in front and pressed on the corner of the sewing box. On her cheek close to the shōji sliding door, the impression left by the pressure of her hand blushed red with her earlobe. The long eyelashes on her beautiful eyelids hung down from above hiding her cool pupils.

From inside those lashes, his younger sister looked keenly at Hajime. Using the flesh on her square shoulders, her slumped body was raised by her elbow.

"Itoko, I've been promised Uncle's gold watch."

"Uncle's?" she quietly asked. Her voice dropped, as soon as she said, "But ..." her black pupils were hidden by long eyelashes. The boldly colored ribbon swung forward for an instant showing her face.

"I'm fine. While in Kyōto, I talked to Kingo."

"Oh." Her face looking down raised halfway. A pitiful, anxious smile rose along with her head.

"If I go overseas soon, what should I buy and send you?"

"You still don't know the test results."

"I'll probably know soon."

"This time, please pass."

"Okay, um. Aha, ha, ha, ha. All right."

"It's not all right. Fujio likes a confident man who does well in his field."

"Am I inept in my discipline and lack confidence?"

"It's not that, but, well, for example, there is Seizō."

"Yup."

"I heard he received a silver pocket watch for academic excellence. He's writing his doctoral dissertation now. Fujio likes that sort of man."

"Really? Oh my."

"What do you mean 'Oh my'? He's a man of distinction."

"I didn't receive a silver pocket watch and am not writing a doctoral dissertation. I failed my exam and am a disgrace."

"Wait, no one says you're a disgrace. You're just too carefree."

"Too carefree is right."

"Ha, ha, ha, ha. That's funny. You don't seem the least bit bothered."

"Itoko, I cannot be a scholar and will fail. Let's drop this. It doesn't matter. Anyway, don't you think your brother is a good brother?"

"Yes, I do."

"Which do you like Seizō or me?"

"I like you, of course."

"And Kingo ..."

"I don't know."

The late afternoon sun passed through the shōji and warmed Itoko's cheek. Only the color of her forehead facing down seemed remarkably white.

"Hey, the needle is stabbing your head. Forgetting is dangerous."

"Oh."

She pressed two fingers on the faint glimmer of her undergarment's sleeve and gently pulled it out.

"Ha, ha, ha, ha. Your hand can deftly reach into an unseen place. If you go blind, you could become a sensitive masseuse."

"I'm used to doing this."

"You're special. Should I make you listen to funny stories occasionally?"

"Like what?"

"The beautiful woman who played the koto next door to the inn in Kyōto."

"You wrote about that in a postcard."

"Ah yes."

"If it's that story, I know it."

"Mysterious things exist in this world. When Kingo and I went to Arashiyama to view cherry blossoms, we saw her. Seeing her was nice, but Kingo was captivated by her and knocked over some teacups."

"Oh, really? Oh my."

"He was probably startled. And then when returning home on the express night train, he rode on the same train as that woman."

"You're lying."

"Ha, ha, ha, ha. They came all the way to Tōkyo to be together."

"Don't people from Kyōto have reasons for randomly coming to Tōkyo?"

"That has something to do with fate."

"People are ..."

"Please listen. Was Kingo on the train with that woman who may become his bride? How about that? It's worrying."

"I've heard enough."

"If it's enough, I'll stop."

"What was the woman's name?"

"Her name? Didn't you say I've said enough?"

"Wouldn't it be better to tell me?"

"Ha, ha, ha, ha. It's good you've become serious. The truth is I lied. I made it all up."

"You're hopeless," said Itoko, smiling happily.

CHAPTER 11

Ants gather around sweetness and people around novelty. Civilized people complain about boredom while living a violent existence. They endure hectic lives where they eat three meals while standing and worry about blacking out on the street. Civilized people complain about the length and breadth of life and crave the length and breadth of death. Without pride civilized people take action, no one suffers from stagnation as much as civilized people. Civilization shaves people's nerves with a razor and blunts people's nerves with a wooden pestle. Every last person numbed by stimulation and thirsting for stimulation gathered at the new exhibition.

Dogs love scents, and people chase after colors. Dogs and people are the most sensitive animals on this point. The purple vestments of the imperial family, the yellow uniforms of those without rank, and the blue coarse clothes of students are nothing more than devices to summon others.

Curious onlookers running along a riverbank always shoulder a variety of flags. Those who fervently manipulate the paddles are taken in by colors.

Nothing is more remarkable in the world than a goblin's nose. A goblin's nose is red, glowing bright since ancient times. Colorful places are not far away. Everyone gathers at a colorful exhibition.

Moths gather around lamps. People gather around electric lights. Shiny objects tug on this world. Categories of silver and gold, giant clam shells, agate stones, lapis lazuli crystals, jambūnada-suvarṇa gold are presented. Their glow astonishes tired eyes and makes tired heads spring up.

At an evening party of civilized people that shortens the day, jewels set on exposed skin alone dominate. Diamonds are more valuable than the human heart because they steal human hearts. The light of a star falling into a muddy sea twinkles more vividly in the observer's heart than on roof tiles in shadow. Pious men and pious women who dance in glimmering shadows empty their houses and gather at the outdoor light display.

When civilization is sifted to the bottom of a bag of stimuli, it becomes an exhibition. If the exhibition is strained in the sands of a dull night, a dazzling light display results. If you live at all, you will look at light displays to seek proof of life and be astonished. Civilized people paralyzed by civilization feel life begins when they experience astonishment.

A train adorned with flowers cuts through the wind to this place. When the living proof is observed, the cargo on board is unloaded near the restaurant named for Yamashita Gannabe, who died long ago. The unloaded cargo is slowly sent toward the forest in an attempt to restore honor when one is about to die.

A hill glances off the night and starts in Hongō. A high platform floats in a haze. A slope starts, descends for nearly ten miles to the east, cuts through the hills to Netsu and Yayoi, and surprisingly passes through to Shitaya. Black shadows stepping on each other gather at the edge of a pond. Nothing there would surprise a civilized person.

Pine trees grow tall and do not hide their flowers. The lights illuminating the night through gaps between branches multiply. The rain falls, and the wind blows. First, lone petals fall and then split in two and scatter. After a few moments, fluttering petals scattered. Meanwhile, a multitude of reds blew onto the ground. Before the blown petals reached the ground, the tips of branches tumbled down after them.

In time, the lively blizzard fades away. At last, the storm in the remaining treetops ebbs. The shadows of flowers that protect the starless night were invisible. At the same moment, the outdoor light decorations lit up.

"Ooh," said Itoko.

"The world at night is more beautiful than the world during the day," said Fujio.

Tufts of pampas grass bent in arcs. The number of half-moons woven in the glittering interior of gold stacked from the left and right is unknown.

Hajime and Kingo stood a foot away from Fujio's obi sash covering a good part of her waist.

"This scene is fabulous. It's the Palace of the Dragon King," said Hajime.

"Itoko, you look surprised," said Kingo, standing with his hat covering his eyebrows.

Itoko turned around. A nighttime smile is like a poem recited underwater. Perhaps, the imagined place cannot be reached. The color of the clothes of the woman who turned around seemed to be yellow and tricked the night. Several black stripes were etched and sliced vertically.

"Were you surprised?" her brother asked this time.

"What about you two?" Fujio turned, ignoring Itoko. Her white face suddenly flashed from the shadow of black hair. Far-off firelight lit the end of her cheek a faint red.

"I was not surprised because this is my third time here," said Hajime, one side of his face brightened by the light.

"Although surprising, this is enjoyable. Women often enjoy themselves and are happy," said Kingo. He stood his long body to its full height and looked down at Fujio.

Black eyes shined in the night and moved.

"That is the Taiwan Hall," said Itoko casually, as she pointed across the water.

"It should come out furthest to the right. It's the best one. Right, Kingo?"

"Seeing it at night ..." Kingo quickly added.

"Hey, Itoko, it probably looks exactly like the Palace of the Dragon King."

"It truly is the Palace of the Dragon King."

"Fujio, what do you think?" asked Hajime, still enthralled by the Palace of the Dragon King.

"Isn't it a little mundane?"

"What? That building ..."

"Your description."

"Ha, ha, ha, ha. Kingo, your opinion is that the Palace of the Dragon King is mundane. Despite being mundane, isn't it the Palace of the Dragon King?"

"Usually, a description becomes mundane when it is accurate."

"If being accurate is mundane, what is it when inaccurate?"

"Perhaps, it becomes poetry," answered Fujio from the side.

"Because poetry is disconnected from reality," said Kingo.

"Because it's greater than reality," Fujio remarked.

"The accurate description is mundane. The inaccurate description is poetry. Fujio, give a bland and inaccurate description."

"Should I say it?

"My brother knows. Please, listen," said Fujio. From the corners of her keen eyes, she spotted Kingo. The corners of her eyes spoke. The bland and inaccurate description is philosophy.

"What's that on the side?" asked Itoko innocently.

A line of flames crossing into darkness and cutting across the sky was the roof. Columns were cut vertically. Roof tiles were cut at a slant. Stars were buried inside a haze. Against the endless night that became a black background, a lightning spike flashed and drew a line across the empty sky. Two were drawn as they dropped from above. A gammadion cross was drawn and rotated close to the ground like fireworks. Finally, the point of the spike reversed, was flung up, and penetrated to the center of the constellation Hercules. The towers met the ridge of the roof that connected to the floor. A picture was created of a huge fire with no gaps filling the area from right to left when looking across Shinobazu Pond from this side.

Embossed gilt lacquerwork not miserly with gold on black paint containing indigo dye drew a temple, a tower, a covered walkway, a curved railing, and numerous rectangular pillars of a round tower. To use up the excess, the drawings went back and forth.

The line of fire running the length and breadth of the sky was alive at each point and line without one misplaced point or segment. It moved, and its motion was unmistakable. As long as it moved, the shape showed no signs of collapse.

"What's next to it?" asked Itoko.

"That's the Hall of Foreign Countries. We can see the front perfectly. From here, it's the prettiest one. The one with the high, round roof on the left is Mitsubishi Hall. That's impressive. How should that be described?" asked Hajime, a little hesitant.

"Only its center is red," said his sister.

"It's like rubies inset in a crown," said Fujio.

"Of course, it looks like an advertisement for a Ginza jeweler like Tenshōdō," said Hajime, feigning ignorance as usual. Kingo faintly smiled and looked up.

The sky was low. During the night approaching the vast, black earth, immature stars wandered lost on the roads and dangled down. Flames at many points connected to pillars and roof tiles immersed the sky upside down and shined on the eyes of drowsy stars. The stars' eyes were hot.

"The sky looks scorched. Maybe, it's the crown worn by the Roman pope."

Kingo's line of sight swept over the large area from Yanaka to the forests of Ueno."

"The crown of the Roman pope? Fujio, what do you think about the Roman pope's crown? You look like you'd appreciate a Tenshōdō ad."

"Either is fine," Fujio concluded.

"Either one is fine. Isn't it a queen's crown? What do you think, Kingo?"

"I can't say anything. Cleopatra wears that kind of crown."

"How do you know?" Fujio shrewdly asked.

"Are there pictures in a book of yours?"

"The water is prettier than the sky," said Itoko out of the blue. The conversation drifted away from Cleopatra.

Water that dies during the day is pressed on by the shadow of a windless night and is placid as far as the eye can see. Since when did it not move? Still waters know nothing. From the water level, if the lake was dug a hundred years ago, it hasn't moved for one hundred years. If dug fifty years ago, it hasn't moved for fifty years.

The rotted roots of the lotus are slowly spewing green sprouts. A carp born from the mud hides in the darkness and gently moves its jaws.

The outdoor light display flipped the tall shadows upside down. Over twenty feet of coastline turned bright red and fell into the serene waters. The dying black waters flashed with colors. The fins of fish hiding in the mud shimmered.

Flickering flames extended just a touch to the shore and crossed brightly to the other side. Everything lying in its path and fully dyed was severed by a long bridge, hanging from west to east. Twenty arches straddled the waves of wild feathers on white stones. Ornamental gibōshi finials capping the railing were white glowing balls illuminating the night.

Accompanying Itoko's voice saying, "The water is prettier than the sky," the eyes of the other three gathered at the water and the bridge. From a distance, the electric lights shining on the stone banisters rising every six feet were visible hanging in the air in a well-behaved row. The crowd gradually passed below.

"That bridge is buried under people," yelled Hajime.

Seizō, joined by Kodō-sensei and Sayoko, were crossing the bridge. A surprised and agitated crowd emerged from a small roadside shrine to the goddess Benten of arts and literature and pushed forward. The distant crowd descended the hill and pushed toward them.

People on the east, west, north, and south abandoned the expanses around the broad forest and the wide pond to gather on the long, narrow bridge. Nothing on the bridge could move.

The string in the center of the bow was raised high. Policemen directed the people coming and going to the left and right. Everyone was jostled around as they passed. There was no time for feet to hit the ground. Only small spaces were discovered for easy steps.

If she thought she finally felt her heel had found a landing, she was pushed forward from behind. She could not believe she was walking. Of course, she couldn't say she was not walking.

Sayoko felt hopeless as if in a dream. Kodō-sensei dreaded being kneaded and massaged by everyone to suppress memories of people from the past. Only Seizō was relatively elated. Standing among the crowd, the man more aware of his superiority than most became elated when moving his body became impossible.

The exhibition is modern. The outdoor light display is an extreme of modernity. Astonishingly, those gathered here are men and women of modern times.

An utterance of surprise was due to the powerful self-awareness of living in modern times. People looked at each other's faces. Their mutual worlds were tacitly understood to be the modern world. After one's power is recognized by many, that person returns home for a sound sleep. Of the many people in this world, Seizō was the most modern man. His elation was understandable.

The triumphant Seizō was, at the same time, in despair. Anyone in the modern world with eyes could see he was alone. There should be no dissent. However, the baggage of being behind the times was carried carefully by two people. Naturally, things seen from the present day together with the past that has no impact are not seen and may seem insufficient. Whether modern or old-fashioned, the size of the crest on the haori formal jacket worn when going to see a play was his only concern as one who did his best to be a spectator. Seizō was ashamed. He walked as fast as the wave of humanity allowed.

"Father, are you all right?" a voice called from behind.

"Yes, I'm fine," came the reply a building away, squeezing out between strangers.

"This seems dangerous ..."

"If you push naturally, there's no need to worry," he said, passing the crush of people and landing at a thorny place with his daughter.

"I'm only being pushed and can't push even a little," said the daughter, unable to calm down but managing to smile on one slender cheek.

"It's best not to push. Only being pushed is being pushed."

While the two conversed, they came out in front. The paper lantern of a policeman glanced Kodō-sensei's black hat.

"Where's Seizō?"

"He's over there," she said, pointing with her eyes. If a hand came out, it was blocked by someone's shoulder.

"Where?"

Kodō-sensei had no time to set his feet. He tilted the front teeth of his dry-weather geta sandals and stood tall. When the sensei's hips nearly lost the center, the impatient civilized people behind him pressed on him. The sensei fell forward. On the verge of toppling over, his fall was stopped by the backs of civilized people standing in front. Instead of the civilized people coming out in front somewhere, they were kind people who did not refuse to help the man with their backs.

Naturally, the wave of civilization advanced. The unreliable parent and child were pushed out close to Benten's shrine. The wave where the long bridge stopped and the feet of the people crossing may or may not land on the ground quickly scattered to the left and right. The heads of black hair broke apart into their desired paths. Eventually, the two people felt like their chests expanded.

He looked into the waning spring evening, the bottom darkened to indigo, and could see the flowers. The aromas from double petals that bloomed late and scattered by rain and wind and the wish for flowers in the night were brightly lit from below by the lanterns of the world of humanity. A faint red mother-of-pearl is engraved, but it is too hard to engrave. Floating means to drift away from the sky. As he wondered how to describe this evening and this flower, Seizō waited for the other two.

"People are frightening," said Kodō-sensei. The word frightening meant its true and ordinary meanings.

"So many have come out."

"I want to go home soon. People are so frightening. Where can we escape this?"

Seizō was grinning. Civilized people who covered the dark forest like baby spiders are in a class of their own.

"Tōkyo is amazing. I never thought it could be like this. It's a scary place."

The number that reveals one's destiny is powerful. A place that creates power is frightening. A place that noisily boils tadpoles in foul water covering less than forty square feet is scary. Not to mention, the horror of Tōkyo that easily vomits up civilized elite tadpoles is expected. Seizō grinned again.

"Sayoko, how are you doing? It's dangerous. You can get a little lost in this place. Kyōto is not like that."

"When passing over that bridge ... I wondered about what would happen. It was scary."

"It's fine now. You look pale. Are you tired?"

"I feel a bit …"

"Poorly? You can't keep walking because you've walked too much. And it's so crowded. Let's rest a little somewhere.

"Seizō, is there a place we can rest? Sayoko isn't feeling well."

"Oh, really? We can try one of the many teahouses," said Seizō, walking ahead.

Fate creates a circular lake. The people circling the lake must meet somewhere. It's fortunate to meet and part as strangers. In gray London that repeatedly froths in a sea of people, attempts at a chance meeting during the morning or evening are futile. Eyes became saucers and legs became sticks of people who asked around in vain. They stared at the sooty air staining the house next door obstructed by a single wall. A man once wrote we will never meet in this lifetime but may meet only after our bones become relics and grass grows over our graves. Fate separates people who care for each other for all time despite the wall between them and creates an unexpected encounter for them at the round lake. Strangely, they spiral toward each other as they move around the lake's perimeter. A mysterious thread sews through the dark night.

"The ladies seem rather tired. Shall we have tea here?" asked Hajime.

"Yes, the ladies are tired, but the men are in worse shape."

"Itoko is in better shape than you. Itoko, how are you? Can you still walk?"

"I can still walk."

"You can walk? That's marvelous. So we'll skip the tea."

"Didn't Kingo say he wished to rest?"

"Ha, ha, ha, ha. That's a clever comment. Kingo, Itoko will rest for your sake."

"Thank you so much," said Kingo, smiling feebly, and added in the same tone, "Fujio may rest for my sake, too."

"If you're asking" was the terse answer.

"I'm no match for women," concluded Kingo.

They crossed the entrance to the makeshift Western-style building constructed to overhang the lake waters. Chairs were arranged around small tables. In the spacious room, small groups of patrons sat chatting.

"Where shall we sit?"

For some time, Hajime looked around at the forty or fifty people in there and tugged on the sleeve of Kingo standing on his right.

Behind them, Fujio was taken aback. However, asking a question would be as indiscreet as questioning the Zen master Yangshan Huiji. Kingo didn't respond with any signal.

"Over there are some empty tables."

He quickly went inside. Tottering behind them, Fujio's eyes took in everything from each corner of the huge room and stored it in her mind leaving nothing out. Itoko looked down.

"Hey, did you see him?"

Hajime was the first to drop into a chair.

The curt reply was "Yeah."

"Fujio, Seizō is here. Look behind you," said Hajime.

"I know," she said but didn't move her head even a little. Her black eyes had a mysterious glow. Her cheeks were a little too hot under the electric lights.

"Where is he?" Itoko casually asked, tilting and turning her gentle shoulders.

Seizō's party took the seats in the second row of tables closest to the wall and to the left of the entrance.

The three people already sitting there were next to the window on the right end. The eyes of Itoko who moved her shoulders ran through the crowd scattered throughout the large room from one end to the other and fell on the profile of Seizō a distance away. She could see Sayoko across from him. Kodō-sensei was only the crest on his back. White threads blending with the spring night were listlessly tugged under his chin. His gloomy beard thrown away and blown away in this world among these people and having accumulated years pointed toward Sayoko.

"Oh, he's with some people," said Itoko, as she turned back around. Kingo seated across from her met her eyes before she turned around but said nothing. He struck the side of a matchbox held vertically over the ashtray. Fujio kept her mouth shut. While sitting back-to-back with Seizō, she might have intended to leave.

"Well, isn't she a beauty?" Hajime teased Itoko.

Fujio's downcast eyes staring at the table could not see. Only her thick eyebrows twitched. Itoko did not notice. Hajime was unconcerned and Kingo, indifferent.

"She is pretty," said Itoko, looking at Fujio who did not look up.

"Uh-huh," she said bluntly. Her voice was muted. When asked a question not worth answering, when too ashamed to acknowledge a companion verbally, a woman will use this technique. Women have the uncanny and superior gift to imply a negative tone in an affirmative phrase.

"Did you see, Kingo? I was surprised."

"Yes, it's a little strange," he said while brushing cigarette ashes onto a saucer.

"That's why I spoke."

"What did you say?"

"You forgot what I said?" said Hajime, looking down and striking a match. Instantly, Fujio's eyes aimed at Hajime's forehead. He did not notice. When he moved the fire to the cigarette held in his mouth and raised his face opposite her, the flash of light had already gone out.

"Oh, that's strange. What are those two talking about?" asked Itoko.

"Ha, ha, ha, ha. Something interesting. Itoko—"

He was interrupted by the arrival of the black tea and Western confections.

"Ah, the sweets of a country in ruins have come."

"What do you mean by sweets of a country in ruins?" asked Kingo, bringing the teacup closer.

"Sweets of a country in ruins. Ha, ha, ha, ha. Itoko should know the history of the sweets of a country in ruins."

While speaking, he dropped a sugar cube into the teacup. Foam-like crabs' eyes made faint sounds as they rose.

"I know nothing about those things," said Itoko, stirring with her spoon.

"Didn't your father say that? He said, 'If students eat Western sweets, Japan will fail.'"

"Ha, ha, ha, ha. Did he say things like that?"

"Didn't he? Your memory is poor. Didn't he say that recently when Kingo ate something with dinner?"

"That's not so. He probably said the students' habit of eating Western sweets makes them aimless."

"Uh-huh, really? They weren't sweets from a country in ruins. Father truly hates Western sweets. He only values curious things like persimmons or miso matsukaze. Bringing things like that close to a stylish person like Fujio will soon end in contempt."

"So it's best not to mention Father's slander. Since you're no longer a student, you are allowed to eat Western sweets."

"Aren't you worried about being scolded? Well, I'll try one. Itoko will also have one. Would you like one, Fujio?

"But it seems that men like Father are gradually becoming few in Japan. That's unfortunate," he said and stuffed a chocolate-covered Castella cake in his mouth.

"Ha, ha, ha, ha. Talking to yourself is ..." said Itoko and looked at Fujio. She didn't respond.

"Fujio, you're not eating?" asked Kingo, as he raised the teacup to his mouth.

"It's too much" is all she said.

Kingo quietly put down his teacup and slightly turned his head toward Fujio. As she thought, He's here. Without blinking, she was engrossed in watching a section of the outdoor light display shining through the window. Her brother's head gradually returned to its original position.

When the four left their seats, Fujio looked toward the front without looking to the side. The doll of a queen proudly walked forward to the entrance and left.

"Seizō has already gone home, Fujio," said Hajime, tapping the woman's shoulder without inhibition. Fujio's chest burned with black tea.

"There is fun in being surprised. A woman is a happy creature," Kingo said when they rejoined the crowd. He wondered, What was I thinking? and said it again.

Being surprised is enjoyable! A woman is a happy creature! Until she returned home and got into bed, those two phrases rang like a bell mockingly in Fujio's ears.

CHAPTER 12

One haiku poem professes poverty in seventeen syllables that proudly intone horse dung or horse piss. Bashō saw a frog jump into an ancient pond. Buson carried an umbrella to see the autumn colors. After the dawn of the Meiji era, a man named Shiki suffering from a disease of the spinal cord drank water from a sponge gourd. To this day, the elegance in poverty has not been exhausted. Seizō disdained this.

An immortal mountain wizard dines on drifting clouds and slurps the morning dew. The food of a poet is imagination. Leisure is necessary to indulge in a beautiful imagination. A fortune is required to achieve a beautiful imagination. The poetry of the twentieth century and the elegance of the Genroku era are different.

The poems of civilization are formed from diamonds. They are created from purple, a rose's fragrance, grape wine, or an amber sake cup. In winter, the bottoms of silk tabi socks are warmed by glossy coal where mottled marble is arranged into a square. In summer, strawberries are served on ice platters, and sweet blood melts into the cream's whiteness. At one time, a greenhouse emits the spectacular fragrance of Qilan oolong tea from the tropics. Paths through fields, the sky, and a field of flowers under the moon are opulently woven into a thick ornamental obi. Chinese brocade short-sleeved kimonos and long-sleeved kimonos brush past each other. The poetry of civilization is in gold. Seizō must obtain money to fulfill the poet's duty.

They say cultivate fields rather than write poems. Few poets have made fortunes throughout time. Civilized people love the actions of poets more than their poems. They bring to life civilized poems every day and night and transform the real life of wealth in flowers and the moon into poetry. Seizō's poems are not worth one *mon*.

No business has as little money as that of poets. At the same time, no business needs money like that of poets. A poet in the civilized world writes poems with other people's money. By using other people's money, a life of beauty must be lived.

Seizō's natural fate was the hope of relying on Fujio who appreciated his true abilities. He heard that the fortune and property in her family were above average. No mother would consent to Kingo's younger half-sister getting married with a simple dowry of a dresser and an oblong chest of drawers. Above all, Kingo had a delicate constitution. Possibly, the mother was inclined to adopt a groom for her daughter into the family. Sometimes, if a roadside fortune-teller is right in an attempt to unravel a problem, it is always good fortune. Rushed work ends in failure. Seizō was mature and waited for events to unfold in the future like the auspicious udumbara flower that naturally blooms once every 3,000 years. Seizō did not initiate sumo wrestling matches and would never win if he did.

Heaven and Earth were eternal compared to this promising youth. Spring was thought about when easterly winds blew endlessly for ninety days over his triumphant brow. Seizō was a gentle, patient man who offered no resistance.

The past descended to this place. From a past in which he turned his back on his dreams of twenty-seven years, a small, dark point comparable to a drop of India ink that should have smoothly flowed to countries in the West pushed forward to the bright city. Something being pushed will fall forward despite no desire to leave. The poet determined to prepare and quietly wait had to hurry into the future. The black dot stopped right above his head. If he looked up, it seemed to be rotating. If it burst and scattered, a deluge would come all at once. Seizō wanted to shrink his neck and run off.

For four or five days, he could not turn his attention to the Kōnos because of assistance to Kodō-sensei or attention to the sensei's business matters. Last evening, he forced an impractical solution. Out of obligation to his former mentor, he chaperoned the sensei and Sayoko to the exhibition. Although the favors were received long ago, the debt of gratitude is current.

I am not a heartless poet who forgets a debt of gratitude. Kodō-sensei taught me the tradition of providing a blessing, like the elderly washerwoman who gave a meal to an impoverished young man who went on to become the great general and politician, Han Xin. From now on, I will endeavor to help the sensei at any time and any place. A beautiful poet must rescue anyone in trouble. As a part of my history amid my current success, I will fulfill my duty, and the remnants of deep human emotions in the poetic material of memories are the most fitting behaviors in me.

However, nothing can be done without money. Unless I marry Fujio, the money will never come. If marriage comes one day sooner, then I could think about caring for Kodō-sensei a day earlier. Seizō developed this logic while sitting at his desk.

He must marry Fujio soon, not to throw away Sayoko but to help Kodō-sensei. Seizō thought his thinking should not be flawed. If asked, he thought he would have a fine defense. He was a man with a sound mind.

Having thought this through, Seizō opened a thick document with richly golden characters on tea-colored paper set on the desk. Inside appeared a bookmark in the art nouveau style with a green willow and a glimpse of a red tile roof. He slid the bookmark to his left hand and read the tiny characters from behind gold-rimmed eyeglasses. Only five minutes were quiet. After a short time, his black eyes jumped from the page and stared at the frame of the shōji door lit diagonally by elongated sun rays.

He was surely thinking, I haven't seen Fujio for four or five days. If the problem were simply time, four or five days or even ten days were of no concern. While being pursued by the past, the time he spent grooming himself was extremely valuable.

If we meet, the target of my hopes moves closer with each meeting. If we don't meet, no fate shortens the length of the rope of the love that should pull you, my former love, to me. Moreover, a demon slips through the tiniest knothole. There's no guarantee the sun will not set after half a day of not meeting, and the moon will enter a cloudy evening. He had difficulty gauging whether a lightning flash fell on Fujio's brow during these few days of neglect. Of course, the diligence needed to write a dissertation is important. However, Fujio is more important than a dissertation. Seizō put down the document.

When he slid open the door covered in Okinawan bashō-fu cloth, he saw bedding on the top shelf of the wardrobe and a wicker trunk below. He took the suit on top of the trunk and quickly changed clothes. His hat waited at the wall for its owner. The shōji clattered open. Just as he thrust the cashmere tabi socks under the red strap of his zōri sandals, the maid entered.

"Oh, you're going out? Could you please wait a moment?"

"What is it?"

He looked up from his sandals. The maid smiled.

"Is something the matter?"

"Yes," she said, still smiling.

"What is it? Is this a joke?"

As he was about to leave, a foot fell out of the brand-new zōri and slid down the polished hallway toward the room with Western lamps.

"Ha, ha, ha, ha. You're in too much of a rush. You have a visitor."

"Who is it?"

"Oh my, you're acting clueless because you were waiting."

"Waiting? For what?"

"Ha, ha, ha, ha. You're too serious," she said with a smile. Without waiting for his response, she turned back to the entrance.

Seizō, looking concerned, peered down the hallway with his zōri sandals in line with the shōji door. He wondered what was about to happen. He straightened to his full height, his dark brown felt hat nearly touched the door frame.

From his vest with a narrow chest, the white shirt, and white collar appeared remarkably elegant given the simplicity of his perfectly creased suit at the side of the dim hallway. Seizō, in stylish attire, calmly settled into a corner of the unpretentious hallway, and looked to the end through his glasses set at an angle. He looked wondering what was about to happen. The man who thrusts both hands into his suit pockets when upset was calm.

"Turn there and go straight."

He thought he heard the maid's voice.

Sayoko's figure gracefully appeared at the end of the hallway. The side covered with maroon silk damask reflected a strange light only at the position of the dragon crest. She wore a lined kimono of ordinary meisen silk that exposed the tops of her white tabi socks.

When she stiffly turned the corner, he glimpsed the color of her long, kimono undergarment. At that moment seven steps separated them in the unobstructed center hallway, the gazes of the man and the woman fell on the other's face.

The man was slightly ill at ease. Only his posture did not collapse. The woman hesitated. Eventually, she hid the rouge flushing her cheeks and slipped her mischievous smiling face to her companion. The wings of vivid color of broad silk shimmering with amber waves extended to her sideburns of black hair untouched by oil.

"Aah."

Seizō's greeting enticed the woman, a distance away, to come closer.

"Were you on your way out?" she asked, still standing. She placed one hand over the other in front and somewhat pitifully stood still but slightly raised her dropped shoulders.

"No. What? ... Please come in. Well ..." he said, pulling one leg into the room.

"Excuse me," she said, sliding her shuffling feet down the hall and still holding one hand on the other.

The man pulled the rest of his body into the room. The woman followed him inside. The window on the bright long day encouraged a youthful conversation between the young couple.

"Thank you for taking time out of your busy schedule last evening," she said as she moved closer to the entrance and bowed, placing her hands on the floor.

"No, it was nothing. You're probably tired. How are you feeling? Have you recovered?"

"Yes, thanks to you." She looked somewhat gaunt. The man seemed slightly worried. The woman immediately made excuses.

"I never before plunged into a crowd like that."

Civilized people held the exhibition for surprise and enjoyment. People of the past viewed outdoor lighting displays with surprise and fear.

"How is the sensei?"

Sayoko did not answer immediately and smiled sadly.

"He probably hates crowded places."

"It may be his age," she said but swiftly regretted her words. She looked away from him to stare at the bogwood teacup saucer placed on the tatami. A *kyoyaki*-dyed teacup rested on her lap.

"It was probably distressing to him," said Seizō, taking a cigarette case from his pocket.

Mount Fuji and the pine trees of Miho no Matsubara were sculpted in detail using the hues of the moon illuminating the darkness. Using the tool of green paint for those pines was slightly commonplace for a poet's possession. It might have been a gift from Fujio who likes gaudy things.

"No, I wouldn't say he was distressed," Sayoko disagreed with Seizō's words.

The man opened the cigarette case. Silver brilliantly flowed on its gold-plated back surface. The lonesome woman thought it was splendid.

"If it were just the sensei, perhaps it would have been best to have gone to a quieter place."

The busy Seizō is forced to make time. Everyone deliberately goes out into the crowds, despite disliking them, because they all think they're precious. Unfortunately, I hate crowds, too. After careful consideration, people who have fleeting encounters and quietly walk together on a spring evening still cannot draw closer. Sayoko hesitated, wondering how best to respond. This was not because of the idea tainted by the state of the world in which she feels constrained by his kindness and the desire to avoid making him feel bad. A slightly more poignant meaning was hiding in Sayoko's hesitation.

Seizō interpreted her hesitation as a sign to ask again.

"As I expected, Sensei prefers Kyōto, doesn't he?"

"Before we came to Tōkyo, he often said he wanted to move soon, but he seemed to prefer a familiar place to live when he came."

"Is that so?" asked Seizō but quietly accepted it. Why did he come out to a place that disagreed with his nature in his heart? Thinking about his circumstances, he felt it was somewhat absurd.

"And you?" he asked.

Sayoko kept her mouth shut. Whether Tōkyo is good or bad is a problem determined by the mindset of the young man smoking cigarettes with the scent of the West before her eyes.

When a boatman asks the passengers, "Do you like boats?" Sometimes you must give one answer, either like or dislike, as if you were going to take the helm. A man controls his likes and dislikes so as not to provoke anger when questioned like this by the head boatman. Nonetheless, he resents being questioned about his likes and dislikes as he wears a look of innocence.

Sayoko shut her mouth again. She wondered why Seizō wasn't being frank.

She saw a watch come out of his vest pocket, immediately understood, and asked, "Where are you going?"

"Oh, no place special," he answered adeptly.

Again, she said nothing. The man seemed a little impatient. Fujio was probably waiting for him. He was silent for a short time.

"The truth is Father is ..." Sayoko spoke her mind at last.

"Oh, is there a reason you dropped by?"

"I'd like to go shopping."

"Yes, of course."

"If you have the time, I came to see if you could take me shopping, even to the shops in Kankōba, as you said you would."

"Oh, yes I did. That's too bad. I'm in a hurry and have to leave now.

"Well, I'll do this. Tell me the items you need. I'll buy them on the way home and bring them to you tonight."

"But that would be too much trouble."

"It's nothing."

Her father's goodwill returned to foam again. Sayoko went home crestfallen. Seizō placed his hat back on his head and rushed out front. At this time, the stage of the dying spring revolved.

Rains gathered to wash the purple on magnolia petals. Flowers on the veranda withered to brown and hid the band of hair drying. If she moved, shimmering heat haze touched her back. Beyond the blackness, the wind and sun teased. Moments earlier, a yellow butterfly playfully fluttered over. Fujio, wearing a blank look, turned inside. In the shadow cast by the sun behind her and in the shadows of the side locks covering her ears and flowing to her shoulders, her profile of toned, chiseled flesh was softly obscured. When she gazed to the far side over her shoulder gleaming with a thousand stripes bathed dark violet on one side, her dazzling eyes quieted. They say the stunning whiteness of flowers, thought to be smartweed at dusk, hides people. In the shadow where copious light streamed onto the veranda through lush hair, on her thin face that barely existed, only the ends of groomed thick eyebrows were perfect. Her long, narrow black eyes beneath her eyebrows did not know what to say. Fujio rested her elbows on a small parquet desk and looked down.

A gold hammer pounded on the door of her heart. Her hot circulating blood of love filled the sake cup of youth. Turning away her mouth from drinking was incomplete. As the moon inclines and pines for the mountains, people age and recklessly preach about the path. The stars are jumbled in the young sky. Cherry blossoms fall to the young earth. Each year passes to reach twenty. Now, the god of love is in full bloom. Her raven hair is disheveled. The thin silk gauze woven from spring winds hung onto the colorful eaves with spider's webs. She waited for the man to entangle himself with her.

The entangled man searched for luminous jewels in a maze and flipped his soul upside down in Christian crosses and Buddhist gammadions made from glowing purple strings. His mind will be in chaos unsettled until the next world.

The woman gazes serenely. A Christian minister says, "Seek salvation."

The Rinzai and the Ōbaku schools of Buddhism say, "Seek enlightenment."

This woman is only lost and moves her dark eyes. This woman is the enemy of anyone who is not lost. When lost, suffering, going mad, and dancing, at first, the woman's approval is fortunate.

She extends her slender hand on the railing and says "Bark." If she says "Bark," she says, "Bark" again. A dog barks over and over. The woman half smiles. The dog barks and runs back and forth while barking. The woman is silent. The dog tucks its tail and goes wild. The woman is more elated. This is love interpreted by Fujio.

A stone Buddha carries no love because the inability to have color is prepared from the beginning. Love is based on confidence in one's qualification to be loved. However, there are those with confidence in the qualification to be loved and those unaware of having no qualification to love. Often these two qualifications are inversely proportional. Anyone who professes the qualification to be loved and does not hesitate brings sacrifice closer to one's companion because the qualification to love another is missing. Someone who drives the soul into beautiful bright eyes is always eaten.

Seizō is in danger. Those who entrust their lives to hearty laughter that exposes dimples always kill people. Fujio was born under the fire horse of the Chinese zodiac. This says she's destined to kill her husband. Fujio understands love for oneself. She never contemplates the existence of love for another person. It is poetic. It has no morality.

The object of love is a toy, a sacred toy. The sole function of an ordinary toy is to be played with. A basic principle is the love toy plays back. Fujio plays with men. The man is not allowed to play even a little. Fujio is a queen of love. The conclusion is love must be disconnected from principles.

She specializes in being loved and focuses only on the love. She is blown around by spring winds, may have a chance meeting before Heaven and Earth in the ebb and flow of a sweet tide, and achieve this peculiar love.

A person who protects her dignity while loving is like someone who drinks sweet sake while wearing a quilted hood for protection. One feels poorly. Love melts everything. Because an illustrated square kite is also a rock candy sculpture, it always melts. Pride will not show signs of softening even when dunked in the waters of love and crossing for three long days and nights. It stays hard forever. One who preserves her dignity while loving is rock candy.

Shakespeare summed up women with these words.

Frailty, thy name is woman!

An awakened love with frailty passing inside her scatters granite sand in the softness of boiled rice and chills the trusting molars munching the rice. The mouth cannot safely move without the flexibility of rubber when chewing thoroughly.

The self-confident Fujio chose to love Seizō who lacked pride. A large brown cicada caught in a spider's web does not thrash wildly even when caught. Sometimes, the net breaks and it escapes. Hajime was easy to catch. However, Fujio found taming Hajime to be difficult.

A woman of pride enjoys whoever comes at once when signaled subtly by her chin. Despite Seizō coming immediately, when he came, a jewel of poetry was always in his pocket. She thought he lacked the will to play with her in dreams and be honored with heartfelt sincerity in becoming her toy. Oblivious to her search for the qualification to love him, the qualification to be loved was a yearning for her genius to be recognized in her eyes, in her brow, and in her lips. Fujio's love had to be Seizō.

Seizō, who should have visited, had not been seen for five days. Fujio wore light makeup every day and hid the sharp edges of her pride in the mirror. It was the last evening on the fifth day! While surprised, she was amused! A woman is a happy creature! A taunting bell still rang at the bottoms of her ears. With her elbows resting on the desk, her body didn't move when the sun shined on her blazing black hair. Living with her back to the veranda and her face in shadow, an ancient rule is to avoid light while in deep thought.

A prisoner bound ten times without rope but captured with a haughty look will come if beckoned and run where pointed. There is no ulterior motive in the play. If a beautiful leaf turns over, a hairy caterpillar is beneath. If she stands beside her beloved and faces a full-length mirror, it is fine to take a picture of only the two of us. She swears to god and has no doubts, but if she looks, she's mistaken. The man remained unchanged, and the one snuggling her was a stranger she'd never seen before. While surprised, she was happy! A woman is a happy creature!

Her sorrowful face with a touch of blue in a brilliant whiteness gazed at the base of an electric light a few tables away. A man who would never approach a young, pretty woman except when by her side, in a thoughtful and friendly way, faced this woman halfway around the square of a Western table. She felt like her heart was struck by a wooden bell hammer. The blood in her bosom rhythmically flushed her entire cheeks. Crimson leaped up in a brilliant red.

Pride stands up ferociously. In that situation, she doesn't turn around or raise suspicion. The word *criticism* is unworthy. Despite there being something, it's dressed up as nothing. It is handled inadequately as a triumph. The aware man surely loses face. This is revenge.

The prideful woman did not have a forlorn expression until this moment. The word resentment is spoken when replaced in the eyes of the person relied on. A suitable word, the opposite of contempt, is fury. Fury blends regret with jealousy. The first principle of a civilized lady is to belittle people. To be belittled by another person is worse than death. Seizō certainly embarrassed the lady.

Love is created from faith. Faith does not allow praying to two gods. As a devout believer in my qualification to be loved, I lower my head, my back of duplicity faces a frivolous public and rings the bell of some Shinto shrine. People selfishly enshrine an ox's head or a horse's bones. Seizō tossed a monetary offering of love to a selfish god and did not look at the paper with the message of wavy lines or characters from a street fortuneteller. Seizō is prey who quickly freed himself from my black eyes and was caught in a plain net woven in invisible light. He cannot rush outside. He must be cherished throughout life as a sacred toy.

Sacred means he becomes a toy and must not be pointed at by another's finger. Since last evening, Seizō was no longer sacred. Only he might have turned me into a toy.

While holding her elbows, Fujio's cast-down eyebrows animated.

If she had been turned into a toy, she could not be left there. Pride shreds love. Spiteful remarks abound. Poverty starves love. Wealth and rank lavish love. A glorious deed sacrifices love. Pride steps on reluctant love. Her thigh is pierced by a pointy drill. "Look at that," she orders and shows her pride to others. Pride is the strength that throws out what one believes is most valuable. If pride stands up, even her life is sacrificed on the altar of vanity. In contrast, the winds of hell that abandon heaven and cut Satan's ear that falls to the center in the darkness of hell shout Pride! Pride! Fujio bit her lower lip while looking down.

After nearly a week of not meeting, she wondered whether she should send a letter. She tried to write immediately after coming home last night. After a couple of lines, she tore it to pieces. She wrote nothing. She's waiting for him to lower his head, yield, and come to her. If I'm silent, he'll surely come. If he comes, I'll make him apologize. And if he doesn't? Pride was a bit of a problem. Pride will not rise into unreachable places.

"Will he come? Of course, he'll come," Fujio said to herself. Unknowingly, Seizō continued to be pulled by pride. He's coming.

Even if he comes, I won't ask about the woman last night. If I did, that woman would appear before his eyes. At the dining table last night, my brother and Hajime spoke in strange codewords. I would upset myself by deliberately hearing about the relationship between that woman and Seizō. I'll lower my head, listen, and surrender. It's fine if those two people want to gang up to make a fool of another. I'll give proof to counter the fact hinted at by the two and put them in their place.

Somehow, Seizō must apologize. He must be hit hard and made to apologize. And my brother and Hajime must apologize, too. Seizō is all mine. There was no point in the mischief provoked by those two with their mocking expressions. I must force them to apologize for showing off their intimacy.

Fujio tried to pierce the two contradictory sides with the word *pride*. She mused over this, her face hidden by freshly washed hair.

She heard footsteps on the quiet veranda. The shadow of a tall figure instantly appeared. The front of the lined kimono with a splash pattern was open. The dark gray woolen undershirt stuck to his skin formed a long inverted triangle that looked nice on his chest. Above were a long neck and a long face. His complexion was pale. His hair swirled into a whirlpool and looked like it hadn't been cut for a few months or combed for a few days. His thick eyebrows and mustache were beautiful. The qualities of his mustache were jet black and wispy. He appeared to be a man who possessed natural grace with no tinkering. A dirty white silk crepe circled his waist twice. The lengthy end was loosely tied under his right sleeve like a cat's toy. The hems did not match at all. She could see black tabi socks peeking from beneath fluttering like a loosely draped priest's robe. Only the tabi socks were new. If it had a scent, it would be deep blue. The man with his old head on new legs walked through the world topsy-turvy and unexpectedly went out to the veranda.

The polished, fine-grained floor planks copied the woven wave pattern on the bottoms of his socks. When she heard the soft footsteps, the black hair on Fujio's back gracefully moved. At that moment, her eyes glimpsed dark blue socks step onto the veranda. Despite not seeing the owner of the tabi socks, she knew who he was.

The dark blue socks quietly walked over to her.

"Fujio."

The voice was behind her. Kingo seemed to stop behind the hemlock pillar that divided the groove of the storm door. Fujio said nothing.

"That dream again?" asked Kingo, still standing and looking down at her straight clean hair.

"Yes?" said the obedient woman, always under his thumb, and turned her face toward him. She resembled a water snake raising its head. Shimmering hot air shattered on her black hair.

The man didn't even move his eyes. His pale face stared down at the woman's forehead.

"Did you have an enjoyable time last night?"

Before answering, the woman quickly swallowed a hot dumpling.

"Yes," she greeted him with chilly indifference.

"That's good," he said calmly.

The woman was impatient. If a woman with a resolute spirit is put on the defensive, she instantly becomes impatient. If her companion is calm, her impatience grows.

As sweat flowed down and tried to penetrate or managed to penetrate, and he calmly leaned against the pillar, the man looking down was a little too selfish, like sitting cross-legged while drinking sake and stealing everything from someone.

"You were probably surprised but enjoyed yourself."

The woman was forced to retreat. The man looked down. He still hadn't moved. No meaningful sign was visible.

Kingo wrote the following in his diary.

A person has ten *sen* in coins and describes this as one-tenth of one yen. Another person has ten sen and describes this as ten times one sen. The same word is higher or lower depending on the person. This is the opinion of a person who uses words. This was the only difference between Kingo and Fujio. The difference in levels results in a strange phenomenon that leads to arguments.

He changed his posture but appeared listless and only said, "Oh."

"Even if I wanted to become a scholar like you and be surprised, I may not have fun because I can't be surprised."

"Fun?" he asked.

Fujio thought but did not ask her question, "Do you understand what having fun means?"

Eventually, her brother spoke.

"It's not fun. Rather, it's peace of mind."

"Why?"

"A person who has no fun does not worry about suicide."

Fujio understood nothing her brother said. His pale face was still looking down. Asking why lacked discretion, so she was silent.

"People like you who have too much fun are dangerous," he said.

Unaware, Fujio made waves in her black hair. She looked up. Of course, her brother was looking down. Did he understand? Not knowing anything, she recalled the line *It is well done, and fitting for a princess descended of so many royal kings.*

"Is Seizō coming as usual?"

Fireworks burst from Fujio's eyes as if the tip of a hammer struck flint. Her indifferent brother asked, "He's not coming?"

Fujio was grinding her teeth. Her brother kept himself from speaking but stayed leaning on the pillar.

"Kingo."

"Yes?" He looked down again.

"That gold pocket watch will not be passed down to you."

"If it's not given to me, who will get it?"

"I'm keeping it for now."

"You're keeping it for now? That's fine, too. Because you're engaged to Hajime ..."

"When the time comes, I'll give it to Hajime."

"From you." He lowered his face and brought his eyes closer to his sister.

"From me. Yes, from me. I will give it to someone."

From her elbows resting on the wooden mosaic desk, she sprung to her feet and stood up straight.

Stripes of dark blue, rich yellow, reddish-brown, and horsetail green stood like poles. Only the hem hit the billowing of four-colored waves and hid the fastening hooks on the sides of her white tabi socks.

"Okay," he said and walked away, exposing the heels of the rippled soles.

While Kingo appeared like an apparition and disappeared like one, Seizō got closer. Every time it rained, the greenish tint trapped in the ground returned to steam and dampened the earth. He stepped on the warm earth to come closer. His handsome shoes covered by the shiny pelt of a goat and not one visible speck of dust carried him in mincing steps closer to the gate of the Kōno home.

On the limp figure that carelessly threw away the world, the cords of his formal haori coat worn out of duty were tied with a round knot. Kingo distracted his idle hands with his thin walking stick and nearly collided with Seizō approaching beside the fence. Nature favors contrast.

"Where are you going?" asked Seizō, touching his hand to his hat and smiling as he neared.

"Good question," Kingo answered. The walking stick no longer moved. Essentially, the walking stick had nothing to do.

"I thought I'd step out for a bit."

"Please, let yourself in. Fujio's home," said Kingo and meekly passed by. Seizō hesitated.

"Where are you going?" Seizō asked again. His attitude of I have business with your sister, and what you do doesn't matter was insufferable.

"Me? I don't know where I'm going. Somehow, I'm only dragged around just as I drag around this cane."

"Ha, ha, ha, ha. That's quite philosophical. A walk, perhaps?" He peered up from below.

"Yes, well, the weather's nice."

"It is splendid. Why not go to the exhibition rather than a walk?"

"The exhibition? I went to the exhibition last night."

"You went last night?" Seizō's eyes were still for a moment.

"Uh-huh."

Seizō thought he would say more but held back. A little cuckoo seemed to enter the clouds with one cry.

"Did you go alone?" Seizō asked.

"No, I went because I was invited."

As expected, Kingo had a companion.

Seizō seemed to have to move forward slightly.

"I see. I guess she's pretty." He made a connection and thought about the next question.

However, Kingo said one word.

"Yes."

Seizō collected his thoughts. I have to settle this matter right away. First, I should ask, "With whom?" but before asking, wouldn't it be better to ask, "What time were you there?" Better yet, I should say, "I went, too." If so, everything would gradually unravel with his answers. But that's unnecessary, too.

For a short time, Seizō debated in his heart and throat. Meanwhile, Kingo moved the tip of his slim cane by just one foot. A foot moved behind the cane. Seizō who glimpsed this sign believed things had already run aground. At the back of his throat, he let go of his painstaking plan.

A man who does not act with the intention to recover, despite his ability to control the future like the dirt under his fingernails, is a fatalist who cannot turn things around with the power of learning.

"Please, go in," Kingo said again. He felt badgered. When he felt fate commanded him to go left, if a push came from behind, he would immediately go forward.

"All right ..." said Seizō, tipping his hat.

"Okay? Well, I'll be going."

The thin cane moved backward only two feet from Seizō. At the same time, Seizō's shoes took one step closer to the gate, they were pulled by the cane and returned to their original positions. Fate placed Kingo's cane and Seizō's feet in an infinite space and fought over the foot-long gap. The cane and the shoes were each man's personality. Our souls reside in the heels of the shoes at the right time and are hidden in the tips of canes at the right time. A novelist who knows nothing about depicting souls depicts canes and shoes.

The shoes, having traveled the entire space of one step, circled the radiant tip and began questioning the cane entrusted to the ground by the desperate slender body.

"Did Fujio go with you last evening?"

The cane held upright like a pole provided the answer.

"Ah yes, Fujio went, too. Depending on the circumstances, today, I may not be able to complete the preliminary reading."

As the thin cane was stuck to and separated from the ground, if thought to be standing, the thin cane was leaning. If thought to be leaning, it was standing and advanced by slicing through infinite space. The shiny shoes, tips covered by a thin layer of mud by his step, walked onto the gravel at the gate and passed through the entryway.

At the same time, Seizō reached the entryway, Fujio, still leaning against a veranda pillar, did not return her toes to her seat but ran them over the guide groove and gazed at the surface of the spacious enclosed garden. Long before she leaned against the veranda pillar, the mystery woman thought with all her might about the inexhaustible time of the coming spring with the ringing iron kettle as her companion in the shut-up room.

Kingo is not a child of my flesh and blood. This statement brought forth all of the mystery woman's thoughts. When elaborated on, this statement becomes the mystery woman's view of life. A view of the universe is possible when the view of life is enlarged. The mystery woman listens to the sounds of the iron kettle every day and creates a view of life in the six-tatami-mat room and a view of the universe. The creators of perspectives on life and the universe are limited to people with leisure time. The mystery woman has the good fortune to pass her days on a silk futon.

A dwelling corrects the heart. A baby chick properly yearning for love is elegant even when eating bugs and chipping its beak. The mystery woman sits gracefully. The view of life in the six-mat room must also be graceful.

Being old and without a husband disheartened her. Having none of the needed children further discouraged her. She was more disgusted than hopeless by the needed children turning into strangers. The mystery woman believes she is an unhappy person and ashamed of herself.

That's not necessarily unsuitable for someone else. Soy sauce and sweet rice wine have been mixed together for ages. However, if sake and tobacco are taken together, a cough develops. Kingo does not pour water that matches its shape to the shape of the parental vessel. As the days pass and pile up, a barrier can be created. Around this time, the feeling was that of a chance encounter in Nagasaki with an Edo enemy. Scholarship is a tool for success in life. This opposes the parent's temperament and not the pursuit of knowledge that misses the rhythm at the year's end and the New Year. It's a disgrace he became an eccentric who deliberately spent money and did not pass into society when he left school. His reputation is bad. She thought he was troublesome for an heir. Despite this, she had no intention of taking stagnant water from this man or working to take it.

Fortunately, Fujio is here. The medake bamboo that survives winter has the power to blow off the powdery snow as the nights multiply. Flashy clothes decorated with embroidered flowers in relief and butterflies are worn by figures in the springtime that attract the attention of people in the streets. The world pushing her out as my child is wide. Each person is free to cheerfully parade around or lose one's way in a sunny world. Whoever is introduced as an ideal man for her husband is led astray and anxious. The honor of the mother who raised him is upheld. By being caught by a stranger like a frozen sea cucumber, my path is to stay for years by my daughter, who is envied and lives flamboyantly day in and day out, and then go to my grave.

Orchids grow in secluded valleys, and a sword returns to the hero. A famous groom must take my beautiful daughter. Men have made many proposals, but my daughter had no interest in them, or they had no interest in her, which was unhelpful. A ring that does not fit her finger will be accepted but thrown out. Whether too big or too small, no one can become her groom. As a result, no man has become her groom to this day. Seizō alone remains from that throng and shines brightly. He is regarded as an exceptional scholar and received a pocket watch as a gift from the emperor. After several more achievements, he'll become a doctor. Not only is he charming, he is kind. He is elegant and has a silver tongue. There is no shame with him as Fujio's husband. Even if he had to be supported, it would feel good.

Seizō is not the perfect son-in-law. His sole flaw is no wealth. However, being cared for by a husband's wealth holds no sway over her no matter how interesting she finds the man. Taking an interest in a certain unique person and making the quiet mother-in-law an important figure becomes Fujio's situation and is for my sake. One problem is her assets. Today, four months after my husband died in a foreign country, naturally, his possessions were returned to Kingo. The scheme starts here.

Kingo says he doesn't need one mon's worth of property. He says he'll give the house to Fujio. If he sheds the clothes of duty and becomes conveniently naked, he won't hesitate to leap without warning into a gushing hot spring. However, clothing worn for show cannot be casually stripped off.

He is also considerate of others. When it looks like rain and someone says, 'Here use this,' and tosses an umbrella to another without hesitation if there are two, as is done in this world. However, some people are expected to extend a selfish hand unconcerned about the person ready to get wet. A puzzle develops there. Giving is, in fact, a lie. Presenting an innocent expression is nothing more than an apology to the neighborhood.

While Kingo looked displeased about transferring his wealth, against his will, to Fujio, his cultured self had to save face. Therefore, the puzzle is solved. The mystery woman explains that giving means not wanting to give and stresses that nothing is accepted given her idea of acceptance. The view of life on the six tatami mats is complex.

The mystery woman scowled at the solution to the problem and finally left the six tatami mats. One method emphasizes accepting nothing until the desire to accept dissipates and acceptance comes one day sooner. This method is not easy to discover even by differentiation and integration. The mystery woman who left the six tatami mats with a desperate, worried look was impatient and could no longer bear sitting on the futon. The day in spring when she went out to look was unexpectedly quiet. The warm air calmly teasing the side locks made fools of people. At last, the mystery woman was becoming more upset.

In the Western-style building abutting the left side of the veranda, Kingo used the room next to the parlor as his study. To the right around a corner was Fujio's six-tatami-mat sitting room, jutting out southward from the bend.

Fujio stood, looking straight at the opposite corner, as though she were about to cross the bottom of a diamond-shaped mochi cake. The area near her wet-looking dark side locks pressed against the hemlock pillar. Closer to the middle of the glossy figure posed at an incline, only her wrists thrust deep into her obi sash looked whiter.

The wanderer gazes at his hometown while lying among the bush clovers and unsettled in the pampas grass. Fujio cannot leave her hometown and doesn't know what she is looking at. Her mother approached from the veranda.

"What are you thinking about?"

"Oh, Mother," she said, separating her inclined body from the pillar. The expression in her eyes did not reveal a shadow of grief as she looked back. The proud woman and the mystery woman looked at the other's face. They were a true parent and child.

"Has something happened?" said the mysterious one.

"What?" asked the proud one.

"That's why I asked what are you thinking about?"

"I'm not thinking about anything, just looking at the garden."

"Oh," said the mysterious one with a meaningful expression.

"The golden carp in the lake are leaping up." The proud one persisted. Of course, splashing sounds came from the muddy water.

"Oh, my. Mother, very little can be heard in your room."

It's not that she couldn't hear. The mysterious one was absorbed in a dream.

"Really."

This time the expression on the proud one's face was meaningful. The world is diverse.

"Look, the lotus flowers are coming up."

"Oh, I hadn't noticed."

"No, this is the first time," said the mysterious one. The mysterious one only thinks about carelessness. When Kingo and Fujio are pulled away, her mind becomes a vacuum. It's not a place of lotus flowers.

After lotus flowers emerge, they bloom. After the lotus flowers bloom, the mosquitoes multiply and enter the storehouse. Then the crickets chirp. Rain comes intermittently. Chilly wintry winds blow. While the mystery woman is worrying about the solution to the mystery, the world changes. The mystery woman intends to sit in one place and solve the mystery. The mystery woman thinks no one in this world is as wise as she and does not think about carelessness in dreams.

The golden carp splash and jump again. Mud sinks in the cloudy water. From the bottom where only the outer layer is slightly warmed, hazy, red shadows move the quiet earth and float closer. When she wonders if its tail swings so as not to scatter the sunshine flashing on the smooth waves, the water is slapped and flies up.

In the thick mud landing on the surface, a faint red object conceals a shadow. The traces left by warm water parting on the back show a swell in a line and tease last year's reeds without wind.

A bird enters a cloud, leaving no trace.

Fish swim, leaving ripples in the water.

Seizō's diary had these couplets written in the standard style and not as Chinese poems or quatrains. Spring sunlight did not cover the world and spontaneously delight people's hearts. Only the mystery woman was not happy.

"Why are they leaping like that?" she asked. Similar to the mystery woman thinking about a mystery, the golden carp leaped recklessly. If whimsical, both acted on a whim. Fujio did not respond.

In praise of a floating lotus leaf, a Chinese poet described a lotus leaf as a folded green copper coin. Naturally, it does not feel heavy like a coin. However, while its young life of yesterday and today is first entrusted at the water's edge, the slim face is exposed to the winds of this corrupt world and is insignificant like a sen coin. The color could not be called green.

A carp jumped above the leaves mixed with a green patina encroaching each day on tender tea leaves, each one much thinner than a sheet of Mino paper, and disliked the heaviness and green. If the remains of spring are blown, they jump up. If they settle down, they become indestructible beads rolling around.

The unresponsive Fujio gazed at the scene before her eyes. The carp jumped again.

The mother gazed above the lake for no reason and eventually had a change of mind.

"Seizō hasn't visited recently. Did something happen?" she asked.

Fujio spun around.

"Did something happen?"

She stared at her mother. Uninterested, she looked away toward the garden. Her mother was startled. The carp from earlier blushed a pale red and passed under floating leaves bouncing on the water.

"If he doesn't come, what will he say when he does? Has he been ill?"

"Ill?" asked Fujio, her voice nearly shrill.

"No. I'm asking if he's not ill?"

"Is he sick?"

The force in her words as if flying down from a stage of spring water stopped at the tip of her nose with a hmph. Her mother was taken aback again.

"When will he become a doctor?"

"When?" she asked with disinterest.

"Did you quarrel with him?"

"Can I argue with Seizō?"

"I simply like to know for the sake of proper etiquette."

Any further explanation to the mystery woman was not possible. Fujio hesitated to answer.

She thought, if I reveal what happened last night, that would be the end. Of course, Mother would become desperate and surely feel compassion for me. I never found telling everything awkward, but willingly seeking compassion was closer to hunger and no different than begging for the compassion of a few sen coins at the door of a stranger.

Compassion is the enemy of pride. Like a puppet dancing on a stage, until yesterday, I spoke with no energy. However, the tip of my little finger commanded standing, sleeping as I wished. In the end, I had a triumphant expression, smiling, teasing, and looking confused and amused. Mother, also admirable and proud, made a special twitch at the tip of her wriggling nose.

Those things are superficial. If the true situation last evening is observed, the beckoning pampas grass flutters in the other direction. If tea were happily drunk with a beautiful woman feigning innocence and an unexpected lid removed, her looks faded in front of her mother.

She said she couldn't agree and explained if a hawk missed its mark, it wouldn't give up. She declared if a dog follows behind and does not sniff, after being hit, it goes away.

Seizō's indiscretion did not go that far.

If left alone, he might go home. No, he will go home. My being compared to Sayoko is my proof. When I come home, I'll meet hardship. After meeting hardship, I'll stand up and lie down. Laughing, teasing, and being confused will happen, too. If I show a proud face that looked interested to my mother, I would save face before her. If I show it to Kingo and Hajime, it would be revenge on those two.

She didn't say this much. Fujio delayed her answer. Her mother forever lost the chance to understand her misunderstanding.

"Did Kingo come earlier?" her mother asked again. The carp jumped. Lotus sprouted. Grass gradually turned green. Magnolia withered. The mystery woman was not concerned about those things.

Day and night, Kingo's spirit is being tormented. She wondered what he was doing while in the study. If he's thinking, what is he thinking about? If he visits her, what did he come to talk about? Kingo was not her flesh and blood. Therefore, she could not afford to be careless with this child she did not bear. This is a major truth innately taught by the mystery woman.

The mystery woman suffered a nervous breakdown when this truth was discovered. A nervous breakdown is a common ailment in civilization. If her nervous breakdown is misused, even her child will suffer a nervous breakdown. She said that illness would cause great trouble. An infection would be a nuisance. The troubled person doesn't know which one is the complaint. Only the mystery woman was thoroughly troubled by Kingo.

She asked, "Did Kingo come earlier?"

"Yes, he did."

"How is he?"

"The same as always."

"Truthfully," Her eyebrows lightly moved closer.

"He's a troubled man." Her brow knitted further and her eyes stared.

"He only speaks sarcastically like something is trapped between his molars."

"Although sarcasm is fine, isn't his incomprehensible, delirious babbling from time to time a problem? Recently, the situation has changed somewhat."

"That may be philosophy."

"But I don't know anything about philosophy. What did he say earlier?"

"He mentioned that watch again."

"Did he talk about returning it? Is giving it or not giving it to Hajime unwanted advice?"

"Where has he gone now?"

"Where has he gone?"

"He surely went to see Hajime."

When the conversation reached this point, the maid placed both hands on the floor and said, "Ono-san has come." The mother withdrew to her room.

When she turned down a bend in the veranda and her shadow disappeared behind the shōji sliding door, Seizō passed through the side of the living room from a side entrance and escaped to the next six-tatami-mat room bypassing the hallway.

A priestly teacher once said when a sounding stone is struck and students enter a room to study under a Buddhist teacher, by only hearing the sounds of their footsteps, the teacher knows who can and who cannot advance spiritually through kōans as sure as if he were holding something in his hands. Any awkwardness will also appear in the way one walks. One saying says even beasts will walk to the slaughterhouse. This phenomenon is not recognized as being limited to a monk in Zen meditation. It is also effectively applied to the genius Seizō. He is always too considerate in the world. Today is particularly strange. A defeated soldier fleeing the enemy is not calmed by swaying pampas grass. Seizō hesitated as the black toes of a sock gently dropped onto a new mat, which had been lightly tread on.

Fujio did not focus on a dark spot or raise her eyes. She glimpsed the tips of the socks dropping to the tatami and knew. Before Seizō sat, he was already being treated with contempt.

"Good morning," he said, smiling as he sat.

"Welcome." She looked serious and looked directly at her companion for the first time. Seizō's eyes quivered under her scrutiny.

"I'm sorry for not visiting—" he quickly added.

"Never mind," she interrupted but said no more.

The man felt frustrated and wondered if he should start again. The sitting room was quiet as usual.

"It has gotten rather warm."

"Yes, it has."

Only those two comments were spoken in the sitting room. After that, the earlier quiet returned. The carp leaped with a splash again. The lake on the east touched Seizō's back. He turned slightly and was about to remark on the carp but looked toward the woman. Her eyes were focused on the magnolias to the south.

After deep purple slipped out, as though coming from a pot, from long flower petals to chase the spring, empty tea stains in the remnants wrinkled up. Only a snapped-off calyx appeared.

About to mention the carp, Seizō stopped again. The woman's face did not come any closer.

The woman who wanted to make the apologetic man explain his long absence but said, "Never mind."

The man knew he had blundered and tried to change the mood by saying "It has gotten rather warm," but saw no positive sign and moved his eyes toward the carp.

The man felt as though he would slip into a place where he could hold his ground but felt uneasy. Nonetheless, the woman stayed seated and motionless. Acting oblivious, Seizō had to rethink everything.

If she's upset because I hadn't come for four or five days, that no longer mattered. A chance meeting at the exhibition last evening presented a slight problem. Nevertheless, many excuses existed. However, had Fujio recognized Sayoko and I among the constantly changing, slow-moving dark shadows? If she noticed, that was it. If she had not noticed, my bold broaching of this topic was identical to thrusting a festering tumor stripped of skin under the nose of the oblivious person to force him to smell it.

Nowadays, a young woman is accompanied when she walks down the street. I cannot say this is a flaw if simply walking is honorable. Only this evening, the dim figures are enthusiastically coaxed and graze each others' sleeves and cuffs of other lifetimes. Later, amid a tumult of black waves in an unknown world, they bury their heads in the east and the west and transform into total strangers. If this is so, it's all right. I'll also say to move forward. Unfortunately, Sayoko and I did not have a shallow relationship like two stones lined up for no reason and drawn closer on a Go board. She escaped from me, and we were apart for five years, a long time. Both day and night, our relationship was held together, although weakly, to this point in the color of a red connection of an unrolled thread.

There's no need to apologize if she is merely called an ordinary woman. On the other hand, it becomes a lie that people hate and she dislikes. A lie is blowfish miso soup. If not cursed only there, it's not that delicious. However, when poisoned, in the end, blood must be vomited in agony. After that, the lie is drawn closer to the truth.

If silent, there are ways to pass through unnoticed. However, trying to disguise myself, enhance my reputation, or embellish my background will easily focus the arrows of distrustful eyes on the target, me. Things patched over tend to unravel.

When the ugly true form fraying from below was seen or appeared, the rust of my being could not be washed away for a lifetime.

Seizō discerned this much and is a clever man who does not grow dim in a relationship of interests. Personal feelings stitch the capital separating east and west using a long thread of thoughts extending over five years. However, he has no desire to tell them to the sulking person seated before his eyes.

At least, the veins of love this time passing new blood are in harmony. He doesn't want to talk until the husband and wife live in a world of blue skies and affectionately tap the wrists of two people.

He'll express these feelings but doesn't want to spew the current lie that pretends not to know the ordinary woman. Without lying, he doesn't want to reveal the situation with Sayoko, not even her name.

Seizō often glanced at Fujio to assess her.

You went to the exhibition last night ... was Seizō's sole thought. He was a little confused over whether she was going out or had gone out.

"Yes, I went."

The nose of a confused man was grazed, and a black shadow suddenly cut across. The man was startled and fell back one step but could do nothing.

"It was pretty."

To say it was pretty was fairly mediocre for a poet. He was

aware of how horrible that was the moment the words left his mouth.

"It was pretty," the woman agreed then gushed, "Most of the people looked pretty, too."

Unwittingly, Seizō looked at Fujio's face. He didn't quite understand and asked, "Were they?"

The tepid answer was a foolish one in an ordinary situation. When the body is weak, a poet willingly accepts folly.

"Most of the people looked pretty," Fujio replied sharply.

This sentence was somehow dangerous. He might not safely pass through. With no way out, the man sealed his lips. The woman stopped and didn't move. Her eyes asked whether he still wasn't in the mood to confess and looked at Seizō.

A story tells about a man named Munemori whose stomach was not cut even when stabbed by a sword. Civilized people who weigh their interests have no reason to act carelessly and harm themselves. Seizō must carefully consider his enemy's slightest movements.

He surprised himself when he asked, "Who did you go with?"

This time she didn't answer. She remained guarded no matter what.

"I just met Kingo at the gate, you went with him, didn't you?"

"If you know that much, why are you asking?" The woman pouted.

"No, I was wondering if anyone else went with you?" said Seizō, a skillful dodge.

"Other than my brother?"

"Yes."

"You should have asked my brother."

He successfully hid a souring mood and navigated through the heart of a whirlpool. Swinging back and forth while dangling from her words, he came out on flat land in no time. Until now, Seizō won each time with this technique.

"I thought about asking Kingo but was anxious to go inside."

"Ah, ha, ha, ha," unexpectedly Fujio laughed loudly. The man was startled.

She took the opportunity to launch these words at him.

"A very busy man was absent with no word for five days."

"No, that time was hectic and I could not come."

"During the day, too," said the woman, pulling her shoulders back. Her long hair moved as if each strand were alive.

"Yes?" he said, a strange look came over his face.

"You were that busy during the day, too?"

"By day you mean?"

"Ah, ha, ha, ha, ha. You still don't understand?"

This time, her high-pitched laughter echoed in the garden. The woman could laugh with abandon. The man was dazed.

"Seizō, is the decorative outdoor light display on during the day?" she asked, one hand placed over the other on her knees. The shining brilliance of a diamond painfully flew into Seizō's eyes. Seizō seemed to have been slapped near his cheek by a Zen master's bamboo *shippei* staff. At the same time, the words "she saw me" rang at the base of his mind.

"If you study too much, you won't get that gold watch," said the woman, her raised face pressing for an answer. The man's battle formation collapsed.

"The truth is a week ago, my old professor arrived from Kyōto."

"Oh, really? I had no idea. So that's the reason you were busy. I didn't know. Excuse my rudeness," she announced and lowered her head. Her jet-black hair moved again.

"While I was in Kyōto, he was a great help to me."

"So, is it all right? If you value something, you treat it with care.

"Well, last night, I went to the light display with my brother, Hajime, and Itoko."

"You did?"

"Yes, I did. There's a food stall called Kameya beside the lake. You probably know of it, Seizō."

"Yes ... I do."

"You know. You may have been there. Everyone has tea there."

The man wanted to stand. Until the end, the woman pretended to have calmed down.

"The tea was delicious. You still haven't been there?"

Seizō said nothing.

"If you still haven't gone, you must take your Kyōto professor there. I intend to go there again with Hajime."

Fujio spoke the name Hajime with an odd echo.

The shadows of spring tilted. The eternal day was not the sole property of the pair for eternity. The Italian majolica table clock decorating the alcove interrupted the relentless conversation. After thirty minutes, Seizō left through the gate. In dreams that night, Fujio did not hear the bell of ridicule. While surprising, it is amusing! A woman is a happy creature!

CHAPTER 13

Two sturdy square pillars were called a gate. He didn't know whether there was a door. When he looked through a hole opened in the wooden fence marked Night Post, it seemed to be closed at night. The front lawn rose to a mound of earth. Pine trees, planted in a pattern, opened like oil-paper umbrellas over the shrubs and blocked the view of the market. If he went around the pines, he traced an arc and, above his head, could see a relief carving of waves on the eaves of the entrance. The shōji sliding door had been left open. Brush strokes, resembling those on a mask for court dances, were scribbled in brushwork in the style of a Taiga-dō temple on the cheerful white fusuma sliding screen door, which acted as the partition in the tatami sitting room.

Kingo turned right at the entryway and gently opened the lattice visible through the shoe rack. He stood tapping the tip of his thin cane on the hard-packed dirt floor. He didn't call out. Of course, there was no response. The mansion's interior was hushed. No signs were seen that suggested anyone lived there. Instead, he heard the lively voices of people in cabs passing before the gate. Taps of the thin cane's tip rang out.

In the quiet interior, the sliding door covered in thick decorative paper made a bright sound.

"Kiyo. Kiyo."

A voice summoned the maid, but she didn't seem to be around. Footsteps approached from the kitchen. The tip of a cane tapped out clicks. The footsteps slipped out from the kitchen and toward the side entrance. The shōji door opened. Itoko and Kingo stood face to face.

The maid was there. A student lived there, too, but he rarely greeted guests despite his easygoing manner.

For a moment, the woman thought about going out. She lowered a propped-up knee and, as usual, sewed the thread a few more stitches. The eternal day having the sensation of hugging a heavy biwa lute sustains a dream that enraptures a buzzing horsefly and collapses unable to bear endless eternity.

She called Kiyo, but she appeared to be out back. Only the teakettle in the open kitchen quietly gleamed. Kuroda was probably in the student's room, as usual, his shaved head buried inside his arm and sleeping like a cat on a desk.

Just as the visitor thought the empty mansion was vacant, the side entrance clattered. When the shōji door feebly slid open, Kingo, the only man in the wide world, was standing there. The sunshine shining through the lattice hit his back. The dim tall figure tapped the cane several times without moving from the center of the hard ground.

"Oh!"

The cane sounds stopped. From under his hat's brim, Kingo looked like he hadn't seen the woman's face in a long time. The woman instantly averted her eyes and stared at the tip of the thin cane. Heat rose from the cane's tip. Her face flushed. Itoko's hair free of oil naturally puffed up and fell forward when she bowed at the waist.

"Is he out?" asked Kingo, the end of the sentence rising.

She only said, "A few moments ago." A wave of charm neared her untroubled eyelids.

"Your father's not home?"

"He went out this morning to a Noh recitation."

"I see," said the man. His tall body turned halfway around. His profile faced Itoko.

"Please, come in. I believe my brother has already come home."

"Thank you," said Kingo and then muttered something toward the wall.

"Please." She pulled back one leg as if luring him in. Her kimono was made from meisen silk with rough stripes.

"Thank you."

"Please, come in."

"Where did he go?" asked Kingo. His face looking at the wall turned slightly toward her. Maybe it was his imagination, but her pale cheeks in the sunshine brushing against her from behind seemed a little thinner than yesterday.

"He probably went out for a walk?" she said, tilting her head.

"I was on my way home but walked too much and am rather tired ..."

"Well then, please come in and rest. He should already be home."

Their conversation went on a little longer. Its length was proof of expanded feelings. Kingo took off his simple, wooden geta sandals and stepped into the sitting room.

In the alcove of an unmoving springtime, heavy nail covers secured the *nageshi* beam construction, and a painting of the cloud dragon by Tsunenobu hung deep inside.

In a bygone age, the color of silk was stained by flowing pale black ink and surrounded by the indigo of patterned silk damask at the corners to quiet the ivory shaft of the scroll. An incense burner with only the mouth of a lion cast on porcelain was set on a table just over a foot long. The mouth blew glossy grease onto the wood grain. The table made of finely-grained rosewood passed from brown to purple and from purple to black.

As the late spring day moved to the veranda, the man who only felt the world's coldness faced the kimono with a splash pattern near its edge. The woman waited at the entrance. Her festive collar of scattered chrysanthemum petals pressed against her full chin. She found the brightness of the sliding door facing her to be dizzying.

The eight-tatami-mat sitting room was so wide the two insignificant people easily stayed away from each other. The distance was six feet.

Kuroda appeared out of nowhere. He was wearing a Kokura kimono and brought in the tea, bouncing from one to the other of his dark red feet below the hem of his hakama trousers with flattened pleats. He also carried in tobacco and a candy dish. The six-foot distance was buried as if by design. The positions of the host and guest were weakly connected by the instruments of hospitality. Kuroda abruptly awakened from a dream in his afternoon nap and mechanically passed a thread of fate between the two. A vague spirit was sealed in his close-cropped hair, then he retreated to the live-in student's room. Later, the empty mansion became as it was before.

"How was last evening? You look tired."

"I'm not."

"You're not tired? Well, you're stronger than me," said Kingo with a hint of a grin.

"The train ride was roundtrip."

"Trains are exhausting."

"Why?"

"That man. I'm tired of that man. Am I right?"

Itoko showed only one dimple on her round cheeks but did not respond.

"Was something amusing?" asked Kingo.

"Yes."

"What was amusing? Was it the lighting display?"

"Yes, the lights were wonderful, too, but ..."

"Other than the lights, was anything else amusing?"

"Yes."

"What?"

"It's a little funny."

She tilted her head and smiled adorably. Missing the point, Kingo wanted to laugh for some reason.

"What's so amusing?"

"Should I say?"

"Please do."

"Well, everyone drank tea."

"Yes, was that tea amusing?"
"No, not the tea. Not the tea but ..."
"Oh, that."
"Seizō was there."
"Yes, he was."
"He was with a pretty woman."
"Pretty? Oh, he was with a young woman."
"You probably know her."
"No, not at all."
"Oh, but Hajime said you did."
"He probably meant I had seen her, but we've never spoken."
"But you know her?"
"Ha, ha, ha, ha. Why must I know her? The truth is I've seen her several times."
"That's why I said that."
"What?"
"I said it was amusing."
"Why?"
"Why not?"

The wave approaching her eyes collapsed along the way and brashly toyed with her black pupils.

Sunshine and shadows leaking through luxuriant young leaves mingled over the vast ground. The wind shook the branches, making the moss shimmer erratically.

Still looking at Itoko's face, Kingo could not find an explanation. She moved forward but offered no reason why. The reason was while he was drowning in her charm, he lost his way before he gained an understanding.

In the world of goldfish happily living day and night in a shallow, gourd-shaped lake dyed the freshly painted yellow of an egg yolk poached in a frying pan, they wave their tails, pass through seaweed, and are not disturbed when rising waves sweep away their bodies. The bones of a sea bream passing through Naruto Straits are jostled by the tides and harden year by year. Passage is not easy whether going or coming back under rough seas bottomless to the depths of hell.

If a wild fish from the open sea is placed in the same box as a goldfish with three round tails, they become friends in an aquarium. A separation barrier cannot be seen, but the partition glass is invisible and only hurts the tip of a nose that attempts to break through. He could not speak about the sea to Itoko who lacked knowledge of the sea. For a moment, Kingo's reaction was to hedge.

"Was the woman that pretty?"

"I think she was pretty."

"I guess so," said Kingo and looked outside at the veranda. He selected an edge of the two-foot-wide path that always looked wet and the dew on the granite on the rough surface. The few untidy flowers of fringed orchids and violets stole the coming spring and stealthily bloomed.

"Pretty flowers are blooming."

"Where?"

Itoko's eyes could only see the red pines in front and the ornamental bamboo grass at their roots.

"Where?"

She extended her warm chin and gazed in that direction.

"Over there. You can't see them where you are."

Itoko slightly raised her hips. As her long sleeves fluttered, she slid on her knees a few steps closer to the veranda. When the distance between the two brought the tips of their noses closer, the delicate flowers came into view.

"Oh," she said and stopped.

"Pretty, aren't they?"

"Yes."

"You didn't know."

"Not a hint."

"I didn't notice because they're tiny. I have no idea when they bloom or disappear."

"Of course, the peach and cherry blossoms are lovely."

Kingo did not answer, but mumbled to himself, "Those flowers are pitiful."

Itoko was silent.

He added, "The flowers are like the woman last evening."

"Why do you say that?" the woman asked doubtfully. The man stared a long time at her face and looking somber, he eventually said, "It's nice to see that you're carefree."

"Am I?" she asked, now serious.

She didn't know whether that was praise or criticism or whether she was carefree or not. She struggled to understand whether being carefree was good or bad. Her belief in Kingo was all she had. Because he's a credible man who speaks seriously, she could only say that he was serious.

Designs and colors steal a person's eyes. Skill tricks a person's eyes. Quality refreshes a person's eyes. When asked if that's so, Kingo felt grateful. When he looks down at a person's soul, the philosopher lowers his head in sympathy and has no thoughts, regrets, or anything else.

"It's good. That's fine. It'd be bad if you weren't. It'd always be bad if it weren't so."

Itoko flashed her beautiful teeth.

"Anyway, this is how I am. I'll be this way forever."

"No, you won't."

"Because it's innate, no matter how much time passes, nothing will change."

"You will change. You will change when you're far from your father and brother."

"Why is that?"

"If you're apart, you will become shrewder."

"I think I want to become shrewder. It's good for one to change if she gets smarter. I think I want to become like Fujio, but being a dummy ..."

Kingo looked at the world with pity and at Itoko's innocent-looking mouth.

"Do you envy Fujio that much?"

"Yes, I am envious."

"Itoko," said the man, suddenly in a gentle tone.

"What?" she asked with a warm heart.

"A woman like Fujio does too much in today's world. It'll be dangerous if she's not careful."

Still, the woman only trickled charming dew onto her large eyes under her fleshy eyelids. She could not see signs of danger even in the shadows.

"When Fujio goes out alone, she will kill five women like the one last night."

The dew trickling on the bright eyes scattered. Her facial expression quickly changed. The word kill terrifies people. Naturally, no other meaning is understood.

"So you are fine. You will change when you move. You must not move."

"Move?"

"Yes, when you love, you will change."

The woman swallowed something about to fly out of her throat. Her face flushed bright red.

"You will become a bride and change."

The woman looked down.

He continued. "That's all right. Getting married is a waste."

Her sweet eyelids winked rapidly a few times. The shadow of a mythical rain dragon swept over her closed mouth. Untidy flowers of orchids and violets bloomed sparsely in the spring.

CHAPTER 14

The electric train lowered the red sign and approached with its whistle blowing. After the switch, winds swept through the town and rushed away over the rails. A masseur estimated the gap and gingerly crossed to the other side. A shop boy at a tea house smiled as he pulled a millstone. The texture of the mohair fabric worn by the flagman collected heaps of dust and yellowed. Western dress approached from a secondhand bookstore. A newsboy cap stood in front of a music hall. The storytelling for the evening was written in white on a painted board. The air was filled with wires. Not one kite was seen. The world is terribly confused below and only quiet above.

"Hey! Hey!" A shout came from behind.

A twenty-four- or -five-year-old woman kept walking but turned slightly.

"Hey!"

This time, a workman's happi coat turned.

Unknowingly, the man being called dodged the man coming from behind and speeded up. He was blocked by two rickshaws that rushed in as they raced each other. The distance between them ballooned. Hajime stuck out his chest and sped off after him. His loosely worn lined kimono and haori coat danced a lively dance each time a foot hit the ground.

"Hey!"

A hand grabbed hold from behind. At the same time, his shoulder came to a dead stop, the tilt of Seizō's slender face could be seen. Both of his hands were full.

"Hey."

He shook the shoulder where his hand landed. While being shaken, Seizō turned around.

"I was wondering who that was ... I'm sorry."

Seizō gave a slight bow, keeping his hat on. His hands were full.

"What were you thinking about? You didn't hear me no matter how many times I called."

"Really? I wasn't the least bit aware."

"You were in a rush and didn't look like you touched the ground as you walked. It was surreal."

"What?"

"The way you were walking."

"Blame the twentieth century ... Ha, ha, ha."

"Is that a new way to walk? How do I say this? You were walking like one leg was new, and the other was old."

"The fact is it's hard to walk carrying this."

Seizō held out both hands and said nothing. He used his eyes to point down. Naturally, Hajime's eyes also dropped below his waist.

"What is that?"

"This is a wastepaper basket. And this is a lampstand."

"You look quite stylish, but carrying a large wastepaper basket is a strange look."

"It's strange, but I had no choice. I was asked."

"It's admirable to become strange when asked. I never thought you possessed the chivalry to walk down the street with a wastepaper basket."

A smiling Seizō said nothing and bowed.

"Where are you going?"

"I'm taking this ..."

"You're taking that home?"

"No, I was asked to buy this. And you?"

"Well, I'm ... I'm going anywhere."

Seizō's mind was a little baffled. He found Hajime's observation that he appeared to be rushing and didn't seem to be walking on the ground exactly matched his present situation. The ground stepped on by shoes has width and firmness, but he felt no sensation of stepping. Nevertheless, he was in a hurry. Meeting the easygoing Hajime and standing there talking to him was grueling. His suggestion of walking together was more of a problem.

Ordinarily, Hajime grabbing me would make me uncomfortable. While knowing or not knowing the relationship between Hajime and Fujio, the relationship between Fujio and me had been established. I don't intend to commit the crime of stealing the fiancée from the formally engaged groom, but I understand Hajime's heart without asking. With each action of the straightforward man, his concerns can be inferred. I didn't go as far as sabotage from the shadows. Unfortunately, however, I have shut down Hajime's hopes. From the perspective of human emotion, it is pity.

Pity is there, but more than pity, Hajime is carefree and would become pitiful over the relationship between Fujio and me. When we meet, we converse without inhibition. There are jokes and laughter. The true nature of men is explained. Governance in the East and West is discussed. Matters of extreme love are hardly mentioned. More than not speaking, it may be an inability to speak. Hajime may be a man who does not understand the truth of love. He is not good enough to be Fujio's husband. Regardless, pity is still pity.

Pity is a word that hides one's sense of self. I am grateful the word hides the self. Seizō believes he pities Hajime in his heart. However, that pity includes his higher self. You'll understand if you consider how you feel when you've been into mischief and have to face your parents. Rather than feeling regret for your parents out of pity, you're overwhelmed by feelings of danger.

When my mischief drops on the head of a person very different from me, the trouble created rings in my head and disturbs me. When someone who hates thunder goes out in front of the peak of a cloud that blocks the thunder, a little hesitation is common. Simple pity looks very different. However, Seizō named this pity. He probably didn't like classifying his feelings as anything worse than pity.

"Shall we walk?" Seizō asked politely.

"Yes. I just got off the train at the corner. Going anywhere is fine with me."

This answer is not the least bit logically consistent, thought Seizō, but logic didn't matter at all.

"I am in a bit of a hurry so ..."

"I'm in a hurry, too, and won't slow you down. We'll go quickly in the direction you're walking. Hand over that wastepaper basket. I'll carry it."

"No, I'm fine. It's unseemly."

"Let me have it. Of course, it's bulky but pretty light. You would say it's unseemly," said Hajime and walked swinging the wastepaper basket.

"As you said, it's a light load."

"It depends on how you carry it. Ha, ha, ha, ha. Did you buy this at a bazaar? It's rather ornate. It's a shame to put wastepaper in it."

"That's why I can carry it through the streets. If it's for actual wastepaper ..."

"I can walk the streets carrying anything. Don't trains filled with human garbage run down the streets with pride?"

"Ha, ha, ha, ha. By doing that, you will be called a wastebasket driver."

"Are you the president of wastebaskets, and is the man who made the request a shareholder? Rare waste can't be dropped in."

"How about dropping in discarded poems or tons of wastepaper?"

"Those things are not necessary. I'd like many old scraps of paper money to be dropped in."

"It'd probably be faster to drop in ordinary wastepaper and be hypnotized."

"Because people will first become wastepaper. Is the beginning a request? If human wastepaper exists, there is a lot even without hypnotism. Why do you want this beginning?"

"I never wanted this beginning. Although it would be convenient if human wastepaper climbs inside the wastebasket."

"It would be nice if someone invented an automatic wastebasket. If it is, all the human wastepaper will jump in themselves."

"Will you get one if there's an exclusive sale?"

"Ah, ha, ha, ha, ha. That would be good. There are probably people we know who want to jump in."

"There may be." Seizō found a way out.

"Anyway, last evening, you went to see the light decorations with odd companions."

His sightseeing had been discovered. He no longer needed to hide it.

"Yes, you were there, too, with friends?" Seizō answered unintentionally.

Kingo feigned ignorance despite having found out. Fujio pretended not to know but tried to extract a confession. Hajime honestly asked face to face. As Seizō nonchalantly answered, but in his heart, thought, Of course.

"Who are they to you?"

"It's a little intense. He's my old professor."

"The young lady is your mentor's daughter."

"Yes, she is."

"Ah, when I saw you drinking tea, you didn't look like strangers."

"Did we look like an older brother and younger sister?"

"A husband and wife. A nice husband and wife."

"I'm terribly sorry," said Seizō, smiling slightly and quickly looking away. The brilliance of Western gilded text in the glass door on the opposite side encouraged a poet's attention.

"Many new books seem to have been delivered over there. Shall we have a look?"

"Books? What will you buy?"

"I'll buy whatever is interesting."

"Great irony lies in buying wastebaskets and buying books."

"How so?"

Before Hajime answered, still holding the wastebasket, he ran through the gap between the train cars to the other side. Seizō trotted behind.

"Ah, a lot of beautiful books are on display. Is there one you want?"

"Yes," said Seizō stooping forward. His gold-rimmed eyeglasses pressed toward the glass window to inspect the display.

The lamb's skin was tanned to softness. Water lilies were finely drawn in gold in the richness of dark bluish green. From near the pedestals of all the petals, straight lines passed to the bases and wrapped around the circumference of the front cover. The back was cut flat and adorned with a pattern of golden hairs meandering over a dark red surface. A cloth texture was crushed onto a hard brass plate. Heavy gold leaf was set in the shape of a shield. The back of the clipped kerf was divided with gray on the top and green on the bottom. Both were inlaid only with characters. He could also see the title page with the book title in red positioned properly on the coarse paper.

"You seem to want them all," said Hajime, not looking at the books but only at Seizō's eyeglasses.

"They all have new bindings. Hmm."

"Only the front covers are nice. That seems to guarantee the contents."

"Unlike yours, these are literary works."

"Because they're literary works, the top parts must be pretty. And because you're a literary man, the need arises to wear gold-rimmed eyeglasses."

"Well, that's severe. But if there is some meaning, literary people may also be works of art," said Seizō and finally left the window.

"Works of art are fine, but security only from gold-rimmed eyeglasses is pathetic."

"Eyeglasses seem to be cursed. Hajime, aren't you nearsighted?"

"Because I don't study, I couldn't be even if I wanted to."

"You're not farsighted either?"

"Stop joking. Well, behave while we walk."

The two men walked off shoulder to shoulder.

"You've probably heard about the bird called a cormorant?," said Hajime as they walked.

"Yes, what about it?"

"At great pains, that bird eats fish but vomits it back up. That's foolish."

"It is foolish. But isn't it all right because fish are kept in the fisherman's fish basket?"

"So it's ironic. When I think about making the effort to read a book, I immediately put it in the wastebasket. A scholar spews out books to earn a living. Nothing will provide me with nourishment. The only and best destination is the wastebasket."

"Saying that is regrettable for a scholar. He no longer knows the best course of action."

"It's action. Not being able to do anything by only reading a book is the same as serenely gazing at a plate full of bean-covered mochi mistaken for a picture of bean-covered mochi. In particular, a literary man spews out pretty things, but he does nothing pretty. Seizō, don't poets in the West often do that sort of thing?"

"That's true," said Seizō, taking a long pause before he asked, "For example?"

"I forget his name, but he deceives women and neglects his wife."

"He probably doesn't exist."

"He does. He definitely does."

"Really? I don't clearly remember."

"It's a problem when an expert does not remember. Anyway, the woman last night ..."

Seizō's armpits dampened slightly.

"I know her well."

If it's the koto incident, he heard about it from Itoko. He knew nothing about any other incident.

"She was in the back of the Tsutaya establishment," he rushed to say first.

"She played a koto."

"Her playing probably embodied virtuosity," said Seizō, not

easily discouraged. The situation altered somewhat when he saw Fujio.

"I guess it was proficient, but I was sleepy."

"Ha, ha, ha, ha. Oh, the irony," said a laughing Seizō. His laughing voice did not stray far from the word *quiet* in any situation and was vibrant with color.

"Don't make fun. This is serious. Making fun of your mentor's daughter, even a little, is not nice."

"But feeling sleepy is a problem."

"It's all right to be drowsy. That's how people are. A drowsy person has some value."

"It's old-fashioned nature is valued."

"A modern man like you somehow manages to go without sleep."

"That's why I'm not valued."

"Not only that. Depending on the situation, an esteemed person is disparaged as being behind the times."

"Today, I've been under constant attack. Shall we part now?" asked Seizō, forcing a smile despite feeling somewhat distressed. He started to leave and simultaneously held out his right hand, curiously, to receive the wastepaper basket.

"No, wait a little longer. We're taking a break."

The two walked again. They walked together, their hearts side by side. Both despised the other.

"You should take time off every day."

"Me? I don't read many books."

"And you don't seem too busy."

"Because I can't see the need to be too busy."

"That's fine."

"As long as something can be done well, that's good enough. It'll be a problem in time."

"That's fine in a fleeting emergency. In the end, it's enough. Ha, ha, ha, ha."

"Are you going to drop by Kōno's home as usual?"

"I was just there."

"I guess you're very busy going to Kōno's home and showing your mentor around."

"I took a break from visiting the Kōnos for a few days."

"The dissertation ..."

"Ha, ha, ha, ha. When?"

"It's best to get it out quickly. But if any time is fine, so it's pointless to rush."

"Then I'll handle it with a temporary makeshift measure."

"About the daughter of that mentor ..."

"Yes ..."

"I have a funny story about that young lady."

Seizō was startled. He didn't know any stories. When he looked askance over the rim of his eyeglasses at Hajime, he shook the wastepaper basket as usual, triumphantly faced forward, and walked off.

When he asked again, "What? ..." he had no energy.

"What? ... Well, I can see a deep bond."

"With whom ..."

"The daughter and us ..."

Seizō was a little relieved but felt trapped. Shallow or deep, I want to sever and throw away the relationships with Hajime and Kodō-sensei. However, despite talent or intelligence, I have no way to do that to things connected by nature.

He thought he'd stay at Tsutaya, one of hundreds of inns in Kyōto. I'll probably stay overnight. The rickshaw yoke will be lowered on Sanjō Avenue, so a stay at Tsutaya may be unnecessary. It's all on a whim. This is too much mischief. I like it despite the stay being worthless to some and inconvenient to others. However, I have no other options no matter how much I rack my brain.

Seizō lacked the energy to answer.

"The daughter ... Seizō."

"Yes."

"Well, I've seen her."

"From the second floor of the inn?"

"I saw her from the second floor, too."

That *too* is a bit worrying. Looking down on the old-fashioned garden with all the weeping forsythia flowers blooming in columns of spring rain has been known for ages. I wouldn't be surprised if he makes inquiries in the future. However, "from the second floor, too" is risky. I believe he has seen other things. I'm willing to listen but feel giddy like I'm creating an illusion.

With a strong push coming from somewhere, he took a few steps.

"I also saw her on the way to Arashiyama."

"You only saw her?"

"I can't talk to a stranger, so I only looked."

"Although it would have been nice if you tried to speak."

Out of nowhere, Seizō joked. His spirit abruptly improved.

"I also saw her eating dumplings."

"Where?"

"Of course, on Arashiyama."

"Is that it?"

"There's more. We traveled together from Kyōto to Tōkyo."

"Of course, thinking about it, you rode the same train."

"I saw you at the station when you came to meet them."

"Really?" said Seizō and gave a strained smile.

"That person seems to be from Tōkyo."

"Who?" Seizō started to say. From the edge of the eyeglass lens, he strangely peeked at his companion's profile.

"Who? Who was it?"

"Who said that?"

Seizō's tone unexpectedly dropped.

"The maid at the inn talked."

"The maid? At Tsutaya?"

He looked as though he was paying particular attention, wanted to hear the rest, or wanted to be sure there was nothing else.

"Yup," said Hajime.

"The maid at Tsutaya is ..."

"Do we turn there?"

"It's a little further. Is that all right?"

"I should already be heading back. Here, take this important wastepaper basket. Carry it so you don't drop it."

Seizō respectfully took the wastebasket. Hajime breezily left.

Alone now, Seizō wanted to hurry. If he sprinted, he'd soon be at Kodō-sensei's home. He didn't want his arrival to be unwelcome and didn't want to rush there. But for some reason, Seizō wanted to hurry. Both hands were occupied. His legs were moving. The watch gifted by the emperor in his vest sounded. The streets were full of life.

Seizō forgot everything and his mind raced. He had to hurry but didn't know whether faster was better. One day and night was reduced to just twelve hours. The car of destiny has no course other than to turn at full speed in the desired direction. He moves forward with no intention of being so thoughtless he breaks natural laws. However, he prefers the natural way of considering the situation, becoming my ally, and acting on my behalf. In that case, if the undertaking were guaranteed, a hundred pilgrimages to a shrine to Kannon-sama wouldn't matter. Conducting the *goma* fire ritual before Fudō-sama to ask for a blessing is fine. Believers of Christianity expect this. As he walked, Seizō felt the need for God.

The man called Hajime can't do academic work, doesn't study, and doesn't understand poetry. I wonder what the future holds for him. I also harbor contempt over his possibilities. Blatantly horrible things will also happen. However, when thinking about it now, his attitude can never be mine. Because he can't, he does not conclude I'm inferior.

There are things I can't do in this world and don't want to. I believe it's more sophisticated to be unable to do the trick of spinning a plate on the tip of a chopstick than to be able to do the trick. Of course, I would find it hard to speak and act like Hajime. Because of my difficulty, I understand the praise of me until now.

When appearing before that man, what sort of pressure will I feel? It's unpleasant. I believe the sole duty of an individual is to give joy to others. Hajime does not pass through the key principle of social life. That kind of man cannot succeed even in a simple world. His failing the diplomat exam makes sense.

The pressure I felt when I appeared before that man was a little peculiar. It's particularly strange that I still have no plan to analyze whether something will come from openness, monotony, or the candidness of so-called old-fashioned directness. Although the scenario that intentionally puts pressure on me cannot be seen in advance from the other side, these feelings somehow come to me.

From inside a natural world in which one behaves as one pleases without a nod of acknowledgment, the pressure shows on my face without having to ask, How are you? I feel self-conscious. The obligations of the hidden side of an apology to that man are a curse.

Although I've persisted in thinking morality added punishments, that alone is never true. For example, rather than saying a mountain that soars with indifference unafraid of the heavens or the earth is uninteresting, it gives no sense of beauty. Dewdrops falling from the stars are received by flower stamens. Occasionally, pretty flower petals are tidings on the wind and flow down streams. I find no enjoyment unless the scenery is like this.

When necessary, the difference between Hajime and me is the difference between the cypress tree forests of Hinokiyama and a flower garden. Because their essential natures do not match, strange feelings certainly arise.

There are times when a person with an incompatible personality is an obvious poor match. Sometimes, I feel pity. There are also wretched and contemptuous times. However, I've never experienced the envy felt today. Whether noble, refined, or close to my ideal, I wouldn't even consider envy in dreams. If I became accustomed to those feelings, compared to the present hardship, envy would rise quickly.

I told Fujio the relationship between Sayoko and me was over. I can't say it exists. To the person who helped me in my past, I declared that the small shadow forlornly accompanying me was separated by mist for five years and the relationship had dimmed when we met again.

I said repaying a debt is the skin of compassion; showing appreciation to a mentor is a disciple's duty; and nothing exists between birds and fish. If possible, the lies endured through hardship are finally told. The lies told in the final thoughts had to be stated despite being lies. The idea that pretends lies are truths does not exist and has a duty to the lies and shows responsibility. Speaking frankly, the advantages and disadvantages of a lifetime come together in lies. The lies are no longer told. It is said god dislikes two lies. Starting today, by all means, lies must pass for truths.

That is troubling. If I go to the sensei now, I must approach with a story that will spout two lies. Despite many ways out, a deadlock will occur, and I lack the courage to refuse outright. If I were born with a little less mercy, there would be no problem. Since I don't intend to create an inconvenience like a legal problem by refusing outright, it will end there. However, I will apologize to my benefactor. While I'm not being pressured by my benefactor and my lies are not discovered, nature whirls around and must proceed so that Fujio and I get married openly.

Then what? I'll think about that later. Nothing is more effective than facts. Once the fact of a marriage is established, everything must be reconsidered with this new fact at the foundation. If this new fact can be generally acknowledged, what sort of untimely sacrifice will come later? No matter how difficult, reconsideration will happen.

Agony lives in this moment. Unable to do anything, my heart races. Moving forward is frightening, but retreating is unthinkable. While I hope the affair evolves rapidly, I'm anxious about how it will unfold. Thus, I envy the carefree Hajime. Someone who negotiates everything envies the levelheaded person.

Spring passed. The departing spring came to an end. Several fluffy layers of pale yellow curtains soft like silk separated the air and hung down covering the top of the ground. The streets with invisible driving winds quieted down as dusk fell. An earthly blue gradually spread. Clouds lightly scorched on the western edge for no reason turned purple.

The narrow streets of Mukōyoko-chō, no wider than twelve feet, waited for the red cheeks that swelled in the dim light to be lit from behind on the proprietress's face on the signboard of a soba shop.

Twilight fell in the narrow gaps between houses. He passed through unchained gates to each door. The interiors of the rooms were probably darker.

He turned the corner and stopped at the third building on the left. This gate could not be called pretentious. He gently slid open the lattice door barely separating the interior from the street to reveal what felt like the early evening approaching darkness descending one more step.

"Hello?"

His quiet voice was too gentle to disturb the tone of a tranquil spring. As he watched through the diamond-shaped black hole in a foot-wide plank, someone moved from beneath the veranda. He waited patiently to be greeted. A response came at last.

A muddled voice blurted something like "yeah" or "huh" or "yes."

Seizō waited for the greeter as he peered at the diamond-shaped black hole. Finally, the person jumped up with a thud on the other side of the shōji-papered sliding door. Its construction appeared questionable. He heard creaking joints so vivid they were nearly palpable. The sliding fusuma screen with an ordinary wallpaper pattern opened. As soon as Seizō stepped out of the two-tatami-mat entryway, the gaunt face of Kodō-sensei in the shadow of the faintly-lit shōji door appeared, beard and all.

He didn't seem any healthier than usual. His bones were thin. His body was frail. His face was gaunt. His many passing years blew uncontested against rain, wind, and hardship. In a harsh world, even the heart barely hanging on only shrinks. Today, his complexion was worse than usual.

Even his greatest pride, his beard, looked different. White buried the black gaps. Wind passed through the white gaps. The shadow of the ancient man was faint until below his chin. Upon close examination of the hairs, each one in the sensei's beard was spindly. Seizō politely removed his hat and greeted him without speaking. His hair in an English-style haircut fell casually in front of the *past*.

A hoop with a diameter of tens of feet was drawn. Many boxes in a metal mesh were placed along its circumference. The toys of fate were placed haphazardly in these boxes. The hoop began to rotate. When the things in this box were lifted closer to the blue sky, the things in that box slowly dropped to the ground that absorbed everything. The inventor of the Ferris Wheel was a sarcastic philosopher.

From now on, the head with an English-style haircut should rise to the clouds in this box. The sensei, who sprinkles a mix of roasted sesame seeds and salt to commemorate a world long gone in the forlorn beard, dropped to a future dark place in that box. Fate is determined so that one side lowers one foot if the other side rises one foot.

The one rising embraced the realization of his rise and freely lowered his head politely before the one who went into the night as he descended. This is the irony created by the gods.

"Ah, it's you." The sensei was in good humor. When the one lowered by the car of destiny meets the one rising in one, his mood naturally improves.

"Please come in," he said and immediately returned to the sitting room. Seizō untied his shoelaces. Before he finished, the sensei came out again.

"Please come in."

After he pushed the bed that extended the daytime without hesitation in the center of the sitting room closer to the wall, he set down new sitting cushions.

"Has something happened?"

"What? I've been feeling poorly since this morning. I soldiered through the morning and fell asleep around noon. You showed up as I was nodding off. I apologize for making you wait."

"No, I just opened the lattice."

"Really? I was surprised someone was here and went out to see."

"Oh? Excuse me for disturbing you. Sleep is good for you."

"Well, that's not important. Sayoko and Granny aren't here."

"Where did they go?"

"They went to the baths and then shopping."

The empty shell of bedding was piled high. The hole to crawl out of faced the shōji door. Its shadow obscured the pattern on the shaded nightclothes. The back of the haori jacket made from glossy brown *kaiki* silk was thrown on top and gathered scant twinkling light rays.

"It's a little chilly. I should put on the haori," said the sensei and stood.

"It may be better if you sleep."

"No, I'll try getting up for a little while."

"What's wrong?"

"It feels like a cold but is nothing serious."

"I'm sorry for taking you out last night."

"Not at all. What? Last evening, I was a nuisance."

"No, you weren't."

"Sayoko had a wonderful time. Thanks to you, she was rejuvenated."

"I have a little more free time and can accompany her to other places."

"You're probably busy. No, you're too busy and don't have to."

"I feel bad for both of you."

"There's no need for you to worry, even a little. Your being busy is our happiness."

Seizō said nothing. The room gradually darkened.

"Have you eaten?" asked the sensei.

"Yes."

"Have you eaten? If you haven't, please join me. There's not much. Would you like green tea over rice?"

He stood unsteadily and cast a long, black shadow on the closed shōji door.

"Sensei, I'm fine. I ate before I came."

"You did? There's no need to hold back."

"I'm not."

The black shadow folded and lowered to its original position. He hacked several coughs.

"Do you have a cough?"

"It's a dry cough."

The moment he started to speak a few more coughs burst forth. Startled, Seizō waited for his coughing to end.

"You should lie down and get warm. A chill is risky."

"I'm fine. I try to move around but can't for a short time. As you age, your will disappears. Those matters are for the young."

I've heard the words "matters for the young" all the time. However, this was the first time they came from Kodō-sensei's mouth. The sparse beard is entrusted to the wind and dust by the person who wonders whether only bones are left behind in this world. For the first time in the last ten or twenty years, the words from his mouth were heard, at least, between rhythmic breaths.

The bong of a midnight bell echoed dolefully. In the dreary room, Seizō heard these words from the gloomy man and reflected on matters for the young and thought you're young only once. He believed not doing something well while young is a lifelong loss.

The feeling after having committed a lifelong loss and now being old like the sensei must be loneliness. It's probably very dull. However, someone who is ungrateful by failing to apologize to a benefactor, a tormented conscience until death may be melancholy by recalling the past when the harm occurred. In any case, youth does not come twice. Matters decided during the exclusive time of youth probably determine one's entire life. I must decide now which matters will determine mine. If I visited the sensei before seeing Fujio today, I might have sidestepped that lie for now. However, if I look at the lies told now, I have no choice. There's nothing to stop me from leaving my future destiny to Fujio. Seizō reasoned this in his heart.

"Tōkyo has changed," said the sensei.

"An energetic place changes every day."

"It's scary. Last night, I was shocked."

"Because so many people came out."

"They did, but I barely saw anyone I knew."

"That's true." Seizō sounded noncommittal.

"Who did you see?"

"Well ..." Seizō was vague. After briefly thinking, he said, "Well, I met nobody."

"Meeting no one is to be expected at an expansive venue," said the sensei, deeply impressed. He seemed to be a bit of a country boy. Seizō looked away from the sensei's lackluster face and down at his knees. His cuffs were bright white. On his cufflinks adorned with seven jewels, pink floated over the edge and warmly surrounded the interior of a delicate gold edge. His suit was a high-quality English weave. When he scrutinized himself, Seizō was unexpectedly self-conscious of the world in which he should live. He was about to involve the sensei, but a forgotten item popped into his mind. Of course, the sensei didn't know.

"It's been a long time since we've gone on a walk together. Won't it be exactly five years this year?"

His words were colored with nostalgia.

"Yes, this is the fifth year."

"Whether the fifth year or the tenth, it'll be fine if I live in one place like this. Sayoko will also be delighted."

The sensei said the last part like an afterthought. Seizō forgot to answer promptly and felt like he was shrinking inside the dark room.

"So Sayoko has gone out," he forced himself to say.

"Yes, but there was no pressing business. If you have the time, why don't we do a little shopping?"

"Unfortunately, I was about to leave."

"Oh, I see. I've probably taken too much of your time. Do you have urgent business?"

"No, it's not an urgent matter."

Seizō hesitated a little. The sensei didn't question him.

"Okay. Well then," he replied, uncertain. Accompanying the vague exchange, the dimness in the room was no longer managed. The evening was moonlit. The moon was out, and there was still time, but the sun set. As an apology to the room, the sensei hung a prized Gitō scroll inside the interior painted dark blue of the alcove on the sand-coated wall. The drunkenness in which tottering shoes nearly step on the kimono and headdress of the Tang period and a long sleeve sloppily drapes the arm leaning against a boy's shoulder is the optimism fulfilled by April in the springtime in contrast to the loneliness of this home.

As if on command, the striking black color of the cap hiding his forehead that caught my attention was a matter for the future. I noticed the ornament ribbon or broad silk flowing to the left and right in the conventional shape mixed in with the lazily approaching evening. The sensei and I hesitated and seemed to disappear like shadows into a hole.

"Sensei, I bought the stand for the Western lamp you requested."

"Thank you so much."

Seizō went out to the entryway from the dim room and carried in the lampstand and the wastebasket.

"Ah, it's become so dark I can't see well. After turning on the light, I'll leisurely look at it."

"I'll light the lamp. Where is it?"

"I'm so sorry. You're trying to go home. Go out to the veranda. It's in the shutter box on the right. It should be clean."

One dark shadow stood and slid open the shōji door. The remaining shadow quietly folded his arms and didn't move. Night suddenly surrounded them. The six-tatami-mat sitting room sealed the lonely man engulfed by gloom. He coughed several times.

Along with the sound of a match striking a corner of the eaves, the coughing stopped. Light moved into the room. Seizō bent the knees of his slacks and placed the lamp core on the new stand.

"It fits perfectly. It's seated perfectly. Is this rosewood?"

"It's probably fake."

"Even fake, it's nice. How much was it?"

"I wonder?"

"I'm not sure. How much?"

"A little over four yen for both."

"Four yen. Of course, this is Tōkyo. Things are expensive. If you have a small pension, Kyōto is preferred."

Unlike several years ago, the sensei had to live on a tiny pension and the interest from a little savings. It was very different from the time he was helping Seizō. Depending on the situation, he appeared to want a little help from Seizō who humbly held back.

"If Sayoko weren't here, there would be no obstacles to staying in Kyōto. But having a young daughter is cause for concern ..." He stopped mid-sentence. Seizō did not respond respectfully.

"It's the same for me to die anywhere. Sayoko, who will be left behind, would be pitiful all alone. So this year, I deliberately came to Tōkyo.

"It has been twenty years since I left my hometown. I have no friends to connect with. It's the same as being in a foreign country. When I came to have a look, sand and dust were stirred up. It was crowded and expensive. I did not think I would ever like living here."

"It's not a good place to live."

"Years ago, my relatives owned several buildings. I haven't been in contact with them for a long time and have no idea where they live. I don't think I can keep going. I think I'll sleep even if just for half a day. It's disheartening."

"Yes, of course."

"I rely on your being by my side more than anything else."

"I've been of no use."

"No, I'm very grateful for your many kind gestures during this busy time."

"With no thesis, I still have free time."

"Thesis. The doctoral dissertation."

"Yes, you're right."

"When will you submit it?"

Seizō thought, I don't know when, but it has to be soon. If it's not accepted, I'll have to write much more. He said to himself, "Now, I will persevere in my writing."

The sensei pulled his hands from the undershirt sleeves, placed his elbows next to the skin inside his kimono, and shook his shoulders a few times.

"I'm shivering," he said, burying his long, thin beard inside his collar.

"Goodnight. Being up is not good for you. I'll be going now."

"What? Our talk. Sayoko will be home soon. If I want to sleep, I'll excuse myself and go to bed. We still have matters to discuss."

The sensei yanked his hands from inside his kimono, put them on his knees, and tapped them once.

"You should relax a bit. It has just gotten dark."

While annoyed, Seizō thought this was pitiful. His wanting to stop himself was not nostalgia for that time or the boredom of the evening. It might have been caused by anxiety over moving to the future destination. Carefully thinking about the destination, he'll probably have peace of mind after death a moment sooner and want to grab onto hands beating with a pulse.

Seizō thought, I still haven't eaten dinner. If we dine together, a conversation I don't want to hear will emerge. Only my hips are floating in space. When I look at the sensei's circumstances, however, there's no need for me to extend my knees in these slacks. This old man fought through illness and forced himself to perk up for my sake. The familiar, cheap futon was lopsided and full of holes. Warmth was something of the past.

"About Sayoko ..." said the sensei while he gazed at the lamp light. Inside the lamp chimney, the lamp wick lit up in a semi-cylindrical shape, the oil filling the jar was silently sucked up. The tongue of a calm flame protected the springtime that just ended without moving. The lonely person and the lonely night compensated for the point of light. The lamp light beckoned the shadows of hope.

"As you know, Sayoko is shy. I'm not concerned because she didn't have the fashionable education like today's women's university students," said the sensei, looking away from the lamp and to Seizō. He had to be grappling with something.

"No ... then why ..." Seizō said and stopped short, but the sensei still had not moved his eyes from Seizō's face. Without opening his mouth, he was waiting for something.

"Don't worry ... that shouldn't be ... a concern," he answered in fragments. The sensei who eventually understood moved forward.

"Because that's also pitiful."

Seizō didn't say "That's true" or "That's not so." His hands rested on his knees. His eyes stared at the backs of his hands.

"My doing this is somehow good. It's good but because my body is like this, there's no guarantee how long nothing will happen to it.

That time will be a problem. The previous promise remains. Because you're not a shallow man who tosses a promise into the wastebasket, after I'm gone, you'll help Sayoko."

"Of course, I will," Seizō had to say.

"That gives me comfort. However, women are narrow-minded beings. Ah, ha, ha, ha. And that's a problem."

The laughter heard sounded forced. The sensei's face looked more lonely when he laughed.

"Worrying that much is unnecessary," he said with no confidence. His words were shaky.

"I'm fine but Sayoko …"

Seizō began rubbing the knee of his pants with his right hand. For a short time, the two were silent. Lamp light without a wick illuminated half of both of them.

"You probably face various issues. But many issues that have arisen have not been fixed."

"That's not so. Only a few."

"Hasn't it been two years since you've graduated?"

"Yes. But with a little more time …"

"How long is a little more? If that's clear, waiting is fine. I often talk to Sayoko. However, there are several problems. Any parent has responsibilities to his children. Will you need a little more time to finish writing your dissertation?"

"Yes, that's it."

"You've been writing for quite a long time, but when do you intend to finish? Around when?"

"I plan to finish writing as soon as possible and will work hard because how much time is a big problem."

"However, could you give me an estimate?"

"A little longer."

"Next month?"

"That's too soon …"

"How about the month after next?"

"We'll see …"

"After you marry, it'll be fine. There's no reason not to write your dissertation after you marry."

"But I'll have more responsibilities."

"You'll be all right if you keep working as hard as you have been. For now, we can't depend on your financial help."

Seizō had no response.

"What is your income now?"

"It's miniscule."

"By which you mean?"

"All together just sixty yen. It's barely enough for one person."

"You're boarding?"

"Yes."

"That's ridiculous. One person using sixty yen is wasteful. Even with a household, you can live easily."

Again, Seizō had no response.

While he says prices are high in Tōkyo, he does not know the difference between Tōkyo and Kyōto. He does not understand the comparison between the era in which Narumi tie-dyed waistbands were tied closed and the cold was staved off with rice gruel and the current situation in which one graduates from the university and must show the appropriate respect to the edges of one's clothes and hat. To scholars, books are the second generation after life. Similar to the walking cane of a blind man, books are indispensable, without them, they can't make a living. If books suddenly sprung up on the desk, surprisingly extravagant spending would converge on some of them. To the sensei, those expenses mean absolutely nothing. Thus, he could not easily answer.

What was Seizō thinking? He placed his left hand on the tatami and extended his right to remove the wick in the lamp. The small six-tatami world brightened as if turned to the east. The sensei's worldview brightened, too. Seizō was still holding onto the knob.

"That's fine. That's a nice amount. Taking too much out is dangerous," said the sensei.

Seizō let go. When he pulled back his hand, he peeked inside his cuff to glimpse at his watch. He pulled a white handkerchief from the inside pocket of his suit and carefully wiped the oil off his fingertips.

"The flame bends a bit," Seizō held his oil-free fingertips to the tip of his nose and sniffed several times.

"Granny cuts them, and they bend," said the sensei, looking at the fully-open lamp.

"How's Granny? Has she been helpful?"

"I've been rude. I haven't thanked you. Little by little I'm causing trouble for you."

"No. I was wondering if she can work at her age?"

"Well, she's all right. She's slowly getting used to everything."

"Really? She was in good health. The truth is I was wondering and worried. Instead, people certainly seem so. Well, Asai vouched for her."

"Speaking of Asai, what does he want to do? Has he returned, yet?"

"He should be back by now. What time is it? Depending on the circumstances, he may return by train today."

"In a letter the day before yesterday, he said he would return in two or three days."

"All right," said Seizō, staring innocently at the head of the twisted wick. He focused his eyes on one point as if meditating to probe the relationship between Asai's return to Tōkyo and the wick.

"Sensei."

His face turned toward the sensei. Oddly, slight resolve settled at the corners of his mouth.

"What?"

"About our talk today."

"Yes."

"Can it wait a few more days?"

"A few more days?"

"Before I respond to the essential parts, I'd like to think about a few things."

"That's all right. Take three or four days or ... even a week. For clarity, I'll wait with peace of mind. I'll speak to Sayoko, too."

"Yes, thank you." As he spoke, he took out the prized watch. After the long shadows heading to summer fell, its glowing night hands seemed to turn swiftly.

"Well, excuse me. I must be going."

"You can wait a little longer. She's probably on her way home."

"I'll come again soon."

"Yes, but I've been negligent."

Seizō stood, feeling relieved. The sensei picked up the Western lamp.

"Please. I understand," he said as he went out to the entryway.

"Ah, it's a moonlit night," said the sensei, holding the lamp at shoulder height.

"Yes, it's a peaceful evening," said Seizō, looking at the street through the lattice while tying his shoe laces.

"Kyōto is peaceful."

The stooped-over Seizō finally left the entryway. He slid open the lattice. Only half of his delicate frame was outside on the street.

"Seizō," called the sensei from the shadow of the lamp to stop him.

"Yes." Seizō turned away from the shining moonlight.

"Oh, nothing. I thought if we came to Tōkyo, we could quickly settle Sayoko's situation. You understand, don't you?"

Seizō doffed his hat. The sensei's shadow disappeared with the lamp.

It was dim outside. Light partly shining on the world and partly blocking the world hung in the sky, which floated in the advancing night like a waist too high or too low but unable to sit. The hanging object was also airy and fluffy. A circle tinted yellow on the round edge gently swelled. The yellow band lost color near its surroundings and oozed into darkened indigo. If it could flow, the moon looked as though it would disappear. In the evening, the moon is easily lost in the sky, and people blend into the earth.

Seizō's shoes hid the heels falling to the ground under the hems of his slacks as if shying away from the damp light. The road slipped out and turned to the left towards the lantern of a soba shop. The streets smelled of humanity. The shadows dragging along the ground did not lengthen. They curled up and approached, swayed in a bunch, and left. The sounds of wooden-soled geta sandals were enveloped by mist and not crisp like frost. White patterns were visible on the telegraph poles brushed past. When bright eyes fixated with doubt, they reflected the black and white of a shared umbrella. Mist moved from daytime to early evening and formed a barricade. Both people coming and going seemed not to understand. If he flees, he'll be in a world of mist. If he goes out, it's into a world of the moon. Seizō walked as if in a dream. He embodied walking slowly and alone in deep sorrow.

He still had not eaten dinner. Usually, when he goes out, the idea is to dive into the first restaurant, even one serving Western food. His slacks with perfect pleats should put a look of pride on his face. No matter how long he stood that evening, he did not feel hungry. He didn't even feel like drinking milk. The weather was too warm. His stomach felt heavy. A pulled-up leg doesn't make one a plover. He didn't feel a vibrant response to his steps. Perhaps, that's the fault of stepping softly. He didn't feel the thud of hitting the ground. Haze is not needed in the world if he walks around like a policeman on patrol. And he had no reason to worry. He could walk like that because he's a patrolman. Seizō, particularly this evening's Seizō, could not mimic a police officer.

Seizō staggered. He wondered, Why am I so timid? Brains do not defeat people. I learned two times more than my classmates. I have confidence in my sophistication in everything from my actions to my style of dress. My timidity is why I lose. Being a loser is fine, but I fell into an unavoidable predicament. I once read in a book that a person sinking into water kicks the water. If I give up and start kicking at the present situation where the stomach can't replace the back, that would be the end of it. But ...

He heard women's voices. Two human shadows approached him from the other side of the road. He could hear speaking voices inside the rhythmic sounds of Azuma geta and low geta sandals leisurely ticking off the warm evening.

"Did he buy the lampstand for you?" asked one woman.

"I think so," answered the other.

"He may be coming around now," said the first voice again.

"Do you think so?" the second voice answered.

"But he said he would buy one, didn't he?" The voice pushed.

"Oh, it's too hot this evening." She tried evasion.

"That's the hot bath. Medicated baths are warm." The other voice explained.

The women's conversation passed from the side opposite Seizō. As he saw them off, only a shadow of his head emerged at a tilt from beneath the eaves and moved toward the soba shop. Seizō who had turned his head and stopped for a few moments began walking again.

If I were a man with few regrets like Asai, I could immediately settle this matter. An untroubled man like Hajime readily acts with ease. An indifferent man like Kingo might find himself caught between a rock and a hard place. However, I cannot. I go to the other side and sink one step deeper. They come here and sink one step deeper. Both sides hesitate, but each side takes one step forward. In other words, the reluctance was wrapped in emotions and a paucity of will.

What are the advantages? The disadvantages? The idea of advantages and disadvantages is the skin of the economic climate covered from behind on the foundation of human emotions. If asked about a person's primary driving force, the immediate answer is human emotions. The ideas of advantages and disadvantages come third or fourth and, depending on the situation, never appear. Of course, I consider possibly falling into the same result. These were Seizō's thoughts as he walked.

Whatever the emotions, I must not be this indecisive. If I fold my arms and leave matters to nature, I don't know how an event will evolve. Imagining becomes terrifying. As much as I worry about emotions, I may witness a scary development. I must do something right now. But I still have a few more days. Even if I decide after several days of serious thought, it won't be too late. If I'm no wiser after a few days, I'll have no choice. I'll grab hold of Asai and ask him to intercede with Kodō-sensei. In fact, I considered this earlier and said I'd take Asai's return home into account and postpone the decision for a few days. Only Asai is not a stickler for emotions in this sort of situation. A person with deep emotions like mine could never decline. Seizō had these thoughts while walking.

The moon still hung in the sky. No signs of flowing without flowing were seen. The brilliance of the light falling to the Earth is sealed in by a heavy, warm atmosphere and pulls a great eternal dream in midair. Scattered stars appeared to dive into the clouds and escape on the other side. They barely flickered, like cannonballs wrapped in cotton. The heavy night was quiet. These thoughts ran through Seizō's mind as he walked. That night, the small temple bells did not ring.

CHAPTER 15

The room faced south. French windows reached five feet above the floor and soon turned to glass. If left open, the sun beamed in, and warm breezes flowed in. The sun stopped at the foot of a chair. The wind knew nothing about stopping and blew relentlessly up to the ceiling and behind the curtains. The study became airy and bright.

A one-legged desk was set up to avoid the French west window on the right. When the semi-cylindrical sliding door is closed, the lock is locked from the top. If light, the center with an edging of green felt was shaved at a slant to the hands, and the back was flat for convenience when opening a book. Underneath, the left and right sides folded down into drawers with metal fixtures, and the fourth section reached the floor of varnished camphor-wood parquet. The soles of shoes in opposition to etiquette shined so brightly they seemed dangerous.

A Western-style table was also in the room. In a combination of Chippendale and Nouveau pieces, drastic modernity was hidden in an elegant past and occupied the center of the room. Of course, the chairs with four legs arranged around the perimeter were built in the same style. Although their satin patterns might have looked like a matched pair, the hips lowered onto and the backs leaned against the white chair covers to block light quickly became a familiar sight. However, they were not a feast for the eyes.

The six-foot-tall bookshelves pushed to a wall were lined up for nine feet to the door. When assembled, they are stacked. When taken apart, one shelf is enjoyed. It held books ordered from the West by his late father. The gold leaf of ornate or block characters was beautifully printed vertically and horizontally on the books crammed onto the shelves and emitted charming lights in dark blue, yellow, and other colors.

Seizō couldn't help feeling envy each time he saw Kingo's study. Naturally, Kingo did not dislike that. Originally, the room served as his father's sitting room. One partition door opened and passed into the parlor. Exiting through the remaining door took one down the inner hallway to the Japanese-style sitting room. The two Western-style rooms were added for his father's benefit by expanding the cramped living space in preparation for the twentieth century. Rather than saying it suited his tastes, the building was entrusted to him for practical reasons and to keep up with the times. The room was not a happy one. Nonetheless, Seizō burned with envy.

When he stepped into this study, he imagined favorite books were read at favorite times. When bored, wonderful conversations were enjoyed with fascinating people. I'll quickly write my doctoral dissertation and show you. After it's written, I will create a literary masterpiece that will astonish the next generation. It may be quite enjoyable. However, in my life at a boarding house, the chaos of the neighborhood swirling in my head is awful. When cornered by the past as I am now, it's horrible to constantly use my mind night and day in a muddle of obligations and human emotions. I'm not boasting, but I do have a fine brain. The profession of a man with a keen mind is to use his brain to contribute to the world. To fulfill this sacred work, this condition is to act to the best of one's ability. This study is an example of that condition. Seizō is desperate to enter this study.

Unlike high school, Kingo and Seizō were in the same year in college. Seizō knew nothing about Kingo's academic ability because philosophy and pure literature were different subjects. He only heard that Kingo submitted a thesis titled *The Philosophical World and the Real World* and graduated. Anyone who hasn't read *The Philosophical World and the Real World* should not understand its value.

In any case, Kingo will not receive a watch, but I will. Not only does a watch gifted by the emperor measure time, but it also measures the quality of a mind. Future progress and academic success are measured, too. I've decided that Kingo who oozes privilege is not an important man. After graduation, he will do no research. He may be storing up deep thoughts internally but should have already published if ideas were being stored. Nothing published is not proof that nothing is stored.

Nevertheless, I am more valuable than Kingo. By rapidly embracing my value, I spend sixty yen each month on food and clothes, but I fold my arms and live each rambling day as a bored man. What a waste for Kingo to occupy this study. If I could become the master of this room like Kingo … The one doing proper work for over two years necessarily endured until today unfairness and suffered the destitution of the inheritance from his father. The superior horse was made to lie down in the stable, too. I've heard that fortune comes back to the unlucky. Every day, Seizō had this wish.

The oblivious Kingo faced his desk alone. If the front window were open, he could pass over one fine stone step and look across the expansive lawn nearby. Cheerfulness connected to the earth constantly flowed into the adjoining room and quietly occupied the space. However, Kingo remained shut in.

A small window on the right was closed and half covered by curtains hanging on the left and right. The transmitted light weakly dropped to the floor. The curtains seemed to have not moved and gathered dust for twenty days with a floral pattern hovering over a maroon woolen fabric. The colors were mostly faded. Naturally, decorations not in harmony with the room worked well in Japan in an age of change. A face pushed to the glass through a gap in the curtains. A peek outside revealed a lake beyond the bushes and trees. It was visible in slices like a wave pattern missing parts horizontally between intermittent stripes. Diagonally across the lake was

Fujio's sitting room. Kingo did not see the shrubbery, the lake, or the grass but leaned heavily on the desk. He contemplated a chilly spring with a single unburned coal from last year in the fireplace.

Eventually, the sound changed to books being shuffled around. Kingo took out an ordinary diary marked by fingerprints and began writing.

> Many persons desire to act wretchedly to us, and at the same time they expect us, under penalty of their hatred, neither to counteract their villainy nor to regard them as villains.

Kingo finished writing the tiny letters and wrote *Leopardi* in katakana at the end. He pushed the diary to the right. He went back to the book set aside and quietly started reading. A pen with a thin blue-shell pen barrel rolled off the desk and onto the floor. A black drop formed under his foot. Kingo pushed on both hands at the corners of the desk and leaned back slightly. He lowered his eyes to gaze at the black drops. A round ring of ink shot out in all directions. The blue shell barrel turned over and released a long, cold light into the dim interior. Kingo shifted the chair. He picked up the Western-style pen, an old souvenir his father bought for him while overseas.

He turned over the hand holding the pen in its fingertips. The retrieved object slid from the valley between his fingers into his palm. When he flipped his palm over, the long pen handle rolled forward and back. With each movement, light shimmered. It was a small remembrance.

While the barrel rolled, he continued reading the book. He turned the page and found this writing.

> When two fencers of equal skill are matched against each other, the art of fencing is in their case reduced to a nullity, since neither of them has any more advantage over the other than if they were both equally unskilled. In the same way it often happens that men resort to falsehood and iniquity gratuitously and to no purpose; for when they find themselves encountered by an equal degree of iniquity

and falsehood in others, the position of the parties becomes neither better nor worse than it would have been if both had been actuated by probity and truth. Thus it is pretty certain that wickedness and duplicity seldom prove effectual save when they are conjoined to superior force, or else where they encounter an inferior degree of these qualities in others, or are matched against positive goodness. Of these cases, the last mentioned is necessarily rare; and the second is not common, since scoundrels are generally about equal in depravity. It is sad to reflect how often, by simply doing good to one another, men might attain with facility objects which they attain with infinite difficulty, and sometimes entirely fail to attain, by wrongdoing one another.

Kingo picked up the diary again and dropped the blue-shell pen barrel to the bottom of the ink pot with a plop. He thought the dropped pen would not easily rise and let go. Leaving the Leopardi open, he placed the diary with a yellow cover on the page. He stretched his legs and leaned against the back of the chair with his hands clasped behind the scruff of his neck. The moment he looked up, his eyes met the gaze of his father in the half-length portrait.

Only two of his vest buttons were visible in this portrait, which was not too big. His clothes could be considered a frock and were absorbed into the darkness of the background. The only spots of brightness were the bit of whiteness of his shirt leaking through and his face with a broad forehead.

They say become the pen of a famous person. When he returned to Japan three years earlier, his father carried home this flat object. The faraway sea rose to the dock in Yokohama. Since then, it has been hanging on the wall each time Kingo looked up. When he wasn't looking up, the wall looked down on him. When he picked up a pen, when he rested his chin on his hands, and when the desk supported his napping head, it was always looking down. Even when Kingo was not there, the man on the canvas always looked down on the study.

He looked down and lived. Discipline inhabited those eyes. They were painted meticulously but were not eyes refined by patience. A natural shadow emerged between eyebrows and eyelashes drawn as a contour in one brush stroke. Sagging could be seen in his lower eyelids. As the years passed, wavy lines stretched from the corners of his eyes. The pupils in them were alive. The ability to drop a static but lively momentary facial expression onto the canvas must be viewed as a remarkable skill that swiftly snags the perfect chance. Each time he looked at those eyes, Kingo thought, He's alive.

If a ripple stirs in an imaginary world, one thousand more ripples follow. When I forgot myself in the realm of thought while embracing turbulent waves, if I lifted my head in agony and our eyes met, I'd think, Ah, he was here. Sometimes, I was also shocked.

When Kingo looked up from the Leopardi and thoroughly trusted the back of the chair, the shock was more powerful than usual.

While a memento for recalling the dead in a kind of memory enables remembrance, it is a form of cruelty to not return the deceased to his original state. In this fleeting world, we embrace several strands of hair clinging to the skin and cry, and time only moves forward. A memento only burns. Since the death of his father, Kingo found it dreadful to look at the picture. A fortress of calm settled in and no unusual changes occurred although separated. A short distance away, a vivid recollection of a compassionate face nearby only revealed the separated parent on the paper of memory or the anticipation for the day to meet again in the springtime. However, the man he thought he would meet had already died. The living part was only in his eyes. Even if he were alive, not even a hair moved.

Kingo was lost in thought with eyes glazed over.

The father also did a regrettable thing. He was at an age where he could have lived a little longer. His beard was not completely white. His complexion was fresh and young. He probably did not believe he was near death. He did something regrettable. If I'm going to die, please let me die after returning home to Japan. He probably decided he wanted to leave things unsaid. He had many things he wanted to hear and say. He did something regrettable. He was no longer a young man and had traveled overseas three or four times. However, he suffered a sudden illness and died a short time later while posted overseas.

His living eyes fixed on Kingo from the wall. Kingo stared up while leaning back on the chair. The eyes of the two men met each time he looked up. The seconds of his staring eyes, not moving, and meeting the other eyes accumulated. After a minute, the other eyes somehow moved toward him. His eyes did not move on a whim but turned to a quiet place. A spirit that gradually strengthened a protective light and deceived steadily came toward Kingo in a straight line.

"Oh, no!"

Kingo moved his head. When the hairs on his head left the back of the chair and moved forward only six inches, the spirit was already gone and, in an instant, appeared to have returned to the interiors of the eyes. Still, the portrait was nothing more than a picture. Kingo again tossed back his black hair to the chair's shoulder.

Nothing made sense. Lately, this has happened occasionally. The fault might have been a weak body or the poor state of my mind. Nonetheless, this picture is awful. I worry and only resemble my rash father. I know nothing starts when the heart remains with the deceased. Being urged to think deeply by dangling a dead body before the tip of one's nose is like thrusting out a wooden sword and urging someone to cut open his belly. Only the annoyance was uncomfortable.

If that is a simple case, it is fine. Each time I remember my father, I pity him. Now, I pity my body and mind. When living in the real world, I only crave famous clothes, home, and food. My mind lives in another country. If I could also forget my mother and younger sister, I'd live this way. If seen in the eyes of a person with advantages and disadvantages that do not understand lifting his heels from the surface of the real world, this may surely be the height of stupidity. I'm ready to throw out everything but don't want to show this messy predicament to my father. Father was simply a man. If Father were watching from the shadows of blades of grass, he'd probably think, What a foolish child! This foolish child doesn't want to think about his father. When I remember, I become miserable.

I can't stand this portrait. When the time comes, I'll put it in storage.

Ten people hold the fates of ten people. Once bitten, twice shy is controlled by the grand principle equivalent to safeguarding your assets and patiently waiting for the right time to profit. During the bright daytime when meals are cooked in many houses, people living underground ready plans for peace in the middle of the night in bed.

While Kingo was alone in the study, lost in his thoughts, Fujio and her mother were chatting in the traditional Japanese room.

"Well, you still haven't talked to him," said Fujio. Instead of unexpected modesty, a brownish lined kimono of knotted silk became bewitching by the presence of a single stripe in a seductive color from the red silk back from behind long, open sleeves. An ancient pattern of red ocher was visible on her obi sash. The name of the textile was not known.

"With Kingo?" her mother asked again. She also wore a subdued striped cloth appropriate to her age. Only the black of her obi sash was tied to catch the eye.

"Yes," responded Fujio and pointed out, "He still doesn't know."

"No, I haven't spoken to him," said the mother and calmed down. She turned up the edge of her sitting cushion.

"Oh, where is my kiseru pipe?"

The pipe was on the other side of the brazier. Fujio gripped the long bamboo stem of the pipe between her thumb and index finger.

"Here," she said as she passed it over the iron kettle with a handle.

"If you speak to him, what will you say?" she asked while pulling back her outstretched hand.

"If we speak, will you please stop?" asked the mother sarcastically. She looked down and packed Kumoi tobacco into the pipe's chamber.

The daughter did not answer. If she had, she would weaken.

She thought she would reply more forcefully but remained silent. Silence is golden.

The mother, who inhaled to her heart's content beneath the kettle stand, opened her mouth as she blew smoke out her nose.

"We can talk at any time. If you like to talk, I will talk. There's nothing to discuss. If you say it's because you intend to do it this way, that's the end of it."

"That is me. Once I've made up my mind, no matter what Kingo says I won't consent."

"He's not a person who will say anything. If I can talk with him, although I didn't begin like this, there are other ways."

"But Kingo has one attitude, and that troubles me."

"True. If that weren't so, talking to him would be unnecessary. Because he's the rightful heir in this family, if he doesn't say yes, I will be left wandering the streets."

"Nevertheless, each time I speak to him, he says he intends to give me the entire fortune."

"Only saying it means nothing, right?"

"Goodness, I can't repeatedly press him."

"Even if you pressed him if I were to be given something, it wouldn't matter. Simply, because it looks bad. Although he's a scholar, it's hard for me to broach the subject."

"Isn't that why it's best to talk?"

"About what?"

"What? That matter …"

"Do you mean Seizō?"

"Yes," Fujio answered.

"Discussing it is fine because it must be discussed at some time."

"If I do, what will he do? If he intends to give me the entire fortune, he will. If he feels like dividing it in some way, he will. If living at home becomes unpleasant, he'll go elsewhere."

"But was I wrong to say I wanted no help from him but asked what he intended to do for you?"

"Did I say help from him was unwelcome? I can't help and don't have any fortune. Well, what do you intend to do, Mother?"

"I intend to do nothing. A wishy-washy man causes problems for others."

"Try to understand my situation a little."

Her mother was silent.

"Recently, even when he said to give the gold watch to Hajime ..."

"Are you saying you will give it to Seizō?"

"Although I'm not saying I'll give it to Seizō, I didn't say I will give it to Hajime."

"He's an odd fellow. I thought he'd say to marry and take care of Fujio. Of course, he wants you to marry Hajime. But isn't Hajime the only son? He would become a son-in-law and take our name."

"Humph."

Fujio turned her slender neck to the side and looked at the garden. The pale blue-green cherry blossoms she gazed at encouraged the night and blew out bright young brown leaves while avoiding all the treetops. She could see a little of the study's window past the three or four shrubs pruned into round shapes and thickly growing on the left. Leaning to one side as much as it pleased, the trunk of a cherry blossom tree with extended branches was a distance from the lake on the left. If the lake dried up, her traditional sitting room would jut out.

Fujio glanced around the quiet garden and turned her head again toward her mother who earlier had turned to Fujio and never looked away. When their eyes met, what was Fujio thinking as one beautiful cheek tensed. The one unable to fix a smile naturally disappeared into an uncertain future on the horizon.

"Hajime will probably be fine."

"If he's not, what could he do?"

"But you probably declined."

"I declined. When I went, I saw Hajime's father and explained why. After coming home, I spoke to you."

"Although I remember that, it seems somewhat uncertain."

"The uncertainty is theirs because his father has patience."

"I may not have made my refusal clear."

"Because there has been an obligation until now, I couldn't humbly decline by saying Fujio said you're awful, like a messenger for a child."

"What is awful? It's best to be blunt because there's no love."

"But the world is not like that. You're still young, you may think being frank doesn't matter, but that's not so in the world. Even if you make the same refusal, they ... of course, you can't speak so harshly. There's no point in making someone angry."

"No matter what you say. I declined."

"Kingo has never said to me he would ever marry because I'm getting older and without hope," she said in one breath and then sipped her tea. "Because I'm old and hopeless."

"Because you've lost hope, if Kingo's intention is to push through like that, the only option is for you to marry a man who will take our name. In that case, Hajime will not come to us because he's the important heir in the Munechika family. And because there is no reason to give you to him."

"It will be a problem if Kingo says he'll marry."

"That's of no concern," said the mother, as an angry frown formed on her tanned forehead. The frown immediately disappeared. Eventually, she said, "If he marries, he will marry Itoko or some other woman of his liking, which is fine. Seizō may soon join this family."

"But Hajime ..."

"He's nothing to worry about," she said sounding irritated. "As long as he does not pass the diplomat exam, he's not marrying anyone."

"If he passes, he'll say something immediately."

"But can he pass? Consider this. If he passes, I promised to give you to him. That's fine."

"You said that."

"No, I didn't. I didn't say that, but it's all right even if I had. He's a man who can't pass."

While smiling, Fujio tilted her head, straightened her posture, and stopped talking.

"Well, I believe Hajime's father will certainly refuse."

"He should. What do you think? Since then, hasn't Hajime's situation changed a little?"

"Of course, it's the same. Now is the same as when we went to the exhibition."

"When did you go to the exhibition?"

Today, she thought, then said, "The evening of the day before yesterday or two days before yesterday."

"If so, it's time for Hajime to know.

"His father is like that, so depending on the situation, the hint might not be understood."

She sounded irritated.

"Because it had to do with Hajime, he may be calm despite hearing it from his father."

"That's true. I can't say which it will be. Well, I'll do this. I'll speak to Kingo.

"If I say nothing, there's no end no matter how much time passes."

"He's probably in the study now."

The mother stood. After taking one step onto the veranda, she turned around and, while leaning over, softly said, "You should visit Hajime."

"I may see him."

"If you do, a little hint would be nice. Didn't you say you're going to Ōmori with Seizō? Isn't it tomorrow?"

"Yes, we have a date for tomorrow."

"It would be a good idea to somehow reveal that the two of you will enjoy a walk together."

"Ha, ha, ha, ha."

The mother left for the study.

She passed by the veranda and half opened the door polished on one side to the pretty wood grain into the dark interior of a Western-style room. As she pushed the knob forward, her leaning body followed the open door. When her feet soundlessly stepped onto the parquet floor, the reverberation of a bolt rang. In the study, curtains blocked springtime and cut off the two dim figures from the world of humanity.

"It's dark in here," said the mother as she walked in and stopped at the table in the center of the room. She only saw the back of Kingo's head above the back of the chair. When the head turned toward the voice, the gap between his eyebrows appeared to widen in confusion. A black mustache along his upper lip naturally drooped and quickly curled at the ends. His mouth was shut. At the same time, his black pupils rubbed against the corners of his eyes. The mother and child recognized the other's position.

"It is gloomy in here," said the mother again, still standing.

The silent man stood. Several steps of his slippers were heard. When his leg reached a corner of the table, he spoke for the first time.

"Shall I open the window?" he leisurely asked.

"Don't bother on my account. I thought you were feeling down."

The silent man again extended his right arm and reached the palm of his hand past the table. The mother being prompted sat in a chair. Kingo sat back down.

"How are you feeling?"

"Better, thank you."

"A little better?"

"Yes, I guess ..." Kingo replied half-heartedly while stretching his back and folding his arms. At the same time, he rested his left ankle on the instep of his right foot. Seated across from him, the mother's eyes saw the shrunken sleeves of his yellowish undershirt.

"When you're not in good health, your mother worries ..."

Before she finished, Kingo pulled his chin into his throat and looked under the table. Two black tabi socks were in a heap. He could not see his mother's legs. She tried again.

"When I'm in poor health, my mood becomes depressed. I'm also not much fun."

Kingo suddenly raised his eyes. His mother instantly changed the subject.

"After going to Kyōto, you seemed a little better."

"Did I?"

"Ha, ha, ha, ha. Did I? As if I'm a stranger.

"Doesn't your complexion look healthier? Did you tan?"

"Perhaps," said Kingo. He turned his head and looked at the window. In the space between the deep pleats in the curtains, the reflections on the glass made one think the new leaves on the photinia trees were on fire.

"Come to the Japanese room and we'll talk. It's more pleasant than this study. It would help your mood and be amusing if, from time to time, you chatted with a tiresome woman as Hajime does."

"Thank you."

"After all, I can't talk enough to become a companion ... but a fool is a fool."

Kingo turned his eyes away from the photinia trees as if they were dazzling.

"The photinias are gorgeous with the sprouts budding."

"They are splendid. They're better than fresh flowers. You can't see them from here, but if you go around to the other side, the pruned ones are round. They are gorgeous."

"The best view may be from your room."

"Oh, have you looked?"

Kingo didn't say whether he did or not.

His mother said, "Lately, perhaps it's the weather, but the red and golden carp in the lake have been leaping a lot. Can you hear them from here?"

"Do leaping carp make a sound?"

"I think so."

"No."

"I can't hear. You probably can't hear. If you stand ... I probably can't hear from my room either. Recently, I told Fujio I've become hard of hearing. She couldn't stop laughing. It makes sense. At a certain age, you can't help being hard of hearing."

"Is Fujio home?"

"Yes, she is. It's about time for Seizō to come for the lesson. Is there a problem?"

"No, nothing."

"She's also full of spirit and may hurt your feelings. I think you should be patient. She is your younger sister. Please watch after her."

Arms still folded, Kingo fixed his deep pupils on his mother. For some reason, her eyes dropped to the table.

"I want to help her," he said quietly.

"Thank you for saying that. That gives me peace of mind."

"I don't want to do anything now but think I want to."

"Hearing that you're thinking about it will probably encourage her, too."

"But ..." He stopped speaking.

She waited for the rest. Kingo uncrossed his arms. Before he leaned his back against the chair, he got so close to his mother that his chest rested on a corner of the table.

"But, Mother. I don't intend to make you worry about taking care of Fujio."

"Well, that ..." This time, his mother pulled her body to the back of the chair. Kingo didn't move an eyebrow. The same soft voice quietly connected.

"The one who says I will care for you is believed by the one being cared for. However, to say believe in me is strange, as if I'm a god—"

Kingo abruptly stopped talking. His mother understood it was not her turn yet or was being reserved as usual.

"It's horrible if no one is trustworthy enough to care for another."

"If abandoned by you, that's it," she said without difficulty but promptly raised her tone. "Fujio is truly pitiful. Don't tell her, but please do something."

Kingo leaned on his elbow and rested his forehead in the palm of his hand.

"But she looks down on me, if I help her, it will only end in a fight."

"What are you saying? Fujio looks down on you."

The gentle mother spoke her denial in a relatively loud voice.

Her voice returned to normal when she said, "Yes, she does but, first, I am sorry."

Kingo said nothing while leaning on his elbows.

"Did Fujio cause some problem?"

Kingo stared at his mother from beneath the hand still holding his forehead.

"If there is a problem, I want to hear everything from you, so don't hesitate to speak. Please tell me. If anything unpleasant happens between us, it will not be amusing."

His five fingers added to his forehead were thin at the joints and slender like a woman's as were the shapes of his fingernails.

"Fujio is already twenty-four."

"She turned twenty-four at the beginning of the year."

"I should have already acted."

"You mean marriage?"

His mother reminded him. Kingo said nothing about brides or grooms. His mother said, "I'd like to discuss Fujio's situation, but before that ..."

"What is it?"

Of course, his right eyebrow was hidden beneath his hand. His eye color had depth. However, a sharp point could not be seen anywhere.

"What should I do? I would appreciate your thinking about it once more."

"About what?"

"About you. Fujio must do something for herself. If you don't marry first, I will be distressed."

Kingo smiled with one cheek in the shadow of his palm. The smile was sad.

"Although you say you're in poor health, there are men with constitutions like yours who marry."

"There may be."

"So you should reconsider, too. You should be fine once you find a wife."

Kingo removed his hands from his forehead for the first time. On the table, a pencil lay on a sheet of ruled paper. He turned over a sheet and saw three or four lines written in English. He realized he was reading it. This paper with an excerpt was a reminder of the book he read yesterday. Kingo laid the paper flat on the table.

His mother subtly frowned and quietly waited for his reply. He picked up the pencil and wrote the kanji character for *raven* on the paper.

"What do you think?"

The *raven* (烏) character became the *bird* (鳥) character.

"It would be nice if you do it for me."

The *bird* (鳥) character became the *shrike* (鴃) character. He added the *tongue* (舌) character below and the *face* (顔) character above to convey a harsh, jabbering face.

"Well, it will be good if Fujio makes her decision."

"If you don't agree, there is no other path."

The mother stopped talking and looked down, dejected. At the same time, triangles were drawn on her son's paper. Three triangles overlapped to form a fishscale pattern.

"Mother, I'll give the house to Fujio."

"Then you ..."

She questioned him.

"I'll also give the fortune to her. I don't need it."

"That will only cause trouble for us."

"Trouble?" he calmly asked. The mother's and child's eyes met for a moment.

"What trouble, you ask? Should I apologize to your late father?"

"Should you? Well, what's best to do?"

He tossed the pencil painted amber onto the table.

"What should you do? An unschooled person, such as me, does not understand. I'm sorry if the unschooled become unschooled."

"Is it awful?"

"Have I ever said something useless like, 'It's awful'?"

"No."

"I also don't intend to. Each time you said that to me, didn't I express thanks?"

"I hear the thanks throughout."

The mother picked up the dropped pencil and looked at its point and the end of the round eraser. She thought he was not the sort of person to extend a hand to help in his heart. While quickly dragging the eraser end along the top of the table, she said, "Well, you have no desire to inherit this house."

"The house is inherited. Legally, I am the heir."

"Although the Kōno home will be inherited, you will not care for your mother."

Before Kingo answered, his pupils fixed on the centers of his sharp eyes carefully watched his mother's face. Eventually, he politely said, "Therefore, I said I'm giving the house and the fortune, everything, to Fujio."

"If you say so, there's nothing I can do."

The mother sighed and left this verse on the table. Kingo was aloof.

"Because there's no other path, you will do as you please, but for Fujio ..."

"Yes."

"The truth is I believe she loves Seizō. What do you think?"

"Seizō?" he said and was silent.

"She can't?"

"It's not that she can't," he slowly said.

"If it's all right, I believe she'll choose him."

"That's probably best."

"Best?"

"Yes."

"Finally, I'll have peace of mind."

Kingo squinted hard at some object in front of him. He seemed to be acknowledging the existence of his mother before him."

"Finally, there's something strange about you."

"Mother, Fujio will probably agree."

"Of course, I know. But why?"

Kingo looked far into the distance. When he blinked, his eyes suddenly got closer.

"Is Hajime a definite no?" he asked.

"Hajime? At first, Hajime was the most preferred. However, Hajime and your father had the relationship you described."

"Was there a promise?"

"I wouldn't call it a promise."

"I recall Father saying something about giving him the watch."

"The watch?" said the mother, cocking her head.

"Father's gold watch. The one with embedded garnets."

"Oh, yes. He had that sort of thing."

She sounded like she remembered.

"Hajime should still be the recipient."

Unconcerned, she only said, "Really?"

"If there was a promise, it's terrible not to give it to him. Obligation is missing."

"Because the watch is in Fujio's hands, I'll be sure to tell her."

"There is the watch, but more important is Fujio's circumstance."

"But there is absolutely no promise to give Fujio to him."

"Okay? Well, she should be fine."

"When you say that, I may be wrong as if I oppose you, but I have no memory of a promise."

"Uh-huh. Then there is none."

"You see, whether there was a promise or not, it's good to give her to Hajime. However, he can't marry while he's still studying because he hasn't passed the diplomat exam."

"That doesn't matter."

"Because Hajime is the eldest son, he must be the heir in the Munechika family."

"Will Hajime marry Fujio and change his name?"

"He doesn't want to, but that's because you don't listen to what your mother says."

"Even if Fujio moves away, I will give the fortune to her."

"About the fortune ... It's a problem for you to misunderstand my idea. I'm not thinking about the fortune at all. My intentions are so pure I'd like to see it divided up. Perhaps, you can't see that."

"I can see," said Kingo. His tone was decidedly serious. He did not even understand his mother's mockery.

"Because of my age and being discouraged ... when I give away Fujio, what follows will be a problem."

"Of course."

"If not, Hajime is good. You two are good friends."

"Mother, do you know Seizō well?"

"I intend to. Isn't he courteous, kind, and a fine man who is an able scholar? Why do you ask?"

"If so, he's fine."

"Don't speak so coldly. If you're thinking of something, please tell me. That's why I've gone to the trouble to come talk to you."

Kingo looked up after staring at the scribbles on the paper for a short time and calmly spoke.

"Mother, Hajime values you more than Seizō does."

"Well," she immediately said but was later quiet.

"Perhaps ... your eyes are not seeing things incorrectly, but this differs from other issues because this alone does not affect the freedom of the parent and older brother."

"Is Fujio insisting?"

"Yes, well ... she's not saying she's sure."

"I know that, too. I know but ... is Fujio here?"

"I'll call her."

The mother stood. When she pressed the electric calling bell in a white section of the wallpaper scattered with dark pink arabesque patterns, the response came before she returned to her seat. The door opened just ten inches. The mother looked back and said, "I need to speak to Fujio."

The door was gently shut.

The mother and child sat face to face separated by the table. Neither spoke. Kingo picked up the pencil again. He drew a circle big enough to brush against the outer edges of the three scales. He filled in the gaps between the circle and the scales, and then carefully drew parallel black lines. The mother idly gazed at her son's sketch.

Of course, their two hearts did not understand. Only the surface looked serene. If the actions of their limbs became signs that carried internal communications to the physical, a mother and child as tranquil as these two could not be readily noticed. The child who outlined a moment of boredom by dozens of lines and meticulously filled in the part outside of the three scales and the mother who placed her hands on her knees as usual and steadfastly protected the interior of the circle blackened by each stroke are a mother and child with sympathetic hearts. They are a mother and child with quiet delight. The two chests faced each other across the narrow table. Behind curtains that shut out the spring, they forgot about the world, people, and conflicts. As always, the likeness of the dead man illuminated the mother and child from the wall.

The painstakingly drawn lines became complex. The black parts gradually grew. When the last part became the position of an arc touching his right hand, he heard the twisting sounds of bolts. The figure of the awaited Fujio appeared in the doorway. The white figure was entrusted to springtime. Against the dark background, her figure above her shoulders seemed to float. Kingo's pencil suddenly stopped halfway while drawing a line. At the same time, Fujio's face slipped out of the background.

As she said, "Why are you using invisible ink?" Fujio walked up to her mother and sat beside her. She asked her mother, "Are you going out?" Her mother only gave her a meaningful look. Meanwhile, Kingo's black lines grew by four lines.

"Your brother has something important to discuss with you."

"Oh?" Fujio said and turned to face him. Many black lines continued to quickly emerge.

"What is it, Kingo?"

"Oh, yes," he said. Finally, he lifted his head but said nothing.

Fujio looked at her mother again. While looking, the shadow of a small smile rose on her lovely cheeks. Her brother broke the silence.

"Fujio, I will give you this house and all the assets Father bequeathed to me."

"When?"

"Today. In exchange, you must care for Mother."

As she said, "Thank you," she looked at her mother again. Of course, she is smiling.

"You're not interested in marrying Hajime. Am I right?"

"Yes."

"You're not? Why is it awful?"

"It's awful."

"Really? Do you like Seizō that much?"

Fujio did not waver.

"After hearing that, what will you do?" she asked, extending her back above the chair.

"Nothing. It will not benefit me. I'm simply saying this for you."

"For me?" These words hung in the air.

"Yes." She dropped this with contempt. The mother started to speak.

"Your brother thinks Hajime is better than Seizō."

"Kingo is Kingo. I am me."

"Kingo says Hajime will take better care of your mother."

"Kingo," said Fujio, then flung these words at him. "Do you understand Seizō's personality?"

"I do," he said quietly.

"Do you?" He stood. "Seizō is a poet. He is a noble poet."

"Really?"

"He's a man who understood his interests and understood love. He is a gentle man. Personality is not understood by a philosopher. You probably understand Hajime. However, you don't understand Seizō's value. Not at all. The person who praises Hajime has no reason to understand the value of Seizō."

"So you will choose Seizō."

"Of course," she replied.

The purple ribbon trembled toward the door. No sooner had a slender hand turned the knob, than the dark background shrouded Fujio's figure.

CHAPTER 16

The pen of this narrative leaves Kingo's study and enters Hajime's home. The day and time are the same.

Taking notes at his usual Chinese-style desk, Hajime's father sat on a cushion with an Oni Sarasa pattern. The wrinkled collar of a disliked, thin, black silk undershirt exposed the scraggly chest hairs on his skin. He was often an Inbe pottery embodiment of the jolly, pot-bellied Hotei Buddha. An unusual tobacco tray was set before the Hotei Buddha. Mountains, weeping willows, and people were painted on the porcelain with the inscription of the potter Goshon-zui. Between the people and mountains drawn around the same size, a line of gold paint meandered endlessly along the rim. The shape opened into a bowl like an earthen pot. The opening on top shrunk drastically into a round edge. For convenience when carry-ing, rattan lightly tinted with persimmon dye was wrapped around a vine that passed under opposing ear-shaped handles.

Yesterday, Hajime's father brought home this heirloom tobacco tray discovered at a secondhand shop. He's been excited since the morning.

"It's a Shonzui. This is a Shonzui."

As a result, he prepared the lighting charcoal, lit the tobacco, and continuously smoked.

The door covered by a thick printed paper smoothly slid open. As usual, the younger Munechika entered full of energy. His father's eyes left the tobacco tray. He saw his son wearing a loose-fitting suit, a hand-me-down from him. His style was mostly seen only in his cashmere socks.

"Where are you going?"

"I'm not going anywhere. I just got home.

"Aah, it's hot. Today is a scorcher."

"Not in the house. You're hot because you're rushing around. Try to calm down a little and walk."

"I intend to calm down enough, but you probably can't see that. I'm weak.

"Oh, you finally lit a fire on the tobacco tray. Of course."

"What do you think of the Shonzui?"

"It looks like a sake jug."

"What? It's a tobacco tray. What are you laughing about? You put the ash in this way. Of course, it looks like a tobacco tray."

The older man held a wire and lifted the Shonzui into the air.

"Well?"

"Yes, I like it."

"You would. There are many fake Shonzui. A real one is not easily purchased."

"How much did it all cost?"

"What do you think?"

"I have no idea. If I speak recklessly, I'll be bawled out just like when I saw the pine in this room recently."

"One yen and eighty sen. It was cheap."

"That is cheap."

"This was a find."

"Oh, I see a new potted plant on the veranda."

"Earlier, I transplanted it with Ardisia crenata. That Satsuma pot is old."

"It's shaped like a hat worn by a Portuguese man from the sixteenth century.

"These roses are quite red."

"They're called Buddha's Smile. It's a strain of roses."

"Buddha's Smile? What an odd name."

"You probably know the verse in the Avatamska sutra. *Buddha on the outside. / A demon's cruel and wicked heart inside.*"

"I only know the phrase."

"That is Buddha's Smile. A flower is pretty but has thorns. Touch it."

"I don't need to touch anything."

"Ha, ha, ha, ha. A Buddha on the outside, a demon's cruel and wicked heart inside. Women are dangerous."

As the older man spoke, he dug around the inside of the Shonzui with the edge of the pipe's bowl.

"They are fussy roses," said Hajime while admiring the Buddha's Smile.

"Yes," said the older man and slapped his knee like he remembered something.

"Hajime, have you ever seen that flower before? One is displayed in the alcove."

As he spoke, the older man turned his head to the back. The flesh that lost a place to go on the twisted neck was bound by three muscles and pushed forward to the shoulders.

A picture scroll with a brush painting of the ascetic priest Kensu Oshō carrying a fishing pole in serenity was placed on the tea-colored platform. A bronze antique jar was set in front. The border of leaves encircled all sides of a cross made by two stems emerging from inside the long crane-like neck. Balls of dew strung like prayer beads bloomed in pairs on the two stems.

"It's a delicate flower. I've never seen one. What is it called?"

"It's a common Chloranthus serratus."

"A common Chloranthus serratus? Common whatever. I've never heard of it."

"You should try to remember this interesting flower. Two white spikes emerge from each one. Hence, the Japanese name, *futari shizuka*, means the quiet of two people alone. The quiet in a Noh song is two people dancing. You probably know that."

"I do not."

"Futari shizuka. Ha, ha, ha, ha, an interesting flower."

"It's only a flower with some sort of karma."

"If you investigate, karma is abundant. Do you know there are many varieties of plums?"

The older man fished the tobacco tray and scooped around the ash with the bowl of the kiseru pipe. Hajime took this opening to change the subject.

"Father, today, I went to the barbershop for a haircut. It's been a while."

His right hand stroked his black hair.

As he said, "Haircut," his father tapped at the center of the stem on the edge of the Shonzui to drop out the ashes."

"Have you become too pretty?" he asked right after his son's return.

"Have I become too pretty? Father, this is not a basic close-cropped haircut."

"A what haircut?"

"You know."

"I don't know?"

"You see now. It's a little longer in the middle."

"Now that you say that, it is slightly longer. Well, you shouldn't do it again. It's disgraceful."

"What's disgraceful?"

"Summer is coming, and the heat will be oppressive."

"However, no matter how horrible the heat, not leaving my hair like this will be a problem."

"Why?"

"That doesn't matter. It's a problem."

"You're an odd one."

"Ha, ha, ha, ha. That's true, Father."

"Yeah."

"I passed the diplomat exam."

"You passed? Well, well. Really? You should have told me sooner."

"In my head, I imagined I would."

"You've always been smart."

"But if I go overseas with a close-cropped haircut, I'll be mistaken for a convict."

"Overseas ... you're going overseas? When?"

"When this hair grows out. It'll probably be at Ono Seizō's graduation ceremony."

"So in about a month."

"Yes, that's about right."

"If it's one month, we can relax. Before you leave, we can have leisurely discussions."

"Yes, I have a lot of time. No matter how much time there is, today is the deadline to return these Western clothes."

"Ha, ha, ha, ha. Why? They suit you."

"Because you say they flatter me, I've worn them until today, but they've become baggy."

"Are they? Well, then it's best to get rid of them. I'll wear them."

"Ha, ha, ha, ha. You surprise me. Then you get rid of them."

"It's all right to get rid of them. Maybe, give them to Kuroda."

"Kuroda is a nuisance."

"But it's funny."

"It's not funny, but they won't fit his body."

"I guess? But that's what makes it funny."

"Yes, the stuffed parts are funny."

"Ha, ha, ha, ha. Have you spoken with Itoko from time to time, too."

"About the exam?"

"Yes."

"I still haven't told her.

"Why not? When did you know about it?"

"I was notified two or three days ago. I was busy and still hadn't told anyone."

"You're too carefree."

"What? I didn't forget. It's all right."

"Ha, ha, ha, ha. It would be terrible if you forgot. But you should be a little more careful."

"I think I'll speak to Itoko next ... because she's worrying ... about the exam and the explanation for this haircut."

"Your haircut is fine, but where will you be going? England? France?"

"I still don't know. The West. It'll probably be in the West."

"Ha, ha, ha, ha. You're easygoing. It'll be fine wherever you go."

"Although I don't want to go to the West, there's nothing I can do because of the procedures."

"Yes, it'd be good to go where you want."

"If it's China or Korea, I'll depart with this close-cropped haircut and wear these baggy Western clothes."

"The West is boisterous. It'll be good training for an ill-mannered lout like you."

"Ha, ha, ha, ha. If I go to the West, I think I'll be corrupted."

"Why?"

"Because the problem is I can't prepare two versions of myself if I go to the West."

"Two versions?"

"An ill-mannered underside and a pretty front. It's inconvenient."

"Isn't that so in Japan, too? The pressure of civilization is intense, so when the top part is not pretty, living in society is no longer possible."

"Instead, you become increasingly rude inside because the competition for survival becomes fierce."

"That's exactly right. The reason is to develop in opposing directions, front and back. People in the future will be punished by being torn limb from limb while still alive. It will be painful."

"Now, when people evolve, only the ones who attached a pig's testicles to the face of god will emerge and may feel at ease. It's terrible to embark on that sort of training."

"Would you prefer quitting? You may like being a man who wears your father's old Western-style clothes at home. Ha, ha, ha, ha."

"The English people, in particular, are unpleasant. They act like England is the model for everything and push through in their way."

"But hasn't the English gentleman gained a fairly good reputation recently?"

"The alliance between Japan and England doesn't deserve that much praise. Curious onlookers don't go to England, will only a flag be raised and Japan disappear?"

"Yes. In any country, when the front develops into only the front, the back should also reasonably develop into the back. It's not just a country, it may also be an individual."

"It will be awful if Japan becomes celebrated and Japan is not imitated in England."

"You will make Japan eminent. Ha, ha, ha, ha."

Hajime did not say Japan would or would not become eminent. When he extended both hands, a cotton print necktie floated out to the center of the collar. The knot was twisted to the side.

"Well, the lapel pin must not slip," he said, while his hands adjusted its position.

"I'll go have a little chat with Itoko," he said and rose to leave.

"Please wait. There's something I wish to discuss."

"What is it?"

He took the opportunity to sit partially cross-legged.

"The truth is because your situation was unsettled until now, I didn't say much."

"About a bride?"

"Well, if you go overseas, will you decide before you leave, marry, or bring her with you?"

"We can't go together because I don't have enough money."

"Going without her is fine. If you settle matters properly and leave her here, I'll take good care of her while you're gone"

"I was thinking along those lines, too."

"What do you think? I assume there is a beloved young lady."

"I intend to wed Kingo's sister. What do you think?"

"Fujio? Uh-huh."

"Is it no good?"

"What's no good?"

"It must be like that for the wife of a diplomat."

"In that case, the truth is while Kingo's father was alive, we discussed this a little. You probably did not know this."

"Her father said he'd give you the watch."

"That gold watch? Fujio was famous for turning it into a toy."

"Yes, that antique watch."

"Ha, ha, ha, ha. I guess the hands turn. Actually, the watch is about that important person. When Kingo's mother visited recently, I brought it up."

"Oh, what did she say?"

"The connection is very good. However, it's unfortunate because his status is undecided."

"By his status is undecided, she meant I haven't passed the diplomat exam."

"Uh-huh, that was probably it."

"You were a little surprised."

"No, the problem is what she says doesn't make much sense rather than being extremely eloquent. Matters to be elaborated on in detail are explained, but I don't understand the main point. In short, she's an impractical woman."

In a somewhat unpleasant mood, the father tapped his knee with the kiseru pipe and moved his eyes to the veranda. The Buddha's Smiles planted the furthest out front now boasted vivid crimson at the border between spring and summer.

"But because not knowing whether she refused or not is worrying."

"It is a concern. There have been a lot of burdens being placed on that woman. Like a cat purring for too long, I hate it."

"Ha, ha, ha, ha. That's fine. Did the negotiation advance?"

"She said it will be fine if you pass the diplomat exam."

"Well, the excuse is gone because I passed this time."

"But there still are problems. A lot of them."

As he spoke, his father placed the palms of his hands on his eyes and rubbed them. The whites of his eyes reddened.

"Despite passing, it's still no good?"

"It's not that it's no good. It seems Kingo said he will leave the house."

"That's stupid."

"If he leaves, the main carer for his elderly mother disappears. That's why whoever marries Fujio must be made the heir. In that case, there's no longer a reason for her to marry you or anyone else. That's what she said."

"That's a ridiculous thing to say. First, there's no reason for Kingo to leave home."

"His motivation to leave home and become a monk probably disappears. In other words, doesn't he say if he marries, caring for his mother will become a burden?"

"Kingo says things like that because he's having a nervous breakdown. That's a mistake. He says leaving is good. Then does his mother feel like sending him away and adopting someone else?"

"That would be a disaster and is a concern."

"In that case, wouldn't it be better if Fujio got married?"

"Better. It's better but thinking about the worst case, I can't stand feeling lonely and helpless, too."

"I don't understand any of it. It's like crawling into an inescapable maze."

"Actually ... I'm at a loss and don't understand the point."

Hajime's father furrowed his brow and stroked his head as he glanced up.

"When did that happen?"

"Recently. I think a week ago today."

"Ha, ha, ha, ha. News of my passing the exam was only two or three days too late, but Father, you saw her a week ago. Only my parent is many times more easygoing than I am."

"Ha, ha, ha. Because you don't understand the point."

"I do not understand the point, but I'll try to understand quickly."

"Why?"

"First, Kingo will be convinced to marry so he doesn't become a monk. Then he should come to candidly discuss whether he will or will not let Fujio marry me."

"You alone are enthusiastic."

"Yes, that's a lot for one person. Because I've done nothing since graduating, at the very least, I'll be bored if there's nothing to do."

"Yes, you should be the one to settle your matters. You should try it once."

"So if Kingo says he'll marry, he'd like you to give him Itoko."

"That's fine. It's no problem."

"For now, I'll ask her about her intentions."

"It's better not to ask."

"But she must be asked because it's different from the other matter."

"In that case, I'll try to ask. Should I invite her here?"

"Ha, ha, ha, ha. The questions must be asked before the father and older brother. In the future, I'll ask. If Itoko agrees, I'll speak with Kingo about her intentions."

"Okay, that's good."

Hajime abruptly stood up in his loose-fitting Western trousers. He left the ornaments of Hotei, the god of contentment, who lived with the bukkenshō, futari shizuka, and kensuoshō flowers, went down the hallway, and climbed up to the second floor.

When he reached the second floor, he saw his sister's obi sash tied in the shape of a taiko drum. The light blue ribbon in the third layer tilted to the side. One plump-looking cheek faced the entrance.

"Today, you're studying. Amazing. What is it?"

Unexpectedly, he sat beside the desk. Itoko gently laid down a book and placed her round, fleshy hand on top.

"Nothing."

"So you're reading an unimportant book. It's *Tenka no Itsumin*."

"Yes, it is."

"Can you remove your hand? It looks like you're picking up a playing card."

"I like it even if that's what I'm doing. Because it's life. Please, go over there."

"I'm going to be such a big pest. Itoko, father said to."

"What?"

"Although you like studying at the women's college, lately, all you read are romance novels. That's a problem."

"You're lying. When have I read those sorts of books?"

"I don't know, but Father told me that."

"It's a lie. Did Father say such a thing?"

"Did he? He said when someone comes, he sees you turn over

the book you're starting to read and hold it down with all your might as if you trapped a mouse under a wooden box. Do you think what Father said is a complete lie?"

"It's a lie. I say a lie, but you're despicable, too."

"Despicable is a grave insult. Am I a traitor to the one being watched? Ha, ha, ha, ha."

"You don't trust what people say. If so, shall I show you the evidence? Okay. Please, wait."

Just as Itoko hid the book she was pressing on under her sleeve, she took a copybook from the desk and hid it in the shadow of her kimono sash so her brother couldn't see it.

"You can't switch them."

"Be quiet and wait."

Itoko fooled her brother's eyes and frequently fiddled with the book hidden beneath her long sleeve. Eventually, she said, "Look," and held it up.

He could see a red seal in the center of the remaining one-inch square of the page she carefully pressed open with both hands.

"What am I looking for? What's that? ... Kōno."

"You see it."

"Did you borrow it?"

"Yes. It's not a romance novel."

"By not showing the genre, I can't say anything. Excuse me for asking, but Itoko, how old will you be this year?"

"Guess."

"I'm not guessing. I could find out right now by going to the ward office. I'm asking for reference. Your forte is you speak without subterfuge."

"I do speak without subterfuge. You say it as if it's a bad thing. I hate being forced to say that."

"Ha, ha, ha, ha. As expected from the disciple of a philosopher, I admire that you don't easily submit to authority. Well, I'll ask again, how old arc you?"

"You're teasing. Who asks that?"

"That's a problem. If I can speak politely, you'll get angry. Maybe twenty-one? Or two?"

"More or less."

"Isn't it obvious? My age isn't obvious. I'm also a little insecure. Anyway, you're no longer a teen."

"Isn't that none of your business? Asking someone's age. Why are you asking? What will you do with it?"

"Nothing in particular, but Itoko, I'm actually wondering whether you'll marry?"

The demeanor of the younger sister who was half joking and being teased instantly changed. When a hot stone is placed on ice, it becomes cold before your eyes. Itoko radiated all her spirit at once. Simultaneously, she secretly cast down cheerful eyes and began counting the tatami mesh.

"Well, getting married isn't a terrible idea."

"I don't know," said a hushed voice. Her eyes kept looking down.

"Not knowing is a problem. I won't go. You will."

"But I'm not saying I'll go."

"So you're not going?"

Itoko shook her head up and down.

"You're not going? Really?"

She didn't answer. This time, not even her head moved.

"If you're not going, I'll have to commit seppuku. How awful!"

The color of the downcast eyes could not be seen. His eyes grazed her full cheeks. The shadow of a smile had flown away.

"This is nothing to laugh about. I will commit seppuku. All right."

"Do as you wish."

Her face jerked up and on it, a broad smile.

"Cutting is good because it's serious. If it's something that will be, isn't living like this beneficial to both of us? It's probably boring for your only brother to cut open his gut."

"No one is saying this is boring."

"That's why I think you will help your brother and say yes."

"But you don't say the reason and said something so impossible out of the blue."

"If you ask the reason, I'll keep talking."

"It's fine. I'm not asking the reason because I'm not getting married."

"Itoko, your answers go round and round like pinwheel fireworks. It's derangement."

"What did you say?"

"What? Anything is fine because it's a legal term ... um ... Itoko, because we'll never get anywhere no matter how long this goes on, I'll tell you everything in confidence, but this is the truth."

"Even if I listen to the reason, you're saying you won't become a bride."

"Do you intend to ask with conditions? It's very cunning. In fact, I think I'll take Fujio as my bride."

"Still."

"Still? This time is the first time."

"However, Fujio said to please break it off because she does not wish to come here."

"You said that recently."

"Yes, isn't it best not to get what you don't want? But plenty of other women exist."

"That's quite reasonable. Your cowardly brother will not coax someone disliked. There's also a connection to your dignity. If it's disliked and determined to be disliked, I'll search elsewhere."

"That happening is probably best."

"But that is uncertain."

"So I'll make it certain," said the shy younger sister, turning her eyes to the desktop as if a bit surprised.

"Kingo's mother recently came here and talked privately downstairs. This was discussed at that time. She said it's not possible now, but if Hajime passes the diplomat exam and obtains a post, she told Father they could talk again."

"And then…"

"Isn't that good? I passed the diplomat exam."

"Huh, when?"

"When? I passed."

"Oh, it's true. I'm surprised."

"You're surprised your big brother passed? You're incredibly rude."

"But you could have mentioned it sooner. I was terribly worried."

"It is all thanks to you. I'm deeply moved to tears. I'm at a loss on what to do because I forgot what moves me to tears."

Unobstructed, the eyes of the brother and sister met. Then, they laughed together.

When the laughter stopped, the brother said, "So I shaved my head like this and intend to travel overseas soon. Father criticized me and said to marry before I leave and build character. He said if I somehow get a bride, she should be Fujio. He said if a diplomat's wife is not sophisticated like that, the future will be difficult."

"If you like her that much, please marry Fujio. Of course, women are better at looking at other women."

"Because there are mistakes in the opinion of the talented Itoko, I also intend to consider that and must make clear demands. If she doesn't like it, she should say so. Because I passed the diplomat exam, I won't say something shallow like I had a sudden change of mind."

Itoko released several gusts of gentle laughter through her nose.

"What can I say?"

"What? If you don't ask ... but if you ask, then you should ask Kingo because you can't be embarrassed."

"Ha, ha, ha, ha. If it's no good, rejection is the usual method in the world. Being rejected is not a disgrace."

"But ..."

"... No, I'll ask Kingo. Asking means to ask Kingo ... But there's a problem."

"What?"

"There's a primary problem. Yes, there is, Itoko."

"So, what is it? You won't ask?"

"There's nothing else, but Kingo will become a monk and cause an uproar."

"That's a stupid thing to say. That's unlucky."

"What? If you're determined to become a monk in today's world, good fortune should be celebrated."

"A harsh state of affairs ... becoming a monk may be a whim."

"I can't say. During days where agony was prevalent like lately."

"Well, please look at what your older brother brings."

"Fickleness?"

"Fickleness, whatever is good."

"Even with a haircut, the difference from a prisoner becomes a shaved head. If stationed at a legation overseas, I can only be considered crazy. As for other matters, because they concern my younger sister, I intend to ask about anything. I wanted to avoid becoming a monk. I've hated short haircuts and fried tofu since I was a boy."

"Well, Kingo said he won't become one either. He doesn't like them?"

"True. The logic is curious, but it should end with no one becoming one."

"I don't know how much of what you're saying is serious or a joke. Are you capable of working as a diplomat?"

"If I didn't talk like this, I wouldn't be fit to be a diplomat."

"People are ... so what will Kingo do? The truth."

"The truth is Kingo ... he said he will give the house and the assets to Fujio and leave."

"I wonder why."

"It seems he's ill and unable to care for his mother."

"How pitiful. A man like him probably doesn't need money or a house. Maybe, it's good for a man to turn out like that."

"If you agree as well, then the primary problem becomes difficult to solve."

"So Kingo has no use for a mountain of money. It's best to give it all to Fujio."

"You prefer generosity, unlike most women, although it's mostly people's belongings."

"I don't need money. It's only a nuisance."

"Certainly not enough for it to be a nuisance. Ha, ha, ha, ha. However, your intentions are admirable. You can become a nun."

"Oh, that's awful. Nuns. Monks. I hate them all."

"On that, we agree. But throwing away your fortune and leaving your home would be idiotic. The fortune is fine. It would be a problem after Kingo left because Fujio would be made the heir. His mother says nothing will be given to Hajime. That's reasonable. In other words, because of Kingo's selfishness, you'll have to break off the engagement."

"For you to receive Fujio, you will tell Kingo to stop."

"Well, that seems right from one perspective."

"Then aren't you being more selfish than Kingo?"

"This time, it's extremely logical. But isn't it trivial? Naturally, an inherited fortune will be thrown away."

"If it's bad, it's over."

"That's not a nervous breakdown."

"Is it any different than an illness?"

"It's not an illness."

"Itoko, today, you're more determined than usual."

"Kingo is that sort of man. Everyone is wrong for treating him like he's sick."

"However, he's not healthy. To propose that sort of action ..."

"You can throw away what is yours."

"That makes sense."

"You should throw away what you don't need."

"Don't need?"

"Kingo doesn't need it. It's not an unwillingness to admit defeat or his being spiteful."

"Itoko, you're Kingo's good friend and know him better than I, but I didn't think you believed that much in him."

"Whether he's a good friend or not, I'm telling you the truth. I'm saying what is right. If his mother and Fujio say that's not so, then they're wrong. I hate lying."

"I'm impressed. I'm impressed because of the confidence that came from truth despite not being a scholar. I wholeheartedly agree with you. Nonetheless, Itoko, we'll discuss this again. Whether Kingo leaves or doesn't leave home, whether he gives away or keeps his fortune, do you want to marry Kingo?"

"That is a whole other conversation. What I just said is only my honesty. I said that because I feel sorry for Kingo."

"Very well. I understand your reason. You're my younger sister, but I look up to you. Now, I'm asking you about another problem. Are you against it?"

"Against it ..." Itoko started to speak and quickly looked down. For a short time, she seemed to be staring at the pattern of her *han'eri* half-collar. Eventually, her blinking eyelashes intertwined, and a tear dropped onto her lap.

"Itoko, what's wrong? Today is a dramatic change in the weather and is only upsetting me."

Her unspeaking lips were still. As he watched, two tears dropped. Hajime snatched a crumpled handkerchief from a pocket of the suit passed down from his father.

"Here's a hanky."

While speaking, he pushed the handkerchief in front of her chest. The younger sister froze like a built-in doll. Still holding out the handkerchief in his right hand, Hajime bent his back a little and peeked at his sister's face from below.

"Are you against it, Itoko?"

She wiped her face but stayed silent.

"Then, you wish to go."

This time her head didn't move.

Hajime dropped the handkerchief onto his sister's lap and returned to his previous posture.

"You mustn't cry," he said, closely watching her face. After a short time, the two broke off the conversation.

Finally, Itoko raised the handkerchief. On her lap of lightly-dyed, coarse meisen silk, she elegantly flattened the handkerchief's wrinkles and folded it into a quarter fold. She pressed down on the corners and raised her eyes. They were like the ocean.

She said, "I'm not getting married."

"You're not getting married," Hajime repeated nearly void of meaning but immediately rallied.

"Don't joke. Didn't you just say you're not against it?"

"But Kingo will not marry."

"I have to ask him that, so I'll go ask him," said Hajime.

"Please don't."

"Why?"

"It doesn't matter. Please stop."

"Well, I can't do anything else."

"It's fine you can't do anything. Please stop. I'm not the least bit dissatisfied with how things are now. So it's all right. I can't marry."

"That's a problem. You've become steadfast in an instant. Itoko, I'm not speaking selfishly to say I will give you to Kingo so I can marry Fujio. As we talk now, I'm only thinking about you."

"I understand."

"If you understand, we can talk later. You probably don't think Kingo is bad.

"All right, it doesn't matter because I see that. Okay? Next, you'll say I shouldn't ask Kingo if he'll marry you or not. I can't make myself understand that logic, but that's fine.

"Since asking is no good, it's fine for you to marry if Kingo says he'll marry you.

"The money and the house don't matter. If you say you'll go to a poor Kingo, it will be to your credit. You are Itoko. Father and I will not object."

"If I marry, will things get worse for others?"

"Ha, ha, ha, ha. Suddenly, a major problem emerges. Why?"

"Never mind why. If things go bad, I'll end up being alienated. I think it's best to stay by Father's and your sides forever."

"Father and I ... Father and I would like to stay with you forever, too. But Itoko, that's a problem. Wouldn't you like to marry, become a better woman, and be adored by your husband?

"Perhaps more than that, practical problems are important. So there was a prior discussion. Despite what was said, I will make a promise."

"What?"

"I said asking Kingo is awful, and I don't know when Kingo would come for you."

"Waiting until who knows when. Do things like that happen? I'm sure about what's inside Kingo's heart."

"So I will promise and make Kingo say yes."

"But ..."

"What? I'll make him say it. I promise because it's my responsibility. What? It's okay? I will slowly grow this hair and must go to a foreign country. When I do, I won't be able to see you, so I'll act in gratitude for your usual kindness. Like my gratitude for the sleeveless fox vest. It'll be fine, okay?"

Itoko gave no answer.

Downstairs, their father was reciting a poem.

"Listen, he's at it again. Well, I'll see you later," said Hajime and went downstairs.

CHAPTER 17

Seizō and Asai came to a bridge. The road they traveled emerged from green barley and entered into green barley. A line stretched before and after. Rail tracks passed over the bottom of a deep valley. As the greenery concealed in the spring blew back, a high embankment surrounded splendid sheer cliffs, bent into an arc like a folding screen, and disappeared far in the distance. This crumbling bridge had iron rails elevated to ten feet and crossed from south to north. Leaning over the railing, they fully took in the green of two vast cliffs and reached the stone wall for the first time. They looked down the wall to the bottom to see a narrow brown road cross. The rails glinted faintly on the narrow road. The two men stopped when they reached the top of the decrepit bridge.

"What a beautiful sight."

"Yes, it's lovely."

The two stood leaning on the railing. They looked at barley endlessly extending in each field. Better than saying the day was warm, it was hot.

One end of a green straw mat laid out with no breaks became a modest forest with a drastic change in tone. Among the dark evergreens, green with bright yellow highlights turned to specks. Blowing around the sky, they appeared to be the young leaves of camphor trees.

"It's been a while since I've been out of the city. It feels good."

"Every once in a while, I enjoy a place like this. But I recently returned from the countryside, so it's not remarkable."

"That's probably true for you. Bringing you along to a place like this is a bit pitiful."

"It doesn't matter. At least, this is enjoyable. It's no good when people have free time to fool around. Is there a way to make a little more money?"

"Making money is not me, but it's a big part of you."

"Lately, studying the law has become boring. It's the same as literature. It's unacceptable without a silver watch."

Leaning his back against the handrail, Seizō took out and opened a silver cigarette case with its usual click. The mouthpieces of the Egyptian cigarettes were lined up perfectly in the box.

"Would you like one?"

"Oh, thanks. Those are excellent."

"They were a gift," said Seizō. After he took one, he threw it into some unseen place.

The smoke from the two men rose in unbroken streams into an empty sky.

"Do you always smoke these first-class cigarettes? Looks like you have spares, can I borrow a few?"

"Ha, ha, ha, ha. I'd like to be the borrower."

"Why do that? Lend me a little. I came to the countryside this time and brought some change, but money is a problem."

He sounded serious. The smoke from Seizō's cigarette blew to the side.

"How much do you need?"

"Thirty or twenty yen would be nice."

"That much?"

"Ten's all right. Even five yen."

Asai kept lowering the amount. Seizō held both elbows from behind with iron hand rests and slightly exposed a goat-skin shoe. Holding the cigarette in his mouth, he gazed at the ornament on the tip of his shoe through his eyeglasses. The shadows of the spring day lengthened and did not begrudge the light. Dust invisible to the eye accumulated on one side of the shiny, brightly polished skin. Seizō tapped the side of the shoe with his walking cane. Dust flew up an inch. Only the part tapped became mottled with black spots. Looking at them lined up, Asai's shoes were like heavy army boots and crudely made.

"I could do about ten yen. For how long?"

"I'll pay you back at the end of the month. If that's all right," said Asai, bringing his face closer. Seizō took the cigarette from his mouth. While holding it between his fingers, he swung it around once and a third of the ashes dropped onto his shoe.

Keeping his body still, when he turned only his head above his white collar to the side, he could see the face six inches down of the man resting his chin in his hands on the railing.

"The end of this month or any time is okay. In exchange, can I ask a little favor?"

"Sure, ask away."

Asai was quick to agree. At the same time, his chin left his hands as he stood. Their faces almost touched.

"The truth is it's about Inoue-sensei."

"Oh, what about him? After returning home, I haven't had time to visit him, so I can't. If you see the sensei, give him my regards ... and to his daughter."

"Aah, ha, ha, ha."

Asai's laughter boomed. He pushed his chest away from the railing. Saliva-like drool spilled down a long way.

"It has to do with his daughter."

"Are you finally getting married?"

"You're going too fast. When you say it like that ..."

He stopped speaking. He gazed at the barley field for a short time and then tossed the cigarette butt toward the field. His white cuffs rattled the pair of seven-jeweled cuff links. Just over an inch of metal brushed the air and fell to the foot of the bridge. The fallen smoke crawled back up from the ground.

"What a waste," said Asai.

"Will you listen to what I have to say?"

"I'm listening. And then ..."

"And then ... I still haven't said anything?

"The money doesn't matter, but I have a special request for you."

"So speak. For my friend from Kyōto, I'll do anything."

He sounded enthusiastic. Seizō lifted one elbow and turned toward Asai.

"I think you'll do it for me. The fact is I was waiting for you to return home."

"So I came back at a good time. Is there something you want to discuss? Marriage conditions? Lately, it has become inconvenient to take a wife who has no money."

"That's not it."

"However, setting the right conditions will benefit your future. That's right. I'll handle it."

"If you do that for me, that negotiation would be nice but ..."

"I intend to receive whatever is given. Everyone thinks that way."

"Like who?"

"Who? Us."

"That's a problem. I'll be given Inoue's daughter, but there's no firm promise."

"Really? No, that's suspicious," said Asai. Seizō thought in the pit of his stomach that he was a worthless man. Because of men like him, engagements are nonchalantly broken off.

"If you cool off starting at the head, talking is impossible," he said in his original mature tone.

"Ha, ha, ha, ha. I like it when you're serious. If you're that mature, it's a disadvantage. You need to thicken your skin a little more."

"Wait a bit longer because I'm still in training."

"Should I take you somewhere for some studying?"

"Please, I'd appreciate that."

"You say that, but a lot of studying is probably going on in the background."

"Not really."

"No, that's not so. Lately, I've noticed many embellishments. Especially, the origin of the earlier cigarette case is quite suspect. This cigarette smells odd."

Asai held the cigarette that burned down to his fingers up to his nose and sniffed a few times. Seizō thought this had become a nonsensical bad joke.

"Let's talk while we walk."

To cut off this bad joke, Seizō stepped out to the center of the footbridge. Asai's elbows left the railing. From the sky, the sun approached the barley pulling out the earth on both sides. The ears snuck out of the warm greenery and climbed up the banks. A layer of shimmering heat blanketed the fields and enveloped the two so powerfully they became dizzy.

"It's hot," said Asai following him. Seizō agreed about the heat, walked out shoulder to shoulder with him, and broached the serious matter.

"I mentioned this earlier, but when I went to see Inoue-sensei a few days ago, he brought up an unexpected marriage condition."

"I've been waiting," responded Asai. He seemed to want to say something, so Seizō rushed the conversation and quickened his pace.

"Because the sensei came with such intensity and I was not about to hurt the feelings of the man who has been a great help to me, I returned home and gave myself a few days to think carefully."

"Good, you were being prudent."

"Please, listen to the end, then I'll listen to your critique without interruption.

"As you know, the sensei has helped me a lot. If I didn't listen to what he said, I would be unprincipled."

"That would be terrible."

"Yes, it would. But unlike other matters, the problems of marriage are serious matters related to happiness over one's lifetime. And I can't submit to a command from the sensei despite my debt to him."

"No, you can't."

Seizō glanced at his companion's face whose serious expression surprised him. He continued, "If he made a firm promise to me or I took the great responsibility of forging a regrettable relationship with his daughter, the sensei wouldn't need to urge me. I intended to proceed from here and marry her. However, I am innocent concerning this point."

"Yes, you're innocent. No human being is as refined and innocent as you. I am proof."

Seizō glanced at Asai's face again. Asai didn't notice. The conversation continued.

"On the other hand, in his head, the sensei believes only I carry a responsibility and deduces everything from that."

"I see."

"Of course, I can't go back to the foundation and identify the error when his thoughts start from the wrong departure point."

"That's because you're too good to people. You'll lose if you're not tested a little more in this world."

"I also know loss, but given my character, I can't blatantly oppose people, especially, when my opponent is the sensei who has done so much for me."

"Yes, your adversary is the sensei who has been your benefactor."

"I told him that I'm currently writing my doctoral dissertation that makes raising this subject a problem."

"You're still writing the dissertation? That's admirable."

"No, it's not."

"What is so great? If a silver watch has no crown, it's useless."

"That's fine, but in this situation, although I'm grateful to him for his great kindness, right now, I want to decline. However, my character toward the sensei is wretched. My reason for asking this favor of you is I can't speak severely. Will you accept?"

"I see, it's nothing. I will meet with the sensei and have a good talk."

Asai readily accepted as if he were going to gulp down green tea over rice. Seizō, as ordered, took a few steps forward during a break, and then he spoke.

"Instead, I think about caring for the sensei for life. Because I don't intend to keep grumbling about this forever, the truth is the sensei's financial situation will be a greater challenge than in the past. It's pitiful. This discussion is not the simple problem of marriage. That is expedient. It appears he wants my support. That I will do. I intend to devote myself to the sensei. Therefore, I don't possess a trace of that shallow idea that I'll be devoted if I marry, and I won't be devoted if I don't marry. I can't deny he helped me. Until I repay the debt, the obligation will not disappear."

"You're a worthy man. The sensei will be happy to hear that."

"Please, tell me as if my intentions will be faithfully carried out because misunderstandings are possible or may later cause problems."

"All right. Without hurting anyone's feelings, I'll do as you say. In exchange, you'll lend me ten yen."

"I'll lend you the money," said Seizō, smiling as he answered.

A drill is a tool for drilling holes. A rope is a means to bind objects. Asai is an instrument for proposing the breaking off of an engagement. There is no plan to pass through a pine plank without a drill. Without rope, he's not prepared to wind a turban shell. From the start, Asai will head to this negotiation with the feeling of going into a bath. Seizō is a genius. He understands the law of effectively using a tool.

When a simple breaking off of an engagement is proposed, the special talent is to tidy up after the proposal to call the marriage off. The raking up of fallen leaves is not limited to the person who rakes the garden. Asai is a brash man who dares to rake fallen leaves on a visit to the Imperial Palace. He's also a courageous man who does not understand the technique of floating and dives into the water. When not diving, a hero does not think the floating technique is needed. It's simply accepted. With the feeling of wanting to try, anything is accepted. That's it. Good and evil. Right and wrong. Lightness and heaviness. If he sets the effects aside and mulls over the issues, Asai is a virtuous man free of ulterior motives.

Seizō was not unaware of this. He asked after he knew because simply proposing the breakup was fine. If they complain, he intends to flee. Even if unable to escape, he is prepared for them to cope. Seizō had plans to go on an excursion to Ōmori tomorrow with Fujio.

Even if most of this matter is exposed after he returns from Ōmori, he probably won't be able to break off the relationship with Fujio. Therefore, he will provide material assistance as promised to Inoue.

Seizō, who was making up his mind, believed he unloaded one burden onto Asai who cheerfully accepted the request.

"When the sun shines, the scent of barley seems to waft before the nose."

Finally, Seizō's topic was naturally touched on.

"There's an aroma? I smell nothing," said Asai, his bulbous nose sniffing.

He asked, "Do you occasionally go to that Hamlet's house?"

"Do you mean Kōno Kingo's home? I still go. I'll go today and in the future," Seizō replied nonchalantly.

"Didn't he recently go to Kyōto? Is he back? I think I smell the faint scent of barley. That sort of man is tiresome. Does he always look glum?"

"I think so."

"It's good when that sort dies young. He's rich, right?"

"He seems to be."

"What happened to his relative? Once in a while, I saw him at school."

"Hajime?"

"Yes, I'm considering visiting him in the next few days."

Seizō suddenly stopped.

"Why?"

"To ask him something. It's bad if you don't exercise as much as possible."

"But Hajime has the problem of not having passed the diplomat exam. There's no point in asking him."

"It doesn't matter. I'm going to talk with him."

Seizō lowered his gaze to the ground and, without a word, moved closer fifteen feet or so.

"When will you visit the sensei?"

"I'll go tonight or tomorrow morning."

"All right."

The barley field turns and becomes a flowing hill of the shadows of cedar trees. The two went down hills in front and behind. There was no time to chat. When they passed a scraggly cedar hedge running alongside the shoulder, Seizō said, "If you see Hajime, please don't mention the matter concerning Inoue-sensei."

"Not one word."

"No, really."

"Ha, ha, ha, ha. You're quite embarrassed. Does it matter?"

"It's a little problem, but please don't say a word."

"All right. I won't say anything."

Seizō thought he was too unreliable and considered withdrawing half of what he requested."

Seizō left Asai at the four-corner intersection and carried his uneasy heart to Kōno's estate. About fifteen minutes after Seizō entered Fujio's room, Hajime's figure stood at the door to Kingo's study.

"Hey."

Kingo deliberately sat back down on the same chair and sketched a geometric pattern as before. He concentrated on drawing three fish scales inside a circle.

When summoned with "Hey," he raised his head. More than out of surprise, enthusiasm, fear, or arrogance, by far, he was looking up. Thus, it was philosophical.

"Oh, it's you."

Hajime strode over to a corner of the table but furrowed his thick eyebrows into a frown.

"The air in here is bad. It's poisonous. I'll open the window a little," he said, released the vertical bolt, possibly grabbed the center knob, and swung, like sweeping a broom over the floor, to open a horizontal space below the front French window. The green of the lawn in the yard and the expansive spring blew into the room.

"This will cheer up this room. It feels good now. The lawn has a nice color."

Hajime returned to the table and sat for the first time on the chair where the mystery woman sat earlier.

"What are you doing?"

"Huh?"

Kingo stopped moving the pencil.

"What do you think? It's rather good."

He slid the paper filled with figures on the table to Hajime.

"What is this? You've drawn quite a lot."

"I've been drawing for more than an hour."

"If I hadn't dropped by, you'd probably continue drawing until evening. Wasting time."

Kingo said nothing.

"Is this related in some way to philosophy?"

"It would be nice if it were."

"You could say it's a philosophical symbol of the world. It lines things up well like in someone's head. Do you have any interest in writing a thesis perhaps called *A Cloth Printer in a Dye Shop and a Philosopher*?"

Kingo did not speak again.

"I don't know why, but you're always procrastinating. You're forever indecisive."

"Today, I'm especially indecisive."

"It's the weather's fault. Ha, ha, ha, ha."

"Rather than blaming the weather, it's the fault of being alive."

"Maybe. Not much seems to be boiling over. We're both pushing thirty. I quietly sob …"

"Forever in the stewpot of this world of the living, I am indecisive."

Kingo reached this point and started laughing.

"Kingo, today, I've come to inform and to negotiate a little."

"You went to some trouble to come here."

"Soon I'll be going to the West."

"To the West …"

"Yes, I'm going to Europe."

"It's good you're going just don't be indecisive like my father."

"What can I say? But it will probably be all right if I cross the Indian Ocean."

Kingo laughed heartily.

"Actually, I passed the diplomat exam this last time, so I cut my hair. Of course, I'll have to leave at the latest opportunity. I'm very busy with mundane matters. I must settle my affairs properly or mostly properly."

"Well, congratulations," said Kingo, scrutinizing his companion's hair across the table. However, he didn't offer a particular critique or ask any questions. Hajime didn't bother to move forward or explain. Thus, his haircut was forgotten.

"That ends the report, Kingo."

"Have you seen my mother?" asked Kingo.

"Not yet. Today, I entered this entryway and did not pass through the traditional room."

Of course. Hajime was wearing shoes. Kingo leaned against the back of his chair. The head of this optimist and a cotton collar with a calico pattern … the collar decoration usually stood out in relief to the middle of the collar. Then he gazed at the suit inherited from his father.

"What are you looking at?"

"Nothing," Kingo said, still looking. "Did you come to speak with my mother?"

This time, Hajime stared without saying no or anything else and started to rise from the chair.

"Breaking off the engagement is best."

From the other side of the table, the phrase was articulated.

The man with long hair abruptly left his chair. As his right hand brushed over his forehead, his left hand pressed on the shoulder of the chair. He looked at the portrait of his late father.

"If I speak to Mother, please speak to that portrait."

The man wearing the suit inherited from his father fixed his round eyes, rose to the center of the room, and observed the owner of hair that looked lacquered. Next, his eyes stared at the portrait of the deceased man on the wall. Finally, he compared the owner of the lacquered hair to the dead man's portrait. When he compared them, the towering man moved his thin shoulder and hovering over Hajime's head said, "My father is dead. That is more certain than my living mother."

With these words, the face of the man resting on the chair naturally turned to the portrait again. For a short time after turning, he did not move. Lively eyes looked down from above.

For a moment, the man resting in the chair said, "Uncle also did a pitiful thing."

The standing man answered.

"Those eyes are alive. They're still alive."

He stopped talking and began pacing the room.

"Let's go out to the garden. You mustn't be melancholy."

Hajime left the chair, went around to Kingo's side to take or not take his hand, passed through the open French windows, and took two steps down to the lawn.

When his foot touched the soft ground, Hajime asked, "What's wrong?"

The lawn stretched over sixty feet to the south, ending at an evergreen hedge. The width was less than half that length. The interior obstructed by dense shrubbery was separated from the nearly 150-square-foot lake. Fujio's desk was placed in a new parlor in the pavilion.

The two leisurely strolled to the end of the grass. They detoured several dozen feet on the way back to the study into the shadow of the shrubbery. Both were silent. By chance, their paces matched. At several paving stones where the shrubbery opened in the center, just as they came to the corner that coaxed people to the lake, a boisterous laugh like a pheasant's crowing blared. Their feet stopped in unison as if agreed upon. Their eyes scanned in the same direction at the same time.

A long, thin empty strip of land extended four feet to the lake's edge. On the opposite side of the lake that dropped straight to the water, a long branch extending from the side of an Asagi cherry blossom tree shaded an area of the building. Seizō and Fujio stood under the eaves looking in their direction and laughing.

They were a picture of two living beings framed on the right and left by a cluster of springtime trees, from above by the sakura branches, and from below by the floating flowers of the lotus with roots in warm water creeping up. The men's eyes converged on the couple on the other side of the water for the border to gather the essence of the natural scenery; to properly shape the border to avoid spoiling the charm and create irregularity so the eyes are not confused; to create the proper spacing for the stepping stones, the water, and the edges; and to properly position them so that the height is not too high or too low; and finally, to blow out in short breaths illusions that suddenly appear. At the same time, the eyes of the two across the water fell on the two on this side. The four people whose gazes met froze each other in place. The moment was perilous. The one who was first to jump to the instant of realization was the winner.

The woman subtly pulled one white tabi sock behind her. From between her obi sash that faded with spring in the brilliance of an old-fashioned pattern dyed red ocher, she jerked out a smooth serpentine object as if to tear it. She gripped the swollen head of a thin snake in her palm and swung a long and slender gold color in the air. A deep crimson light burst from the tail. In the next moment, a brilliant gold chain hung like a bolt of lightning across Seizō's chest.

"Ha, ha, ha, ha. This looks best on you."

Fujio's shrill voice hit the sluggish water and rebounded to the two men's sharp ears.

"Fuji ..."

Kingo pushed forward nearly poking Hajime's side.

The picture of the lively couple disappeared from Hajime's eyes. Kingo's face leaned over from behind as if to cover up and landed near his best friend's ear.

"Be quiet ..." he said softly, pulling the man shrouded in smoke into the shadow of the shrubbery.

Kingo put his hand on Hajime's shoulder to push him up the stone steps and returned to the study. He didn't speak and shut tight the left and right sides of the French window that resembled a door.

He shut the vertical bolt with flair. Next, he went to the door at the entryway. When he inserted and turned the key, the lock easily opened.

"What are you doing?"

"I'm shutting up the room to keep people out."

"Why?"

"Any reason will do."

"What has happened? Your complexion looks terrible."

"What? I'm fine. Please sit," he said and dragged the frontmost chair closer to the desk. Hajime obeyed the order like a child. After Kingo calmed his companion, he quietly sat on his usual armchair. His body turned to the desk.

He faced the wall and called out, "Hajime." Only his head turned and said, "It's over between you and Fujio."

His calm tone somehow carried a tepid warmth. To prepare all the branches to return to green, the pulse of spring passing unseen through the desolation was Kingo's compassion.

"I see."

With arms folded, that was all Hajime said. Later, he became somber and said, "Itoko said so, too."

"Your little sister understands better than you. Fujio is no good. She has leaped away."

The doorknob clattered as it was twisted. The door did not open. Taps came from outside the door. Hajime swung around. Kingo didn't even move his eyes.

He said coldly, "Leave me."

Tittering laughter got louder like a mouth was pressed against the door. The sounds of footsteps retreated toward the traditional room. The men exchanged glances.

"It was Fujio," said Kingo.

"Really?" answered Hajime again.

Then it became quiet. The clock on the desk ticked.

"The gold watch is also gone."

"Yes, it seems so."

While Kingo's head was still turned to the wall, and Hajime's arms stayed folded, the clock ticked. The party in the traditional room laughed one time.

"Hajime," said Kingo, turning his head again. "Fujio dislikes you. It's best to say nothing."

"Yes, I'll keep my mouth shut."

"Fujio does not understand a personality like yours. She's a shallow, impetuous woman. She will marry Seizō."

"I had my hair cut like this."

Hajime took his thick-jointed hand off his chest and tapped the top of his shaved head.

Kingo may or may not have brought a wave of laughter to the corners of his eyes and solemnly nodded. Then he said, "If you could do that, you probably don't need Fujio."

"Uh-huh," Hajime feebly agreed.

"And my mind is at peace," said Kingo. He raised his resting leg and placed it on the knee of the other. Hajime lit a cigarette. From inside the blown smoke, he spoke as if beginning a monologue.

"From here on ..."

"From here on ... Life will begin for me, too."

Kingo's answer also sounded like a monologue.

"You're beginning, too? What will you do next?" Hajime pushed through the cigarette smoke, bringing his healthy face closer.

"From now on, I'm turning over a new leaf starting from essentially nothing."

With his fingers holding the Shikishima cigarette, Hajime came over but forgot what he was about to say and fell dumbstruck. Again he asked as if he doubted his brain, "What do you mean by turn over a new leaf and start from essentially nothing?"

A serene Kingo calmly answered in his usual tone, "I gave everything, this house and all the assets to Fujio."

"What? You gave her everything? When?"

"A short time ago. When I was drawing all those figures."

"That is ..."

"When I was drawing the three scales in the circle. That pattern is the best one."

"You gave it away so easily."

"What do I need? The more there is, the more trouble there is."

"Did your mother agree?"

"She did not."

"She didn't agree. That troubled her."

"Not doing it would mean trouble."

"Is she worried about you acting rashly?"

"My mother is a fake. All of you have been fooled. She's not my mother. She's a mystery. A special product of a civilization in a stagnant age."

"That's a little too much …"

"You probably think I'm warped because she's not my birth mother. It's fine if you do."

"But ..."

"Don't you trust me?"

"Of course, I trust you."

"I'm taller than my mother. Wiser. I understand the reason. And I'm more virtuous than she."

Hajime said nothing. Kingo continued.

"To say 'Please, don't leave your mother's house' has the same meaning as saying 'Please leave.' To say 'Take the assets' has the same meaning as saying 'Give it to me.' To say 'I want to be taken care of ' has the same meaning as saying 'Being helped is awful.'

"Therefore, from the outside, it looks like I'm opposing my mother, but the truth is, I'm following her wishes.

"Look, after I leave home, my mother will say I was awful to leave, and the world will believe that. I will be the only sacrifice and planned this for the sake of my mother and sister."

Hajime sprang from his chair, went to a corner of the desk, propped one elbow on top, and peeked at Kingo's face as if trying to cover it.

He said, "You're insane."

"I agree in my head about the madness. Until now, it's been in the shadows. I was constantly called crazy and stupid."

This time, tears trickled from Hajime's big, round eyes and fell onto the Leopardi on the desk.

"Why didn't you say something? Wouldn't it have been better to send her away?"

"Send her away? Her character would only degrade."

"Naturally, even if I don't send her away, there's no way I could leave."

"If I don't leave, only my character will degrade."

"Why did you give her all the property?"

"I don't need it."

"You should have discussed this with me."

"There was no need to discuss giving away what is not needed."

"Uh-huh," said Hajime.

"For money I don't need, there's no merit in causing degradation in my mother and sister whom I am obligated to."

"You finally want to leave home."

"I will go. If I stay, both will degrade."

"Where will you go?"

"I don't know."

For no reason, Hajime picked up the Leopardi on the desk and stood up the leatherbound book. While lightly tapping a square of zelkova wood attached at an incline, he engaged in light meditation. Eventually, he said, "Will you come to my house?"

"There's no point in going to your house."

"Is it bad?"

"It's not bad, but there's no point."

Hajime stared at Kingo.

"Kingo, I've come here with a request. Perhaps for my sake and my father's, but please come for Itoko's sake."

"For Itoko?"

"Itoko is your dear friend. Your mother and Fujio misunderstand you. Even if I misjudge you, even if you are persecuted throughout Japan, only Itoko is steadfast. She doesn't have an education or wisdom but explains your value well. She thoroughly understands your heart. Itoko is my younger sister but is a superior woman. She's a precious woman. Itoko is not a woman who worries about degradation even without money.

"Kingo, please marry Itoko. It's all right if you leave home.

Going to the mountains would be good. Wherever you go, it doesn't matter, even if you become a vagrant. Because everything will be fine, please go and take Itoko with you.

"I am responsible and made a promise to her. If I don't listen to what you're saying, I couldn't face my sister. I'd have to kill my only sister. Itoko is a precious and honest woman. I'm telling the truth. I'd do anything for you. It's a waste to kill."

Hajime shook Kingo's bony shoulders on the chair.

CHAPTER 18

Sayoko received a bag of confections from Granny. When she placed them on an Izumo pottery plate, the pattern of a blue Chinese phoenix in the center was hidden by Japanese-style cookies. Most of the yellow edge remained. She carried the plate from the traditional Japanese sitting room to the parlor. The two bamboo chopsticks were set side by side to not fall off.

Asai was in the parlor as the sensei's companion mulling over the old joys of Kyōto. It was morning. Shadows were creeping toward the veranda.

He asked her, "You are quite familiar with Tōkyo?"

She placed the candy dish between the host and his guest and gently pulled back her shoulders.

"Yes," she answered in a quiet voice and stood.

The sensei filled the void.

"She grew up in Tōkyo."

"Oh, she has gotten big," he said, quickly moving to another matter.

Sayoko lowered her sad, smiling face and refrained from speaking this time. Asai's tactless face gazed at Sayoko. While mulling over the ruin of her marriage, he looked unconcerned. Asai's opinion of her marriage problem was uncomplicated like that of a street-corner fortuneteller. He showed little compassion for the woman's future and lifetime happiness. Because he was asked, he knew it would be fine to carry out the request. He recognized that the matter is chiefly in the realm of legal scholars, that legal scholarship is inherently practical, and that realism is the ultimate approach.

Asai was a man of little imagination and never once thought his lack of imagination was a flaw. He believed the power of imagination was completely different from the action of intelligence. He believed the action of intelligence was always obstructed by the power of imagination. No professor in a law classroom has ever made the case that proper handling waits for imaginative power, does not return to the entirety of human nature, and comes to life outside of the pure actions of wisdom and discernment.

Thus, Asai knew nothing. He thought the matter would end with a simple refusal. The unthinkable problem in Asai's dreams became could the fate of the lonely Sayoko change with a few words from a sage?

As Asai blankly gazed at Sayoko, Kodō-sensei stifled several strange coughs. Sayoko turned to her father, who looked uncertain.

"Have you taken your medicine?"

"Yes, I've taken my morning dose."

"Are you cold?"

"No, I'm not, well, maybe a little."

The sensei placed three fingers of his left hand on his right wrist. Sayoko forgot Asai was there and only stared at the sensei's face as he measured his pulse. The sensei's bearded face grew thinner each day.

Concerned, she asked, "How is it?"

"It seems a little fast. Of course, the fever isn't gone."

His forehead wrinkled a little. Each time the sensei measured his temperature, he looked uncomfortable, as if he were irritated, and Sayoko saddened. There is gratitude for a single cedar tree available as shelter from evening showers in the middle of a field, but the treetops are searched for a lightning flash. More than saying it's scary, it's pitiful for an older person. If irritability emerges from inadequate care, his mood is indulged. If a disease can't be overcome with spirit, filial devotion will never be exhausted.

When he went around to the shadows to ask about a fleeting cold and the recent cough he did not believe was serious, a doctor said his condition would not improve. He said if the fever does not go away after a few days, this illness is not mild and is cause for concern. You will worry if you know. If not spoken, it passes through by spirit. Also, a neurosis will develop. If this condition advances, after a year, nerves become raw and exposed. Even if touched by the air, he may jump up. Last evening, Sayoko could not meet his eyes.

"Maybe, you should put on your haori coat."

Kodō-sensei did not answer. Sayoko said, "Where is the thermometer? We'll take your temperature."

She went to the sitting room.

"Did something happen?" casually asked Asai.

"No, just a little cold."

"Oh, okay. Most of the young leaves have come out."

He showed no compassion or concern over the sensei's illness. The sensei missed the mark in thinking Asai would listen to details about the cause, progress, and state of his illness.

He turned toward the adjacent room and in a voice louder than usual, "Hey, did you find it? What happened to it?" Then he coughed twice.

"I'm coming," she quietly answered. She appeared without a thermometer. The sensei turned to Asai.

"Oh, really?" His answer lacked energy.

Asai became bored and thought about quickly wrapping up this business and going home.

He said, in a haphazard order, "Sensei, Seizō is absolutely no good and has been completely Westernized. He has no desire to marry your daughter."

Kodō-sensei's sunken eyes sharpened instantly. Eventually, the sharpness spread to the surface, and resentment spread over his face.

"It's better to break off the engagement."

In the adjoining room, Sayoko searched for the misplaced thermometer and gently stopped her hand pulling out the second drawer of the oblong brazier at about four inches.

The sensei's disgusted face softened slightly. The unimaginative Asai did not expect that result at all.

"Lately, Seizō became extremely Westernized. Going to him would harm your daughter."

No longer able to restrain his disgusted face, he said, "It seems you came here to bad mouth Seizō."

"Ha, ha, ha, ha. Sensei, that's true."

Asai laughed loudly at a strange place.

"That is unneeded meddling and superficial," Sensei said pointedly in rejection. His voice had taken on a different tone. For the first time, Asai was surprised. Both were silent for a short time.

"Hey, have you found it? What is taking you so long?"

He couldn't hear the reply from the other room. During the silence, a shadow was cast on the shōji door pushed slightly to the side. A narrow plain wood tube quietly came from beyond the wooden panel. The sensei picked it up from the tatami, popped it open, and removed a tube. He held the thermometer over his head and shook it vigorously a few times.

"What is this about? Making these uncalled-for remarks?" he asked while gazing at the markings. Half of the sensei's mind was on the thermometer. Meanwhile, Asai's energy was restored.

"Actually, I was asked."

"Asked? Who asked you?"

"Seizō did."

"Seizō?"

The sensei forgot to hold the thermometer under his armpit. He was confused.

"Because he's the man who says those things, I couldn't refuse to go to the sensei's home, so he asked me."

"Uh-huh. Tell me more."

"Because he had to give you an answer in a few days, I came as his representative."

"So what's the reason for the rejection? Is it a good idea to tell you the details?"

Sayoko blew her nose in the shadow of the sliding screen door.

It sounded reserved, but the person on the other side of one layer was detected. The person close to the lintel who heard seemed to be standing at the sliding door. She probably had no idea what Asai felt about what he heard.

"Here's his reason. He said he can't marry because he must become a doctor."

"He said the doctorate is more important than Sayoko."

"That may not be the reason, but not becoming a doctor would be a great disadvantage in the future."

"All right I understand. Is that the entire reason?"

"He also said no definite contract exists."

"A contract means a legally binding contract. It's an exchange of written documents."

"He said there is no written proof. Instead, in gratitude for the many years of assistance, he wants to provide material help."

"Does that mean he'll give money every month?"

"Yes."

"Hey, Sayoko, come here. Sayoko ... Sayoko," his voice gradually got louder. No answer came.

Sayoko did not move but stayed crouched in the shadow of the sliding screen door. The sensei could only turn toward Asai.

"Are you married?"

"No. I'd like to marry but a job is important."

"If you don't have a wife, you should listen for reference.

"A man's daughter is not a toy. Could you bring yourself to exchange a doctorate for Sayoko? You should think about it. Even the daughter of a poor man is a living being. I will say she is my precious daughter. Please ask Seizō if he wants to become a doctor even if someone is killed. From now on, please say it that way. Inoue Kodō is a man who respects a moral contract more than a legal one.

"Will he give me money each month? Who asked him to give me anything? The man who helped Seizō was kind because he came in tears to beg and was pitiful, so I acted out of kindness. Offering any material help is rude.

"Sayoko, I'm going out for a little while for some errands. Hey, are you here?"

Sayoko was sobbing in the shadow of the sliding screen door. The sensei coughed many times. Asai panicked.

I'm confused. I didn't think the sensei could get so angry. He had no reason to get this angry again. I'm stating this clearly. To stand in the world and be a success, a doctorate is vital in anyone's eyes. I couldn't accept the neglect of my social obligations by saying, Please end this vague contract. It may be a problem to accept help with nothing to give in return. However, had I brought material compensation for what had been given, he would have been delighted. Then, my sense of duty would have been satisfied. Unexpectedly, that sparked his anger.

Now, Asai was stunned.

"Sensei, it's no use getting so angry. If it's so troubling, you should meet with Seizō and discuss this with him."

This was a serious issue.

The sensei paused, then calmly said, "You think the decision to marry is a simple matter, but that's not so."

He sounded regretful.

He didn't understand what the sensei meant, but Asai's spirit was moved slightly by the sensei's appearance. However, Asai believed it was fine to get engaged for convenience and break off an engagement for convenience but had no particular reply.

"Because you don't understand a woman's heart, you came as a messenger."

Of course, Asai said nothing.

"You don't understand human emotion. That's probably why you speak nonchalantly about that sort of thing. You probably think if Seizō broke off, Sayoko could wonder where to go starting tomorrow. Is there a woman who, after suddenly being rejected for no special reason by the man she was convinced for the past five years would be her husband, could immediately move on untroubled to be a bride in another family?

"There may be, but Sayoko is not that shallow a woman. She was not raised to be frivolous.

"You are the agent of an impulsive break-up and will mistakenly ruin Sayoko's life. Does that feel good?"

The sensei's sunken eyes boiled. He coughed frequently. Asai was impressed if that were the truth. In the end, he felt wretched.

"Uh, please wait, Sensei. I'll talk with Seizō one more time. I came here to make that simple request but knew none of the details."

"No, I'm fine with no more talking. I wouldn't want to force him if he finds it dreadful. However, it would be acceptable for him to come and explain his reasons."

"But your daughter thinks so ..."

"Seizō should understand Sayoko's thoughts," said the sensei firmly, as if his open hand slapped his cheek.

"Because that may be a problem for Seizō, too, one more time ..."

"Please, tell Seizō that Inoue Kodō is not a despicable man who would bow his head to a man who said his beloved daughter was no good. Hey, Sayoko, are you out there?"

On the other side of the sliding screen door, what looked like a sleeve made a sound near the bottom edge of the thick paper covering the door.

"That response may not be an obstacle."

No answer came. Her voice rose from her amazed face buried in her sleeve.

"Sensei, I'll talk to Seizō once more."

"Not talking is fine, too. Please tell him to come here and decline."

"Anyhow ... I'll tell him that."

Asai finally stood. The sensei saw him off at the entryway. When he bowed his head, the sensei said, "Having a daughter is a burden."

Asai stepped out front and sighed. He had never felt like this before. He left the side street and passed by the standing paper lantern of a soba noodle shop on the right. When he reached the place where a train came to a sudden stop, he hopped on.

A little over an hour later, Asai, who boarded the train on a whim, unexpectedly appeared at the gate to the Munechika home. Next, two rickshaws left, one after the other. One headed to Seizō's boarding house. The other left for Kodō-sensei's house. About fifty minutes later at the base of the pine tree at the entryway, the rickshaw puller raised the shaft of a rickshaw with a lowered black canopy, pointed to Kingo's estate, and ran off. This novel must successively explain the missions of these three rickshaw cabs.

When the sounds of the wheels of Hajime's rickshaw went silent in front of Seizō's boarding house, Seizō had just finished lunch. The tray was out. He left untouched the wooden container of cooked rice. The hero moved his seat to the front of the desk and was thinking as he watched the thick smoke he blew from his mouth.

Today, I promised to take Fujio to Ōmori. I have to go because it's a promise. However, I have qualms about having to go. I'm anxious. If no promise existed, I'd probably be a little more at peace. I might have wanted to have another bowl of rice. Of course, I tossed dice from the beginning. The faces showed one and six.

I must cross the Rubicon. However, Julius Caesar, who crossed that river with ease, was a hero. After this decisive moment, an ordinary person thinks this over again. Each time he reconsidered, Seizō regretted not ending it definitively.

When he stepped one foot onto the boat, when the boatman said, "We're off," and manipulated the pole, he wanted to say, "Please wait."

Anyone would think it would be nice to be towed from the shore. If he just boarded, he still had a chance to return to shore. While a promise is left unfulfilled, similar to a boat at the shore, the situation is not desperate with no way out.

This is a story from a novel by George Meredith. A man and a woman conspired to meet at a train station. If during the execution of the plan, the steam whistle blew, the honor of the two people would end there. At the moment in time the fates of the two people closed in, the woman had not come to the station. The man put his face tired of waiting in a box-shaped carriage and went home to an empty house. Later when asked, some friend said he detained the woman and deliberately got the promised time wrong.

If Seizō, who promised Fujio, could break the promise like this, he thought he might be happy as he gazed at the cigarette smoke. Also, Asai's response still hadn't come.

If there is agreement, whichever way he goes is fortunate. If a rejection is heard, the plan should be to push in advance to the point of no return, and then, after turning back, break through any barrier by taking a flexible approach. Therefore, it ends if he goes to Ōmori a moment sooner. Of course, it's not necessary to wait for the 'no.' It is 'no,' but he's anxious as the moment to act approaches. The plan crafted in his head is destroyed by human emotions. He pulls back because imaginative power is not employed. Seizō, being a poet, is rich in imaginative power.

Because I'm rich in imagination, I'm unable to bring myself to go in person and decline. I get two alternatives when I look at the sensei's face and Sayoko's face, the room decor, and the living circumstances, extend what I see into the future, and stare at what I imagine in the mirror of imagination.

When I weave myself inside the mirror, springtime, abundance, and total happiness exist. When my image is erased from the mirror's surface, darkness comes and sunset falls. Everything becomes tragic.

The negotiation over detaching only my spirit from the spirit of this group is like stealing firewood from the small wood-burning stove while imagining smoke will rise. It is unbearable. A man shuts his eyes and downs a bitter drink.

The eyes of the imagination cannot be opened when this tangled edge is cut into two equal parts. Therefore, Seizō asked Asai whose eyes were shut. After asking, it ends if the imagination is killed. He was uncertain but resolved.

However, even killing one dog is not an easy task. Painting black only over inconvenient places and completely erasing the innate actions of the heart are desperate measures tested on tens of millions of people since ancient times and is a lowly plan equally failed by tens of millions of people. A person's heart is different from a manuscript. Imaginative power was restored from the evening Seizō made this decision.

Gaunt cheeks are drawn. Sorrowful eyes are drawn. Disheveled hair is drawn. Breaths like a bug's are drawn. Then the imagination switches.

Blood is drawn. A frightful night, wind, and rain are drawn. A cold light is drawn. A white paper lantern is drawn.

The horrifying imagination stops.

When his imagination stopped, he instantly remembered the promise. He remembered the unpleasant effects arising from carrying out the promise. The effects create turbulent twists and turns in imaginative power.

The conscience can be pawned. Paying off the debt of life is impossible. Benefits are heaped on benefits. The back becomes heavy, hurts, and bends. Getting up from sleep is hard. Society talks about you behind your back.

He gazed dumbstruck at the cigarette smoke. Every second, the imperial gift of a watch reminds him to fulfill the promise. This object was like having entrusted a powerless body to a sled. If he folded his arms and did nothing, he would naturally slide into the abyss of the promise. Nothing slides as accurately as a sled of *time*.

"Should I go after all? As long as it's not a liaison in the shadows, there should be no problem. If I'm cautious, it can be undone. What I will do about Sayoko depends on Asai's response."

When the cigarette smoke densely lingered and obscured future shadows, Hajime's sturdy figure appeared in the real world and drove off all imagination.

Somehow, in no time, had the maid escorted him in unnoticed? Hajime entered out of nowhere.

"There's too much confusion," he said as he placed the tray finished with reddish-brown lacquer in the hallway. He took out the round, black rice container and set it beside the earthenware teapot.

"What's going on?" the guest asked as he sat in the middle of the room.

"Excuse my rudeness," said the host, turning his bowing body around. Fortunately, the maid entered and left with the serving tray and tea kettle.

The one who surrenders his heart for an entire day and does not dare move one hand has the destiny where one must act to fulfill the promise. The uneasy heart is weighed down every second and slowly moves to a scary place. Leaping out in an attack from the side, Hajime blocked the advance of the person forced to fail. At the same time the blocked person is held back, he can indulge in the momentary calm at an earlier place.

I have decided the promise should be kept. However, I am not the one who removed the conditions needed to accomplish this. Feelings are different when a promise is broken and when obstacles arise and the promise cannot be kept. When a promise becomes perilous, I'm happy when someone prevents me from carrying out the promise so that I'm not blamed. If chastised by my conscience over why I did nothing, a sense of duty to go was present. The answer is it was unavoidable when Hajime became an obstacle.

Seizō gave Hajime a friendly welcome. However, the friendliness of this point is fenced in on all sides by regrettably dreary emotions.

Hajime and Fujio are distant relatives. Whether he breaks up with Fujio or she with him, a risky promise capable of creating an irreparably broken relationship between two people was made with faces feigning innocence. On the verge of starting to act, the one who charges in becomes a nuisance and feels great guilt. If it's unrelated, that is fine, too. The one who charged in is, of all people, a relative of the other party.

It would be better if they were just relatives. Hajime has had feelings for Fujio for a long time. He had been given permission to be the groom of the daughter of the man who died overseas. Unaware of the relationship between the two people until yesterday, Hajime stayed linked to his old hopes. Without knowing the whereabouts of the stolen money, Hajime guarded an empty safe.

A cloud of secrets was split in half by a flash of lightning from a golden chain that radiates springtime. After the golden chain awakened sleepy eyes, Asai went to talk about the Inoue matter. That's a problem. Pitiful is a word that's only said about the other side. Guilty feelings are used when business is unfinished on my part. When trouble comes, greater skill emerges and is used when advantages bounce back directly onto me. Seizō looked at Hajime's face and was troubled.

The core of a shred of kindness to express the will to welcome Hajime's visit was awkwardly surrounded by rings of wretchedness. On top, a ring of guilty feelings piled up unpleasantly. The outermost troublesome ring connected to an endless future like spreading black ink. Then, Hajime seemed like the hero who ruled over the future.

"I was rude yesterday," said Hajime. Seizō blushed and looked down. Thinking he'd bring up the gold watch later, he uneasily lit a cigarette. Hajime could not see his expression.

"Seizō, Asai deliberately stopped by earlier to discuss that matter," he said bluntly.

Seizō's nerves twitched. After a short time, he blew cigarette smoke mournfully out his nose.

"Seizō, you mustn't think an enemy has come."

"No, I'd never ..." said Seizō, startled again.

"I am not the type of man to make insinuations and take advantage of another's weakness. I'm clear about this. I don't want to turn free time into a drug. Even so, it goes against the traditions of my family."

He understood what Hajime meant but not its conception in his mind. However, he was silent because he lacked the courage to ask again.

"If I can be thought of as a despicable man, it's not worth it for me to make time to come when I'm so busy. I'm a man who understands the reason for education. Once I'm seen as that sort of man, in the end, whatever I say to you becomes entirely invalid."

Seizō remained silent.

"I'm an idle man but would not fly here by cab to be held in contempt by you.

"Anyhow, it's probably as Asai said."

"What did he say?"

"Seizō, I'm serious. All right? There are situations when a man must be serious once a year. If one lives superficially, an opponent finds no rival. Even if he becomes a rival, it would be dull. I came to make you my rival. All right? Do you understand?"

"Yes, I do," Seizō gently answered.

"If you understand, I see you as an equal. Aren't you always anxious? You seem far from calm."

Seizō artfully confessed, "That … that may be so."

"You speak plainly. It's all pitiful, but that may be the truth."

"Yes."

"People may be uneasy and calm but are unbothered by living in a shallow society. Many people act with arrogance despite being riddled with anxiety. I may be one of those people, too. No, I know. I am one of them."

For the first time, Seizō began to actively block his opponent.

"I'm jealous. The truth is I often think it would be nice to be like you. That's sums up what I think. When I go to that place, I'm nothing more than a tedious man."

He couldn't believe he could be as charming. The superficial culture had ruptured, revealing true internal feelings. Although dejected, his voice was flush with sincerity.

"Seizō, I've noticed that in you."

Hajime's words held some warmth.

"I am here," he answered. After a short time, he again said, "I am here," and looked down. Hajime stuck his face forward. His companion kept looking down.

"My character is weak," he said.

"In what way?"

"I can't help it. I've been this way since birth," he said, still looking down.

Hajime brought his face closer. He propped himself up on one knee and rested his elbow on the other to support his pushed-forward face. Then he said, "You are more able than I as a scholar. Your mind is also sharper than mine. I respect you. I came to help because of that respect."

"To help …"

When he raised his head, Hajime was at the tip of his nose. He spoke as though he would press against Seizō's face.

"In these dangerous times, when one's innate nature is not reshaped, life is fraught. No amount of studying or becoming a scholar can undo this. From here on, Seizō, I will be serious. How many people in this world will live their lives and never understand seriousness? People who live only superficially are no different than dolls made of clay. If there is no seriousness and if there is, becoming a doll is a waste. After becoming serious, one feels good. Have you ever experienced that?"

Seizō hung his head.

"If not, try to do it one time. This situation will not occur twice in a lifetime. When this chance is gone, it'll be gone forever. You'll die never knowing the charm of seriousness in life. Until you die, you will only be restless and anxious like a shaggy dog. A person can accumulate as many chances as possible to become serious. Human-like feelings will come.

"It's not a boast. You don't understand until you have the experience. I'm what I am. I'm not a scholar. I don't study, fail, and lie around idly. Nevertheless, I'm calmer than you. My sister Itoko thinks it's because my nerves are numb. Of course, they probably are.

"However, if I'm so insensitive, even today, I wouldn't do this and rush over in a cab. Isn't that so, Seizō?"

Hajime smiled. Seizō did not.

"I'm calmer than you, but it's not because I'm a scholar, my studies, or anything else. It's because sometimes I become serious. More than saying I become, saying I can become is more appropriate. I can become more serious, but my self-confidence does not emerge. I become more serious, but I'm unable to settle down. I become more serious but am unaware of the presence of spirit. The notion that I exist before the universe is self-awareness first obtained after becoming serious. You see, seriousness means you don't play fight, you fight with real swords. It means to finish off your enemy. It means I must eliminate my enemy. It means all of humanity acts.

"No matter how cleverly I use my words or deftly move my

hands, I'm not serious. My feelings become serious the first time I fling what is in my mind into the world. Then I have peace of mind. The truth is my sister became serious yesterday. Kingo became serious yesterday, too. And I was serious yesterday and am today. You also became serious during this affair. When a person becomes serious, not only that person is helped. The world is saved.

"What do you think, Seizō? You don't understand what I'm saying."

"No, I understand."

"This is serious."

"I seriously understand."

"That's good."

"Thank you."

"So ... because that man Asai is a man who is completely useless as a human being, it's difficult to take his words seriously. In essence, Asai came here and said this and that. I will tell you point-by-point what he said to me. Then after comparing it to what you say, I may be able to determine the truth. No matter how dumb I may be, I will understand that much. However, it's a grave problem whether I become serious or not. The one who made the promise slipped and tumbled down. If I marry, I can't become a doctor. If I don't become a doctor, my reputation will be spoiled. It looks like something seen by a child, it may not matter which is which. Does it matter?"

"Yes, it doesn't matter."

"When needed, a serious measure should be applied. That is what you do. If it's not a nuisance, I will ask for advice. It's fine to make every effort."

Seizō, dejected and head hanging down, corrected his sitting position, raised his head, and looked right at Hajime. His eyes were uncommonly unyielding.

"The serious measure is to marry Sayoko as soon as possible. I'm sorry I abandoned Sayoko and will apologize to Kodō-sensei. I've been horrible. The rejection was entirely my fault. I also apologize to you."

"Apologize to me? There's no need for that. You'll understand later."

"I'm absolutely sorry. It's all right to not decline. If I don't decline, but Asai has probably already declined."

"He declined as you requested. However, Inoue-san said you should come and decline in person."

"Well, I'll go. I'll go right now and apologize."

"But now, my father has gone to Inoue-san's home."

"Your father?"

"Yes. According to Asai, Inoue-san was furious because his daughter wept and sobbed. So while I came here to talk with you, he went to console and connect because it would be bad if anything happened."

"Thank you, you're so kind," said Seizō, lowering his head close to the tatami.

"Because the old man is wiling away the days, he's delighted to offer some help. So, I did it like this. If a negotiation is arranged, call on his daughter and bring her here by cab.

"If she comes, the declaration from your mouth in front of me will be, 'My future wife will be you.'"

"I'll do it. It's fine to leave here."

"No, because I have business other than calling her here. If that's done, the three of us will go see Kingo. You will make your declaration once more before Fujio."

Seizō seemed to flinch slightly. Hajime immediately followed.

"Should I introduce your wife to Fujio?"

"Is that necessary?"

"You're becoming serious.

"In front of me, you should cleanly break off the relationship with Fujio. Sayoko will be brought along as proof."

"Bringing her is fine, but it will be too spiteful. If possible, a little discretion ..."

"I don't like using a pretext, but I have no choice but to help Fujio. Her kind of personality is not repaired through ordinary means.

"But ..."

"They'll say you have no honor. This has become a mess. Grumbling about embarrassment and awkwardness are certainly superficial actions. Didn't you just say you've become serious? To me, seriousness reduces everything to the words *take action*. Becoming serious only in your words means only your words are serious, but the man does not become serious. If the assertion is an individual like you has become serious, there is nothing if the only evidence of the assertion is not seen in practice."

"I'll do it. It doesn't matter how many people are there. I'll do it."

"Good."

"But I will reveal everything. The fact is I have an engagement to go to Ōmori today."

"To Ōmori. With who?"

"Her ... today's person."

"Fujio? When?"

"We're to meet at the train station at three."

"Three. What time is it now?"

A snap was heard from inside Hajime's vest.

"It's already two. Shouldn't you be going?"

"I'm not going."

"It's not good for Fujio to go alone to Ōmori. If you do that, she'll probably go home if it's after three."

"If I'm just one minute late, she'll have no interest in meeting and immediately go home."

"That's true.

"What's that? Is it raining? Did you promise to go even if it rained?"

"Yes."

"This rain doesn't look like it's going to stop. Anyhow, I'll send for Sayoko with a note. Her father is waiting impatiently and is surely worried."

This strong rain fell at a slant, unlike spring rains. The bottom of the sky was immeasurably deep. A multitude of unending stripes descended from its depths. It was so chilly a brazier would be welcomed.

The note was written amid the echoes of raindrops. The story moves to the time the messenger trembled in the rain hitting the colors of the hood and left in a hurry. A short time ago, the second cab left the gate of the Munechika home and had already arrived at the residence of Kodō-sensei as the rider continued to fulfill his mission.

Kodō-sensei had come down with a fever and was sleeping. Sayoko held an ice pack to cool his hairline as he lay with his eyes on his treasured Gitō scroll. Crouching at his bedside, her eyes were swollen and red from crying. She seemed to be counting the wrinkles near the folds of the ice pack. She did not easily raise her head. Hajime's father sat dignified about two feet from the bedding with a checkered pattern. At his thick kneecaps sticking out from the sitting cushion and lightly pressing on the tatami, there was something dignified and majestic compared to Kodō-sensei's face where the blood receded and his flesh drooped.

The elder Munechika's voice was loud, as always. Kodō-sensei's voice was louder than usual. The conversation between the two continued.

"My sudden visit was due to the situation you mentioned. I'm sorry for making you feel uncomfortable. Please excuse my abrupt appearance."

"No, this is a highly offensive mess. I'm the one who is ashamed. I am awake and must welcome you."

"Thank you. It's easier for you to stay there and talk. I ended up in this condition. Ha, ha, ha, ha."

"I'm grateful for your kindness and this opportunity to ask."

"In bygone days, they said warriors helped each other. Ha, ha, ha, ha. I have no limits on how long I'll help. However, your move back to Tōkyo after many years and being under the weather may be the problem."

"This is the twentieth year."

"My, my, twenty years. Two decades. How are your relatives?"

"It's like having none. We've had no contact for years."

"Of course. Only Seizō has helped. But that has become troubling."

"I should have seen something was wrong."

"No, how could you? Don't worry about that."

"I'm not worried, but I should have known. A short time ago, I explained to my daughter how this would affect her."

"However, it's unfortunate the one who has been so diligent until now is being harshly abandoned. For now, please leave it to us. Also because my son said he will make every effort and do his best."

"I'm truly grateful for your kindness. However, since the rejection from the other side, my daughter may no longer want to visit. Even if she says she will, I can never do that."

Sayoko gently lifted the ice pack and carefully wiped the moisture off his forehead with a towel.

"Let's stop the cooling for a short time. Sayoko, it's all right if you don't go."

Sayoko placed the ice pack on a tray. She pressed both hands against the tatami and stuck out her head as if she would cover the top of the tray. Tears slowly dripped onto the ice pack. Kodō-sensei twisted his salt-and-pepper head halfway around to the back as he said, "It'll be fine."

He could see tears drop onto the ice pack.

"That's reasonable. That's reasonable ..." said the elder Munechika, repeating himself. Kodō-sensei's head turned back. His shining sunken eyes fixed on the older man.

Eventually, Kodō said, "Even if Seizō took Fujio as his wife, I feel sorry for your son."

"No, that's nothing to worry about. Hajime will not marry her. Perhaps, no, he won't. Even if my son says he'll marry, I will not approve. I will not allow him to marry a woman who dislikes him even if he says he wishes to."

"You see, Sayoko, Hajime's father says so, too. It's the same thing."

"I ... even if I don't go ... that's fine," sputtered Sayoko from behind the pillow. Amid the noisy rain, finally, she was heard.

"No, if not, that's a problem. My flying here was in vain. Somehow, as in the earlier conversation, I'd like you to listen to what my son has to say because of the possible situation developing with Seizō.

"Talking about my son is strange, but that fellow understands the reasons. He will not make a plan that will later turn into a problem. If he thinks breaking off the engagement is for your sake, he will recommend that.

"This is our first meeting, but please trust me. They should be here by now, unfortunately, it's raining."

The rattling wheels of a lone cab pounded by rain stopped before the lattice. At the moment the door flung open, drenched straw sandals stepped into the area for removing footwear. The story moves to the mission of the third cab.

As the third cab carrying Itoko came running while sending out ringing echoes to the Kōno gate, Kingo tidied the study. He pulled out each desk drawer, ripped up, and threw out papers of correspondences saved for a long time. The papers torn in half piled high on the floor at his knees. Kingo stepped on the scattered papers and stood.

This time, he took a few sheets of paper written with fine characters from the drawer. Among them, sets of five or six pages were bound together. The papers were mostly Western, as was the writing. Kingo glanced and immediately stacked them on the desk. Without reading as much as half a line, he easily arranged them. In a short time, the stack was just short of a foot high. The drawers were mostly empty.

Kingo held the pile by the top and bottom, carried it close to the fireplace, and, without a word, tossed it in. When the hero's hands released the pile, it collapsed to one side.

An ashtray with a flowering grapevine cast in bronze was on the Western-style table. Matches were on the ashtray. Kingo reached out for the box of matches. He turned to the side to pick it up. After the sounds of five or six faint strikes were heard, he returned the matchbox to the desk.

He picked up a diary bound with a yellow cover beside the Leopardi and returned to the fireplace. He watched the sheets fly past like rain as his thumb pressed down. Black ink and gray pencil marks danced until he reached the yellow cover. He had no idea what he had written. He wrote before falling asleep last evening.

> A silent visitor becomes a priest
> A monk with an unshaven head leaves the
> house

He recalled only the last verse on the last page of this couplet. He despaired and placed the diary on the loose papers. He squatted in front of the fireplace rug and listened to the hisses. In the quiet, the scattered papers lazily stretched as they heated up from below. The scent of burning rose through the gaps between the papers. The papers moved out from the bottom.

"Yes, I still have things to write," said Kingo. He stood on his knees and rescued the diary from the smoke. The paper turned brown. Inside the fireplace, a whoosh and then a plane of fire burned.

"Oh my, what's happening here?"

His mother stood in the doorway, staring doubtfully into the fireplace. Kingo leaned back in response to her voice. When the end of his sleeve caught fire, he faced his mother.

"It's cold, so I'm warming up the room," he said, looking down into the fireplace. The fire burned a light amber. The smoke blended, occasionally bringing indigo and purple to mind, and rose inside the chimney.

"Use the soft coal."

Just then, rain lured by the wind hit the window and broke into four or five streaks.

"It has started raining."

His mother did not respond and took three steps into the room. Kingo seemed to look through her.

"If it's cold, shouldn't you burn coal?"

The blazing fire disappeared in a flare after rising in a quivering purple tongue. A pop and the fireplace was pitch black inside.

"That was enough. It's already gone."

Kingo finished talking and turned his back to the fireplace. His late father's eyes occasionally dropped in a flash from the wall. The rain swooshed.

"Goodness, papers are scattered all over. Are all of them useless?"

Kingo gazed at the floor. The documents ripped and thrown about created a huge mess. Some scraps had a couple of lines or five or six lines were shredded in half. At the extreme one line was torn in half.

"I don't need any of them."

"I'll straighten up a little. Where's the wastepaper basket?"

Kingo did not answer. His mother peeked under the desk. She could barely see a Western-style wastepaper basket beyond the footstool. She squatted down and reached out. Light from the window fell on her dark blue satin obi sash.

Kingo extended his arm fully to the right and grabbed the chair's backrest draped with a sun cover. He slanted his thin shoulders and slowly dragged the chair closer to the desk.

His mother slid the wastepaper basket from under the desk, picked up each scrap of paper off the floor, and placed them in the wastepaper basket. She carefully flattened out the twisted ones. She tossed in one with the writing *I have the pleasure of* ... and one with ... *for receiving permission. As circumstances permit,* ... and turned over and read one with ... *only with patience* ....

Kingo stared at his mother from the corners of his eyes. He grunted from exertion on the chair's back to pull it closer to a corner of the desk. Dark blue tabi socks were swiftly lined up on the white sun cover. Soon, the lined-up socks jumped onto the desk.

"What are you doing?" asked his mother, holding a paper scrap and looking down. The frightened expression in her eyes was easily read.

"I'm taking down the portrait," he said calmly from above.

"The portrait?"

The fright changed to surprise. Kingo placed his right hand on the gilded frame.

"Wait a moment."

"Yes?" His right hand still hung onto the portrait.

"You will take down the portrait and do what?"

"Take it with me."

"Take it where?"

"I'll take the portrait when I leave this house."

"You will leave. Well, even when you leave, wouldn't it be better to gently remove it?"

"Am I wrong?"

"No, it's not. Take it if you want it. That's fine. It's better not to rush when doing anything."

"If I don't remove it now, I won't have time."

His mother made a strange face and stood overcome with surprise. Kingo placed both hands on the frame.

"Leave, you say. Do you truly want to go?"

"Yes, I do."

Kingo directed his answer to the back.

"When?"

"I will leave after this."

Kingo used both hands to jerk the frame upward once, removed it from the brads, and lowered it. The frame was attached to the wall by a fine wire. When he let go with one hand, the wire seemed to break, and the frame was about to fall. He reverently raised the frame with both hands. From below, his mother said, "But it's pouring rain."

"The rain doesn't matter."

"At least, do me the favor of saying goodbye to Fujio."

"She's probably out."

"That's why I'm asking you to wait. Won't springing this on your mother cause problems for me?"

"I don't intend to cause problems for you."

"Even if you didn't, people will talk. Go, if you're going, then go, and I will be shamed."

"People," he started to say while holding the frame. When he only turned his head around, Kingo's narrowed eyes dropped down once to his mother. Eventually, he did not move to the door at a distance away from his mother.

The mother looked uncomfortably over her shoulder.

"Oh, my!"

As if she fell from heaven, Itoko stood quietly and gently lowered her face. When her hair styled in a puffy *hisashigami* settled down, she walked over to the desk. When her two white tabi socks were side by side, she said, "I came to see you," and looked up at Kingo.

"Please, hand me the scissors," he said from above. His chin pointed to the scissors beside the Leopardi.

With a snap, the frame separated from the wall. The scissors dropped to the floor with a clang. Kingo raised the frame with both hands and turned around on the top of the desk to face forward.

"I came because my brother said go and get Kingo."

Kingo slowly lowered the raised frame from just below eye level.

"Please, take this."

Itoko took a firm hold. Kingo jumped down from the desk.

"Let's go. Did you come by cab?"

"Yes."

"Can this portrait come, too?"

"Yes."

"Well then." He picked up the frame and headed to the door. Itoko followed. His mother called to stop them.

"Wait a moment. Itoko, please wait a little longer, too. I don't understand what displeases you enough to leave your parent's home. Can't you understand my feelings even a little? Won't I lose face in society?"

"Society does not matter at all."

"You say something so unreasonable like a child who can't tell right from wrong."

"If I'm a child, that's fine. If I could become like a child, that's fine, too."

"That's ridiculous. Haven't you grown from a child into an adult? You have yet to make a serious effort or two. Please, think this over a little."

"I'm going because I've already thought about it."

"Why are you saying such unreasonable things?

"All of this began with my negligence. I had no choice but to cry again and cajole, but I ... for your late father ..."

"Father is all right. He says nothing."

"He says nothing. Wouldn't it be nice if you weren't so stubborn and didn't bully me?"

Kingo held on to the portrait and didn't answer. Itoko quietly went to his side. Rain enveloped the room and blew closer. Distant winds gathered with expanding echoes of loud whooshing sounds. Within the echoes, Kingo stood quietly, as did Itoko.

His mother asked, "Do you understand a little?"

He was still silent.

"I've said this much, but you still don't understand?"

Kingo didn't open his mouth.

"Itoko, this is a miserable situation. When you return home, please explain this to your father and brother.

"It's shameful to show all of you this side of me."

"Auntie, Kingo wants to leave, so it should be fine to let him leave without resistance. I think nothing will come of forcing him to do anything."

"If you believe that, then nothing else can be done. I may be rude, but you're still young and don't think too deeply.

"However much he wants to leave, he's not a man to live in a house in the mountains. If he just decided and leaves now, more than he, the ones left behind will have difficulties."

"Why?"

"Isn't what people say annoying?"

"Why is what people say bad?"

"If we both show our faces in public, aren't we spending today doing this? The obligations to society are more important than those to me."

"But to leave in this way, isn't that pitiful?"

"That is an obligation."

"That obligation is unimportant."

"It is not unimportant."

"But it doesn't matter what Kingo does."

"It doesn't matter. Of course, that's for Kingo's sake."

"More than Kingo, isn't it for Auntie's sake?"

"It's one's obligation to the world."

"I don't understand. The one who wants to leave wants to leave despite what the world says. That should not trouble you, Auntie."

"But the rain is coming down hard."

"Despite the rain, Auntie, does it matter to you because you can't get wet?"

That was an issue in times before trains existed. A mountain man and a seafaring man quarreled.

The mountain man said, "Fish are salty."

The seafaring man asked, "Are fish salty?"

The quarrel did not quiet down for some time. When a train dubbed *education* runs and a convenient method for freely raising and lowering the stages of reason cannot be used, mutual thoughts do not understand each other.

At times, when no one is too pickled by the secular world and seems dizzy at a glance, he will not be accepted as human. He will not acknowledge the lie or the fabrication even after hearing an explanation. Until the end, he asserts the pickled taste.

The interactions between the mystery woman and Itoko only ran in parallel no matter how far they went and never converged to a point. Similar to the mountain man and the seafaring man who held different basic ideas concerning fish from the beginning, the mystery woman and Itoko held different ideas about people.

Kingo who understood the sea and the mountains said nothing and looked down at the two women. Itoko's words were unembellished and incapable of mounting a defense. His mother's assertion was so stupid and common, it alienated him. While waiting for the women's dialogue questions and answers, Kingo stood hugging the portrait. His mood didn't seem particularly bored. He also didn't appear impatient or anxious. He thought, If these women talk until sunset, I'll probably be standing in the same position and holding the portrait until then.

A shout rose in the rain. A cab stopped at the entryway. Footsteps approached from the entrance. Hajime appeared first.

"You haven't gone, yet?" he asked Kingo.

"No," he answered.

"You're here, too, Auntie. That's good," Hajime said and sat. Seizō entered behind him. Sayoko followed like Seizō's shadow coming out only a bit.

"Auntie, you have a full house despite the rain.

"Sayoko, this is my sister."

The active child both greeted and introduced herself in one phrase. Hajime was in a hurry. Kingo still stood supporting the portrait. Seizō had nothing to do but did not sit on a chair. Sayoko and Itoko politely lowered their heads with a touch of mischief. Of course, there was no chance for the exchange of candid words.

"The rain is falling hard, very hard."

The mother sprinkled this charm on the surface.

"It's pouring out there," Hajime immediately answered.

"Seizō is —"

The mother started to speak, but Hajime interrupted again.

"Seizō made a promise to take Fuji to Ōmori today. But they can't go now."

"But, Fujio went out earlier."

"She still hasn't come home?" Hajime quietly asked. The mother looked slightly displeased.

"Why a place like Ōmori?" she said to herself and turned around slightly.

"Would you all like to sit? All this standing is tiring. Fujio will probably return home soon," he warned.

"Please," said the mother.

"Seizō, please sit. You too, Sayoko? Kingo, what happened there?"

"He took down his father's portrait and said he was leaving with it."

"Kingo, please wait a bit longer until Fujio returns home."

Kingo did not respond.

"Let's wait a little longer," said Itoko softly.

"What?" asked Kingo, propping the frame lowered to the floor against the wall. Sayoko looked quietly through her cast-down eyes at the portrait.

"Do you have business with Fujio?"

These words were her mother's.

"Yes, I do."

This was Hajime's answer.

Later, the rain fell. No one spoke. This time, one cab carried Cleopatra's fury in a quick run from Shimbashi, like the swift-footed god of war, Skanda.

Hajime said curtly above his padded vest, "It's three-twenty."

No one responded. The cab jetted away causing a thousand rain streaks to bounce off the black hood. Cleopatra's fury leaped above the futon.

"Auntie, shall we talk about Kyōto?"

To beat the rain falling to the ground, the riding fury lashed the back of the rickshaw man to run faster. When the wind fanning to the side cut to the front, and the gears twisted in reverse, the gravel spread inside Kōno's gate in two long lines burst before the entryway.

When the fury gathering at the dark purple ribbon passed under the hood, a trembling Cleopatra flew up to the entryway.

"Twenty-five—"

Before Hajime stopped speaking, the embodiment of fury stood in the study like a humiliated queen. The eyes of six people focused on the purple ribbon.

"Ah, she has returned," said Hajime, holding a cigarette between his lips.

Fujio was too proud to respond with a word of greeting. She curved her long back and looked sternly around the room. Her scanning eyes finally reached and stabbed Seizō. Sayoko was hidden by his suit's shoulder. Hajime abruptly stood. He tossed the half-smoked cigarette into the green grapevine ashtray.

"Fujio. Seizō did not go to Shimbashi."

"Stay out of this. Seizō, why didn't you come?"

"I'm sorry I didn't go."

Seizō's pause was conspicuous. Lightning flashed from Cleopatra's pupils and brazenly shot at Seizō's forehead.

"If a promise is not kept, an explanation is required."

"Because keeping a promise is a serious matter, Seizō broke it," said Hajime.

"Be quiet. Seizō, why didn't you come?"

Hajime took several long strides toward him.

"I will make the introductions," he said, pushing Seizō to the side to reveal the diminutive Sayoko.

"Fujio, this is Seizō's wife."

Fujio's expression filled with hate. The loathing gradually morphed into jealousy. When the jealousy etched its deepest point, it fossilized.

"She is not his wife, yet, but will be in time. It appears they've been engaged for five years."

Sayoko lowered her slender neck, her eyes swollen from tears. Fujio froze with clenched white fists.

"That is a lie. A lie," she repeated. "Seizō is my husband. My future husband. What are you talking about? How rude."

"I will report only the facts out of goodwill. Incidentally, her name is Sayoko."

"You are insulting me."

Behind the fossilized expression, veins burst. Purple blood poured a second wave of fury over her entire face.

"It's kindness. It's goodwill. A misunderstanding would be a problem," said Hajime, of course, calmly.

Finally, Seizō opened his mouth.

"Everything Hajime said is true. Sayoko is my future wife.

"Fujio, until today, I've been a frivolous man. I give my sincerest apology to you. And to you, Sayoko. And you, too, Hajime.

"I will reform starting today. I will become a serious man. Please forgive me. Had I gone to Shimbashi, it would have been bad for you and me. So I didn't go. Please, forgive me."

Fujio's expression changed three times. Blood from the ruptured veins was absorbed into pure white. Only the color of contempt remained. The shape of a mask rapidly crumbled.

"Ha, ha, ha, ha."

A hysterical laugh collided with the rain outside the window and loudly welled up. As a clenched fist punched through a thick panel, she slowly pulled out a long chain. The dark crimson tail emitted a mysterious light and swayed from right to left.

"Well, this is of no use to you. That's fine.

"Hajime, I will give this to you."

Her white hands stretched out to expose slender arms. A watch dropped into the reddish-brown palm of Hajime. He took a big step closer to the fireplace. A shout of "Ah!" and the reddish-brown palm danced in space. The watch broke apart on a marble corner.

"Fujio, I didn't create this crazed disturbance because I wanted a watch. Seizō, I didn't take part in this mischief because I want a woman who someone loves. If it ends like this, all of you probably understand my soul. This is a part of the action of the first principle. Am I right, Kingo?"

"Yes, it is."

Fujio's face showed surprise, and her muscles stopped moving at once. Her hands hardened. Her legs hardened. She kicked away a chair, like a stone statue that lost its center and collapsed to the floor.

CHAPTER 19

The rain that pierced the bottom of a freezing cloud and fell at a slant in the air for nearly a day seeped into the core of the Earth and stopped. Spring ran out here. The red remaining on plum blossoms, cherry blossoms, and peach blossoms scattered as if in a dream. Every source of pride in the spring died. The selfish woman ingested the poison of vanity and died. The winds that lost the companionship of the flowers mischievously began to fill the room with the scent of the dead woman. Fujio now slept with her pillow to the north, as is proper for the dead.

Katawaguruma, the phantom of a naked woman in pain and tormented while riding on an ox-cart with a single, burning wheel, was undyed in a form not of the earthly realm under a Yuzen quilt lightly draping her. On top, ivy nearly half colored crawled over the surface. The pattern was melancholy. There was no sign of movement. The futon stacked two layers of thick Gunnai weaving. From beneath a dust-free sheet smoothly spread out, each line of yellow and olive brown of a coarse grid was visible.

Only her black hair was unchanged. The purple ribbon was picked up and discarded. All was left in disarray on the pillow. The mother who thought about the world until today seemed to not have even inserted the teeth of a comb. The disheveled hair spilled over onto the pure white sheet connected to the velvet in the quilt band, and surrounded her upturned face. Yesterday's flesh changed color. Her eyebrows were as thick as they had always been. Moments earlier, her eyes were closed by her mother. Until she slept, her mother tenderly caressed her. Nothing but her face was visible.

The watch was on the bedding. The nanako basket weave deeply etched in its metal had been destroyed. Only the chain was untouched and wrapped around the edges of both lids. At the center of the glow from the gold color bent in half, a pomegranate bead sat like the eye of the crooked lid.

A silver-leaf folding screen with two panels was standing upside down. Within six feet the frosty color of the moon vividly shined on one surface, a rusty green patina was used without reservation to draw only a tangle of supple stalks. Sawtooth leaves were drawn in a jagged, lopsided pile. Thin flower petals were drawn as large as the palm of a hand at the tops of stalks that used up all the rusty green patina. If a stalk burst open, it was lightly drawn only fluttering down and in red and purple to fold into the multiple folds of shrunken Yoshino paper. Everything sprouted from silver metal. They bloomed in silver. The fallen ones were drawn to appear to be inside the silver. The flower was a poppy. The signature was Sakai Hōitsu.

The familiar, small parquet desk was placed in the shadow of the folding screen. A Takaoka lacquered inkstone box decorated with silver was moved to the staggered shelves holding books. A vessel for pouring oil was placed on top of the desk. During the day, the wick of a lamp was lit. The wick was new. The nozzle pulled to extend three inches taller than the vessel was slender and white when empty of oil.

There was also a white porcelain incense burner. The faded red of an incense pouch stuck out at a corner of the desk. The five or six sticks standing in the ashes smoked from red points and disappeared. The fragrance resembled that of Buddha. The color was a fluid indigo. The smoke densely rising from the base swayed to the left and right. Its width expanded with each undulation. The color paled as the width expanded. A thick stripe flowed gently inside a faint band. The destinations of the broad width and the band were unknown. The consumed ashes toppled over in a line.

The Takaoka lacquerware on the staggered shelves swelled up in the blue of an old tree trunk on a dark reddish-brown backdrop. Several red blossoms on a winter plum tree were crafted from mock mother-of-pearl. In the background, a lone bush warbler flew over a black field. Until yesterday, pomegranate beads that released intense light on the dark bottom were embedded in the embossed lacquer-ware of a row of reed geese. A gold case watch embossed with a woven nanako pattern had no gap between the lids. A book was set on the embossed lacquerwork. Only the small openings of gold foil that cut four corners were brilliantly visible. The long length of a purple bookmark tassel dangled. The seventh line from the bottom of a page sandwiching the bookmark was:

It is well done, and fitting for a princess descended of so many royal kings.

A thin line had been drawn by a colored pencil beneath this sentence.

Everything was beautiful. Among the pretty things was the beautiful face of the laid-out woman. Haughty eyes were shut for eternity. The eyebrows of Fujio with sleeping proud eyes, her fore-head, and her black hair were as beautiful as those of a celestial maiden.

"Perhaps, I should cut the incense stick," said her mother standing in the antechamber.

"I just went in," said Kingo. He lined up his knees and folded his arms.

"Hajime, please come in."

"Thank you."

The fragrance of the incense blew as remembered from Fujio's room. Columns of burnt ashes gently tipped over in the incense burner. No one noticed the fragrance released by the silver-leaf folding screen.

"Has Seizō come yet?" asked his mother.

"He probably has. I notified him," said Kingo.

The room was closed tightly on purpose. Only the sliding fusuma partition was open. Only the Yūzen-dyed hem of the Katawaguruma was visible. Later, everything was hidden by thick banana-fiber paper. The edge delineating this world and the netherworld is black. It ran an inch wide straight from the top of the door frame to the threshold.

The mother seated by the fusuma door sometimes tilted her head and turned her back as though she was peeking into an invisible place. She worried more about the cold face than the cold legs. Each time she peeked, the black edge neatly cut the Yūzen quilt at a slant. If copied, it would be a replica of the pattern.

"Auntie, she has flown away. It's tragic, but there's nothing to do now. May you find enlightenment."

"Sadly, it has come to this."

"I cried. There's nothing to be done now. It is fate."

"It was truly an unfortunate event," she said, wiping her eyes.

"Crying too much is not good for a memorial service. More than that, what will come is important. After this, Kingo has no choice but to stay. Your worrying only troubles you."

The mother burst into tears. The ones that reminisce over the past are easily suppressed. Spontaneous tears come when one suddenly realizes one's future fate.

"What would be best to do? ... What do you think? ... Hajime."

The scattered words spilled out between tears and snot.

"Auntie, excuse me for saying, but the usual way of thinking is no good."

"Because of my negligence, Fujio turned into this ... and was going to be abandoned by Kingo."

"Therefore, crying doesn't help."

"I'm truly embarrassed ..."

"Thus, from here on, I will slightly adjust my thinking. Kingo, that's probably best."

"Everyone, I've been awful, haven't I?" said the mother to Kingo. At last, the man with folded arms opened his mouth.

"It's best not to distinguish a stepchild from one's birth child. It's best to be simple and direct. It's best not to hold back or to think hard about trivial things."

Kingo punctuated his words. His mother looked down and could not answer. Or he thought, she may not have understood. He spoke again.

"You wanted me to give the house and the assets to Fujio. Because I said I would, it's awful that I was always under suspicion and not believed. You might not have been pleased by my staying at the house. Therefore, I said I would leave this house, but it could not be spurred by spiteful remarks or negative thoughts.

"You probably wanted Seizō to marry Fujio and take our family name. You thought I'd disapprove and sent me to Kyōto for rest. During my absence, Seizō and Fujio's relationship deepened day by day. That strategy was unacceptable. You probably told me and other people that my going to Kyōto was to cure my illness. That was a terrible lie.

"Even if I changed my mind over this matter, there's no particular need to leave home. I am fine with caring for you forever."

Kingo stopped. Still looking down, his mother paused to think and answered in a quiet voice.

"When you say that, I've been horrible. From now on, I will listen to your opinion and intend to correct deficiencies."

"That's fine. Right, Kingo? For you and your mother. You are fine at taking care of matters at home and will have a serious talk with Itoko."

"Uh-huh," Kingo only answered.

When the incense sticks in the adjacent room burned out, Seizō held his pale forehead. The indigo-blue smoke rose, grazing the silver-leaf folding screen.

Two days later, the funeral ended. On the final night of the funeral, Kingo wrote the following in his diary.

Tragedy finally came. I expected tragedy for a long time. My reason for letting the anticipated tragedy unfold was I understood that not lifting a hand to make the slightest effort reflected the powerlessness of one hand in the face of actions by a deeply sinful person. Also, I understood the magnitude of the tragedy. At last, I experienced the great power of tragedy. I could not wash away karma, which crossed over the three generations of the past, the present, and the future, at its root. It was not out of unkindness. If I raise one hand, I lose one hand. If I move one eye, one eye loses sight. Although I have injured one hand and one eye, the karma of the other person remains unchanged. A chisel cuts deeper moment by moment. There is no fear of shoving hands into sleeves and closing eyes. More than hands and eyes, natural punishments are kindly accepted and are nothing other than the nuanced meaning of a brief encounter with one's true nature.

Tragedy is greater than comedy. I'll explain this. Death blocks all obstacles and, consequently, is said to be great. Falling into and being unable to escape from the abyss of an irreparable fate is said to be great because flowing water that goes and does not return is said to be great. Fate does not become great because it simply reveals the conclusion. Tragedy is great because life suddenly changes into death. It is great because a forgotten death is high-lighted in an unguarded moment. It is great because someone fooling around quickly straightens his collar. It is great because self-control is regained, and feeling the need for morality prevails. The first principle of human life is great because the notion of morality is founded in the mind. The movement of morality is great because it confronts and starts in tragedy and doesn't hesitate.

The practice of morality is grueling to us despite the ardent desire for this in people. Tragedy is great because it compels an individual to follow this practice. The practice of morality benefits others the most and is adverse to oneself. When the power of human beings reaches this point, ordinary happiness is encouraged, and society is guided to an authentic culture. For that reason, tragedy is great.

Problems are countless. Millet or rice is comedy. Craft or busi-ness is also comedy. That woman or this woman is comedy. Tapestry or satin with raised figures is comedy. The English or German language is also comedy. Everything is comedy. In the end, one problem remains. Life or death. This is tragedy.

Ten years last 3,600 days. The problems in which the ordinary person works his body and spirit hard from morning to night are all comedy. Ultimately, the person who acts out comedy throughout the 3,600 days forgets the tragedy. The agony in the problem of being unable to explain life places death in one's mind. The biggest problem of life and death is neglected because of the preoccupation with the choice of this life and that life.

The one who forgets death becomes extravagant. One both floats and sinks during life. No one worries about dancing, going crazy, or fooling around during life because putting in the least effort is a part of life. Extravagance becomes audacity. Boldness tramples morality and runs wild with total freedom.

All people start with the serious problems of life and death. They say this problem is solved and death is thrown away. They say to love life. Here, all people advance in life. In simply throwing out life, the implicit agreement should be to mutually preserve morality with the requirement that death should be discarded because everyone agrees. However, morality becomes unnecessary because all people advance in life day after day, fade away in death day by day, and have self-confidence without the fear of running free and wild with the ultimate freedom and escaping life even a little.

All people who value morality specialize in sacrificing morality and acting out a comedy. They joke, make merry, deceive, ridicule, make a fool of, trample, step on, and kick. All people derive pleasure from comedy. Because this pleasure specializes as it evolves while advancing in life and is enjoyed for the first time by sacrificing morality, no one knows where the advance of comedy reaches the bottom and stops. Also, the notion of morality diminishes day by day.

When a society of people, who deplete the notion of morality and want life, is maintained satisfactorily, tragedy strikes unexpectedly. The eyes of all people are directed toward one's departure point. They know death lives next to life. When dancing wildly with no regard for the rules, people know they will step outside of the boundary of life and enter the realm of death. I know that death abhorrent to other people and me becomes an eternal trap that should never be forgotten. I know that the rope of morality that decays in the domain of the trap leaps over the rules. I know the rope must be stretched anew. I understand the meaninglessness of the actions of the second and later principles. First, however, I realize the greatness of tragedy ...

Two months later, Kingo sent a summary of this entry to Hajime in London. This was Hajime's response.

"Only comedies are popular here."

HAIKU

This haiku was published at the end of the final installment of *Gubijinsō* (*Poppy*) published in *The Tōkyo Asahi Shimbun* on October 29, 1907.

秋の蚊の鳴かずなりたる書齋かな

—— 夏目漱石

In a hushed study
Mosquitoes no longer buzz
The time is autumn

—NATSUME SŌSEKI

CREDITS

Japanese Text

Natsume, Sōseki. *Gubijinsō (Poppy)*. *The Tōkyo Asahi Shimbun*, serialized from June 23 to October 29,1907 (in Japanese).
Aozora Bunko, accessed October 11, 2023.
Input by: Shibata Takuji
Revised by: Itō Tokiya
https://www.aozora.gr.jp/cards/000148/card761.html

Natsume, Sōseki. "Gubijinsō Yōkoku" *(The Press Release for Poppy)*, *Sōseki Zenshū (The Complete Sōseki)*, Vol. 20. Tōkyo: Sōseki Zenshū Kankōkai, 1929: 277 (in Japanese).
National Diet Library Digital Collections, accessed May 26, 2024.
https://dl.ndl.go.jp/pid/1193058

Natsume, Sōseki. *The Complete Sōseki*, Vol. 15 (Shoki no Bunshō oyobi Shika Haiku). Tōkyo: Sōseki Zenshū Kankōkai, 1928: 303 (in Japanese).
National Diet Library Digital Collections, accessed May 26, 2024.
https://dl.ndl.go.jp/pid/1193048

Quotations in English

Plutarch. *Parallel Lives.* Loeb Classical Library edition. Vol. IX, 1920.

Shakespeare, William. *MacBeth*. Barbara Mowat, Paul Werstine, Michael Poston, Rebecca Niles, eds. (Washington, DC: Folger Shakespeare Library, n.d.), accessed June 22, 2024.
https://folger.edu/explore/shakespeares-works/macbeth/

Shakespeare, William. *Hamlet*. Barbara Mowat, Paul Werstine, Michael Poston, Rebecca Niles, eds. (Washington, DC: Folger Shakespeare Library, n.d.), accessed June 22, 2024.
https://folger.edu/explore/shakespeares-works/hamlet/

Leopardi, Giacomo. *Essays, Dialogues, and Thoughts*. Translated by Major-General Patrick Maxwell. London: Walter Scott, Ltd., 1893.

Front Cover Image

Tanigami, Kōnan. *Seiyō Kusabana Zufu* (*Western Flower Collection*). Tokyo: Unsōdō, 1917 (in Japanese).
National Diet Library Collections, accessed October 29, 2024.
https://dl.ndl.go.jp/pid/1184991

Back Cover Images

Okamoto, Ippei. *Bungei Bijutsu Manga* (*Literary Art Manga*). Tokyo: Senshinsha, 1930 (in Japanese).
National Diet Library Digital Collections, accessed July 18, 2024.
https://dl.ndl.go.jp/pid/1178239

Natsume, Sōseki. *The Complete Sōseki*, Vol. 4, Edited by Sōseki Zenshū Kankōkai.
Tōkyo: Sōseki Zenshū Kankōkai, 1936 (in Japanese).
National Diet Library Digital Collections, accessed October 11, 2023.
https://dl.ndl.go.jp/pid/1883210

Author Portrait Taken May 1907
Handwritten Gubijinsō Manuscript

Natsume, Sōseki. *The Complete Sōseki*, Vol. 3 (Gubijinsō, Kōfu). Edited by Sōseki Zenshū Kankōkai. Tōkyo: Sōseki Zenshū Kankōkai, 1925 (in Japanese).
National Diet Library Digital Collections, accessed October 11, 2023.
https://dl.ndl.go.jp/pid/3458507

Natsume Sōseki in study in Waseda Minami-chō (December 1914)

Natsume, Sōseki. *The Complete Sōseki*, Vol. 14 (Hyōron Zappen). Tōkyo: Sōseki Zenshū Kankōkai, 1929 (in Japanese).
National Diet Library Digital Collections, accessed May 27, 2024.
https://dl.ndl.go.jp/pid/1178969

Study in Waseda Minami-chō

Natsume, Sōseki. *The Complete Sōseki*, Vol. 12. Tōkyo: Sōseki Zenshū Kankōkai, 1936 (in Japanese).
National Diet Library Digital Collections, accessed May 27, 2024.
https://dl.ndl.go.jp/pid/1883306

Remembering Sōseki Natsume-sensei

Terada, Torahiko. "Natsume Sōseki Sensei no Tsuioku," *Terada Torahiko Tsuihitsushū* (*Collected Essays of Terada Torahiko*), Vol. 3. Tokyo: Iwanami Bunkō, Iwanami Shoten, May 15,1948 (in Japanese).

Aozora Bunko, accessed October 11, 2023.
Input by: Momo Co.
Revised by: Katō Kaori
https://www.aozora.gr.jp/cards/000042/card2472.html

Sketch from Diary

Natsume, Sōseki. *The Complete Sōseki*, Vol. 11 (Diary and Notes). Tōkyo: Sōseki Zenshū Kankōkai, July1924 (in Japanese).
National Diet Library Digital Collections, accessed June 8, 2024.
https://dl.ndl.go.jp/pid/1901084

ABOUT THE AUTHOR

Remembering Natsume Sōseki-Sensei

by Terada Torahiko

This recollection occurred around the time of final exams for second-year students in residence at Kumamoto Fifth Higher School. A sports committee member was selected to visit the homes of the teachers to get points for the two or three students in the prefecture under their charge who probably failed the exams. Fortunately or unfortunately, I was a committee member.

At that time, a male relative had failed Natsume-sensei's English class. His family was poor and received school expenses from others. The fear was if he failed, the assistance would end.

Sensei's home, which I was visiting for the first time, was built on the banks of the Shirakawa River in a quiet town near Fujisaki Shrine. He was also the sensei, who would absolutely turn away a student who came to his door "to get points." Nevertheless, Natsume-sensei was calm and saw me without hesitation.

He listened quietly to each detail of the tearful plea, but of course, he did not intend to say whether he'd give or not give me the points.

Anyway, at the end of the small talk after this important mission of the committee member was accomplished, I raised a question stupid to anyone in the world.

"What on earth is haiku?"

My reasons were Sensei was already recognized as a famous poet, and around that time, my interest in haiku was dawning. The gist of the sensei's answer left an impression that remains vivid today.

"Haiku condenses rhetoric."

"He described it as a focal point like the rivet of a folding fan that hints at an associated world radiating from there."

"Conventional depictions such as saying flowers scatter like snow are dubbed mediocre."

"A verse such as

> Autumn winds have come
> Over a plain wooden bow
> A lone string is stretched

is a fine verse.*

"No matter how much they try, some people are incapable of writing haiku. Others are talented from the start."

Hearing his explanation, I immediately wanted to try writing haiku. During summer vacation that year, after I returned home, I grabbed any supplies I could get my hands on and wrote only twenty or thirty verses.

When summer vacation ended, a little before I arrived in Kumamoto in September, I visited Sensei and brought them to him. On the manuscript he returned to me on my next visit, he had written brief comments and synonymous verses, made corrections, and added a star or two in front of a couple of them.

Later, I fell ill, zealously wrote verses, and went to the sensei's house two or three times a week. Around that time, he moved from the house on the banks of the Shirakawa to Uchitsuboi. It was quite far from my boarding house in Tatsutasanroku, but I went there feeling like I was on a rendezvous to meet a lover.

A driving rain seemed to have drenched the stone for removing shoes placed at the entryway after passing through the roofless gate

---

* 秋風や白木の弓につる張らん
向井去来 (Mukai Kyorai)

facing east. I remember scrubbing my muddy feet with a hand towel on rainy days but felt ashamed as I sat on a silk cushion.

A six-tatami sitting room was to the left of the entryway. An eight-tatami room was next door on the west. Both rooms shared an outside corridor that crossed over to a garden on the south side.

The garden was flat and grew next to nothing. Farmland was on the far side of a split-bamboo fence in front. A vine of morning glories wrapping the fence had crumbled and remained after winter began. The six-tatami room was an ordinary reception room. The eight-tatami one seemed to serve as a sitting room and a study. I believe the sensei composed this verse.*

> A morning glory
> Clambers to an empty hook
> For a hand towel

That hand towel hook was fastened to the corridor outside of the six-tatami room.

Sensei always seemed to wear a black haori jacket and sit properly. His young, newlywed wife, who wore a black silk kimono with a family crest, sometimes came to the entryway. To the eyes of a country boy like me, Sensei's home was quite attractive and refined. High-quality, fresh sweets were always offered. Sensei seemed to enjoy and often requested treats, such as beautiful, fresh, red and white kudzu cakes.

He sent the manuscript of poems I brought appended to the end of his manuscript of poems to Masaoka Shiki. He returned them with red added. Some of the verses were published in the newspaper *Japan* in the haiku column, located at the bottom left corner of the front page. Imitating Sensei, I enjoyed cutting things out of newspapers and saving the clippings in a paper bag.

I was elated when my early writings became movable type and appeared in print.

In those days, in addition to me, others taught haiku by the

---

* 朝顔や手ぬぐい掛けにはい上る

sensei included Kuriyagawa Senkō, Hirakawa Sōkō, and Gamō Shisen, who became a medical doctor.

This group started a poetry meeting. At first, we held the meetings at the sensei's home. Later, we rented another house. Sometimes, Sensei faced a student in a challenge to create ten fully-formed verses. At those times, a novel verse far better than mundane burst forth one after another from me like the sensei. Even I was amused and chuckled.

I once asked Sensei if I could become a live-in student/houseboy at his home. He said the storehouse in the back was available and to come over to see it. Well, the room he showed me had ripped tatami and was a true storeroom filled with junk. Disheartened, I turned it down. However, if I said okay and moved in, he probably would have laid down tatami and cleaned it up. But I wasn't brave in those days.

Kanō Kōkichi, Oku Taichirō, and Yamakawa Shinjirō were fellow professors and close colleagues of Sensei in those days. Oku-san, said to be a man in Sensei's novel *Nihyaku Tōka* [*The 210th Day*], had a fine reputation.

In school, Sensei taught *Opium-Eater* and *Silas Marner*. In those days, verbatim explanations were employed in the meticulous teaching methods at Matsuyama Middle School. Our method centered on lucidity in contrast to other methods. Simply, Sensei fluently read aloud and then asked, "Well, did you understand?"

While thinking about it, he also wrote various quotations related to a passage in the text on the blackboard.

During exams, I wrote answers that exactly copied recitations of several of Homer's verses previously quoted by Sensei. I was proud and happy.

When he entered the classroom, he took out a nickel-plated watch with no chain attached from his vest pocket, propped himself on a corner of the desk, and began the lecture.

After he satisfactorily explained any slightly complicated matter, his habit was to extend his index finger and lightly press on the bridge of his nose. If a fellow who loved asking questions while learning persisted in his queries, Sensei pushed back by saying, "You wouldn't understand that even if you asked the man who wrote it."

The sensei of those days terrified some of the school's alumni. To me, he wasn't scary at all. Rather, he was my nicest and most cherished sensei.

He lectured on Othello from seven to eight in the morning mainly as an extracurricular lecture for literature students. When it was cold and I looked out the second-floor window, I would see Sensei wrapped in a black overcoat hurrying this way as if he were swimming away from the front gate. There were some who made fun of him.

"Oh goody, here he comes."

He looked stylish with the buttons on his black overcoat buttoned up. In his home, however, Sensei in his black haori and sitting properly as though chilly possessed a classic look, reminiscent of a ronin from the Mito Clan.

While back home for summer vacation, Sensei sent me a post-card with a simple picture he drew of a man napping on his back with his legs stretched out and a verse he wrote. *

> A tanuki
> Grabs a noontime nap

The tanuki's face wore a mustache like Sensei's. From then on, it seems he made the habit of an afternoon nap.

When I entered college after high school, Sensei introduced me to Masaoka Shiki in his hospital bed in Kaminegishi Uguisuyoko-chō. At that time, Shiki talked about his hard work and actions to get Natsume-sensei a job and help in other matters. Shiki and Sensei deeply respected each other and had the nicest friendship. However, when I asked Sensei, he smiled and said, "I swear Shiki thinks he's celebrated. He's a cocky guy." As he spoke, he seemed to deeply understand their mutual feelings of indulgence and nostalgia.

Sensei had traveled to the West and was seen off in Yokohama.

---

* たぬきの昼寝かな

The ship was a Preussen owned by Lloyd's of London. When the ship sailed, his fellow passengers, Haga-san and Fujishiro-san, waved their hats to say farewell to the people sending them off. Only Sensei leaned heavily on the railing away from the others, did not move, and stared at the dock. The moment the ship started to move, he saw his wife raise a handkerchief to her face. He sent a postcard from Kōbe with this verse.*

> Autumn winds blowing
> On a solitary man
> Adrift on the sea

While Sensei was studying overseas, I fell ill, took a year off from school, and spent time on the shore in my hometown. I was bored, wrote a long letter, and sent it to Sensei in London. I was delighted when news came from Sensei. I got better and went back to Tōkyo. Soon after, Sensei returned to Japan around the time my wife died while we were living in a boarding house in 5-chōme in Hongō.

I went to welcome him in Shiodome near Shimbashi Station. He stepped off the train and lifted his daughter's chin to make her look up, and stared at her. As I recall, he eventually let go and smiled enigmatically.

After his return, Sensei temporarily stayed at the home of his Nakane in-laws in Yarai-chō. During a visit there, a large wooden box stuffed with books arrived. A man called Tsuchiya-kun opened it and took out the books.

Sensei showed me photographs of famous paintings in English museums. I said I liked a few of them. He gave me Reynolds' *Portrait of a Girl* and Murillo's *Maria Magdalene*. Sensei took a bouquet of artificial white roses from his satchel. I asked, "What are those for?"

He said, "Someone gave them to me."

At that time, he surely enjoyed sushi. I didn't realize it back then but later heard that if Sensei ate sushi rolls, I also ate sushi rolls. If Sensei ate eggs, I adopted eggs. If Sensei left the shrimp alone, I left

---

* 秋風の一人を吹くや海の上

it alone. In a note that came after Sensei's death, he had written *How T eats sushi*. It seemed to be from that time.

After he decided to live in Sendagi, I visited before three days passed, just like the old days. Still a teacher of English literature and a haiku poet, his entryway was not very lively, but I was quite a nuisance. Even if he said, "I'm busy today. Go home," I'd talk about some selfish matters, lazily remain seated, and look at the studio pictures close to where Sensei was working. At that time, Sensei liked Turner's paintings and often spoke about the painter. When was that? When Sensei received only a few manuscripts from somewhere, he wanted to see the set of watercolor paintings, sketchbooks, and an ivory buck knife I bought for him and looked happy. He wrote postcards with those painting materials and sent them to people close to him.

After *Cat*, he exchanged picture postcards with Hashiguchi Goyō and Ōtsuka Naoko.

I shaved and fixed the nicked end of the ivory buck knife with my small knife. Often saying it's the times, he always rubbed his cheek or nose, oil soaked in turning them amber.

Calligraphy on half-size paper of a monk of the Ōbaku school of Buddhism hung on a wall of the study. An object like a feather fan of a long-nosed tengu goblin was placed to the right of his seat. Notes written in fine characters in sepia ink were always on the desk. A silhouette of the profile of a self-portrait of Suzuki Miekichi was mounted on the wall. While he loved the shape and color of a bottle of Curacoa given to him by someone, he said this liquor had the scent of pine flowers. I remember he had me drink a little. He enjoyed the dark-green, jellied yōkan dessert. When we went to restaurants, he always asked if they served green soybean soup.

I Am a Cat brought Sensei fame in one leap. A literary gathering of people associated with the literary magazine *Hototogisu* was held in the Sensei's home from time to time. Takahama-san always recited from the continuation to Sensei's *Cat*. Sometimes, Sensei looked quite embarrassed, steeled himself, and listened to the recitation.

I was looking at an old philosophical magazine at school and discovered an amazing paper that discussed the mechanics of hanging written by Reverend Haughton. I borrowed it from the school and brought it to show Sensei because I found the paper to be interesting and useful. It appeared in the lecture by Kangetsu-kun in *Cat*. Sensei was excellent in mathematics in high school and had a thorough understanding just by reading the paper, an exceptional ability in a literary man.

When Takahama, Sakamoto, Samukawa, Sensei, and I went for lunch at a restaurant in Renjaku-chō, Kanda, Samukawa-san talked as we walked through the Suda-chō area. He said the incident in which an eccentric newspaperman jumped off a bridge appeared as one of the behaviors of Kangetsu-kun in a passage of *Cat*.

Sometimes, Sensei and I attended concerts at the Meiji Musical Society held every month at the Ueno Music School. There were musical programs where the pieces mixed in chirping voices and the sounds of popping champagne corks. That was hilarious. While strolling past a restaurant serving Western food on the way home, Sensei imitated a snoring sound and had a good belly laugh. He often seemed to still be so much like a young student.

Sensei remarked that my white flannel muffler was so dirty it was gray and had the maid wash it. He looked sharp like a man born and raised in Tōkyo and liked a variety of clothes. When he went out, he always looked sharp. He'd say things like "You should have one nice suit made and show it to me." I received a failing grade in clothes from Sensei. My cotton flannel underclothes extended two inches beyond the cuffs and were a seed for Sensei's laughter.

By nature, I'm selfish. For example, when he moved, I didn't help even a little. On this point, too, I failed.

One time, Sensei said, "Torahiko brought me one slice of dried bonito as a souvenir from his home province," and laughed. However, the generosity of a loving father to all the weaknesses and flaws appeared to the young people who gathered as students with hearts like children. Instead, his extreme sensitivity to hostility and selfishness hidden at the bottom of social skills are seen in Sensei's works.

While he was writing *Gubijinsō* (*Poppy*), he said, "Show me the laboratory where you conduct your experiments."

One day, I brought him to school and meticulously explained the test equipment in the basement room. I photographed the waves of air before and after a flying bullet by Schlieren photography.

He asked, "Would this be good to write in a novel?"

If I said that would be a little difficult, he said to tell him about another experiment. By chance, I told him about an experiment related to the measurement of radiation pressure conducted by a researcher named Nichols. He heard this only one time and wrote with a clear understanding of the essentials in the laboratory scene of Nonomiya-san. He realistically depicted an experiment he only heard about but had never seen. This was also astounding in a literary man in Japan.

Not only this, he was deeply interested in general science and particularly enjoyed talks on scientific methodologies. Major themes like scientific research methods for literature moving around constantly in Sensei's head were probably imagined concepts from his essays or notes. However, he was busy creating original works in his last years and seemed to have no time for this research.

For a short time, Sensei lived in Nishikata-machi and then moved to Minami-chō, Waseda. As always, I frequently visited him. After Thursday was designated as the visiting day, I found some reason to intrude on other days of the week.

During my studies overseas, Sensei fell seriously ill at Shuzen-ji Temple and roamed between life and death. At that time, he had Komiya-kun send a picture postcard of the lodgings of Sensei that I received at my boarding house in Göttingen. After returning to Japan, I hadn't seen Sensei for a long time, but he seemed a little different from the sensei of long ago. It was probably aging. Sensei who mimicked a frog's voice was no more.

He enjoyed creating paintings following the Nanga school of Chinese painting considered to be an extension of watercolor paintings drawn long ago. When a rude criticism was attempted, his mouth opened in surprise, and his face looked aggrieved. Nevertheless, he accepted the criticism and made revisions.

On one hand, Sensei was very headstrong, but on the other, he was like a good-natured older man who kindly receives another's words. I feel that rude critiques with the conceit of making it better were unjustified.

One time, I pulled Sensei from a crowd. I took him to Asakusa and got him to ride on the merry-go-round at Luna Park. He looked puzzled but became a youngster and got on a wooden rocking horse to go round and round.

In those days, he often went window-shopping at antique shops in Akagishita, searching for "a three-yen work by Ryūrikyō." He invited me and made me come once.

When the First Hyūzan-Kai Art Exhibition was held at Yomiuri Shimbun Company at the edge of Kyōbashi. I was drawn to one picture. I mentioned thinking about splurging and buying it. He said, "Okay, I'll go see it." We went together.

"Of course, this is nice, so buy it," he said.

In his final years, he wrote zealously. Takita Tachoin-kun began in the morning of Thursday's meeting and refused to leave before he wrote some number of pages. Sensei would write whatever he had to in order to not be defeated.

Whenever I had a hunch he would write me, but I received no painting or writing, sometimes Sensei would deliberately send a gift of a Chinese poem written on a silk canvas with an attached letter. Also, a picture postcard from the Sendagi era became a unique memento. After Sensei died, his family gave me the hanging scroll of the painting on the postcard.

He learned a Noh song from Hōshōshin-san. One time I listened to Sensei chant. I pointed out that he chanted with a trill. I'll always remember he said, "I was the guy who said that awful thing."

During another conversation with Sensei in the reception room in Waseda, a strange man in rough clothing stumbled in like a drunk from the hallway. He looked about to sit in front of Sensei but suddenly started cursing in a loud, rude tone. I later heard that he was O, a formerly famous literary man who came with M-kun. It seems M-kun was totally confused and left speechless by this unexpected scene. However, Sensei's response to this drunkard was amusement. In contrast to the other man's drunken threats, both took on the same attitude and tone to not be outdone by the other and had a delightful exchange. At that moment, I felt I could see Sensei, a Tōkyo native, had an invincible spirit by nature.

At the time of Sensei's final serious illness, I had fallen ill with the same disease and was weak. I searched for a potted begonia at a florist on the banks of the Edogawa River and went to visit him in his sickbed but wasn't allowed to see him. His wife said, "My, my, these are pretty," and took the flowers to his sickroom. Near the hearth in the kitchen, I was speaking to his physician M. Suddenly, I heard groans coming from the sickroom. He had vomited a large amount of blood.

I didn't see him before he died, but I swayed in the human-powered cab to Waseda after K-kun flew to inform me of his death. On the way, the street lamps seen through the celluloid window in the front of the cab's hood looked like oddly blurred stars and mysteriously danced a frenzied dance.

I learned many things from Sensei. Not only did he teach me the techniques of haiku, he also taught me how to use my eyes and body to discover natural beauty. He taught me how to distinguish between the truth and fiction in a person's heart, and to hate the false and love the truth.

However, I was told by the extreme egoist in me, it didn't matter whether Sensei created good or poor haiku, or understood more or nothing through English literature. It mattered much less whether Sensei became or did not become a literary master. That sort of thing didn't matter. Instead, I wonder if would have been better for Sensei to have never become famous and remained a simple school teacher. If Sensei hadn't become a major figure, I felt, at least, he might have had a longer life.

When various misfortunes weighed down my mind, I'd go and talk to Sensei. In no time, the load on my mind lightened. In dark times in my heart caused by dissatisfaction and worry, I'd consult with Sensei, and then the black cloud in my heart was swept away. With renewed feeling, I poured all my power into my work. The existence of Sensei nourished my spirit and became medicine. Mysterious influences flowed out from somewhere inside Sensei. I don't think I could view Sensei objectively the more I analyzed him.

Many young people traced a narrow path under flowers and gathered at Sensei's gate. Their hearts were probably the same as mine. If these rambling recollections I write here appear to the readers as if I monopolized Sensei, I think they should understand that my memories represent the genuine feelings of each of the many other students at the gate.

Today after Sensei's death, along with those fellow students at his gate, inside the indescribably fond memories felt each time we had a chance to see his face, memories of the pleasant gatherings long ago in the Sensei's home in Sendagi or Waseda lurk in the background.

Perhaps the records of these memories from my faulty memory are mistakes of the era or misunderstandings of the facts. I intended to conscientiously write a profile of Sensei to the best of my ability in my simple subjective vision of the world. By introducing a profile of Sensei from my perspective as a student, a writer, and a human being, I only pruned away many unimportant branches and leaves. In light of this, I earnestly pray for the generosity of the readers and fellow students.

December 1937, Haiku Course

Sketch from diary